Rhys Bowen is the *New York Times* bestselling author of the Royal Spyness Series, Molly Murphy Mysteries, and Constable Evans. She is a recipient of the Agatha Best Novel Award and an Edgar Best Novel nominee.

Praise for Rhys Bowen

'The latest addition to Molly's case files offers a charming combination of history, mystery, and romance.' *Kirkus Reviews* on *Hush Now, Don't You Cry*

'Engaging . . . Molly's compassion and pluck should attract more readers to this consistently solid historical series.' *Publishers Weekly* on *Bless the Bride*

'Winning . . . The gutsy Molly, who's no prim Edwardian miss, will appeal to fans of contemporary female detectives.' *Publishers Weekly* on *The Last Illusion*

'This historical mystery delivers a top-notch, detail-rich story full of intriguing characters. Fans of the 1920s private detective Maisie Dobbs should give this series a try.' *Booklist* on *The Last Illusion*

'Details of Molly's new cases are knit together with the accoutrements of 1918 New York City life. . . . Don't miss this great period puzzler reminiscent of Dame Agatha's mysteries and Gillian Linscott's Nell Bray series.' *Booklist* on *In a Gilded Ca*

RHYS BOWEN

The Twelve Clues of Christmas

Constable • London

CONSTABLE

First published in the US in 2012 by Berkley Prime Crime, The Berkley Publishing Group

This edition published in Great Britain in 2016 by Constable

Copyright © Janet Quin-Harkin, 2012
Published by arrangement with The Berkley Publishing Group,
a member of Penguin Group (USA) LLC

1 3 5 7 9 10 8 6 4 2

The moral right of the author has been asserted.

*All characters and events in this publication, other than
those clearly in the public domain, are fictitious
and any resemblance to real persons,
living or dead, is purely coincidental.*

All rights reserved.
No part of this publication may be reproduced, stored in a retrieval system, or transmitted,
in any form, or by any means, without the prior permission in writing of the publisher,
nor be otherwise circulated in any form of binding or cover other than that in which it is
published and without a similar condition including this condition being imposed on the
subsequent purchaser.

A CIP catalogue record for this book
is available from the British Library.

ISBN 978-1-47212-078-6 (paperback)

Typeset in Berthold Baskerville by TW Type, Cornwall
Printed and bound in Great Britain by CPI (UK) Ltd, Croydon CR0 4YY
Papers used by Constable are from well-managed forests and other responsible sources

MIX
Paper from
responsible sources
FSC® C104740

Constable
is an imprint of
Little, Brown Book Group
Carmelite House
50 Victoria Embankment
London EC4Y 0DZ

An Hachette UK Company
www.hachette.co.uk

www.littlebrown.co.uk

Chapter 1

Castle Rannoch, Perthshire, Scotland
December 14, 1933
Weather: cold, dreary, bleak.
Atmosphere here: cold, dreary, bleak.
Outlook: cold, dreary, bleak. Not in a good mood today. I
wonder why. Could it have something to do with the fact
that Christmas is coming and it will be utterly bloody?

Ah, Christmas: chestnuts roasting; Yule logs crackling merrily; tables groaning under roast goose, turkey, mince pies and flaming plum puddings; carols and mistletoe; goodwill to all men. I'm sure there were some houses in Britain where this was going to be the case, in spite of the depression – just not at Castle Rannoch, on the bleak Scottish moors, where I was currently trapped for the winter. No, I was not snowed in or being held prisoner. I was there of my own volition. I happen to be Lady Georgiana Rannoch, sister to the current duke, and that bleak castle is my family home.

There is actually no way to make Castle Rannoch festive even if one wanted to. Firstly it would be impossible to heat

Rhys Bowen

those cavernous great rooms no matter how many Yule logs you piled on the fire, and secondly my sister-in-law, Hilda, Duchess of Rannoch, commonly known as Fig, was in full austerity mode. Times were hard, she said. The country was in the grip of a great depression. It was up to us to set an example and live simply. We even had to endure baked beans on toast as our savory at the end of dinner, which shows how dire our situation had become.

It is true that times are hard for the Rannochs, even though we're related to the royal family and my brother inherited Rannoch Castle and a London house in Belgravia. You see, our father lost the last of his fortune in the great crash of '29, then went up on the moors and shot himself, thus saddling poor Binky with horrendous death duties. I had my allowance cut off on my twenty-first birthday and have been struggling to keep my head above water ever since. Not that our situation is as dire as those poor wretches in the soup lines. I was supposed to marry well, to one of those chinless, spineless and half-imbecile European princes, or, failing that, become lady-in-waiting to an elderly royal aunt.

So far I had chosen neither of the above, but as Christmas approached and the wind whistled down the hallways of Castle Rannoch, either option began to seem more desirable than my present situation. You might wonder why I stayed in such dreary surroundings. It had started through the famous Rannoch sense of duty that had been rammed down our throats since birth. We'd been raised with stories about ancestors like Robert Bruce Rannoch, who had kept fighting when his arm was hacked off in battle and merely changed his sword from his right hand to his left. I don't think my sense of duty was that strong, but it was definitely there.

You see, that summer, in London, my sister-in-law, Fig, had given birth to a second little Rannoch. Although she looked as if she had the constitution of a cart horse, she had been rather ill. She had gone home to Scotland to recuperate and had actually begged me to come to keep her company (which shows how jolly sick she was!). I, being a kind-hearted soul, had agreed.

Summer had turned to autumn and there were the royal relatives at Balmoral to visit, house parties, grouse shoots – all of which we hoped might bring Fig out of her blue funk. But she had remained languid and depressed, hardly showing any interest in little Adelaide – yes, that was what they named the poor child. Adelaide Gertrude Hermione Maude. Can you imagine saddling any poor baby with such monstrosities? They hadn't even come up with a good pet name yet. One could hardly call her Addy or Laidy, could one? Then she'd be Lady Addy or Lady Laidy and that wouldn't do. To date she was addressed as 'baby,' or occasionally 'diddums.'

And so I had stayed on. Nanny coped admirably with little Adelaide, Fig lolled about, getting more and more petty and bad-tempered, and Binky wandered the grounds looking worried. I was starting to wonder how long I could endure this, when things were decided for me. Fig's mother, Lady Wormwood, arrived to take charge. It only took an instant to see where Fig's pettiness and bossy nature came from. If Fig was a trial, Lady Wormwood was utterly bloody. (Yes, I know a lady is not supposed to use words like 'bloody,' but in describing Lady Wormwood the adjective is actually rather mild. Alas, my education was sadly lacking. If I knew stronger words, I'd have used them.)

She had been in the house for about a week when I came

back from a walk to hear her strident voice saying, 'It's not healthy, Hilda.' (She was the only person who called Fig Hilda, being responsible for the ghastly name.) 'It's not natural for a young girl to shut herself away like this, doing nothing all day. Does she not think at all about her future?'

I froze in the entrance hall, shielded by a suit of armor. I expected Fig to leap to my defense and tell her mother that I was only shutting myself away at Castle Rannoch because she had begged me to stay with her. Instead I heard her saying, 'I really don't know what she thinks, Mummy.'

'She can't possibly expect that you'll go on supporting her. You've done your duty and more. The girl has had her season, hasn't she?' (People like Lady Wormwood pronounced the word 'gell'). 'Why isn't she married? She's not bad-looking. She has royal connections. You'd have thought someone would have taken her off your hands by now.'

'She's already turned down Prince Siegfried of Romania,' Fig said. 'I don't think she has any idea about duty. The queen was really angling for that match. They are Hollenzollern-Sigmaringens, you know. Related to the queen's family. And Siegfried was a charming young man, too. But she turned him down.'

'What on earth is she waiting for – a king?' Lady Wormwood asked, her voice dripping with sarcasm. 'It's not as if she's next in line to the throne, is it?'

This was true. I had been thirty-fourth until Adelaide was born. Now I had been relegated to thirty-fifth.

Fig lowered her voice. 'Between ourselves, she's mooning after some disreputable chap called Darcy O'Mara. Absolutely rotten sort.'

'O'Mara? Son of Lord Kilhenny?'

'That's the one. Their family is in a worse state than ours.

One gathers his father has had to sell off the family seat and the racing stables to cover his debts. So there are no prospects in that quarter. This O'Mara chap has no fortune and no career. He'll never be able to support a wife.'

'Well, she wouldn't be allowed to marry him anyway, would she?' Lady Wormwood's voice echoed around the great hall. 'They are a Catholic family. As a member of the line of succession she'd be barred from marrying a Catholic.'

I took an involuntary step back, knocking into the suit of armor and just managing to grab the mace before it clattered to the floor. I knew that the royal family was not allowed by British law to marry a Catholic, but surely that didn't apply to me. It wasn't as if I'd ever find myself queen, unless a particularly virulent epidemic hit or invaders wiped out numbers one through thirty-four. Not that Darcy had asked me to marry him. In fact, we did not even fit the traditional concept of sweethearts. When I was with him it was bliss, but most of the time I didn't even know where he was. I certainly didn't know how he earned his living. He appeared to be another young man-about-town, spending his days in idle pursuits like most peers' sons, but I suspected he was also employed by the British government as some kind of spy. I had questioned him on several occasions but he remained enigmatically mum. When I last heard from him he was on his way to Argentina. I felt a lump come into my throat.

'The girl needs taking in hand, Hilda.' Lady Wormwood's voice boomed again. 'Make it quite clear to her that she is expected to do her duty like everyone else. None of us mooned around waiting for an unsuitable chap, did we? We married whom we were told to and got on with it. Such a stupid notion that one marries for love.'

'Hold on a minute, Mummy,' Fig interrupted. 'I'm jolly

fond of Binky, you know. I consider myself very lucky in that department.'

'Nobody is saying that love doesn't come later in some cases,' Lady Wormwood said. 'If I remember correctly, you had a distinct crush on the local curate until we set you straight. So will you speak to the girl, Hilda, or shall I? Give her an ultimatum – tell her you can support her no longer and it's up to her to find herself a husband right away.'

I couldn't stand there for another second. I turned and pushed open the front door, stepping out into the full force of the gale that had begun brewing during my walk. It had started to snow, a driving kind of sleet that stung like needles then stuck to my clothing, hair and eyelashes, but I didn't care. I walked, faster and faster, away from the house and out into the storm. As I walked I concentrated on my anger, to keep my fear at bay. How dare she! Castle Rannoch was my ancestral home, not hers. She couldn't turn me out. And then the fear began to creep in . . . if they did turn me out, where would I go? God knows I'd tried to find ways to support myself, but with the world in the grips of a great depression even those with qualifications and experience were standing in bread lines. And then the bigger fear – the real fear. What if I couldn't marry Darcy? Was I waiting for an impossible dream? Hadn't I better start facing reality?

The snow turned to blizzard, coating me in a white blanket and making it hard to breathe. Well, one thing was sure – I was not going to conveniently die in a storm just to please Fig and her mother. I turned around and made my way back toward the looming black shape of the castle. Since my presence was no longer appreciated, I'd not stay any longer. I'd have my maid, Queenie, pack my trunk and we'd leave for London in the morning. I had become rather good at camping out in our London house. My grandfather was nearby and my friend Belinda always seemed to have exciting things to do. And who knows, Darcy might be returning to London any day now. It was time for me to take my life into my own hands again.

Chapter 2

As I entered the front hall I was greeted by Hamilton, our aged butler. 'I've been looking everywhere for you, my lady,' he said. 'I had no idea you had gone out in this inclement weather. Let me help you out of your coat.'

As a well-trained butler he appeared not to notice that I was leaving a large lake of melted snow around me on the tiled floor. Instead he removed the coat with deft hands. Nor did he ask what had possessed me to go tramping out in a blizzard in the first place. 'No doubt you'll want warming up,' he said in his light Highland voice. 'I'll have Cook send you up some cocoa with brandy in it right away if you'll go through to His Grace's study.'

'My brother's study?'

'Yes, my lady. You're wanted on the telephone, and I believe it's rather more private on the extension in there.' He gave me the hint of a knowing smile.

My heart did a flip. It was Darcy. He was back in England and I was going to see him again after all. I sprinted with unladylike haste across the great hall, my footsteps sending up a clattering echo not unlike the time Murdoch Jamie

Rannoch rode his war horse into the castle and up the stairs on returning from battle, having heard a rumor that his wife was in bed with the steward. The rumor proved to be right and Murdoch Jamie dispatched both of them on the spot with a wield of his trusty claymore. We Rannochs can get rather hot-headed where love is involved.

I was so breathless by the time I picked up the receiver that I could hardly gasp out, 'Hello?'

'Darling, is it you?' came a feminine voice.

My first thought was that it was my friend Belinda Warburton-Stoke, one of the few people I knew who called me darling. But then I realized that the voice was deeper, smoother, sexier, polished by years on the London stage. 'Mummy?' I replied. 'What's wrong?' In my impecunious world the telephone was used only for the direst emergencies and I hadn't spoken to my mother in months.

'Nothing's wrong, darling,' she said indignantly. 'I was just looking forward to a chat with my only child.'

'Where are you calling from?' The line had that hollow crackle of long distance.

'I'm in London, darling, where I hoped I'd find you.' She sounded peeved now, as if I were deliberately avoiding her. 'What on earth are you doing up in Scotland at this time of year? My God, it must be bleak.'

'It is, rather,' I agreed. 'I've been keeping Fig company.'

'From choice?' She sounded horrified.

'More from a sense of duty, I suppose,' I said. 'She's been awfully down since she had the baby and Binky begged me to stay on and cheer her up. He's been rather at a loss for what to do for her, poor chap.'

'I'd have pushed her off a cliff long ago if I were he,' Mummy said.

'Mummy, you're terrible.' I had to laugh. 'Anyway, I had hoped that going down to London for Christmas might cheer her up, but you know Fig. She's sure it's cheaper to stay in Scotland rather than open up the London house. So we're stuck up here. But what about you? What are you doing in London? I thought you'd be looking forward to a jolly German Christmas with Max.'

'Max is having the jolly German Christmas. I'm not,' she said. 'He's gone to spend the holiday with his aged parents in Berlin and he thought it wiser that I not accompany him, since they are very prim and proper and don't know about me.'

'Oh, dear,' I said. 'I thought he was anxious to marry you.'

'He still is,' she said, 'but he thought this wasn't the right moment to spring me on the old folks. And frankly I'm delighted to have a chance to spend Christmas in England for a change. I'm already looking forward to carols and Yule logs and flaming plum pudding and crackers.'

A wonderful picture floated into my mind – Mummy and I sharing Christmas with all the trimmings at a swank London hotel. Glorious food, glamorous parties, pantomimes . . .

'Are you at the Ritz?' I asked.

'At Brown's, darling. I had this great desire to be horribly English for once and they are so lovely and old-fashioned. What's more, they've conveniently forgotten that I'm not a duchess anymore, and one does so enjoy being called Your Grace.'

'You were the one who walked out on Daddy,' I reminded her. 'You could still have been Your Grace if you'd wanted to.'

'Yes, but it would have meant spending half the year on those ghastly Scottish moors, wouldn't it? I'd have died of boredom. At least now I'm having fun.'

With a great many men on all six continents, I wanted to add but didn't. My mother was one of the first of the notorious bolters, having left my father for a French racing driver, an Argentinian polo player, a mountain climber, a Texas oil millionaire and most recently a wealthy German industrialist.

'So you're going to be spending Christmas at Brown's Hotel, are you? Or do you think you may come up to Scotland to visit us?' Of course I was angling for an invitation to join her in London, but I was too proud to come out and say it.

'Come up to Scotland? In winter? Darling, I'm very fond of you, but wild horses wouldn't drag me to Castle Rannoch in winter. Perhaps you could pop down to London when I'm back in the new year and we'll go shopping and do girlie things.'

'Back? I thought you said you were spending Christmas in England.'

'Yes, darling, but not in London. Don't laugh, but I'm off to a village called Tiddleton-under-Lovey of all things. Isn't it a divine name? I thought Noël was making it up when he told me. It sounds as though it comes straight from one of his plays, doesn't it?'

'Noël? You mean Noël Coward?'

'Is there any other Noël, darling? Remember I mentioned earlier this year that he wanted to write a play for us to star in together? Well, he's demanded that we hole up together over Christmas and work on the dialogue. Imagine, little *moi* in a play with Noël. Utter heaven. Of course he'll hog the limelight and give himself the best lines, but who cares?'

'Will Max approve of your holing up with another man?'

She laughed. 'Darling, it's not another man. It's Noël.'

'And what about your going back into the theater? Will Max approve of that?'

'Max can like it or lump it,' she said breezily. 'I'm not Frau Von Strohheim yet, and anyway Max wants me to do anything that makes me happy. And I've been away from the theater for too long. My public still yearns for me.'

I could find no response to this except to wonder how a mother with such supreme confidence in her own wonderfulness managed to produce a shy and awkward daughter like me.

'Where is this Piddleton-under-Lovey?' I asked.

She gave another tinkling laugh. 'Tiddleton, darling. Not Piddleton. In Devon. Tucked at the edge of Dartmoor, one gathers. Noël chose it because of its name, I'm sure. You know what a wicked sense of humor he has. But also because it was featured in *Country Life* as one of England's most charming and quaint villages. He's rented a thatched cottage on the village green and promises me roaring fires and hot toddy and all the delights the countryside has to offer.'

'It sounds lovely.' I tried not to sound disappointed.

'I'd invite you to join us, darling, but it really is a working holiday and Noël insists that he wants no distractions. He can be so intense when he's creating. He's already slaving away furiously in his London flat and naturally he's left all the domestic details of this Tiddleton-under-Lovey business to me. I'm supposed to come up with a good cook who can produce plain old-fashioned English food and someone to look after us, which means, I suppose, that I'll have to abandon Brown's and go down to Devon ahead of him. I can't see any staff I'd hire in London wanting to go down to Devon in the bleak midwinter, can you?'

If I'd known how to cook, I'd have volunteered for the job

myself. But since my repertoire didn't go beyond toast, boiled eggs and baked beans, I didn't think I'd prove satisfactory.

'Anyway, I must toddle off, darling.' Mummy cut short my thoughts. 'I've a million and one things to do. Should I order the hamper from Fortnum's or Harrods, do you think? I seem to remember I was rather disappointed in Harrods last time – terribly bourgeois in their choices.' (This from someone who was raised in a two-up, two-down house in Barking where luxury consisted of an extra helping of chips on Saturday night.) 'So have a lovely Christmas, won't you, my sweet, and afterwards we'll meet in London and I'll treat you to a lovely shopping spree as a Christmas present. All right?'

Before I could say good-bye the line went dead.

Chapter 3

Still Castle Rannoch
Blizzard still continuing.

I came down to dinner with what I hoped was a confident and jaunty air. I was not going to let Fig and her mother know that I had overheard their conversation.

'Beastly day,' I said as I took my place. 'Did any of you go out?'

'Absolutely not,' Fig said. 'I have to be careful that I don't catch a chill after all that I've been through.'

'Nobody in their right mind would go out in weather like this,' her mother added.

'I went for my usual walk,' Binky said in his jolly fashion, oblivious to the fact that he had just admitted to not being in his right mind. 'It wasn't too bad. Blowing a bit hard, but one expects a good stiff blow at this time of year. You didn't go out riding, did you, Georgie?'

'Of course not. I would not expose Rob Roy to this weather, poor thing. But I did tramp around the estate a bit this afternoon before I was nearly buried in the blizzard.

One does need some exercise, doesn't one?' I gave Fig a swift glance. She frowned. 'So have you decided what we're going to do about Christmas?' I went on cheerfully. 'Don't you think it would be more fun in London? It's so remote up here and nobody will come to visit.'

'On the contrary,' Lady Wormwood said, 'we are expecting the rest of our family to join us. Hilda's sister, Matilda, and her husband and daughter. I believe you met them in France earlier this year.'

Oh, God. Not Ducky, her lecherous husband, Foggy, and their dreadful daughter, Maude!

'Maybe you can help Maude with her French lessons again while she's here,' Fig said. 'You two became great chums, I remember.'

In fact, it had been a case of mutual loathing. I cleared my throat. 'Ah, well, I don't think I'm going to be here after all. I've decided to go down to the London house, if it's all right with you. There are parties and things going on, and I know you all want me to meet a suitable chap, don't you?'

There was a silence you could cut with a knife, punctuated only by the clink of silver spoon against tureen as the footman ladled out soup.

'I'm afraid that's out of the question, isn't it, Binky?' Fig said.

'Is it?' Binky looked up from his soup, clueless as usual. 'If that's what Georgie wants to do I think it's a splendid idea. Young thing like her needs her Christmas parties, what?'

'Binky!' Fig's voice developed a knife edge to it. 'We discussed this before, remember? We decided it was far too expensive to open up the London house in winter, even with the small amount of coal and electricity that Georgiana would use. So I'm afraid you're stuck here with us, Georgiana, and you can make yourself useful for once keeping Maude amused.'

With that she turned her attention to her cock-a-leekie soup.

I sat fuming, but could find nothing to say. I wanted to remind her that I had only come here in the first place because she had begged me to keep her company. I had only stayed on so long because Binky had begged me to do so. Surely they owed me something for my months of enduring Fig. But she didn't seem to think so. Rannoch House was the property of the current duke and I no longer had any claim to it. In fact, nothing belonged to me. I began to feel like a Jane Austen heroine. I was stuck in Scotland with relatives who didn't like me and didn't want me there. Frankly, I couldn't think of a worse Christmas ahead, but I also couldn't think of a way to escape from it.

Then a lovely idea popped into my head. I'd stay with my grandfather! That would shake them up. You see, my mother's father is a retired Cockney policeman who lives in a little semi-detached house in Essex with gnomes in the front garden. All the years I was growing up I wasn't allowed to meet him. I had since made up for those years and I adored him.

I took a deep breath. 'Then I think I may go and stay with my grandfather if the London house isn't available to me.'

Spoons clattered. Someone choked.

'Your grandfather?' Lady Wormwood said in the same tones Lady Bracknell used regarding a handbag in the Oscar Wilde play. 'I thought your grandfather had been dead for years.'

'Her mother's father,' Fig said coldly.

'Oh, her mother's father. I don't believe I ever met him.'

'You wouldn't have met him,' Fig said. 'He's not . . . you know.' Then she lowered her voice and muttered, 'N.O.C.D.' (which is upper-class shorthand, in case you don't know, for 'not our class, dear').

Binky was looking rather red around the gills. 'I say, Georgie. Your grandfather's a decent old stick and all that, but it's simply not on. We've been into this before. You can't stay in a cottage in Essex. Think of the embarrassment to Their Majesties if the press found out about it.'

'Anyone would think it was the Casbah or a den of ill repute,' I said hotly. 'Anyway, how are they going to find out? It's not as if the society reporters follow me around the way they do my mother. I'm nobody. Nobody cares if I stay in Belgrave Square or in Essex.'

Suddenly I felt tears welling at the back of my eyes, but I was not going to allow myself to cry in public. 'I'm over twenty-one so you can't stop me from doing what I want to,' I said. 'And if Their Majesties are embarrassed by my behavior, they can give me an allowance so I don't have to live as a penniless hanger-on all the time.'

With that I got up and walked out of the dining hall.

'Well, really, such hysterics,' I heard Lady Wormwood say. 'Takes after her mother, obviously. Bad blood there.'

I had just reached the top of the first flight of stairs when the lights went out. This was a normal occurrence at Castle Rannoch, where electricity was a recent addition to a centuries-old building and the wires were always coming down in gales. Thus we had candles and matches all over the place. I felt my way up the last two steps, then along the wall until I came to the first window ledge. There, sure enough, was a candle and matches. I lit the candle and continued on my way. Outside, the wind was howling like a banshee. Windows rattled as I passed them. A tapestry billowed out to touch me, making me flinch involuntarily. I had grown up in this environment with stories of family ghosts and ghoulies and things that go bump in the night and usually I took them all in my stride. But tonight even I was on edge.

The hall went on forever with darkness looming before and behind me. My candle flickered and threatened to go out every few yards. There was no sign of another living soul although the house was full of servants. I realized that they must all be at their supper down in the depths of the servants' hall. At last I reached my door. As I stepped into my room a great gust of wind blew out my candle. I felt my way to my bed, knowing there were more matches on the bedside table. As I reached out for the bed my hand touched cold, flabby flesh. I stifled a cry as a white shape rose up at me, looming larger and larger until it seemed to fill the room.

'Bloody 'ell?' muttered a voice.

'Queenie?' I demanded and fumbled to light my candle. My maid stood before me, hair disheveled, cap askew, blinking in the candlelight.

'Cor blimey, miss,' she said. 'You didn't half give me a nasty turn there. Scared me out of me ruddy wits.'

'I scared you?' I tried not to sound too shaky. 'How do you think I felt when I touched a cold hand when I was expecting to feel an eiderdown? What were you doing on my bed?'

She had the grace to look somewhat sheepish. 'Sorry, miss. I came up after me supper to put your hot water bottle in and I just sat down for a minute on the bed and I must have nodded off.'

'I've told you before about lying on my bed, haven't I?' I said.

'I know. And I didn't mean to, honest. But I get so sleepy after all that stodge they feed us in the servants' hall. I swear we've had stew and dumplings three nights in a row.'

'You should be glad you have enough to eat,' I said, trying to sound like a mistress putting her servant in her place. 'When I was in London you should have seen all those poor wretches queuing up for soup. You have a job and a roof over your head, so you should work harder to make sure you keep them.'

Her eyes brimmed with tears. 'I do try, miss,' she said. 'Honest I do. But you know I'm thicker than two planks. You knew that when you took me on.'

'You're right, I did.' I sighed. 'But I had hopes that you might improve, given time.'

'Ain't I improved at all, then?'

'You still haven't learned to call me "my lady" and not "miss."'

'Strike me pink, so I ain't.' She chuckled. 'I try, but when I'm flustered it goes right out of my head.'

I sighed. 'What am I going to do with you, Queenie? My sister-in-law is badgering me every day to get rid of you.'

'Spiteful cow,' Queenie muttered.

'Queenie. You're talking about the Duchess of Rannoch.'

'I don't care who she is, she's still a spiteful cow,' Queenie said. 'And ungrateful too, after all what you've done for her. Staying up here, month after month, because she wanted company, and now she turns on you like this. If I was you I'd get out while the going is good and leave her to get on with things by herself.'

'I may just do that,' I said. 'Can you find me another candle? I want to write a letter.'

'Bob's yer uncle, miss,' she said, instantly happy again.

'I'll go and take the one out of her bathroom – then just see how she likes going to the lav in the middle of the night in the dark.'

'Queenie, you're incorrigible,' I said, trying not to laugh. 'There's a perfectly good candle on top of my chest of drawers. Then tomorrow morning I want you to bring my trunk down from the attic.'

'Are we really leaving, then?'

'Maybe. But I want to be ready, just in case.'

The candle was lit and Queenie departed.

I started to write the letter. *Dear Granddad* . . .

Then I paused, my pen in midair. Was it even right to ask him if I could stay? He had very little money himself and his health had not been the best lately. The last time he wrote to me his bronchitis had returned, aggravated by the London fog that crept out across the marshes into Essex. In truth I worried about him. At least Mrs Huggins, his next-door neighbor, would be taking care of him and making sure that he ate well. She had designs on marrying him, I knew, but I wondered if he was more fond of her cooking than he was of her. In fact . . .

I gasped as a flash of brilliance struck me. A wonderful thought had entered my head, so wonderful that I hardly dared to think it. Mrs Huggins was a good plain cook and she and Granddad had acted brilliantly as housekeeper and butler one time when I'd needed to produce servants for a visiting princess. I sat there in the darkness, waiting until I heard everyone go to bed. Then I tiptoed down to Binky's study and picked up the telephone. I knew that Fig would have a fit if she knew I was making a trunk call, but for once I didn't care. This was more important.

'Brown's Hotel,' came the polished voice at the other end

of the line after what seemed like hours of waiting for the operators to make the necessary connections. I asked to speak to the former duchess of Rannoch.

'I cannot disturb Her Grace at such a late hour,' said the voice sternly. 'It wouldn't be seemly.'

I wondered if this was a polite way of saying that my mother was not occupying her bed alone. It wouldn't be the first time. 'This is her daughter, Lady Georgiana Rannoch, calling on a matter of great importance,' I said. 'So if you could possibly see if Her Grace is still awake?'

He was instantly gushing. 'Yes, yes, of course, my lady. Please hold the line and I will try to connect you.'

I waited, thinking of the minutes being added to Fig's telephone bill. At last an agitated voice said, 'Georgie darling? What's wrong?'

'Nothing's wrong, Mummy, but I just had an absolutely brilliant idea for you.'

'I was sound asleep,' she said.

'You'll be glad that I telephoned. Listen, you know Granddad's next-door neighbor Mrs Huggins cooks decent plain food,' I said. 'I thought you could ask her and Granddad to come down and run the cottage in Tiddleton-under-Whatsit for you. They were frightfully good at playing butler and cook when I had to entertain that German princess.'

'I can't ask my own father to wait on me,' she said. 'Besides, he'd never do it. He's too proud.'

'Persuade him, Mummy. I know you can if you try. It would be a perfect solution for both of you. You wouldn't have to look around for suitable servants and have people in the house you didn't know. He'd benefit from fresh air and country living. London in winter is so bad for his chest.'

'It would make things awfully simple, wouldn't it? And

give me more time for shopping. I'd have to put it to him in the right way, so that he felt he was being invited and not as a servant.'

'You could suggest that Mrs Huggins come and cook for you and naturally she wouldn't want to travel alone so you suggest that you pay his way to accompany her. You know what he's like. He hates not being busy, so he'd be bringing in the firewood and that sort of thing without being asked. And then you hire a local girl to clean, and bob's your uncle, as he would say.'

My mother laughed that wonderful bell-like laugh that had enthralled theatergoers for years. 'You're becoming as devious as I am, darling. All right. I'll do it. And by the way, guess who I saw going into the Café Royal this evening? None other than the delicious Darcy.'

'Darcy? But I thought he was in Argentina.'

'Not any longer, obviously. I'm sure it was he. Nobody else has those roguish black curls – so very sexy.'

I wanted to ask if he was alone, but I couldn't make myself. 'Then I expect I'll be hearing from him in due course,' I said, trying to sound breezy and unconcerned, 'although he won't come up to Scotland, I'm sure. Fig is so jolly rude to him.'

'Then escape to London and meet him in a hotel, darling. You'd have a blissful time.'

'Mummy, you're not supposed to suggest things like that to your unmarried daughter. Besides, think what the royals would say if they got word of it.'

'Oh, bugger the royals,' Mummy said. 'It's time you stopped trying to please other people and started living for yourself. I always have.'

* * *

It was only when I climbed into bed and curled into a tight ball in an attempt to bring back life to my frozen feet that I realized what I had done. I had condemned myself to spending Christmas with Fig and her family.

Chapter 4

Still Castle Rannoch
December 15
Stopped snowing, at least for a while.

I was awoken in the morning by loud bumping noises and
muttered curses. Queenie appeared and instead of bringing
in my morning tea she was dragging my trunk.

'Here you are, miss,' she said. 'Your trunk like you wanted.
I hope I got the right one. It does have your name on it.'

I sat up, my breath coming out as steam in the freezing
cold of the room. 'Yes, it's the right one, Queenie, but I'm
afraid I won't be going anywhere after all.'

'Ruddy 'ell, miss. You mean I got to take it back up all
them stairs again?' she demanded.

'Just leave it for now and go and get my tea,' I said. 'I'll feel
better when I have something warm in my stomach.'

'You should see what's going on downstairs, miss,' she
said, pausing to look back from the doorway. 'Apparently
them people what we stayed with in France are coming to

stay. You know, the stingy ones what only had one piece of cheese and crackers for their dinner?'

'It was lunch, Queenie,' I corrected. 'Remember I told you that people of my class eat luncheon in the middle of the day and dinner at night.'

'Well, whatever it was, there weren't enough food to feed a ruddy hamster,' she said bluntly. 'I expect they're coming here for Christmas so they can eat your brother's food instead of their own.'

'That's not for you to comment on,' I said. 'You must watch what you say. If my sister-in-law ever heard you, I really would be forced to sack you. You realize that.'

'Sorry, miss. My dad always said my big mouth would get me in trouble, if something else didn't first.'

'So the servants are getting their rooms ready, are they?' I asked. 'That must mean they are arriving very soon.'

'It's a pity you aren't going away after all,' Queenie said. 'I don't see a very happy Christmas shaping for us.' With that she made a grand exit.

I got up and went over to the window. The world was covered in a blanket of white, apart from the black water of the loch, which lay mirror-still reflecting the crag and the pine trees. For once the scene looked almost like an Alpine picture postcard and I tried to cheer myself up by thinking of the fun I'd have building snowmen and going sledding with little Podge, my nephew. He was almost five years old now and splendid company.

When I came down to breakfast, however, I learned that Podge had developed a cold and was not to be allowed out in the snow. 'But you can take Maude out tobogganing when she comes,' Fig added, as if that were an incentive. Maude probably wouldn't want to do normal things like tobogganing, I thought. I'd never met a drearier child. Nor a worse know-it-all. I looked up as Hamilton came in with the morning post on a salver.

'Anything for me, Hamilton?' I asked hopefully. If Darcy was back in London, surely he would have written. . . .

'I'm afraid not, my lady. Only a letter for His Grace and some magazines.'

Magazines were better than nothing, I supposed. I took *Country Life* and *The Lady* and went to curl up in an armchair by the fire in the morning room, which was the only room in the house that became passably warm. I flicked through the pages, trying not to feel anxious and depressed. Every page seemed to show pictures of jolly Christmas house parties, hints on how to decorate with holly and mistletoe, amusing cocktails for New Year's bashes. . . . I put down *Country Life* and thumbed idly through *The Lady*. I was about to put it down when some words leaped off the page at me: *Tiddleton-under-Lovey*.

It was an entry in the advertisements column. *Wanted: young woman of impeccable background to assist hostess with the social duties of large Christmas house party. Applications to Lady Hawse-Gorzley, Gorzley Hall, Tiddleton-under-Lovey, Devonshire.*

I stared at it as if mesmerized. What an astounding coincidence. Here was a place I had never heard of before and now it had come up for the second time in two days. That ought to be a sign from heaven, surely. As if I were destined to go there. My breath was coming in rapid gulps. I could escape from Fig and be paid for it. It really did seem too good to be true, an answer to a prayer. I was about to rush to the writing desk and send in my application when I felt a warning siren going off in my head. Maybe it *was* too good to be true. I had come up with brilliant ways to make money before and they had all turned into disasters. I couldn't face a repetition of the escort service fiasco, and I had never heard of Lady Hawse-Gorzley.

I went back into the breakfast room, where Fig and her mother were working their way through the *Tatler*, making catty remarks about the society pictures.

'Does either of you know anyone called Hawse-Gorzley?' I asked.

They looked up, frowning. 'Name sounds familiar,' Fig said.

'Sir Oswald, I believe,' Lady Wormwood said. 'Only a baronet. West Country people, aren't they? Why, what have they done?'

'Nothing. I read the name in *The Lady* and I'd never heard of them. Just curious, that's all. Interesting name, don't you think?' I wandered out of the room again, trying not to let my excitement show. They were legit. Lady Wormwood had heard of them. West Country people. Now I just hoped that I wasn't too late. Heaven knew how long our copy of *The Lady* had taken to reach us up in the wilds of Scotland. There were probably hundreds of applications from suitable young women winging their way to Gorzley Hall at this very moment. I decided I needed to act fast. I was about to make a dash to the telephone when I decided that wouldn't be the right thing to do at all. It might fluster and embarrass her. The correct method would be to write to her on Castle Rannoch writing paper, crest and all, but it would be too slow. Drat and bother. Suddenly I brightened up. I could send her a telegram. I'd learned about the effectiveness of telegrams when I was in France, and all the best people sent them.

'I'm going into the village,' I said, popping my head around the breakfast room door. 'Does anyone want anything?'

Fig peered at me over the *Tatler*. 'How do you propose going to the village in this weather? You're certainly not taking the motor and I don't want MacTavish to have to drive you.'

'I suppose I could ride,' I said.

'I thought you said it would be criminal to take your horse out in this weather,' Lady Wormwood said with the smirk of someone who is scoring a point.

'I could walk if necessary. It's only two miles.'

'Through snowdrifts? Dear me, it must be urgent.'

'It's probably a letter to that Darcy person,' Fig commented. 'Am I right?'

'Not at all,' I said. 'If I can't have the car I'd better start walking.'

'Dashed slippery out there. Who is going out walking?' Binky asked, appearing in the doorway.

'I am,' I said. 'I have to go to the village and I've no other way of getting there.'

'I'm going in myself later,' Binky said. 'If you don't mind sticking around a bit, you can ride in with me.'

Fig glared at him as if he had let the side down by actually wanting to help me, but it was his car, after all.

'Thank you, Binky.' I beamed at him. 'Let me know when you're ready.'

I went upstairs and worked at composing my telegram. Would it make me seem too eager and pushy? I wondered. But then other girls in more southerly climes would have had a couple of days' head start on me, and Christmas was rapidly approaching. I had to take the risk. I scribbled, crossed out, scribbled again and ended up with:

COPY OF THE LADY JUST REACHED ME. HOPE I'M NOT TOO LATE TO APPLY FOR POSITION. SENDING MY PARTICULARS BY POST. GEORGIANA RANNOCH.

Of course anyone who sends telegrams on a regular basis would know that this amount of verbiage would cost me a fortune. I blanched when Mrs McDonald at the post office-cum-general store told me the amount, but Binky was hovering and my pride would not let me take it back for rewriting. Besides, I didn't actually know what I could have left out. So I handed over the money, hoping that it would result in a paid position shortly. I realized there had been no mention of money in the advertisement. Perhaps the only recompense was to be the joys of a big house party. Ah, well, no matter. Anything would be better than a house full of Fig's relatives.

I waited all that day and all the next, sinking further and further into gloom. I was too late. Some other young woman of impeccable background would be enjoying the delights of that big house party while I ate baked beans on toast and dodged Foggy's grabbing hands. Then the next morning a miracle happened. Hamilton appeared with the post while we were at breakfast.

Fig took it. 'Oh, something for you, Georgiana,' she said. 'Who do you know in Devon?'

I snatched the letter and went out of the room to read it. 'It will be a rejection,' I kept muttering as I opened the envelope. Instead I read:

My dear Lady Georgiana:
    I was overwhelmed to receive your telegram. I had no idea that someone of your rank and status would ever consider gracing our small house party in the Devon countryside. We

would be more than honored for you to join us. As mentioned in my advertisement, your duties would only be those of a young hostess, making sure that the younger guests have a good time. Could you be here by the twentieth and stay until after the New Year?

I hardly like to discuss remuneration, but of course we will cover your traveling expenses as well as the fee for your services. I think you'll find us a jolly crowd and we'll have a really gay Christmas.

> *Yours sincerely,*
> *Camilla Hawse-Gorzley*

I bounded up the stairs, two at a time.

'Queenie, I need my trunk again. We're going away!' I shouted.

'Cor blimey, miss,' she muttered. 'Now I suppose you want me to go back up all them stairs and get the ruddy trunk out of the attic again.'

Chapter 5

On my way to Tiddleton-under-Lovey
December 20

I'm delighted to say that Fig was seriously miffed when I told her I had been invited to a house party for Christmas.

'But you don't know anybody in Devon,' she said.

'I know all sorts of people,' I said. 'I just don't mention them to you.'

'Well, if that doesn't take the cake,' she snapped. 'And Maude was so looking forward to seeing you again, and having more French lessons too.'

I smiled sweetly. 'I expect you'll all survive without me. Do give my love to Foggy and Ducky.' Then I made a grand exit. I can't tell you how good it felt.

I also can't tell you how excited I was when I got my first glimpse of Tiddleton-under-Lovey. Queenie and I had traveled on the night express to King's Cross and then across London in a taxi to Paddington. I glanced out the taxi window as we inched our way through the London fog, wondering if Darcy was still somewhere close by and I had no way of contacting him. I had actually received a postcard on the day I left Scotland. It said, *I gather you're celebrating Christmas with the family. I've also been roped in for a family do. But I hope to see you in the new year. Happy Christmas. Love, D.* It was so frustrating. He wrote *Love, D*, but did he mean it? And why hadn't he telephoned me if he was back in Britain? Some of the time I felt hopeful about a future with him and then chance remarks like my mother's dashed those hopes. If you loved somebody, didn't you want to be with her? At least to telephone her to hear her voice? I tried to face the fact that Darcy really was not good husband material, even if I were allowed to marry him. He was one of those men who could not be tamed or made to want to settle down.

I was glad to board the Great Western Railway at Paddington Station and leave the depressing cold and grime of London behind. We had to change trains in Exeter and then take a branch line. The little train huffed and puffed its way beside a lively stream with snow-dusted hills on one side until it reached the small market town of Newton Abbot. The Hawse-Gorzley chauffeur was waiting with a splendid, if rather old, Bentley. As we set off through the country lanes the sun was sinking in a red ball behind the hills. Rooks were cawing as they flew home to their trees. On a great sweep of upland moor I saw a line of Dartmoor ponies silhouetted against the sunset.

We came around a bend and there it was, Tiddleton-under-Lovey, nestled under a snowcapped tor. Was that rocky crag the Lovey? I wondered. It didn't look very loving to me. Or was it perhaps the noisy little stream that passed under the humpback bridge as we approached the first houses? On one side of the village street was a small row of shops and a pub called the Hag and Hounds – complete with a swinging pub sign depicting a witch on a broomstick with baying dogs below her. On the other side was a pond, on which glided several graceful swans, and a village green. Behind this were some thatched cottages and the square tower of a church. Smoke curled up from chimneys and hung in the cold air. A farmer passed, riding a huge cart horse, the clip-clop of its hooves echoing crisply in the evening air.

'Stone me, miss, it looks just like a ruddy picture postcard, don't it?' Queenie said, summing up my thoughts.

I wondered which of the cottages was to be occupied by my mother and Noël Coward. I wondered if my grandfather had consented to come and my heart leaped with hope. Christmas at an elegant house party and my loved ones nearby. What more could I want? Darkness fell abruptly as we drove between a pair of tall gateposts, topped with stone lions, and up a gravel drive. Lights shone out of a solid, unadorned, gray stone house, its severe façade half covered in ivy. This then was Gorzley Hall. It didn't exactly look like the site of an elegant house party – more Bennet residence than Pemberley, but who was I to judge by appearances?

We drew up at the front entrance and the chauffeur came around to open the door for me.

'My maid will help you with the bags,' I said, indicating to Queenie that she should stay, even though she was looking apprehensive. Then I went up to the front door. It was a massive studded affair obviously designed to keep out past invaders. I rapped on the knocker and the door swung open. I waited for someone to come then stepped gingerly into a slate-floored hallway.

'Hello?' I called.

On one side a staircase ascended to a gallery and I spied a pair of legs in old flannel trousers up on a ladder. They belonged to a stocky chap with shaggy gray hair, wearing a fisherman's jersey, and he was wrestling with a long garland of holly and ivy.

'Excuse me,' I called out.

He spun around in surprise and I saw that it wasn't a man at all but a big-boned woman with cropped hair. 'Who are you?' she demanded, peering down at me.

My arrival wasn't exactly going as I had expected. 'I'm Georgiana Rannoch,' I said. 'If you could please go and tell Lady Hawse-Gorzley that I have arrived. She is expecting me.'

'I am Lady Hawse-Gorzley,' she said. 'Been so dashed busy that I completely forgot you were coming today. Come up and grab the other end of this, will you? Damned thing won't stay put. It looked so simple in *Country Life*.'

I put down my train case and did as she requested. Together we secured the garland and she came down the ladder. 'Sorry about that,' she said, wiping her hands on her old slacks. 'I don't want you to think we're always this disorganized. Had a hell of a day here. Police tramping all over the place, not letting the servants get on with their work. That's why we're so behind. Must have the decorations up, y'know. First guests arriving day after tomorrow.'

She led the way back down the stairs, then stuck out a big hand. 'Well, here's a pretty first introduction to Gorzley Hall, what? Camilla Hawse-Gorzley. How do you do? Dashed good of you to muck in like this. Nearly had a fit when I saw my little advertisement answered by the daughter of a duke. You should have seen the other applications I got – their ideas of impeccable background and mine weren't at all the same, I can tell you. Parents in trade, I shouldn't wonder. So you were an answer to our prayers and here you are.'

She beamed at me, making me realize she wasn't as old as I had first thought. 'Well, don't just stand there. Take off your coat. Come on through and have a sherry, then I'll give you a quick tour of the house. Brought a maid with you, I expect?'

'Yes, I brought my maid.' I realized it was going to be hard to get a word in edgewise.

'Jolly good. If I can round up Martha, she can show the girl where you're sleeping and take up your things.'

She rang a bell furiously. 'Damned girl is probably entertaining the policemen in the kitchen. Got too much of an eye for the other sex, that one. Going to come a cropper, you mark my words.'

While she was talking she had led me through to a comfortable-looking drawing room with armchairs and sofas set around a blazing fire in a hearth almost the size of our one at home. Lead-paned bay windows looked out across an expanse of lawn. The walls were wood paneled and the ceiling had great beams running across it. What's more, it was delightfully warm. Lady Hawse-Gorzley motioned me to sit in one of the armchairs then went over to a table in the corner and picked up a decanter. 'Sherry all right for you? Or would you prefer something stronger? A brandy maybe, after your travels?'

'No, sherry would be lovely, thank you.'

'Always have one myself before dinner. I suppose the sun has to be over the yardarm, wouldn't you say? What time is it, by the way? Damned grandfather clock has given up the ghost again. It's been in the family since 1743, so I suppose one can allow it the odd temper tantrum, but dashed awkward time for it.'

'It's about five thirty,' I said, consulting my wristwatch.

'Is it, by George? A little early for sherry, but in the circumstances, I suppose we can bend the rules, what?' She poured two generous glasses and handed me one. 'God, how the time has flown today. I don't know how we're going to get everything ready for the guests in time. Those damned police tramping around all day.' She perched on the arm of a nearby chair and knocked back her sherry in one gulp. 'Like another?' she asked, and looked surprised that I hadn't yet started mine. 'Come on. Drink up. Do you good.'

I knew that good breeding did not allow one to ask too many questions, but I was dying of curiosity. 'Lady Hawse-Gorzley, you mentioned that the police had been here all day. What exactly have they been doing?'

'Tramping all over the place and upsetting my servants, that's what. Damned impertinence. All because our stupid neighbor had to go and kill himself in our orchard. Of all the inconsiderate things to do, especially when he knew I had people coming. Still, that was par for the course with him. Didn't care a hoot about anybody but himself.'

I tried to digest this while she knocked back a second sherry. 'Your neighbor killed himself? Committed suicide, you mean?'

'I hardly think so. If you wanted to kill yourself you probably wouldn't bother to climb a tree first, would you? Not unless you wanted to fall and break your neck, and our fruit trees aren't that big. No, the police think it was an accident. Carrying a loaded rook rifle with him, somehow slipped or knocked the gun and it went off in his face.'

'Had he come onto your property to shoot rooks then, do you think?'

'Wouldn't have thought so. The big elm by the church is where the rooks go to roost for the night. He could have stood in the churchyard, fired with his eyes closed and not been able to miss at dusk. No, my husband agrees with me – it was probably designed to be another of his practical jokes. Going to rig up the rifle so that it went off when someone walked past, or maybe aiming it to shoot at one of our windows – that's what the inspector suggested.'

'He was aiming to kill one of you?'

'No, just give us a nasty scare. That was young Freddie's stock in trade. M'husband reckons that he wanted to pay us back because Oswald found him shooting grouse on the moor the other day. I mean to say – everyone knows the grouse shooting season ends on the tenth of December. And there he was, bold as brass on the eighteenth. Gave him a damned good talking-to. Obviously he didn't like that and decided to get back at us.'

She took another swig of sherry. 'Inherited the property behind ours from his father a few years ago. Still hadn't married and amused himself by being absolutely bloody to his neighbors. In his thirties but still acted like a ten-year-old boy.' She paused and sighed. 'Still, I wouldn't have wished an end like that for the poor chap. He might have turned out all right if he'd married and had to settle down.'

She broke off at the sound of footsteps outside and several blue uniforms passed the window.

'Ah, they are finally off home,' she said. 'I told them they were wasting their time looking for clues on my property. Quite clear the fellow shot himself while trying to rig up some kind of trap. Had the wire with him. Fool. Well, let's hope that's the end of it. The last thing I want is to have my guests greeted by policemen all over the place. I was worried they'd all cancel when they read about the breakout last week.'

'Breakout?'

She looked up in surprise. 'Don't tell me you didn't hear about it! I thought it was in all the newspapers. There have certainly been enough pressmen hanging around here.'

I shook my head. 'Sorry. It takes a long time for news to reach us in the wilds of Scotland.'

She leaned closer. 'Three convicts escaped from Dartmoor Prison, only a few days ago. Supposed to be model prisoners and they were part of a gang working in the quarry. It was all very well planned. They lingered behind on some pretext, hit the guard over the head with a rock and made off over the moor. They were shackled, of course, but apparently one of them made his living as an escape artist. Two of them were entertainers of some sort, but they were all nasty pieces of work. History of violent crimes.'

'And they haven't caught them yet?' I glanced up nervously at the window. It was now completely black outside, with no lights showing anywhere.

'Not seen hide nor hair of them. We've had men with dogs up on the moor, police checkpoints along all the roads, and not a sign of them. We think they must have had a vehicle waiting on the nearest road and were whisked away before anyone could sound the alarm. Which means they are well away from here, thank God.' She stood up. 'I tell you, it's been a hell of a business. Quite upset m'husband. He's a quiet man, is Sir Oswald, doesn't say much. But I could tell it upset him, especially as he was the one who found the blighter slumped in our apple tree today.'

As if on cue I heard the sound of boots in the hall and a big, florid man came in. He had a face like a British bulldog, all jowls and sad eyes. And he was wearing an old tweed jacket that made him look more like a tramp than a lord of the manor. 'Well, they're finally off, then,' he said. 'What a bloody business. What did the blighter think he was doing? If he hadn't shot himself I'd have wrung his bloody neck.'

'Language, Oswald. We have a visitor.'

He broke off as he saw me sitting there. 'Oh, hello. Who's this?'

'Georgiana Rannoch, y'know, sister to the duke.'

'Are you, by George? What on earth are you doing here?'

'She's graciously agreed to join our little house party,' Lady Hawse-Gorzley said, giving me a warning frown that I failed to understand.

'So you've been invited to join this bun fight, have you? Idiotic idea, if you ask me. No good can come of it.'

'I'm sure Lady Georgiana will enjoy herself like everyone else and we'll all have a splendid time,' Lady Hawse-Gorzley replied with great vehemence, all the time glaring at her husband.

He stuck his hand into his pocket and produced his pipe. 'Can't think why. Dull as ditch water down here,' he said, going over to the mantelpiece to find a match. 'I'd have thought you'd be hobnobbing with your royal kin at Sandringham.'

'I wasn't invited,' I said. 'And anyway I'm sure it will be loads of fun here.'

'Well, we've got our share of excitement, as it turns out. You heard the ghastly news, I suppose.'

'I told her about the escaped convicts and about the man managing to kill himself in our apple tree.'

'It was a pear tree, as it happens,' Sir Oswald said, 'but it makes no difference. The local bobbies were full of bright ideas. Suggested he might have come into our orchard to poach pheasants. Utter rubbish, I told them. You don't shoot pheasants from trees. They are ground birds. Idiots, the lot of them. And you don't shoot pheasants with a rook rifle either. No, it's quite obvious to me that he was rigging up some kind of stupid trap. He had the wire with him. Then his weight broke a branch, he slipped and the gun went off in his face. Nasty way to go, but the blighter had it coming.'

He looked down at himself. 'God, I look a sight, don't I? Been out with the damned police all day. Dinner at the normal hour then?'

'If the servants have managed to cook it and set the table while being cross-questioned by police all day,' Lady H-G said.

'I'd better go and change.'

Lady Hawse-Gorzley got to her feet. 'And I should give Georgiana a tour of the house and show her where she will be sleeping so that she has time to freshen up and change for dinner. Come along, my dear. This way.'

She led me on a whirlwind tour – lovely old dining room with a polished table running the length of it, library, morning room, music room and at the back even a ballroom with the air about it of being long out of use. Lady Hawse-Gorzley chatted incessantly like one who hasn't had company for a long time, which made me wonder why she had suddenly decided to have a large house party this Christmas.

'So how many guests are you expecting?' I asked when she paused momentarily for breath. 'You said a large party.'

'Let me see.' She stared out across the expanse of the ballroom as if trying to picture people in it. 'Colonel and Mrs Rathbone. Charming couple, just back from India, you know. Looking forward to a good old-fashioned English

Christmas again. Then there are Mr and Mrs Upthorpe from Yorkshire, with their daughter, Ethel. He owns some kind of large factory up there. Trade, I know, but delightful people nonetheless.'

She paused to take a breath. 'Now, where was I? Ah, yes. Mr and Mrs Wexler from America with their daughter. Most looking forward to some lively transatlantic conversation, I can tell you. And then there is someone I'm sure you already know. The dowager countess Albury and her companion. Do you know her? No? I'm surprised. She's someone who has moved in the highest levels of society, but maybe not in your time.'

While she talked she ran her finger over a couple of marble statues, looking for dust, adjusted sprigs of holly in vases and then led me out of the ballroom again, talking over her shoulder. 'And then a couple of local friends – Captain and Mrs Sechrest. He's a navy man. You'll like them. And Johnnie Protheroe. You can't have a party without Johnnie. Life and soul of any gathering. Most amusing. Let me see – that makes thirteen, doesn't it?' She stopped her forward progress and turned back to me with a fleeting worried look. 'Oh, dear. I'm glad I'm not superstitious or that would be unlucky, wouldn't it? But then, I haven't counted you and you can count as a guest, can't you? So that would make fourteen. And the rest are family, brought in to boost the numbers.'

I wondered why she wanted to boost the numbers, since it was already going to be expensive to feed that many guests. Was there a requisite amount of guests needed at a house party? But she had already gone on ahead, out of the ballroom, down the hall and back to the stairs, while hurling out a commentary as she passed. 'M'husband's study and the land office on your right. And servants' quarters through that door. Kitchen, laundry, all that kind of thing. Haven't seen a servant in hours. Hope the police haven't arrested them or scared them all off.'

Then she set off up the stairs at a lively clip.

'Where did your things go? I wonder. Did someone take them up for you?'

'I expect my maid was shown where to put them.'

She turned back. 'I'm so glad you brought a maid with you. Of course you would. Of course. Well, she'll be jolly useful. She can help the female guests with their attire. I don't suppose they'll all think of bringing maids with them. Of course they won't. I don't have a personal maid any longer. Had to let her go. It's not as if I need help getting dressed and Martha handles the washing and cleaning admirably. So here we are.'

We had gone along a main corridor, lined with family portraits, hunting scenes, with old china vases adorning the deep windowsills. I saw that this must have been the original manor house and that wings had been added on either side to make an E shape. The walls were also oak paneled with all kinds of nooks and crannies. At the moment I observed this, Lady Hawse-Gorzley said, as if reading my mind, 'Perfect place to play sardines, don't you think? I'm hoping for some splendid game nights.'

She turned in to one of the side wings now and paused outside a door. 'I've put you in here. Not quite as big as the main bedrooms but should be all right. We're camping in this hallway ourselves for the duration. Given over our bedroom to guests, y'know.'

Then she flung open the door. I was expecting to see a spartan room like the ones we had at school. Instead it was a pretty room, little and old-fashioned with roses on the eider-down, a matching dressing table skirt and curtains, a white wardrobe, a white chest of drawers and a fireplace waiting to be lit.

'It's charming,' I said.

'Used to be my older daughter's,' she said. 'She's married now. Lives on the Continent. Can't drag her back to England for love or money. Will it do, do you think?'

'Absolutely. It's lovely,' I said. 'Much nicer than my room at home.'

'Is it, by George?' She looked pleased. 'Oh, and I see your maid has unpacked your stuff. Dashed efficient girl, is she? French?'

'No, she's English,' I said, not wanting to reveal Queenie's normal lack of efficiency or that I'd probably find she'd hung up my stockings and shoved my ball dress into a drawer.

'Well, then, I'll leave you to dress for dinner,' she said. 'We're not usually that formal when it's just family, but over Christmas we'll be going the whole hog. Living up to the spirit of the thing, y'know. You'll hear the first gong at quarter to eight for sherry.'

And with that she left me. It was only when I looked in the mirror that I realized I was still wearing my hat. I grinned to myself as I sat down. This was a good place. The house had obviously seen better times, that was clear. So had the Hawse-Gorzleys. Which made me wonder why they had chosen to embark upon such a lavish house party this year and who these guests were, coming from Yorkshire and India and even America to be part of it.

Chapter 6

Gorzley Hall, Tiddleton-under-Lovey, Devon
December 21
Good dinner last night. I think I may have fallen on my feet here!

I awoke to find Queenie standing over me, with a tea tray in her hands.

'Morning, my lady,' she said. 'I've brought your tea.'

I sat up, examining her closely to see if she had been bewitched overnight or whether someone else was actually impersonating her.

'Are you feeling quite well, Queenie?' I asked.

'Yeah. Never felt better,' she said. 'I like it here, miss. Them servants don't look down their noses at me. In fact, I'm the only lady's maid what is in residence at the moment so the cook asked me if I'd prefer to have my meals brought to my room or I'd like to eat with the rest of them. How about that, eh?'

'And what did you say?' I took a sip of deliciously strong hot tea.

'I said I wasn't too proud to sit down with the rest of them. And she said good, 'cause they were going to be run off their feet with this house party.'

'Lady Hawse-Gorzley has asked that you assist the other ladies who will be coming,' I said. 'You can do that, can't you? I do hope you won't let me down and do anything too dreadful.'

'Oh, no, miss. I'll be real careful, I promise. I won't set anyone on fire or nothing. I'll stay away from candles.' (This because she had set her former employer on fire with a wayward candle.)

'I am glad to hear that, Queenie. I'll be wearing my Rannoch tartan skirt and my green jumper today.'

'Bob's yer uncle, miss. It's going to be a lovely day.'

I got out of bed and went over to the window, to find that my room faced the orchard where the body had been found. What a strange thing to have happened. I stared down at the bare trees, wondering which one he had been climbing and what exactly he'd intended to do. They weren't very big trees. Had he really been intending to aim the rifle at one of these windows – at this one, maybe? I shivered and turned away. Well, I wasn't going to let the accidental death of a man I didn't know spoil my Christmas.

I came downstairs to find the front hall taken up by the most enormous Christmas tree, which four men were attempting to raise into place while being bossed around by Lady Hawse-Gorzley.

'Morning. Slept well?' she barked up at me. 'Splendid. Breakfast in the dining room. Can't stop now or they'll smash the chandelier.'

I went through into the dining room to find places set at one end of the long table and a good smell coming from a number of silver tureens on the sideboard. I was just filling my plate with kidneys and bacon and wondering if it would be greedy to add some kedgeree to the mix when a girl came into the room. She was wearing riding breeches and a hacking jacket and her face was glowing as if she'd just come from the cold air.

'Hello,' she said, looking at me curiously. 'Who are you?'

'Georgiana Rannoch,' I said, wishing that Lady Hawse-Gorzley had let a few more people know I was coming so that I didn't have to keep on explaining myself.

'Oh, you're the famous Lady Georgiana, are you? Mother's done nothing but talk about you. She's frightfully excited. You count as a coup.'

'Really?'

'Well, yes, I mean it's close to claiming you have royalty at your party, isn't it?' Her face lit up. 'I say, isn't your mother Claire Daniels? Used to be a famous actress? Well, the village is buzzing with the rumor that she's come down here for Christmas. Is that true?'

'I gather it is,' I said. 'But nobody's supposed to know. She's working on a new play with Noël Coward.'

'Noël Coward? I say. How frightfully exciting. That livens up our dull little corner of the world a bit, doesn't it? Is that why you agreed to take up Mother's little offer?'

'Partly,' I said. 'And partly because I wanted to escape from an even duller place than this.'

'Can there be anywhere duller?' She laughed. 'I'm Hortense, by the way. The daughter of the house. Sorry I wasn't here last night. I was staying with friends in Exeter.'

Hortense Hawse-Gorzley, I thought. What on earth made people choose such names for their poor children? She must have read my thoughts because she grimaced. 'I know. Dreadful name, isn't it? But I'm usually called Bunty. Don't ask me why. No idea.'

'And I'm Georgie,' I said.

'Jolly good. I was dreading we'd have to go through the title and formality stuff. I hate that, don't you? I suppose it's because I don't have one. Complete envy.'

I laughed. 'You wouldn't find my current situation very enviable.'

'Really? I should have thought you'd have a frightfully glamorous life – balls and parties and chaps lining up to marry you.'

'Hardly lining up. There have been a few, but they were all half imbecile and utterly awful. I wouldn't have turned down a halfway decent offer.' I noticed her gear. 'Have you just been out riding?'

'Yes, I have. Splendid morning for it. Do you ride? Stupid question; of course you do. You've probably got stables full of oodles of horses.'

'Not oodles, but I do have a horse at home.'

'Better than the ones we have here, I'm sure. We used to have splendid horses, but of course that's all past now. I gather the family used to be quite rich once. Tin mines in nearby Cornwall. But they closed and Daddy invested the last of the money in America. Right before the crash of '29, as it happened. So we've been in reduced circumstances ever since. But I shouldn't be talking about it. Mummy doesn't like to be reminded of it.'

'Your family eats a good deal better than mine does,' I said, sitting down with my heaped plate.

'Ah, well, we have the home farm. We live on what we can grow and raise most of the year. And Daddy is building up a breeding herd of Jersey cows. Lovely clotted cream, as you'll soon find out.'

She pulled up a chair and sat beside me. 'If you like I'll show you around the village after breakfast.'

'I think I'm supposed to be helping your mother,' I said. 'Doesn't she have masses to do before the first guests arrive?'

'Oh, I don't think you're supposed to actually do anything.' She grinned. 'You're just supposed to be yourself. Lend authenticity to the whole charade.'

'Charade?'

She lowered her voice and whispered, 'They're all paying guests, my dear. Only don't for God's sake let her know that I told you. It's Mummy's brilliant idea to make some money. Ye Olde English Christmas with ye olde aristocratic family. Apparently some people are prepared to pay a lot for that.'

So now it made sense – the diverse guest list and Lady Hawse-Gorzley's flustered preparation for them. And that was why she wanted a young woman of impeccable social background.

'It should be rather fun, actually,' Hortense, or rather Bunty, went on. 'Better than the usual dreary Christmases we've been having lately. My brother's arriving tomorrow and bringing an Oxford chum and Mummy's invited a cousin who is absolutely dreamy and we've been promised a costume ball as well as all the usual village festivities, which are rather amusing in their way.' She paused and a worried look came over her face. 'Oh, Lord. I hope they won't cancel the village things because of what happened to poor old Freddie. You heard, did you, that our neighbor Freddie Partridge shot himself on our land yesterday? I quite liked him, you know. At least he wasn't boring like most people around here. And he played some jolly good tricks on people. I loved it when he bunged up the pipes of the church organ with dead rooks and the organist pumped harder and harder and suddenly they all came flying out all over the congregation. Mr Barclay, the pompous little chap who plays the organ, was furious. But then, it's very easy to upset Mr Barclay. He takes himself far too seriously.'

While she talked she had managed to consume large amounts of food. She got up to refill her coffee cup. 'I think my father really wanted me to marry Freddie, so that he could get his hands on all that extra land. Now I'm not sure who will inherit it. I don't think he had any close relatives.'

At that moment Lady Hawse-Gorzley came in, pushing back her hair from her face. 'Oh, there you are. You girls have met, I see. Splendid.'

'Is there something you'd like me to help you with, Lady Hawse-Gorzley?' I asked.

'We could use more holly and some mistletoe too, if you girls would like to take a basket down to the churchyard. I want the whole place decorated with greenery – festive atmosphere in every room, y'know. Oswald has gone out looking for the Yule log.'

'Yule log?' Bunty laughed. 'Aren't you taking this a bit far?'

'Nonsense. It's part of the traditions of Christmas. We'll go out with the guests on Christmas Eve and have one of the horses drag in the Yule log. If only it snows we can put it on a sledge and drink hot toddies and sing carols as we bring it home.'

Bunty shot me a look. 'While the happy peasants dance in the snow and tip their forelocks, I suppose.'

'Don't be facetious, Bunty. I'm counting on you to get into the spirit of the thing. So off you go and bring back as much holly and ivy as you can carry. And you might see if the vicar could spare us some more candles. We'll need an awful lot, especially to light the ballroom for the costume ball.'

'We do have electric light, Mummy.'

'Yes, dear, but candles are so much more atmospheric, aren't they? A masked ball by candlelight. Think of it.' And she looked quite wistful.

'Come on, then, Georgie,' Bunty said. 'I'll find some shears and off we go.'

'And could you possibly stop at Dickson's cottage and tell him I'd like to go through things with him later this morning, if he doesn't mind?'

Bunty turned to me. 'Dickson's our former butler. He grew so ancient that he had to be put out to pasture, but we dust him off for formal occasions. He's an old dear, actually. Almost like one of the family.'

I put on my coat, hat, and gloves and we set off down the driveway. We stopped first at the gate cottage, where we were shown into a spotless little room and Bunty gave her message to the former butler. He looked extremely elderly and frail, but was dressed formally with stiff collar and black jacket, as if ready to spring back into action again. When she introduced me he gave a correct little bow.

'What an honor, my lady, that you would choose to grace our little corner of England. And how is the health of their dear majesties?'

'I haven't seen them since Balmoral but they were well then, thank you.'

He sighed with relief. 'One does worry so much about His Majesty's chest,' he said. 'Given the current behavior of the Prince of Wales. Tell me, have you actually met the American woman?'

'Yes, I have,' I said. 'Many times.'

'And is she . . .' He paused, searching for the right words.

'As dreadful as they make out?' I smiled at his embarrassed face. 'Oh, yes. Quite as dreadful.'

'I feared as much. The boy was always weak. Still, one hopes that he will buck up and do the right thing when the time comes.'

Privately I didn't share his optimism, but I nodded and smiled and we took our leave. As we came out of the gates and into the village we noticed several groups of villagers, standing in tight knots, talking animatedly. A cluster of men outside the pub glanced furtively in our direction, then went back to their chatter. There was something unnerving about this, a tension in the air as if something was being plotted. Bunty didn't seem to notice there was anything odd in their behavior.

'So here's the sum total of Tiddleton-under-Lovey,' she said. 'One pub, two shops, one school, one church on the green and a few cottages.'

'What about that nicer house beside the school?' I asked. 'Is that where the schoolmaster lives?'

'Oh, no, he has a cottage on the Widecombe road. That house belongs to the Misses Ffrench-Finch. Three elderly sisters who have lived there all their lives. Their father left them quite well off and they never married. We used to call them the Three Weird Sisters and spy on them when we were growing up. You'll meet them over Christmas, I'm sure. Mummy always invites them to Christmas lunch.'

'And what about the pub?' I asked, looking at the sign swinging in the chill morning breeze. 'The Hag and Hounds? What's that about?'

'Local history.' Bunty grinned. 'We had a local witch, you know. Back in the 1700s. They wanted to catch her and bring her to trial, but she escaped onto the moor. They chased her to the top of Lovey Tor with a pack of hounds and then burned her at the stake. We have a festival to celebrate it every New Year's Eve. You'll be able to see just how primitive we are down here in Devon. This way.'

And she turned from the street to the path around the village green, then stepped through the kissing gate into the churchyard. Rooks rose cawing and flapping.

'Damned nuisance,' she said. 'They peck out the eyes of newborn lambs, you know. So let's see where there might be any good holly left.'

As we made our way between ancient gravestones the church door opened and a woman came out. She had spinster written all over her, the sort of woman one always sees coming out of churches and doing good works. She wore an old fur coat that might have been 'good' once and a shapeless hat and those strange lace-up shoes that old women seem to favor. And she came toward us, head down against the wind, holding her hat on with one hand.

'Good morning, Miss Prendergast,' Bunty said and the woman started in surprise.

'Oh, Miss Hawse-Gorzley, you gave me a start,' she replied in a breathless, twittering little voice. 'I was completely lost in thought. I have just been working on the church flowers for Christmas. I was planning to surround the crèche with holly but Mr Barclay told me absolutely not. He said that holly did not grow in the Holy Land and thus it would not be authentic. Really, he is such an objectionable man, isn't he? An absolute stickler for detail and always insists on his own way. I'm sure our Lord wouldn't mind being brightened up with some nice red holly berries around him.'

'I'm sure he wouldn't,' Bunty said. 'And may I present

our guest Lady Georgiana Rannoch? Georgie, this is Miss Prendergast.'

'How do you do,' I said.

She looked stunned. 'Oh, my goodness. It's almost like having royalty visit the village, isn't it? Delighted to make your acquaintance.' She bobbed an awkward half curtsy. 'So you're here to enjoy the splendid festivities Lady Hawse-Gorzley has planned, are you? I am so looking forward to them myself. Lady Hawse-Gorzley has been kind enough to invite me to join you for the Christmas banquet. Such a treat when one lives a simple lonely life like mine. But I mustn't keep you.'

And she went on her way.

'Another weird woman?' I asked.

'No, she's no weirder than the average village spinster. A bit twittery and rather nosy, I suspect. And she's a relative newcomer, too. She moved here about five years ago. Looked after her aged mother somewhere like Bournemouth. When the mother died she sold the family home and bought that cottage next to the church. Used to come here on holiday as a child, one gathers. And I must say she's proving to be an asset. Every village needs a willing spinster, don't you think? Always volunteering for good deeds.'

We found some good holly bushes and started cutting branches. Isn't it interesting the way they always love to grow near graves?

'We still have to find mistletoe,' I reminded Bunty.

'I don't really see why.' She gave me a grin. 'I'm not sure there will be anybody for you to kiss, apart from old colonels whose mustaches will be frightfully spiky.'

'Nonetheless, your mother asked for some. And didn't you say you have a dreamy cousin coming?'

'I didn't say there was nobody for *me* to kiss,' she replied with a wicked grin. 'I believe I saw some on the big tree next to the middle cottage. Yes, look up there. I hope you're good at tree climbing.'

We came to the big elm and saw there was indeed mistletoe growing from an upper branch.

'I suppose I'd better go up,' Bunty said. 'Mummy would never forgive me if you fell and broke your neck. Here, give me a leg up.'

I was just hefting her off the ground when she looked down the path, squinted into the sunlight and said, 'Hello, who is this?'

I looked too. A small round silhouette was coming up the path toward us. He recognized me at exactly the same moment I recognized him.

'Blimey, strike me down with a feather,' he said, his face lighting up. 'What the dickens are you doing here?'

'Granddad,' I said and rushed to him, leaving Bunty suspended in the tree.

Chapter 7

'Granddad, you came! I am so glad.' I hugged him fiercely, feeling the familiar scratchy cheek against mine.

'Well, I couldn't very well let Mrs Huggins travel all this way on her own, could I?' he said. 'She ain't been no further than Margate before. But what on earth are you doing here? Did your mum invite you and not tell me?'

'No, she doesn't know I'm here. I'm actually helping out at the house party at Gorzley Hall. Pure coincidence.'

His little boot-button eyes twinkled. 'You know I always say there ain't no such thing as coincidence, don't you?'

I laughed uneasily. 'Yes, well, we're both here and it's going to be a wonderful Christmas. I take it Mummy is already in residence?'

'So is that Coward bloke. Bit of a poofta, isn't he? And awfully fussy. Likes his eggs boiled three and a quarter minutes, not three, not three and a half.'

I laughed, then heard a slithering sound and saw Bunty lowering herself from the tree.

'Oh, sorry,' I called. 'I've just had a lovely surprise. Come and meet my grandfather. Granddad, this is Bunty

Hawse-Gorzley. She's the daughter of the house where I'm staying.'

'Pleased to meet you, miss,' Granddad said, holding out a big meaty hand.

Bunty looked surprised, but was too well bred to comment. 'Lovely to meet you too,' she said. 'I hope you don't mind but we're getting mistletoe from your tree.'

'Not my tree, ducks. Take all you want.'

'I should go inside and say hello to my mother.' I turned to Bunty. 'Maybe my grandfather can help you see if there is a ladder in the shed. That will be easier than trying to climb the first bit.'

I knocked lightly and went into the cottage. It was everything a cottage should be and I could tell why Noël had chosen it. Big beams across the ceiling, brass warming pan on the wall, fire crackling merrily in the hearth, copper pots hanging over the kitchen stove. All it needed was a spinning wheel and a white-haired old lady to complete the picture. Instead there was my mother, curled up like a cat in an armchair by the mullioned window, reading *Vanity Fair*. She looked up and those lovely blue eyes opened wide.

'Good God, Georgie, what are you doing here?'

'That's a nice welcome, I must say.' I went across the room to kiss her cheek. 'How about, "Hello, darling daughter, what a lovely surprise to see you"?'

'Well, it is, but I mean – what *are* you doing here? I told you Noël and I were going to be working and there's actually no room and–'

'Relax, Mummy. I'm staying at Gorzley Hall. Pure coincidence that we're in the same village. I just came down to say hello.'

Relief flooded over her face. 'Well, in that case, lovely to see you, darling.' And she kissed my cheek in return.

'Everything all right? All settled in?' I asked her.

'Splendid. Noël's up in his room, pounding away at his typewriter. Your Mrs Huggins is doing very well, in spite of Noël's food fads, and we've found a local girl, Rosie, to come and clean for us. At least I hope she's coming to clean. She should have been here by now.' She glanced at her watch.

I looked out the window and saw a woman break away from one of the tight knots of gossipers and hurry in our direction with a worried expression on her face. It occurred to me that perhaps the gossip was because the villagers had found out about my mother and Noël Coward.

The front door was flung open and the woman came in. 'Awful sorry I'm late, ma'am,' she said in a broad Devon accent. 'I know I said ten o'clock, but I were that upset – I don't know if you've heard the news, ma'am.'

'About the man who killed himself yesterday? Yes, we were told about that.'

'No, ma'am. Not about him. 'Tis Ted Grover I'm talking about. He were found drowned in Lovey Brook this morning.'

Mummy sat up. 'And who is Ted Grover?'

'He were my uncle, ma'am. Owned a big garage just outside Bovey Tracey. Doing awfully well, he were. Owned charabancs and gave tours of the moor. And now he's gone.' She put her red, work-worn hands up to her face and started to sob noisily. Mummy put a tentative arm around her shoulder. 'I'm very sorry, Rosie. I'll have Mrs Huggins bring you a cup of tea.'

'What happened to him?' I asked as Mummy headed for the kitchen, calling, 'Mrs Huggins!' in strong theatrical tones.

'Well, he was always popping over for a drink at the Hag and Hounds,' Rosie said. 'Leastways everyone knew why he came to this pub and not the Buckfast Arms, which was right next to his garage. And it weren't the quality of the ale either. He and the publican's wife were sweet on each other, you see. They'd meet out behind the pub and then he'd cut back across the fields to his place, thinking that nobody saw him. Of course we all knew about it – well, in a village everyone does, don't they?'

She paused, taking out a big checked handkerchief and blowing her nose. 'Well, he had to cross a little stone bridge over Lovey Brook. It's just one of them simple clapper bridges like you see around here made of big slabs of stone balanced on rocks, and they are not always very stable. So they reckon he'd drunk quite a bit last night and lost his balance, see. Fell into Lovey Brook and hit his head on a rock. Terrible tragedy, just before Christmas. And my poor auntie – knowing how he died, having gone to see that woman.'

I gave a sympathetic nod.

'And of course you know what everyone in the village is saying, don't you?' She looked up at Mrs Huggins, who had come in personally with the cup of tea, not wanting to miss out on anything, I suspect. Rosie brightened considerably, having now a larger audience. 'Two deaths in two days? They are saying it's the Lovey Curse, striking again.'

'The Lovey Curse?' Mummy looked amused.

Rosie beckoned me, my mother and Mrs Huggins into a tight little circle. 'You've heard about our witch, no doubt? Well, when she was being burned at the stake, she cursed the village, saying every Yuletide she'd be back to take her revenge. And sure enough, something bad always happens here around Christmastime.' She folded her arms with satisfaction. 'You mark my words. It's the Lovey Curse, all right.'

'What in God's name is all this weeping and wailing?' Noël Coward appeared in the doorway, wearing a striped silk dressing gown, with a long cigarette holder between his fingers and a pained expression on his handsome face. 'I thought I chose this place for peace and quiet.'

'There's been a tragedy, Noël. Rosie's uncle fell off a bridge last night and drowned.'

'Ah, the transience of life.' Noël gave a dramatic sigh. 'Frightfully sorry to hear about your uncle, Rosie dear, but could you grieve more quietly, do you think? The muse was doing splendidly until a few minutes ago, when she fluttered out the window and simply vanished.'

'Do you want me to go looking for it for you, sir?' Rosie asked. 'Some kind of pet bird, is it?'

Noël sighed again. 'I shall return to my room, I think. Could you be an angel and produce some drinkable coffee, Mrs Huggins?'

He was about to make a dramatic exit when my mother called after him. 'Look who has come to visit, Noël. My daughter, Georgiana.'

He spun around. 'Georgiana, of course! I thought the face looked familiar but I couldn't quite place you. Lovely to see you, my dear. Are you just passing through?'

'No, I'm actually here for Christmas,' I said wickedly as I watched Noël struggling to hide his annoyance.

'She's staying at Gorzley Hall,' Mummy corrected hastily. 'They are going to have a frightfully jolly house party there, so I gather.'

'Well, bully for you,' Noël said. 'Claire and I will be

working. Slaving away, actually, but do come down for a drink sometime, won't you?'

With that he stomped back up the stairs.

Mummy gave me a commiserating smile. 'You mustn't mind him. He's awfully grouchy when he's working. I'm glad you're here, darling. We must have some girl time together.'

Mrs Huggins was loitering at the kitchen door. 'Does that mean my Queenie has come down here with you, my lady?' she asked.

I remembered that Queenie was her great-niece. 'Yes, she's here with me. I'll send her down to say hello to you.'

'Is she proving to be satisfactory, my lady?'

I couldn't tell the brutal truth that Queenie would probably never be satisfactory in her life. 'She's definitely improving, Mrs Huggins,' I said.

'Well, that's nice to know, isn't it?' She beamed at me as she went back into the kitchen.

Noises outside indicated that a ladder had been found and that Bunty was attempting to go up the tree. 'I should go,' I said. 'I'm supposed to be gathering mistletoe.'

'I hope there is someone worth kissing at your party,' Mummy said. 'Such a waste of mistletoe otherwise.'

I came out to find Granddad steadying the ladder while Bunty clung to it precariously. 'I volunteered to go up for the young lady,' he said, 'but she wouldn't hear of it.'

'Quite right. No ladders at your age,' I said.

'I'm not over the hill yet,' he said. 'By the way, what was all that fuss about in there? I heard weeping and wailing.'

'Rosie's uncle was found drowned in a brook this morning. Rosie's saying it's the Lovey Curse striking again. Two deaths in two days in the village.'

'Hmm,' Granddad said. 'You know what my old inspector would say about that, don't you?'

'Well, in this case your inspector would be wrong, I suspect,' I said. 'One man shot himself by accident and the other fell off one of those little stone bridges in the middle of the night after he'd drunk too much. I don't think you can read a curse or anything else into that, can you?'

'Let's hope not,' Granddad said. 'I'd like a nice quiet Christmas, personally, with no complications.'

Bunty had just climbed down, waving a sprig of mistletoe triumphantly, when a motorcar drew up.

'Oh, Lord,' Bunty said as several policemen got out. 'I thought we'd seen the last of them.'

Chapter 8

One of the policemen headed straight for us. He was wearing a fawn raincoat and a matching fawn hat and had a droopy fawn mustache. If he'd had the words 'detective inspector' tattooed to his forehead it couldn't have been more obvious. 'Morning, Miss Hawse-Gorzley,' he said, raising his trilby to reveal thinning fawn hair, neatly parted down the middle.

'Good morning, Detective Inspector.'

'I suppose you've heard this latest news. Two deaths in two days. And just when I thought I'd be getting time off to do some Christmas shopping with the wife, too.'

'But they were both accidents, surely,' Bunty said.

'Let's hope so, Miss Hawse-Gorzley, let's hope so,' he said. 'But I have to wonder about Ted Grover. Not usually the type who goes stumbling around drunk, would you say? Holds his liquor pretty well, so I've been told. Which makes me ask myself whether one of them convicts might still be hiding out in the neighborhood and encountered Ted last night.'

'If I were those convicts I'd have headed for Plymouth as quickly as possible and boarded a ferry for France,' Bunty said.

'You would, no doubt, Miss Hawse-Gorzley, but then you're a young woman of the world. Those criminal types would be lost on the Continent, not knowing how to parley-vous and all that. They'd stick out like sore thumbs and be caught instantly. If you want to know what I suspect, I suspect that they haven't strayed too far. What's more, I suspect that someone around these parts is hiding them.' He looked at my grandfather. 'Now, take the folks who are renting this cottage, for instance. Moved in just around the time of the breakout, didn't they?'

'Yes, but one of them is Claire Daniels and the other Noël Coward,' I said. 'They're supposed to be in seclusion, writing a new play together, and I'm pretty sure they won't be harboring escaped convicts.'

'And how about you, sir?' the inspector asked. 'Are you one of their servants?'

'I am Claire Daniels's father, Albert Spinks,' Granddad replied stiffly, 'and what's more I was on the force for thirty years with the Metropolitan Police.'

The inspector took a step back, then stuck out his hand. 'Pleased to meet you, sir. Inspector Harry Newcombe. What a stroke of luck that you're here. I'll be calling upon your expertise, if you don't object. So you've been at the cottage these last few days. And I notice that the cottage garden looks directly onto the orchard where the man shot himself. So did you happen to hear a shot in the early hours of yesterday morning?'

Granddad shook his head. 'No, I can't say I did, but then, I sleep quite soundly. Have they ascertained the time of death?'

'No, I haven't had the doctor's report yet,' the inspector said, 'seeing that he was off delivering a baby at Upper

Croft Farm on the moor, but we reckon it had to be early yesterday morning. I can't imagine that anyone would go tramping through an orchard and climbing trees in the dark, so that would make it seven thirty or later. And it had to be before Sir Oswald went on his morning rounds with his dogs.'

'I was up by seven,' Granddad said. 'But maybe I was shaving or getting the fires started and a little rifle like that doesn't make much noise.'

'It's strange that nobody heard the shot, though,' the inspector said. He patted my grandfather heartily on the shoulder. 'It's going to be a boon to have someone like you on the spot here. You'd be in the position to notice any strange goings-on in this village, wouldn't you? My men can't be everywhere and there are so many little villages like this where the blighters could be hiding.'

'These convicts,' Granddad said thoughtfully. 'I did read something about the breakout when I was coming down on the train, but I didn't take in the details. Local men, are they, then?'

'No, I wouldn't say that. Two of them were entertainers of sorts – an escape artist turned safecracker; we reckon he picked the locks on their shackles – then a bloke who used to have an act in the music hall and the third one was a bank clerk who'd been involved in a railway heist. We reckon he was the brains. Quiet little man on the surface but absolutely ruthless. Slit your throat as soon as look at you.'

Bunty shivered.

Granddad nodded. 'But none of them with connections around here?'

'Well, the bank clerk had a sister in Plymouth. You can bet we've got a close eye on her place. And of course that big heist was on the Penzance-to-London express, but further up the line in Wiltshire. You no doubt remember it.'

Granddad nodded. 'Very well,' he said. 'The money was never recovered, was it?'

'It was not. So the Wiltshire police will be keeping their eyes open near the spot where it happened. And both the entertainers had spent a fair amount of time in the West Country – played summer shows on the piers in Torquay and Weston-super-Mare. What's more, this music hall bloke, Robbins, he was inside for swindling his landladies out of their life savings. And we reckon that he bumped off a few, including the last one down here in Newton Abbot.'

'Why wasn't he hanged for murder, then?' Bunty asked.

'Got off on a technicality. Couldn't actually prove that he pushed her down the stairs, so it was reduced to manslaughter and he got twenty years. Nasty bit of work he was, too.'

'But he'd have no reason to linger in these parts, would he?' Granddad asked.

'I wouldn't if I were him. He was a Londoner. And they'd be queuing up to turn him in around here.'

Granddad shook his head. 'In my experience there's not much that gets past the locals in a village like this. If someone were hiding here, they'd know it.'

Inspector Newcombe sighed. 'I reckon you're right. And I am probably reading too much into a couple of unfortunate accidents. I don't see how the first could be anything other than suicide, and the second – well, there's no sign of a struggle. And those convicts – well, they'd have bashed someone over the head, wouldn't they?'

'Have you dusted the rifle for fingerprints?' I asked.

The inspector seemed to be aware of me for the first time. 'Ah, we've an amateur detective here, have we, miss? Like to read those Agatha Christie books, I've no doubt. They've turned half the population into know-it-alls.'

'I have had some experience with murder,' I said. 'And if I were you I'd have checked the rifle for prints and also I'd conduct an autopsy on the body. That way you can be sure nobody else was involved.'

Inspector Newcombe gave me a patronizing smile. 'If I were planning to kill somebody, young lady, I'd wait until he came down from his tree. If he was up a tree with a rifle, I'd feel rather vulnerable as I approached him.'

This was, of course, a valid comment and I nodded.

'Are you also staying at the cottage, miss?' he asked.

'This is Lady Georgiana Rannoch, the king's cousin,' Bunty said grandly, 'and she's staying with us at the hall.'

'Well, I never,' Inspector Newcombe said. 'No offense, I hope, my lady. Honored to make your acquaintance, but I suggest you go back to the hall and have a nice Christmas celebration and you leave the detective work to the police.'

'Obnoxious little man, isn't he?' Bunty muttered as we retraced our steps to the hall. As we turned onto the village street the door of the general store opened and a strange-looking figure came out. He was so bulky that he almost filled the narrow door to the shop and he was dressed in bright motley clothing with a shapeless red hat on his head and a mop of unruly curls. He set off with a strange lumbering gait, like a giant in a children's pantomime.

'Who on earth is that?' I turned to Bunty.

'Oh, that's only Willum. He's the village idiot. Every village has to have one, don't they?' She laughed. 'Actually, he's the son of Mrs Davey at the shop. He's a bit simple, but quite harmless. Just wanders around, helping people for the odd coin occasionally. 'Morning, Willum,' she called out.

He turned his innocent child's face to us and touched his cap. 'Morning, Miss Hawse-Gorzley. Did you hear the news? They are saying that Ted Grover from over Five Corners way fell into Lovey Brook last night. What were he doing walking across the fields in the dark, that's what I'd like to know.'

'Returning home from the Hag and Hounds,' Bunty said.

Willum frowned. 'That's what comes of drinking, don't it? He should have been safely home with his mum like I am of an evening.'

'Quite right, Willum.' She chuckled. 'Rather sweet, actually,' she added to me as we moved away. 'Oh, and you'll probably meet Sal at some stage. She's our wild woman.'

'You're making it up.' I laughed.

'I am not. We have our idiot and a wild woman to boot. Sal is one of those strange untamed creatures you find sometimes in the country. She lives up on the moor in a stone hovel, picks herbs, dances around barefoot in the moonlight. The locals swear she has magic powers – in fact, there is a rumor that she is a direct descendant of our witch. She's tough, I'll tell you that much. You'll see her out in the foulest weather running around barefoot in a flimsy dress.' She glanced across at me. 'Oh, dear, I hope I haven't scared you off. Mummy says I mustn't mention her or Willum or the unfortunate events to the guests or they'll all want their money back.'

'I gather the first ones are arriving tomorrow,' I said.

'Yes, and Mummy's not happy about it. She wanted everyone to arrive at the same time for the grand welcome, but the Americans insisted on coming a day early. Mr Wexler cabled from the ship that they'd be arriving on the twenty-second to give them plenty of time to settle in, and that they were bringing their son as well, because he refused to be left behind.'

'Oh, dear, I hope they are not going to be difficult,' I said. 'I'm afraid people with lots of money do seem to be rather arrogant.'

'Let's hope that the presence of one who is related to the royal family will awe them into submission.' Bunty gave me a wicked grin. 'Oh, Lord, I'm afraid you'll have to meet Mr Barclay now.'

A small man with hair neatly parted in the middle and a perfect little mustache was coming out of the church.

'Morning, Mr Barclay,' Bunty called merrily.

'It is not a good morning, Miss Hawse-Gorzley. Not at all. That dreadful Prendergast woman has absolutely no taste. You should see what ghastly things she wants to do with the decorations. And the vicar only wants the good old hymns. He shot down my version of "*In Dulci Jubilo*." Positively shot it down – after the choirboys have been practicing it, too. Oh, well, if he wants a boring midnight mass, he shall have one.'

And he swept away with small mincing steps before I could be introduced. Bunty and I exchanged a smile. 'He's always upset about something,' she said. 'Always complaining to the parish council and seething with indignation.' We approached the gates leading to Gorzley Hall. 'So now you've seen what a strange lot we are. Hopelessly inbred, all crackers.' And she laughed.

Chapter 9

Gorzley Hall
December 21 and then 22

As we were about to turn in to the drive an ancient motorcar drew up across the street and three birdlike old ladies were helped out by an equally ancient chauffeur.

'We've been shopping, Miss Hawse-Gorzley,' one of them called excitedly. 'Such fun. Almost forgot the crackers, and we were afraid that Hanleys would have sold out, but they hadn't.'

'And your dear mother invited us again to join you for Christmas luncheon,' the second old lady called to us. 'We look forward to it all year.' She turned for affirmation to her two companions, who were handing packages to the chauffeur. 'And I hope you won't forget to come caroling at our house. Cook has made enough mince pies to feed an army.'

With that they tottered like a line of ducklings into their house. I knew, of course, they could only be the Ffrench-Finch sisters.

'They are rather sweet, really,' Bunty said. 'Never married. Lived here all their lives. How boring, don't you agree? But they seem content enough. Of course, Effie, the oldest, bosses the other two around. They have a really good cook. Mummy's tried to lure her away several times, but she won't leave them.'

With that we continued up the drive toward the house. We spent a pleasant afternoon putting up holly and mistletoe. I thought that Bunty made a big fuss about the correct situation of the mistletoe sprig, as the only younger males were to be her brother and her cousin. I also made note of where it was so that I could avoid standing there. I really dislike being grabbed and kissed by aged colonels.

The decorations were complete, apart from the tree, which would be decorated by the guests on Christmas Eve. Then after a fairly simple dinner, by their standards, during which Lady Hawse-Gorzley got through rather a lot of wine, I went to bed early. I must have slept in rather late and I woke with a start to see Queenie looming over me.

'Morning tea, my lady,' she said. 'Guess what? It's been snowing all night. It looks lovely out there.'

I sat up and examined the scene with pleasure. The pine trees beyond the orchard and then on Lovey Tor made the scene look almost alpine. To the left smoke was curling up from the chimney of my mother's cottage. 'It does look lovely,' I agreed. 'Perfect for Christmas.'

'Good food here, eh, miss?' she said, setting down the tray. 'Will you be wearing your tartan skirt and the jumper again?'

'No, I think the gray jersey dress and my pearls. The Americans will expect me to look like royalty.'

'Yer gray dress and pearls?' Queenie said. 'Won't you be a bit cold in that?'

'No, the house is actually quite warm,' I said. 'You can put them out while I go and have a bath. Let's hope the bathroom is free at this hour.'

'I thought I might pop down and visit my auntie 'ettie after breakfast, if that's all right with you,' she said, handing me my robe.

'Of course. She asked after you.'

Reluctantly leaving the warmth of my bed and taking a good swig of tea, I slipped on my robe. I had just assembled my sponge bag and towel and was halfway down the hall when I heard a violent hammering at the front door. I paused, looking down from the gallery with unabashed curiosity. Was this the first visitors arriving so early?

The aged butler went to the door and I heard a young woman's voice, thick with the local accent, saying, 'Oh, Mr Dickson. Terrible news. It's Miss Effie. We just found the gas turned on in her bedroom and Miss Effie stone dead. We don't have a telephone in the house so Miss Florrie sent me to call the doctor – though what he can do, I can't imagine. Stone dead, she were, God rest her poor soul.'

This outburst brought Lady Hawse-Gorzley through from the dining room. 'What's going on, Dickson? What's this all about?'

'It's the girl from the Misses Ffrench-Finch, my lady,' Dickson said, his voice wavering a little with emotion. 'It seems that one of the ladies has been found dead in her bed, and this girl wishes us to telephone for the doctor.'

'How awful. I'm so sorry,' Lady Hawse-Gorzley said. 'Come on in, my dear. What a shock for you. Which of the Misses Ffrench-Finch was it?'

'Miss Effie,' the girl said, swallowing back a sob that rose in her throat. 'I don't know what the other two are going to do without her. She was always the strong one, the one who bossed us all around.'

Lady Hawse-Gorzley put an arm around her shoulder. 'Well, she was no longer young, was she? I suppose it was her heart?'

'Oh, no, ma'am. Like I were telling Mr Dickson, we found the gas turned on for her gas fire, but no flame lit. She must have been breathing that gas all night.'

Lady Hawse-Gorzley sprang into action. 'Dickson, please telephone Dr Wainwright and tell his receptionist he is wanted immediately at the Misses Ffrench-Finch. I had better come over right away, hadn't I? I imagine there is chaos.'

'Well, ma'am, Miss Prendergast is already there. I expect she'd be comforting Miss Florrie and Miss Lizzie. She just happened to be passing on her usual morning walk, so she went straight inside and was her usual efficient self. But of course she doesn't have a telephone neither, so that's why she sent me here.'

I didn't wait a second longer, but headed straight back to my room. Queenie hadn't got around to laying out my clothes. 'I thought you was taking a bath, miss,' she said when confronted. I didn't have time for explanations and hurriedly put on the kilt and jumper I had worn the day before, then ran down the stairs and along the drive to catch up with Lady Hawse-Gorzley. The snow now lay several inches deep and I wished I had taken the time to put on sturdier shoes.

'You heard the ghastly news, I take it,' she said, hearing my footsteps behind her. 'They must have made a mistake.

The poor old thing probably died in her sleep from natural causes. It wouldn't be like Miss Effie to forget to light the gas or to turn it on by mistake. She's the efficient one of the three. She was the one who looked after the other two and kept them in line.' She sounded genuinely upset. 'It's not right,' she added. 'Three deaths in three days. We'll have people really start to believe in the Lovey Curse and then my guests will all want to go home.'

'I've always heard that bad things come in threes, haven't you?' I said to her. 'Three deaths in a row is not unprecedented, especially as they are all so very different. Perhaps we'll find there was a malfunction with the gas fire. Perhaps the wind blew out a low flame. All kinds of simple explanations.'

She looked at me as if she had only just realized to whom she was speaking. 'Lady Georgiana, I really can't expect you to get involved in our local unpleasantness. Why don't you go home and have breakfast? I'll join you as soon as I can.'

'I thought maybe I might be able to help,' I said.

'Well, all right. Won't say no. Could use the company. Dashed awful, isn't it?'

We were just crossing the road when I heard my name being called and saw my grandfather waving. 'Just been out to get the morning papers,' he said, striding toward us. 'Mrs Huggins likes her *Daily Mirror* and Mr Coward likes the *Times* and I like a morning walk. Lovely down here, ain't it? Smashing, eh?'

'Yes, it's lovely,' I said.

He picked up something in my manner. 'Why, what's the matter, love?'

'One of the old ladies who lives in this house has just died in suspicious circumstances. This is Lady Hawse-Gorzley. You met her daughter yesterday.' I turned to her. 'This is my grandfather. He used to be in the Metropolitan Police. Perhaps it might be a good thing if he came with us.'

'Oh, dear.' Lady Hawse-Gorzley looked worried. 'Surely we're only dealing with another ghastly accident, aren't we? You yourself just said that deaths come in threes.'

'I said bad things come in threes,' I corrected. 'And I hope we are just dealing with a ghastly accident. But it couldn't hurt if my grandfather came with us to take a look.'

'But the ladies won't be ready to receive gentlemen callers at this hour,' Lady Hawse-Gorzley exclaimed in horror. 'They may still be in their night attire.'

Granddad laughed. 'I've seen worse than night attire in my thirty years on the force,' he said. 'Still, I won't come in if I'm not wanted.'

Lady Hawse-Gorzley relented. 'It might be useful to have a trained professional eye on the scene. And I suppose the police will have to be called eventually.'

We went up the path to the front door. It was a solid, square Georgian house in local Devon sandstone and was of pleasing proportions. The type of house the old wool merchants built for themselves when wool meant prosperity. We found the front door still ajar. Lady Hawse-Gorzley pushed it open and we were met in the front hall by a frantic-looking housekeeper. Her apron was on askew and her hair an unsightly mess.

'Oh, it's you, Lady Hawse-Gorzley. What a terrible thing to happen. Poor Miss Effie. We sent the girl to telephone for the doctor.'

'Dickson is helping her do so at this moment,' Lady Hawse-Gorzley said. 'This gentleman is a former detective from Scotland Yard. He may be able to throw some light on what happened.'

'Throw some light,' the woman said. 'There was something wrong with that gas, that's all. What else could there be?'

We went up a broad curved staircase and were met at the top by Miss Prendergast, who was trying to give an impression of being calm while clearly being considerably agitated.

'Thank God somebody else has come,' she said. 'What a terrible business. I didn't believe it when the maid ran out in hysterics. But I'm afraid it's true. See for yourselves.'

She opened the door to a bedroom. The faint odor of gas still lingered, but the windows were wide open and an ice-cold breeze blew in. I glanced at the small white figure in the bed. She looked so tiny, so frail. I looked away hurriedly and rather wished I hadn't come. What had made me think I could be of any use?

Granddad looked around. 'I don't know how she managed to kill herself in a big room like this with the windows open,' he said.

'Oh, no, I opened the windows,' Miss Prendergast said quickly. 'Everyone here was in such a state, they hadn't even thought to do so. So it was the first thing I did. I turned off the gas and opened the windows or we might all have suffered the same fate as Miss Effie. They were shut tightly. The smell in here was horrible. Poor woman. It had to have been a malfunction. Either that or one of the servants turned it on and forgot to light it properly. Of course, you'll never get her to own up to it now.'

Lady Hawse-Gorzley sniffed contemptuously. 'That's what comes of sleeping with the windows shut. Nasty, unhealthy habit. Good fresh air never hurt anyone.'

'Well, that's the strange thing, ma'am,' the housekeeper said. 'Miss Effie usually slept with her window open, and the door open too. Miss Florrie is prone to nightmares, so Miss Effie kept her door open in case her sister cried out in her sleep.'

'But they were both closed last night?' I asked.

She nodded. 'They were indeed. I suppose it was snowing and she didn't want the snow to come in. And maybe the wind blew the door shut.'

'Then maybe it was a gust of wind that blew out the fire,' I suggested.

'Yes, that would be it,' Miss Prendergast agreed. 'Temperamental things, gas fires. I won't have them in the house.'

Granddad was prowling the room, not touching anything, but checking. 'This lady – she hadn't given any signs of being depressed or worried lately, then?'

The housekeeper, who had been lurking close to the doorway, gave a little cry. 'Suicide, is that what you're suggesting, sir? Never. Not Miss Effie. She was the one who kept this place going. Had us all on our toes and took good care of her sisters. No, she'd never have left them in the lurch.'

'Did you have any visitors at all yesterday evening?' Lady Hawse-Gorzley asked.

The housekeeper shook her head firmly. 'Oh, no, ma'am. The ladies never entertain in the evenings anymore. It's an early dinner, then bed for all three of them. They might manage a little game of cards after dinner, but not for long.'

'I must have been one of the last visitors, then,' Miss Prendergast said. 'I was here for tea and Mr Barclay stopped by so of course he was asked to join us. Most awkward, since Mr Barclay and I have not seen eye to eye on the decorations. Miss Effie was most tactful about it. Smoothed things over wonderfully. It was a knack of hers. Oh, and when we were leaving Willum arrived, didn't he, Mrs Bates?'

'That's right. The ladies had asked him to come over and bring down the decorations from the attic for them. He brought them all down and then helped us bring in the Christmas tree. It's all there in the drawing room. They never decorate it until Christmas Eve. It's their tradition.'

'So after Willum nobody came?' Lady Hawse-Gorzley persisted.

'No, ma'am. I believe we locked the doors when Willum went.' She stopped talking at the sound of a car drawing up outside. 'Oh, Lord,' she groaned. 'It's that policeman. He was here the other day. Nasty bullying way with him. Made our girls quite upset, scaring them with talk of convicts hiding out in the sheds.'

There was thumping on the front door. One of the maids must have answered it because we heard heavy footsteps coming up the stairs.

'Quite a little party we have here, I see,' Inspector Newcombe said, coming into the room. 'I was at the police station in the next village when the call was put to the doctor, so Gladys on the switchboard saw fit to try to locate me. Bright girl, that one. She said the old lady gassed herself?'

'Not deliberately, sir. Miss Effie would never do that,' the housekeeper said. 'Something went horribly wrong somewhere. The windows were shut; the door was shut. That wasn't right.'

'Are you sure you're not reading too much into this?' He went across to the body and leaned down over it. 'A lady of her age – it could just as easily have been heart failure.'

'But the smell, sir. There was this gas odor something terrible,' Mrs Bates said.

'It only takes a little gas to leave a bad smell,' he said. 'Maybe there was a small gas leak.'

'The gas was turned on,' Miss Prendergast said firmly. 'I had to turn it off myself before I could even get into the room to open the windows. Somebody had turned it on, by accident or intention we don't know.'

'This is all I need,' Inspector Newcombe said. 'At this rate my family is not going to see me at all over Christmas, and as for buying presents . . .' He rubbed angrily at his mustache. 'Now the rest of you go on home, please. I don't want you touching everything.'

'Nobody has touched anything except for my turning off the gas and opening the windows, which I've already told you.' Miss Prendergast gave him a withering look. 'But we will leave you to it. I'd question those housemaids if I were you. I wouldn't be surprised if one was slipshod in her duty – thought she had lit the gas properly but didn't wait to see.'

'Well, that's a rum do,' Granddad said as we came down the stairs. 'Three deaths in three days. Talk about coming to the country for peace and quiet!'

Chapter 10

The home of the Misses Ffrench-Finch
December 22

There were policemen standing outside the house, or I think I might have persuaded Granddad to join me in a little snooping around outside. Unfortunately the snow now covered any footprints that might have shown that someone climbed in through that open window. I wasn't sure who or why. Perhaps one of those convicts came in to grab supplies and Miss Effie saw him and he stifled her and then made it look as if the gas was to blame. I wished the police would hurry up and catch them or that they were already far, far away. I didn't think I'd linger close to Dartmoor Prison if I ever got out.

'I'm not sure what to do now,' Lady Hawse-Gorzley said as we left Granddad and Miss Prendergast and made our way back to Gorzley Hall. 'Tomorrow night when the guests arrive we are supposed to go sing carols around the village. But that wouldn't be seemly, would it, with poor Miss Effie lying there and her sisters grieving.'

'Probably not,' I said. 'Take the guests to find the Yule log instead.'

She brightened up. 'Excellent idea. I'm so glad you're here, my dear. You're sensible. So is my daughter. No hysterics, no nonsense. I hope you both make good matches. Do you have a young chap in mind?'

'Not really,' I replied, blushing.

'I rather feel Hortense has her eye on her cousin. Not sure of the legality of that. Also not sure if it's him or the title she wants more.' She managed a weary smile. 'And I would appreciate it, my dear Lady Georgiana, if you did not mention our unfortunate events to the guests when they arrive. They might find the news . . . unnerving.'

I nodded, thinking that I found the news of three dead bodies in three days a trifle unnerving myself. Not that they could be in any way connected – such different kinds of deaths and all explainable as accidents. Myself, I was inclined to believe in the Lovey Curse.

As soon as I took off my coat I went back upstairs. 'Queenie,' I called. 'Where is my gray dress?'

Queenie opened my wardrobe and shut it again hastily. 'Remember you said that dress was a bit long? You said it wasn't quite fashionable?'

'Yes.' A feeling of dread was creeping over me.

'Well, it's not too long anymore,' she said and produced from the wardrobe a dress that was now about a foot shorter than when I last saw it.

'My dress. What did you do to it? You didn't cut it off, did you?' I could hear my voice rising dangerously.

'Oh, no, miss. I wouldn't do a thing like that. It was just that . . . well, I saw this thread hanging down and I yanked on it and the whole thing started to unravel. Lucky I stopped or it would have turned into a jumper.'

'Queenie,' I wailed. 'Is there no piece of clothing of mine that you haven't tried to ruin? That gray dress is the only smart winter item I own, apart from my suit, and I can't wear a suit in the house. Now I'll have to look like a school-girl in my tartan kilt all week.'

'I could try knitting it back up for you,' she suggested hopefully.

'Of course you can't knit it back up. I honestly don't know why I keep you. You know I can't afford to buy new clothes.'

She was now turning those big cow eyes on me, brimming with tears. 'I'm awful sorry, miss. I didn't mean no harm.'

'You never do, Queenie. But the dress is ruined all the same.'

'It might not be too very short,' she suggested. 'You did say hemlines are up this year.'

'Yes, but not up to mid-thigh!' I held the dress up against me. 'Well, there's nothing to be done. I'll just have to wear what I wore yesterday. And please do not touch my dinner dresses. Don't try to clean them or iron them. I'd rather wear them crumpled. I don't want to find there is a big hole or the nap has been rubbed off the velvet.'

She nodded bleakly. 'Bob's yer uncle, miss,' she said.

'And Queenie,' I called as she started to creep away. 'Remember when Lady Hawse-Gorzley suggested that you might assist other ladies if they hadn't brought their own maids?'

'Yes, miss?'

'Don't,' I said. 'I can't afford to pay for ruined outfits or be responsible for anyone set on fire.'

'That was only the once,' she said. 'I don't go around setting people on fire all the time.'

'I'm just being cautious, Queenie. You are a walking disaster area and I think you should confine your activities to making my life a misery.'

'Yes, miss,' she muttered and crept away, leaving me feeling rotten. Why did she have this ability to make me feel bad when it was always her fault? I finished my toilet and went downstairs to face the arrival of the first guests – the Wexlers from Indiana.

The Americans arrived late that afternoon. We received a telephone call from Newton Abbot Station. The car was dispatched and we were urged to walk to the end of the drive to meet them at the gates. 'As a gesture of welcome and goodwill,' Lady Hawse-Gorzley put it. She even made the servants line up as if to receive the new lord of the manor.

'Bloody rubbish if you ask me,' Sir Oswald muttered. 'And don't think I'm going to change out of my old cardigan either. I'm not dressing up for anybody. They can take me as I am.'

'Oswald. It has a hole in the sleeve. You look like a tramp,' Lady Hawse-Gorzley said. 'At least put on your tweed jacket.'

As we stood at the gates, feeling cold and silly, it started to snow.

'You see, it is going to be a white Christmas,' Lady Hawse-Gorzley said happily. 'All your gloom and doom, Oswald, and it will be splendid. Absolutely splendid.'

At last the Bentley was spotted approaching the village. We waved and welcomed them all the way up the drive and Lady Hawse-Gorzley insisted on opening the car door herself.

'What kind of antique automobile do you have here?' The

father of the family uncurled himself from the back seat. 'Real quaint. I guess you dust it off to fetch guests from the station. Helps to create the right atmosphere, I reckon.'

'This happens to be our only motorcar,' Lady Hawse-Gorzley said.

'Gee, at home it would be in a museum,' he replied.

The rest of the family climbed out of the motorcar, staring around them as if they had landed on Mars. They consisted of an impossibly tall Mr Wexler, a blonde and very painted Mrs Wexler, a pouty daughter whom Wexler called Cherie, and a freckled son named Junior.

'I sincerely hope we are not the only guests,' Mr Wexler complained as he stepped through the front door and looked around. 'We were promised a big house party.'

'The other guests are not arriving until tomorrow,' Lady Hawse-Gorzley said, 'except, of course, our member of the royal family. Lady Georgiana is already here.'

As Bunty had predicted, that changed everything. Mrs Wexler bobbed an awkward curtsy. Mr Wexler muttered, 'Well, gee whiz. How about that, Mother. Didn't I promise you a Christmas you'd never forget?'

'Hey, Pa, take a look at those swords on the wall. Are they real?'

'They certainly are, little boy,' Lady Hawse-Gorzley replied, 'and they are so sharp that they'd take your hand off.' Junior withdrew his hand hurriedly.

They were shown their rooms. The parents found them quaint and charming, but the daughter, Cherie, commented that they were 'real small' compared to the palatial suites they had at home in Muncie, Indiana. Mrs Wexler suggested her hosts turn up the central heating a few notches and was horrified to find that there was none.

'Well, I guess it's so darned cold in here because someone left the window open by mistake,' she said and promptly shut it.

'We always sleep with the windows open. Much healthier,' Bunty said with a bright smile.

'Well, little lady, you must be tougher than we are,' Mr Wexler replied. 'We like our rooms nice and warm in the winter, so if you wouldn't mind making sure there's a good fire by the time we get ready for bed . . .'

'Oh, yes, the servants always light the fires well before bedtime,' Bunty said.

Junior looked under the bed. 'Hey, Pa, there's a chamber pot under here.' He shrieked with laughter.

'It goes with the décor, honey,' Mrs Wexler said. 'It's old world.'

'No, it's there because the nearest lavatory is a long walk down the hall,' Lady Hawse-Gorzley said. 'One never knows.'

'You mean we don't have our own bathroom?' Mrs Wexler said, looking with big hopeless eyes at her husband.

'This house was built in 1400,' Lady Hawse-Gorzley said. 'In those days they weren't very good about indoor plumbing. We are fortunate to have two on this floor – one at the end of this hallway and one down there at the other end.' She paused. 'And I should probably get Bunty to show you how the geyser works. It can be temperamental.'

'A geyser? Don't tell me your hot water shoots up from the ground like at Yellowstone?'

'Shoots up from the ground?' Lady Hawse-Gorzley looked bemused. 'It's a perfectly normal water-heating device. A little gadget above the bath. Ours just happens to be slightly temperamental, that's all.'

'It's not what we're used to,' Mr Wexler said.

'Of course not,' Lady Hawse-Gorzley said brightly. 'That's why you came, isn't it? For an old-fashioned English Christmas. There would be no point if it was just like your home.'

With that she marched away down the stairs, leaving them to stare after her.

'I guess you've upset a British aristocrat, Clyde,' Mrs Wexler said in a low voice. 'You know how highly strung they are.'

Lady Hawse-Gorzley was clearly ill at ease with the Americans all afternoon, trying to keep from them the news of three unexpected and unexplained deaths. She suggested that the younger ones go out and make a snowman, to take advantage of the snow – which produced mirthful laughter. Apparently it snowed all winter where they lived, so snowmen were not a novelty. So I was left to cheer them up. I started telling them stories about my cousins the little princesses and the good times we had together. Luckily they really lapped this up.

'Fancy that, Clyde. She went out riding with Princess Elizabeth and she says the princess can ride as well as any grown-up. And that little Princess Margaret – a real fire-cracker, from what she says. They're going to have trouble with that one when she grows up.'

They seemed to perk up when tea was served. Apparently tea was a novelty to them and they all approved of the cakes and scones.

'We do dress for dinner,' Lady Hawse-Gorzley said. 'Just to warn you. Sir Oswald is very hot on keeping up standards.'

I thought this was a bad example, as Sir Oswald was still in his old Harris tweed jacket and faded corduroy trousers and had made no effort to be hospitable.

'Do some people sit down to dinner in their underwear in England, then?' Junior asked, making his sister giggle.

'No, but the lower classes do not change out of their day clothes. The better class of person usually dines formally in evening wear, even when we are eating alone. It's the done thing,' Lady Hawse-Gorzley said.

'I don't have no evening wear, do I, Ma?' Junior asked.

'You won't be dining with the grown-ups, young man,' Lady Hawse-Gorzley said. 'We'll have Cook bring up a tray to your nursery.'

'Of course Junior will eat with us,' Mrs Wexler said. 'Junior always eats with us. What a horrible idea, making him eat alone like a convict in his cell. No wonder the British grow up so cold and unfriendly.'

'I assure you we are not cold or unfriendly,' Lady Hawse-Gorzley said. 'I suppose the young man may join us if he wishes.'

'And stay up late, huh, Pa?' Junior asked.

'Sure, son, why not? How often do you get to sit up with quaint British people?'

Lady Hawse-Gorzley pressed her lips together and walked away. During dinner, however, it transpired that the Wexlers did not drink, thus raising Lady Hawse-Gorzley's spirits considerably because it would keep down the costs and mean more wine for her. She waxed poetic about all the quaint and lovely English customs that awaited them. 'We've been out searching the grounds for the perfect Yule log,' she said, 'and when everybody is here, we'll all decorate the Christmas tree. And there will be caroling door to door of course, and a hot mince pie and toddy at each house, I shouldn't wonder.'

'Sounds boring to me,' Junior said. His sister nodded agreement.

Lady Hawse-Gorzley went on, 'Ah, but Lady Georgiana has some splendid things planned for the young folk. Party games and indoor fireworks and of course the costume ball. Then, after Christmas, all the traditional village events: the hunt, the Lovey Chase and of course the Worsting of the Hag on New Year's Eve.'

'What's that?' Junior demanded, interested now in spite of himself.

'It's all to do with the Lovey Curse,' Bunty said dramatically. 'We had a witch in the village who was burned alive at the stake. And she swore she'd come back every Christmastime to get revenge. So every year on New Year's Eve the villagers go from house to house with drums and pots and pans, making a lot of noise to scare out the hag and ensure a safe year ahead with no bad luck.'

'There's no such thing as curses and witches, is there, Pa?' Junior said uncertainly.

'Maybe not in America,' Lady Hawse-Gorzley said. 'There certainly are in England. We are a very old country, you know. This house was built one hundred years before Columbus even discovered your country.'

After dinner Mr Wexler declined to stay with Sir Oswald for port and cigars and insisted on accompanying the ladies into the drawing room, where it transpired that the Wexlers did not drink coffee at night. 'But if you have any malted milk instead . . . ?' Mrs Wexler said.

'Malted milk?' Lady Hawse-Gorzley looked baffled. 'I suppose Cook could have cocoa sent up to your rooms when you are ready for bed.'

'That would be any time now, wouldn't it, Mother,' Mr Wexler said. 'Early to bed, early to rise, that's our motto. What time is breakfast? We're always ready for it about seven.'

'Since you didn't bring a maid, Lady Georgiana has graciously agreed to lend you hers if you need help,' Lady Hawse-Gorzley said.

I thought of the jersey dress, had temporary misgivings, then asked, 'Would you like my maid to help you undress?'

They found that most amusing. 'Help me undress?' Mrs Wexler dug her husband in the ribs. 'She thinks I'm too feeble to undress myself, Clyde.' She patted my arm. 'Honey, at home women are raised to do everything for themselves. We don't believe in having servants. It doesn't seem right.'

'Heaven help us,' Lady Hawse-Gorzley replied when the Wexlers had gone, leaving us alone with our coffee. 'I didn't think guests could be so–'

'Difficult?' Bunty suggested.

'I was going to say "different,"' her mother said, 'but I'm afraid I have to agree with your choice.'

'Tell them that's how we do things in upper-class British households and that was why they came here – to see how the other half lives,' Bunty said firmly.

'I did try.' Lady Hawse-Gorzley sighed. 'But I do hope the other guests won't prove so . . . different.'

We went to bed. For some reason I couldn't sleep, but lay staring at the ceiling, listening to the hoot of an owl in the stillness. Random thoughts flew around my head concerning the three mysterious deaths, escaped convicts, the village idiot, the wild girl and the assertion that they were 'all crackers' around here. After a while I realized how still it was. The complete silence of the world indicated to me that it must still be snowing and I thought how jolly it would be to have a white Christmas. My dear ones were nearby. There was loads of lovely food and drink and a house that wasn't freezing. And no Fig for miles and miles. I wasn't going to let those three deaths, the escaped convicts or difficult Americans spoil it for me.

Chapter 11

Gorzley Hall
December 23
Other guests arrive today. Hoping they won't be as difficult as the Wexlers. Not sure I'm cut out for the role of social hostess!

I was awakened early the next morning by the Wexlers tramping down the corridor talking loudly. I didn't wait for Queenie and morning tea, but went down the hall to the bathroom, then came back and dressed, this time in the skirt from my tweed suit plus a blouse and cardigan – not exactly smart but at least different from the day before. As I came downstairs the butler was standing in the entrance hall. 'It's still not working, my lady,' he called.

He heard my feet on the stairs and looked up at me, then continued. 'The telephone line appears to be down. Maybe it snowed during the night, but there is certainly no connection this morning.'

Lady Hawse-Gorzley came through from the breakfast room looking harassed. 'It's too bad,' she said. 'Now I'll have to send the motor into town to deliver the message, I suppose.'

'Is there something I could do?' I asked.

'Well, I suppose you could go to the police station and ask to use their telephone,' she said. 'It is an emergency, after all.'

'Emergency?' I felt my pulse rate quicken.

'Yes, I need to let the butcher know that I changed my mind. I do want the geese to go with the turkeys. I'm not a big fan of goose myself – so rich and fatty, isn't it? But Oswald reminded me that it is the traditional Christmas fowl, so I'm afraid we must serve some. The guests will be expecting it.'

'So you'd like me to put in a telephone call to the butcher?'

'Yes. Skaggs, the butcher. The girl on the switchboard will connect you. Tell him that Lady Hawse-Gorzley changed her mind and she does want the geese delivered early tomorrow morning to go with the turkeys.'

'I can certainly do that for you,' I said.

'Go and have your breakfast first, dear,' she said. 'The Wexlers have already finished theirs. It appears they only take some kind of cereal that resembles twigs at home, and they absolutely refused to try the kidneys.' She shook her head as if they were already a lost cause. 'There is no huge hurry, although I'm sure the butcher will be busy all day today. And we don't exactly know when the other guests will arrive so I will be tied to the house all day. And the Wexlers asked about stockings. What exactly do people do with stockings at Christmas?'

'Hang them up for Father Christmas, I believe.'

'Hang them where?'

'Over the fireplace.'

'My dear, with this many people it would look like a Chinese laundry, wouldn't it? No, I think we'll dispense with stockings. I'll have a present for everybody inside a snow house and those who want to can exchange gifts privately or put them under the tree.'

'Oh,' I said, staring at her as the thought struck me. 'Are we supposed to give presents?'

'Not you, my dear. Absolutely not necessary.'

I nodded, my brain still racing. We didn't go in for presents much at Castle Rannoch. I always gave my nephew, Podge, a little something. Binky and Fig occasionally managed a box of handkerchiefs or a pair of gloves. Mummy sent a check when she remembered, but Christmas was certainly a no-nonsense affair with us. This time I had actually brought a small gift for Queenie, but it occurred to me now that I should give my grandfather something too, and also my mother. The problem was that Lady Hawse-Gorzley hadn't reimbursed me for my train fare yet and I was seriously lacking in funds. I didn't think that my mother would be satisfied with Ashes of Roses perfume from Woolworths instead of Worth. I'd love to have given Granddad a really nice present – a cashmere scarf or a warm pullover. It felt so frustrating to have no money. For a second I wondered if I could ask Lady H-G for an advance, but my pride wouldn't let me. At least I'd look in the village shop for small tokens and hope for a miracle.

I ate a hearty breakfast and set off for the village, crunching down the driveway, where the snow had frozen hard all night, and stood admiring the village scene – small boys with sleds, a snowman on the village green, villagers bundled against the cold staggering home with baskets laden with good things and mysteriously wrapped packages.

Suddenly it was impossible not to be caught up in the spirit of Christmas.

At the police station I was met by a worried-looking young constable. 'Sorry I can't help you, miss,' he said, 'but our telephone isn't working either. I don't know what can be wrong. It's not as if there was a storm last night, was there? Maybe it's the cold what's done it.'

I looked around the village shop, but there was nothing that was remotely suitable for Christmas presents, the most exotic items being long woolen underwear and white handkerchiefs. But my spirits were raised when I realized that someone would now have to go into town to deliver Lady H-G's message.

'Their telephone's not working either?' she said, running a hand through her hair. 'What a nuisance. There is always a last-minute hitch, isn't there? I don't suppose you'd be an angel and go into town for me, would you? I absolutely have to have those geese and I know he'll sell out if I wait any longer.'

'Of course I'll go into town for you,' I said, delighted that I would now get a chance to shop.

The car was summoned and I rode in solitary splendor into the little market town of Newton Abbot. If the village had depicted the rural Christmas scene, this was straight out of Dickens. Little shops with lead-paned bow windows, a cheery pub, children singing carols on every street corner and people staggering under loads of provisions and presents. I delivered my message to Mr Skaggs, who looked pleased with himself.

'I told her ladyship, didn't I?' he said in his thick Devon burr. 'I said she'd be needing the geese as well. Right, my lovey, you tell her that I'll be delivering them bright and early on Christmas morning. She don't need to worry.'

'Lady Hawse-Gorzley tried to telephone you,' I said, 'but it seems that the line is down or something. Even the police station telephone was not working.'

'Ah, well, they wouldn't be, would they?' the butcher said, giving me a knowing look. 'Fire last night at the exchange. Didn't you folks hear about it? Terrible it were. Seems there was something wrong with the wiring and one of the poor telephone operators plugged in her headphones and she were electrocuted right away. Then the whole thing caught on fire. Took the fire brigade hours to put it out. Such a terrible shame so near to Christmas.'

'So the girl was killed?' I asked, swallowing back my rising fear.

He nodded. 'Not exactly a girl anymore. Poor old Gladys Tripp. She's been operator at the local exchange for years. Bit of a nosy parker if you ask me, always listening in on people's calls, but a good enough soul. Didn't deserve to die like that.'

'Did she live out toward Tiddleton-under-Lovey?' I asked.

'No, right here in town. Born and bred here. She and I went to primary school together.'

I couldn't think of anything else to say. I came out and walked down the high street, no longer noticing the lively Christmas-card scene. The fourth death. Again it could have been a horrible accident – wiring that had been badly done. Electric wires too close to telephone wires. I didn't exactly know how telephones worked, but I didn't think that kind of accident would happen too often. And the telephone operator who had been killed was the type who loved to listen in, to gossip. Had she overheard something she shouldn't? At least I couldn't tie her to the Lovey Curse when she had always lived in a town ten miles away.

There was nothing I could do to help and I couldn't see any way that her death was related to the others, unless a madman in the area was randomly targeting people to kill in different ways. Then I remembered there was one connection: I had heard her name before. Inspector Newcombe had mentioned that Gladys Tripp was the quick-thinking operator who had been sharp enough to alert the police after she had received the emergency call about Miss Effie. A link between two deaths at last, but a tenuous one. I toyed with it as I walked down the high street, being buffeted by round ladies with shopping baskets. By the end of the street I was none the wiser and tried to turn my mind back to the job in hand – finding Christmas presents in a hurry. I looked in dress shops, shoe shops, newsagents, even a haberdashery, and found nothing that looked nice but cost little. I paused to look in the bow window of a small jeweler and saw some lovely pieces of antique jewelry that made me sigh with longing. There was some high-quality stuff here. I wondered how many people in a small Devon town had the sort of money to patronize a place like this. I was about to walk on when a small display at the bottom of the window caught my eye.

Lucky Devon Pixies, said the sign.

I'm a lucky Devon pixie, from the legend old and true,
Kiss me once and turn me twice and I'll bring luck to you.

The pixies were silver charms in pretty little boxes with the verse on the lid, obviously put there to attract tourists and bring people into the shop. I decided that Granddad could use some luck and that maybe my mother might be charmed by the pixie too. I was about to buy one for each of them when, on impulse, I took an extra one for Darcy, if and when I had a chance to see him again. If anyone needed luck it was he, since he was as impoverished as I and was always popping off to dangerous places.

The man who served me was an elderly Jewish man, presumably Mr Klein, since the shop was called Klein's Jewelers. He treated me with great deference even though I was buying such humble items.

'I've just acquired some fine pieces from Paris if you'd care to look, miss,' he said as he wrapped up the boxes for me.

'I'm afraid that I don't have the money for your lovely things,' I replied, giving him a regretful smile.

'I understand.' He handed me the boxes. 'It's not easy to survive these days for most of us, is it? It's rare that I have a call for my better-quality items these days. My compliments of the season to you, miss.' Then he added astutely, 'Or should I say "my lady"?'

I came out of the shop with three pixies then went into the sweet shop next door and bought a box of chocolates for Mrs Huggins and Black Magic for Lady Hawse-Gorzley. I wasn't going to attempt to buy anything for the invisible Mr Coward.

Chapter 12

The next lot of guests arrived around two o'clock. They were Mr and Mrs Upthorpe and their daughter, Ethel – a large girl with a rather vacant moon face and Marcel-waved hair that somehow didn't make her seem smarter. Both mother and daughter wore well-cut clothes that shouted Paris, but they still seemed ill at ease. The Wexlers and the Upthorpes regarded each other suspiciously. I showed Ethel up to her room.

'I'm glad to see there's someone else ordinary here,' she said in a whisper. 'I was afraid they'd all be lords and ladies. We're plain folks really, except that my dad has made a lot of money. But that's not enough, is it? They wanted to have me presented at court, but I got turned down. So now my mum has set her heart on my marrying into the aristocracy; that's why she decided we had to come here. But I don't actually see any young men around.'

'I gather that three of them are due later today,' I said. 'The son of the house, his friend from Oxford and his cousin. I can't tell you what they are like because I haven't met them yet.'

'So what does your dad do?' she asked.

'He used to be Duke of Glen Garry and Rannoch,' I said. 'He's dead now.'

She put her hand up to her mouth. 'Oh, crikey. I know who you are. I've seen your picture in the society pages. Oh, I do feel a fool.'

'That's all right,' I said. 'I am quite ordinary, really. I'm unattached with no job, so probably worse off than you are.'

'But you have royal relatives,' she pointed out.

'Well, yes, that's true.'

'I should be curtsying and calling you "my lady."'

'Not at a function like this. We're all friends together this week. Why don't you call me Georgie?'

She beamed at me. 'You're a good sport, Georgie. Just wait till I tell the girls at home about this.'

At least I'd made someone happy. We came downstairs to find that Colonel and Mrs Rathbone had arrived. They looked exactly as I would have expected. He was portly with a small military mustache. They were both wearing country tweeds and she had a good-quality Cairngorms brooch in her lapel.

'Of course it can be dashed uncomfortable in Calcutta in summer,' he was saying. 'I usually send the memsahib up to the hills, don't I, old thing?'

'It's lovely up in the hills. Tea plantations for miles and miles. Have you ever been to India?' Mrs Rathbone looked at the Wexlers and the Upthorpes, only to be met with blank stares.

'I wouldn't like a place like India at all,' Mrs Wexler said with a shudder. 'All that dirt and disease and cows running around the streets. No, sirree.'

'Damn fine place, India,' the colonel said. 'You should see the maharajas' palaces, and the tiger shoots, and the lake in Kashmir. Damn fine place.'

'Are you home on leave or back for good?' Lady Hawse-Gorzley asked.

'Long leave. We take one every five years. We used to have a house in this part of the world, but not any longer, unfortunately. Circumstances being what they are. Not at all sure that we'll come back to England to settle when I leave the army. Life is just so pleasant for the memsahib in India, isn't it, old girl?'

'Apart from the heat and the diseases, I must say life in India is very easy. Our servants are devoted. There are always parties and dances. No, I think I'd find it rather dull in England. I did when we were last home four years ago, especially as Reggie was gone most of the time – weren't you, my dear?'

'Dashed inconvenient, I called it. Only here for a few months and I got summoned to–'

'Oh, I believe that must be the dowager countess now.' Lady Hawse-Gorzley sprang to her feet. 'Please excuse me while I go to greet her. We'll be serving tea shortly and you'll have a chance to try our Devonshire cream.'

She motioned to me to follow her as an ancient Rolls-Royce drew up and a very distinguished-looking lady was helped from the back seat. She was dressed in a long sable coat with matching fur hat. She held an ebony and silver cane and she lifted a lorgnette to survey the scene as another woman, a mousy little creature, scurried around to lead her to the front door.

Lady Hawse-Gorzley came forward to greet her, arms open.

'Countess Albury – what a delight. Welcome to Gorzley Hall and the compliments of the season to you.'

'How do you do,' the countess said stiffly, holding out a black-gloved hand before she could be touched.

'Have you been traveling long?'

'Not too bad. Drove from London yesterday. Spent the night at the Francis in Bath. One of my favorite cities. Always loved shopping for antiques on Milsom Street. Not anymore, of course. Nowhere to put them.'

'Come inside, do,' Lady Hawse-Gorzley said.

'I fully intend to,' the countess sniffed. 'Certainly don't expect to stand out here in the cold all week.'

Lady Hawse-Gorzley gave an embarrassed little titter and tried to help the dowager countess up the steps. The latter fought her off. 'I am not quite decrepit yet, you know. People have tried to put me away in mothballs, but I won't let them.'

She made it up the steps unaided.

'I'm sure you'd like to go to your room to freshen up before you join our other guests for tea,' Lady Hawse-Gorzley said.

'Freshen up? Is that some horrible transatlantic slang? If you mean for a rest, a wash, a change of clothes, then please say so. People always said what they meant in my day. There was no "freshening up" and "needing to relax" when I was a girl.' She glanced up the long sweep of stairs. 'Given the condition of my right knee, I think I will forgo the "freshening up," if you would please show my companion where we are to sleep and have someone escort me to a salon or wherever one sits in the afternoon.'

'There's a lovely big fire in the drawing room,' Lady Hawse-Gorzley said. 'Maybe Lady Georgiana will find you a comfortable chair.'

The lorgnette was turned onto me. 'Georgiana? Not Bertie

Rannoch's daughter! Yes, I see the family likeness.' She put a hand on my arm for me to lead her. 'I knew your grandmother and of course your terrifying great-grandmama, Queen Victoria. I nearly toppled over when I was presented to her, I was so nervous. Your grandmother was a shy woman, I remember – well, she would be, wouldn't she, not daring to say a word in her mother's presence. But we became quite close after she married Rannoch and I married Albury. I remember your father as a boy. Sweet-natured child. Always loved company and was always so lonely. It was a shame they couldn't provide him with brothers and sisters. He would have thrived in a big household.'

'Like me,' I said. 'My brother was so much older than me that it was like being an only child.'

'At least your grandmother produced a son and heir before she died,' the countess said. 'I wasn't able to do that, I'm ashamed to say. In consequence the estate has gone to a no-good nephew and I was unceremoniously expelled.' She paused, staring out at the snowy scene through the window. 'Well, I was offered the gatehouse, but his lower-class wife made it quite clear that she wanted nothing to do with me. So I'm living in a small place in Kensington these days. Most of my friends either share my reduced circumstances or are dead. And I had a hankering for the old days – the grand old Christmases of my youth.'

I gave her an encouraging smile. 'I'm sure you'll have a lovely time.'

She leaned closer. 'What about the other guests? Anyone I'd know?'

'I don't think so,' I said tactfully. 'But I think you'll find them pleasant enough.'

'That's the problem,' she said. 'There aren't many people

I know left alive. Outstayed my welcome on this earth, I fear.'

'You are very welcome here anyway,' I said.

She patted my hand. 'A kind girl, I can see. Your father was kind, wasn't he?'

'I hardly knew him,' I said. 'He spent most of his time on the Continent.'

'I remember now. There was some kind of scandal, wasn't there? His wife ran off and left him. Not that that kind of thing causes a scandal anymore. People are always doing it. Look at the Prince of Wales. One hears he's trailing around after some American woman who is married to someone else. I don't know what the world is coming to.' She turned to look behind her. 'Don't just stand there, Humphreys. Go and find out where I'm to be sleeping and put my things away.' She looked back at me. 'She's a poor specimen. No backbone. But she's loyal. Been with me five years now.'

We arrived in the drawing room and Lady Hawse-Gorzley made the introductions. The other guests were suitably over-awed by the dowager countess, except for the Rathbones. When they found out she had been to India, they entered into a lively session of name-dropping and one-upmanship with the countess.

'And Simla? How did you like Simla? Our of our favorite places, but of course we adore Ooty. Did you ever meet the Maharaja of Udaipur? Such opulence.'

'Yes, he was comfortably off, shall one say, but nothing to compare with dear old Pixie of Hyderabad. And did you ever go to Government House when dear Tommy was vice-roy? Now, those were parties.'

The countess was winning the name-dropping handily when tea was announced. Low tables were produced, and a trolley was wheeled in, laden with all the items I particularly adore: warm scones with cream and strawberry jam as well as smoked salmon sandwiches, éclairs, brandy snaps, mince pies, slices of rich fruitcake and a Victoria sponge. Everyone's mood lightened enormously. The Wexlers and the Upthorpes exchanged boasts about how much they spent on their motorcars and their wives' furs. The Rathbones and the countess agreed that the good old days had gone and would never return. Even Junior Wexler had to agree that the scones and cream were 'swell' and ate an impressive number. I was enjoying my own scones when Lady Hawse-Gorzley suddenly looked up at the doorway. 'Why, the boys are here and I didn't see them arrive,' she said. She got to her feet. 'Monty, darling. How lovely to see you. So you made it safely, then.'

'No, Mother, we're lying dead in a ditch,' Monty said, giving a grin to his sister. 'Of course we made it safely. We're here, aren't we?' He was tall and slim and looked absurdly young.

'And Badger. You are most welcome.' Lady Hawse-Gorzley held out her hand to a red-haired, freckled young man. 'Come on in.'

'Thanks, Lady H-G,' the freckle-faced lad nicknamed Badger replied, giving her a hearty handshake. 'Looking forward to it awfully. Frightfully decent of you to invite me.'

'May I introduce my son, Montague, and his friend Archibald, usually known as Badger,' Lady Hawse-Gorzley said to the company. Then she looked around. 'Didn't your cousin come down with you on the train? He said he was going to.'

'He came in with us,' Monty said. 'Ah, here he is now.'

And Darcy stepped into the room.

Chapter 13

He hadn't seen me. Before he could cross the room Bunty rushed at him. 'Cousin Darcy. How absolutely lovely to see you again. It's been ages and ages. Haven't I grown up a lot since you saw us last?'

'You certainly have,' Darcy said, accepting the hug and the kiss on his cheek. 'And how are you, Aunt Camilla?'

'All the better now that you are here,' she said, beaming at him. 'Lovely to see you again after so long, dear boy. I'm not sure where Oswald has disappeared to. Really, it's so hard to make him be sociable. But here are our guests, all dying to meet you: Colonel and Mrs Rathbone, recently home from India. Mr and Mrs Wexler, all the way from America, and their children. The Upthorpe family from Yorkshire, and may I present you to the dowager countess Albury. Countess, this is my nephew, the Honorable Darcy O'Mara.'

Darcy went over to her and kissed her hand. She squinted at him through her lorgnette. 'Kilhenny's son? Yes, you have the look of him about you. I've no doubt you're as big a rogue as he was as a young man.'

'Indubitably,' Darcy said and grinned.

'And this,' continued Lady Hawse-Gorzley, 'is Lady Georgiana Rannoch.'

I had been about to eat a bite of scone, but had stood frozen with a mouthful unchewed. Now I tried to swallow it rapidly, which resulted in a fit of coughing.

It was hardly the traditional meeting of sweethearts. We didn't rush across the room into each other's arms. In fact, I read mixed emotions in Darcy's astonished stare. 'Good God, Georgie, what on earth are you doing here?' he said.

'Hello, Darcy,' I said, trying to recover my dignity from the coughing fit. 'The same as you, apparently. Looking forward to a jolly good Christmas.'

'Ah – you two know each other. How splendid,' Lady Hawse-Gorzley said. 'But of course you would. You bright young things go to all the same parties in town, I've no doubt.'

'Shall I take Cousin Darcy up and show him his room?' Bunty asked, slipping her hand through his arm.

'You most certainly shall not,' her mother replied. 'A young lady does not escort a young gentleman to a bedroom, Hortense, even if he is your cousin.'

'We'll show Darcy his room later, Mother,' Monty said. 'But at the moment we are all in dire need of refreshment and I notice scones and cream. Come on, Badger. Dig in, old chap.'

The two young men pulled over a sofa and attacked the scones. Darcy accepted a cup of tea, then came over and perched on the arm of my chair, which I found reassuring. Given his less than exuberant greeting when he saw me, I wasn't sure how to treat him. I reminded myself that he hadn't even contacted me properly when he arrived back in England. And a succession of wild thoughts was rushing through my head: that he might have been meeting a girl when my mother had spotted him in London at the Café Royal, and was embarrassed to find me here when he'd hoped to find her. Or, a second alternative, that Lady Hawse-Gorzley was no more his aunt than I was, and this was actually some kind of secret meeting of spies into which I had blundered by mistake. This one made more sense, since I suspected he secretly worked as some sort of spy. I gave him a polite little nod and waited for him to make the first move.

'How are you?' he said in a low voice. 'What a lovely surprise.'

'I'm well, thank you,' I replied. 'And if you'd taken the trouble to talk to me, you might have heard about my plans to come here.'

'But they told me you were spending Christmas in Scotland with the family,' he muttered to me.

'Who told you?'

'I tried to telephone you. Your sister-in-law instructed the butler to tell me,' he said. ' "Her Grace wishes me to tell you that Lady Georgiana will be unavailable over the Christmas celebration. It is to be a family affair." Those were the very words, I seem to remember.'

'The absolute cow,' I said. Darcy laughed. 'She never mentioned that you'd telephoned. How utterly spiteful of her.'

'She doesn't approve of me. I lead you astray, remember? So what made you leave the bosom of the family Christmas?'

'Fig's family was descending en masse. More than body and soul could endure.'

'But what are you doing here of all places? I had no idea that you knew my aunt.'

'Darcy dear, do help yourself to tea,' Lady Hawse-Gorzley said.

I could hardly say that I had answered an advertisement in front of the paying guests, so I leaned forward and poured Darcy a cup of tea. Our fingers touched as I handed it to him and I felt a shiver run all the way up my arm.

'And, Georgiana, perhaps after tea you can take the young people into the study and make plans for the things you'd like to do over Christmas. I do so want you young folk to enjoy yourselves.'

'I expect you'd like to go out for a ride in the morning, Darcy,' Bunty said, pulling up her chair closer. 'Do you remember what fun we had the last time you were here and we went out riding on the moor?'

'I hardly think we'd be wise to take the horses on the moor in the snow, Bunty,' he said. 'We'd never see the bogs.' He looked up with a grin. 'By the way, how is your wild girl – Sally, is she? Still going strong?'

'Wild girl?' Mrs Wexler asked nervously.

'Not really wild, just strange,' Lady Hawse-Gorzley said rapidly. 'A strange young woman who lives alone on the moor.' She attempted a gay laugh. 'Yes, she's still going strong.'

'And how is the village where nothing ever happens?' Darcy went on gaily. 'That's what you said last time I was here, Bunty.'

'Just as quiet and peaceful as ever,' Lady Hawse-Gorzley said again rapidly. 'A perfect little backwater. England the way it used to be. And that's how we love it. Ah, here is my husband, finally.'

And Sir Oswald came in, still wearing his dreadful old tweed jacket, plus fours, old socks and boots. 'Damned fellow didn't muck out the pigs properly,' he said. 'Had to do it myself.' And he promptly sat down next to Mrs Rathbone.

'God, I'm famished. Mucking out pigsties certainly brings on an appetite.'

I heard Darcy stifle a chuckle as Mrs Rathbone moved hastily to the far end of the sofa.

'And those damned police johnnies have finally departed, thank God. Blasted inconvenient of people to go and kill themselves over Christmas. And those wretched convicts, too. Time of peace and goodwill, isn't that what it's supposed to be?'

'Killed themselves?' Mrs Upthorpe asked nervously. 'Who killed themselves? Where?'

'Just a couple of unfortunate accidents in the area. Nothing to be alarmed about,' Lady Hawse-Gorzley said hastily. 'Have another scone, do. And Alice, bring us some more tea. This is getting cold.'

'And the convicts?' Mrs Wexler interjected.

'A couple of men escaped from Dartmoor Prison, which is several miles from here. They'll be far away by now. The police have combed the moors.'

'How exciting. Perhaps we'll be taken hostage,' Cherie Wexler said and got a dig in the side from her mother.

'Well, something exciting has to happen or we'll all die of boredom,' the girl retorted.

Lady Hawse-Gorzley leaped to her feet. 'Georgiana – why don't you take the young people now and make your plans?'

'We just got here, Mother. We've hardly eaten anything yet,' Monty said, his mouth half full of éclair.

'And I'm still hungry,' Junior Wexler said.

'Of course, I don't mean to rush you,' Lady Hawse-Gorzley said. 'In that case, why don't I take the grown-ups and give them a tour of the house. So many fine historical features.'

The Wexlers, Upthorpes and Rathbones rose obediently, but the dowager countess stayed put. 'Does the woman think I've never seen an historic home before? I used to be a frequent guest at Blenheim and Longleat, and Albury Park was not too shabby either. Gardens by Capability Brown.'

'Lady Albury, I do realize that you'd find the stairs too much for you,' Lady Hawse-Gorzley said. 'Perhaps you'd like Hortense to take you through to the little library. There is a nice fire and you'd find it more peaceful than being with the youngsters.'

'I like young people. Make me feel alive again,' the countess said. 'I shall relish all the latest gossip from London. Go on, off you go.'

The adults departed dutifully, except for Sir Oswald, who was eating away merrily, quite oblivious to the fact that he smelled of pig. Lady Albury moved to the sofa, closer to Darcy and me. 'So do tell me all the latest London scandal.'

'I'm afraid I've been in Scotland for the past few months,' I said.

'And I in South America,' Darcy said.

'But have you met this notorious American lady? Simpson, is that it?'

'Yes, I have met her,' I said. 'And I think the term "lady" is stretching the definition.'

She threw back her head and laughed, patting my hand. 'I like you,' she said. 'Good sense of humor like your father. And you, young man' – she turned to Darcy – 'what were you doing in South America? Up to no good, I'll wager.'

'A little of this and that, you know,' Darcy said.

'Dealing in arms, no doubt. That's how people make money in South America, isn't it? Help to start another revolution then supply both sides with arms.'

'Certainly not,' Darcy said. 'How can you suggest such a thing?' But he was smiling, his eyes teasing her.

'I know a thing or two about how the world works.'

'I thought we were supposed to be planning what we want to do,' Bunty said peevishly.

'When Junior has finished polishing off the cream buns, we'll get started,' I said.

'Junior, you'll make yourself sick,' Cherie Wexler said. 'He is such a little pig. I don't know why we had to bring him along. You should have stayed with Aunt Mabel, Junior. You aren't old enough for polite society yet.'

'Go and jump in the lake, sis,' he said and made a grab at the last cream bun.

'So,' I said brightly, 'what would we like to do? I gather there is to be a fancy dress ball one night, and we should play charades, don't you think?'

'Oh, yes, charades,' the red-headed Badger agreed.

'And the place is perfect for sardines,' I went on.

'Sardines? What on earth is that?'

'Like hide-and-seek but when you find someone you join them, until you are all crammed into a cupboard or wherever you are hiding,' I said.

'That sounds really juvenile,' the Wexler girl said.

'Ooh, I don't know. Could be fun,' Ethel Upthorpe said, eyeing first Darcy and then Monty and clearly visualizing herself pinned into a wardrobe with them.

'What would you like to do?' I asked Cherie Wexler. 'Any suggestions for us?'

'When I go out with friends we dance the quickstep and

smoke and drink cocktails in secret,' she said. 'Or we go to the talkies.'

'I don't think the cinema constitutes part of an old-fashioned English Christmas,' I said.

'I think we should go out and have a snowball fight before it gets quite dark,' Monty said.

'Dashed good idea,' Badger added. 'Who's up for it?'

Everyone except for Cherie Wexler thought it might be fun. We put on coats, scarves and gloves and went outside. The sun had just sunk below Lovey Tor and the sky was a brilliant blood-red, turning the snow pink. Rooks were cawing madly as they came home to roost. Darcy came up beside me.

'All right, now spill the beans,' he said, still looking incredulous and a trifle suspicious too. 'What brought you here, of all places? I mean, I had no inkling that you knew my aunt.'

'Lady Hawse-Gorzley really is your aunt, then?'

He nodded. 'Of course. My mother's sister. I don't suppose I ever mentioned her, because I've relatives dotted all over the place. But things are rather strained between my father and me, so when I received this invite, I was happy to accept.' He moved closer to me. 'Even happier now.'

I felt a glow of happiness go through me too.

He leaned closer. 'Look, I know you're hot stuff as a detective,' he said. 'Did you find out where I'd be staying and wangle yourself an invitation?'

'No, I did not,' I said, feeling myself blushing. 'I was absolutely amazed to see you. I had no idea you were connected with the Hawse-Gorzleys.'

'I had no idea you knew them either.'

'I didn't,' I said. 'Between ourselves – and this is not to go any further – I applied to an advertisement to help a hostess with her Christmas house party. I had never heard of the Hawse-Gorzleys or Tiddleton-under-Lovey before. But I'd have applied to the North Pole to escape from Fig's relatives.'

I saw relief flood across Darcy's face and he laughed. 'It must be fate bringing us together,' he said.

A snowball came flying through the air and struck me full in the face. 'Whoops, sorry, Georgie,' Bunty said.

Chapter 14

Gorzley Hall and around the village
December 23

We actually had a jolly good snowball fight and were just going inside, with fingers and noses tingling with cold, when a white shape came walking up the drive toward us. It was the little maid who had come to us in such distress that morning.

'Beg pardon, miss,' she said to Bunty, 'but I've a message for your mum from the Misses Ffrench-Finch. Miss Florrie and Miss Lizzie want me to tell your mum that they'd like the carol singing to go ahead, in spite of what happened yesterday. They say that Cook has made so many mince pies and Miss Effie would have hated them to go to waste, so would you please come round as planned.'

'Oh, jolly good,' Monty said. 'Nothing like a good bout of carol singing, is there? Everyone up to scratch with their "Good King Wenceslas"? Or do we need a practice session first?'

We trooped back into the house, where Lady Hawse-Gorzley was thrilled to hear the news.

'Breeding will tell,' she said, rather undiplomatically, I thought. 'We will try to find a subdued and reverent carol to sing outside their house. How they must be suffering, poor dear ladies.'

When we had taken off our coats and hats we found that more guests had arrived: a smartly dressed middle-aged couple and a suave, fortyish man with a jaunty, pencil-thin mustache and canary yellow silk cravat at his throat.

'Our party is now complete,' Lady Hawse-Gorzley said. 'Some of our neighbors have come to join us. Captain and Mrs Sechrest – he's a local sea dog, home on leave. Mrs Sechrest is my bridge partner and I must say she plays a fine hand. Has a fine seat in the saddle too.'

'Pretty decent seat out of the saddle,' the lone man said, getting a titter from Mrs Sechrest.

'Johnnie, you're terrible. Can't you behave for one second?' she said.

'Sorry, old bean. You know me. Got an eye for the ladies, what?' He gave her what could only be described as a smoldering look.

'And this disreputable character is Johnnie Protheroe. He's a writer of sorts.'

'A renaissance man, Camilla dearest, if you don't mind,' Johnnie said. 'I paint, I sail, I hunt and I'm fun to be around, aren't I, Sandy?'

Mrs Sechrest tried to give an imitation of my great-grandmother being not amused, but it didn't quite come off. Captain Sechrest sat there, whiskey in hand, looking frightfully bored and correct, while his wife clearly enjoyed Johnnie's attentions.

'If you don't mind, we'll be having a simple supper tonight

after our carol singing, and I don't think that we'll expect you to dress, given the lateness.'

'We're only getting a simple supper?' Pa Wexler demanded. 'Yesterday's dinner was kinda simple too. I thought we were promised sumptuous multicourse banquets.'

'It has been our experience that guests are rather full of mince pies and good cheer by the time we return from the carol singing. I think you'll find our simple meal quite adequate, Mr Wexler.'

As we left the room Mrs Upthorpe muttered to her daughter, 'Eee, that's too bad. I was looking forward to wearing one of those evening dresses we got in Paris last summer, weren't you, Ethel?'

'It's certainly not worth wearing them up in Bradford,' Ethel said. 'They don't know a Chanel from Woolworths, do they?'

I went upstairs thinking about the irony of this. I was the daughter of a duke. My dresses did not come from Paris. In fact, I'd be lucky to find one of them undamaged by Queenie's ministrations. I was worrying about this as I turned the corner to go to my room and found my path blocked by Johnnie Protheroe. 'Well, hello,' he said, looking down at me with what could only be described as a lecherous leer. 'And who do we have here?'

'Georgiana Rannoch,' I said frostily. 'How do you do?'

'I do very well,' he said. 'So you're the famous Lady Georgiana. One hears that your delectable mother is in the area. Is that correct?'

'I really couldn't say,' I answered, uncomfortable now with his closeness. He had one hand on the wall and was leaning down toward me.

'And are you as much fun, I wonder, as your mama?' he said.

'Do you know my mother?'

'Not personally, but one reads delicious tidbits in newspapers.'

'You shouldn't believe what you read in newspapers,' I said and ducked under his arm. I heard him chuckling as I opened the door to my room.

We assembled as instructed, bundled into our warmest clothes, and found that lanterns on poles had been stuck in the snow for us to carry. Bunty also handed out a supply of music books for those who didn't know the words.

'I thought we'd start off with "Good King Wenceslas" as we walk down the driveway,' Lady Hawse-Gorzley said, 'to warm up our voices, so to speak, and then we'll switch to "O Little Town of Bethlehem" when we reach the Misses Ffrench-Finch. And we'll keep it suitably subdued.'

Darcy slid into the line beside me as the singing began and we moved off. 'Why are we keeping it subdued?' he whispered. 'Are they true aficionados of music who would be offended by our out-of-tune renditions?'

'No, they had a death in the family yesterday morning,' I whispered back. 'One of the three elderly sisters was found dead in her bed. Someone had turned the gas on and closed the windows.'

'Suicide?' he asked.

'I don't think so.'

'Then one of the other sisters wanted her out of the way, probably. Jealous, or wanted a better share of an inheritance. Or was simply batty.'

I shook my head. 'No, one gathers that they adored their sister and relied on her. She was the strong one who made the decisions.'

'When the snow lay round about, deep and crisp and even,' went on the singing.

He turned to me sharply. 'Are you saying it was murder?'

'They'd all like to believe it was an accident,' I said. 'But there have been three deaths in three days in this small village. That seems to be stretching the law of averages, doesn't it?'

'Were the other two similar old ladies?'

'No, quite different. A landowner found shot with his own gun in a tree in the Hawse-Gorzleys' orchard. A local garage owner fell off a bridge into a creek as he went home from the village pub – where it is said he was fond of visiting the publican's wife. No hint from the police that they have found any evidence of foul play. The old ladies' house was locked for the night at six and nobody seems to be able to come up with a reason for wanting Miss Ffrench-Finch dead.'

'They say deaths come in threes, don't they?' he said. 'The most logical thing is that they were all accidents.'

'There are a couple of other things I should mention,' I said. 'One of them is the Lovey Curse.'

'The what?' He was laughing, his eyes sparkling in the light of the lantern.

'Apparently there was a local witch who was burned alive on New Year's Eve, hundreds of years ago. As she died she cursed the village that tragedy would strike them at Yuletide every year.'

'And has it?'

'I've no idea,' I said, 'but the other thing is more serious. You might have read that three convicts escaped from Dartmoor Prison a few days ago. The police seem to think they haven't gone far. So maybe they are hiding out on the moor and they've killed the people who have spotted them.'

'You mean the man out shooting?'

I nodded. 'Very early in the morning. Maybe he ran into them.'

'And the man crossing a bridge in the middle of the night? Yes, he could have run into them. But I don't see how that could apply to your old lady. She didn't go wandering around on the moor looking for trouble, did she?'

'No, I'm sure she didn't. I suppose she could have spotted the convicts through her motorcar window. But then she would have telephoned the police straight away, wouldn't she?'

'And they are hardly likely to have gassed her in her bed. Not the modus operandi of most criminal types. Bashed her head in or suffocated her.'

'Besides,' I said, 'they couldn't get into the house.'

We reached the end of the driveway just as the singers broke into a lusty rendition of:

In his master's steps he trod, where the snow lay dinted.
Heat was in the very sod, where the saint had printed.

Darcy was frowning, staring up at the big square shape of the Ffrench-Finch house and its plain stone walls. 'I don't think there's any way that three convicts could be hiding out in a village like this,' he said. 'Village eyes are too sharp. They'd notice something. And even if someone was hiding them, the villagers would notice someone buying more food than usual.'

'Your aunt has certainly been buying more food than usual,' I pointed out. 'I expect everybody has for Christmas.'

We crossed the deserted street to the Misses Ffrench-Finches' front door and switched to 'O Little Town of Bethlehem.'

A maid opened the door and was joined by two tiny ladies with neat gray buns. They were now dressed in black with fringed Spanish shawls around their shoulders. The first thought that struck me was that their name was so apt. They both listened with their heads to one side, bobbing like little birds.

'So good of you to come,' one of them said in her soft child's voice. 'Effie always loved the carol singing. We won't invite you in, I'm sure you understand, but do have some of Cook's delicious mince pies and try some of our home-made elderberry wine.'

Two trays were produced. The mince pies were wonderful – warm, flaky pastry and plenty of spicy filling. The elderberry wine was not unpleasant and I had a second glass. We drank a toast to their health and to their dear departed sister and went on our way.

Mr Barclay welcomed us gushing and bowing and requested that we sing a couple of carols none of us knew, before settling on 'Hark! the Herald Angels Sing.' I hope the herald angels sang a little better than we did, but he seemed to appreciate the effort. He offered hot cheese straws and mulled wine. From him we went to the vicar, who invited us into his well-worn but comfortable sitting room where we gave him a rousing rendition of 'Oh, Come, All Ye Faithful.' He had more mince pies laid out for us and a traditional wassail bowl. I was beginning to feel the warmth of the food and alcohol as we left and made for Miss Prendergast's cottage, singing 'In the Bleak Midwinter.'

She met us at the door, looking flustered. I decided she was probably one of those spinsters who always looks flustered. 'I'm so embarrassed,' she said. 'I was doing a crossword puzzle and completely forgot the mince pies. I do so love my little puzzles and I was so engrossed that I only remembered the pies when I smelled something burning. And of course by then it was too late to go into town to buy more mincemeat. I feel like such a fool. My mince pies are usually so good too, aren't they, Lady Hawse-Gorzley? So I'm afraid you'll have to settle for biscuits and ginger wine.' She retrieved a tray she had put on a low table beside the front door. 'Here we are. Ginger to keep out the cold. Nothing better,' she said, offering the tray around. 'And I am so looking forward to joining you for the Christmas festivities, Lady Hawse-Gorzley,' she twittered. 'So good of you to invite me. So generous. I can't tell you how much one appreciates company when one is all alone in the world like me.'

The ginger wine was so powerful that it took my breath away and made my eyes water. I stumbled along, half blind, as we headed for my mother's cottage. I was interested to see whether they would pretend to not be at home, but lights shone out between heavy curtains and the door was opened by my grandfather. I wondered whether he would be playing the role of jolly butler, but instead he said, 'I won't ask you in, because they've been working hard all day and consequently have retired with headaches. But we do have a hot rum punch ready and Mrs Huggins has made some lovely sausage rolls. So if you could possibly manage a quiet carol, it would be appreciated.'

We obliged by singing 'In the Bleak Midwinter' again and then Granddad ladled out the punch. He winked as he handed me my glass. 'That will put hair on your chest,' he said. 'Oh, and by the way, your mum and Mr Coward have been invited to join you for Christmas dinner.'

'What about you?'

'Not me, my dear,' he said. 'Me and Mrs Huggins will be

a lot happier here on our own than where we don't belong. We ain't posh and we never will be.'

'I'll come down to visit on Christmas Day when I get a chance,' I said.

'That will be lovely. Anytime. We'll be here.'

I took my glass of punch. It was hot and the fumes from the rum were strong enough to make me cough. But it slipped down deliciously and I was feeling that all was right with the world as we left the cottage and headed on our way. We'd only gone a few yards, however, when I had the strangest sensation. We were being watched. I decided that it was probably my mother and Noël Coward having a good chuckle at our expense upstairs in the cottage, but I also sensed something else. I sensed danger.

Chapter 15

***Somewhere in the darkness, in the village of
Tiddleton-under-Lovey
December 23***

I had been in enough difficult situations to know what
danger felt like and I was clearly sensing it now. A hostile presence was watching us. I turned to look around.
The village green lay in perfect stillness and repose. Early
moonlight glistened on crisp snow. Smoke curled up from
chimneys. Lights peeped out of cottages. Some curtains
were not fully drawn and I saw Christmas trees and paper
chains and all kinds of greenery decorating cozy front
rooms. Here was a picture postcard of the pretty and
peaceful English village. And yet three people had died
here in three days. I wondered if there was to be a fourth
– if someone was stalking our column of singers, panther-
like, waiting to pounce.

We sang outside the rest of the cottages. Willum beamed in
delight and did an ungainly dance when we sang 'God Rest
Ye Merry, Gentlemen' outside the shop, while his mother

looked on, smiling. I found myself looking around to see if we passed any empty cottages or anywhere else a dangerous presence might be hiding, but every front door seemed to be open to us. I noticed as Lady Hawse-Gorzley instructed villagers to come up to the hall for their Christmas box on Boxing Day and they bowed reverently, muttering, 'God bless you, your ladyship.'

If one of the convicts was nearby, I was certain that nobody in this village knew about him. And certainly none of these happy villagers, their children peeping shyly around their parents' legs and skirts, was harboring him. And yet the feeling did not go away until we were walking back up the drive. Actually, it was overtaken by another feeling – one of unsteadiness. I've never been a great drinker and all of those various punches and drafts from wassail bowls were suddenly having an effect on me.

'That was fun, wasn't it?' Darcy drew close to me again. 'Like reliving one's childhood.'

'Marvelous fun,' I said. 'Absolutely marvelous fun.' At least that was what I wanted to say. It came out 'Absholuly maavlus fun.'

Darcy eyed me critically. 'You've been drinking.'

'Only the punches and the elderberry wine,' I said, trying to look haughty and dignified, which effect was lost as I tripped over an unseen rock in the snow and would have fallen on my face if Darcy hadn't grabbed me.

'Whoopsie,' I said and started to giggle.

'The elderberry wine?' he said. 'My dear girl. Don't you know that home-made wines, especially those created by old spinsters, are always lethal?'

'Silly me. I had two glasses,' I said, as I staggered and giggled again.

Darcy took my arm firmly. 'You'd better give me that lantern,' he said. 'And hold on to my arm.'

'You are so kind.' I gazed at him adoringly. 'You take such good care of me. But you always go away again. Why do you always go away?'

'A little thing called money,' he said. 'One needs to earn some occasionally.'

'What does money matter?' I went on. 'Why don't we run away and live in a little cottage on a desert island and we'll be wonderfully happy.' I don't know how much of this he understood. I was having trouble forming words by now. What's more, the world was swinging around.

We reached the house and Darcy leaned his lantern against the portico. 'I think I'd better get you up to bed before anyone else sees you like this,' he whispered. 'Come on. Up the stairs with you.'

'I'm perfeckly all right,' I said at the same moment that my foot started to slide on the polished floor. 'Who put in an ice rink while we were away? Wasn't that clever of them?'

'Up the stairs. Now.' Darcy gripped my arm firmly and half carried me up the stairs and then down the hall to my room.

'Finally,' I said as he bundled me inside the door. 'We're alone together, just you and me and a bed. What's taken you so long, Darcy? I've been waiting for this a long time.' I kept talking while he pulled off my various outer garments and then sat me down to take off my shoes. 'Do you know how boring it is to be a virgin?' I went on. 'Boring, boring, boring. Everybody thinks virgins are boring. And do you know what? They are.'

Darcy undid the leather strap that held my kilt in place and it dropped to the floor.

'Arms up,' he said and yanked my sweater over my head. 'There. You'll do until your maid can finish undressing you. I'll bring you up a tray from supper. You should eat something if you can. And a cup of black coffee.'

'Where are you going?' I asked plaintively.

'Down to tell them that Lady Georgiana is not feeling well.'

'You're not going to leave me alone, are you? Not when there's this big and beautiful bed and I'm in it all by myself. And you are such a good kisser too.'

Darcy smiled and leaned to kiss my forehead. 'As tempting as this offer is, my lady, I'm going to wait until you'll remember what you've done. In spite of what your sister-in-law thinks, I happen to be a gentleman.'

'Oh, Fig. Don't talk about Fig. If I am boring, then she is boring times ten. The most boring person on the whole Earth. I bet she never invited a young man to her bedroom. Never never.'

Darcy looked down at me with a mixture of amusement and concern. 'Now, you're to stay put and try to sleep. I'll find your maid and have her come to keep an eye on you. And I'll bring you something to eat later. All right?'

'I wish you weren't going away,' I said in a small voice. 'I'd rather fall asleep with your arms around me. So nice. So warm. So safe . . .' I closed my eyes. When I opened them again, he had gone.

I lay back, half dozing, half awake, until I heard the click of the door latch and a shaft of light came from the hallway outside. This was rapidly extinguished as the door closed again and I sensed someone coming toward the bed.

'Is it suppertime already?' I asked sleepily.

'Supper is over,' said a deep voice. 'They're all having

coffee, so I thought I'd slip up and see how you were faring.'

And someone sat on my bed. I fumbled for my bedside light. In its rosy glow Johnnie Protheroe's face loomed close to me.

'What are you doing in my room?' I demanded, fear giving me control of my tongue.

'Just came up to see how you were, old thing,' he said. 'I heard you were feeling poorly. Thought you might need cheering up, what?' And to my horror he put a hand on my bare shoulder, caressed it, then started to slide it down my front.

I mustered all my energy and sat up. 'Unhand me, churl,' I said, knocking at his hand as if it were an annoying insect. 'Be gone, I say.'

For some reason he found this really funny. 'You really are quite delightful,' he said. 'I thought I'd be bored to tears this Christmas but now I can see it's going to be rather jolly.'

He grabbed my hands as I lashed out at him, and pinned me back to the pillow. 'A spirited little miss, eh?' he whispered as I tried to break free of him. 'I do enjoy a good struggle. The prize is so much sweeter. All of the dried-up prunes around here are all too ready to leap into the sack at the slightest invitation.'

His face was close to mine and I smelled the unpleasant mixture of alcohol, tobacco and some kind of scented pomade or hair oil. That sobered me up more quickly than any black coffee would have done.

'Go away or I'll scream,' I said.

This made him laugh even more. 'My dear, bed hopping is a time-honored country sport. Everyone does it. It's only a bit of fun, what?'

'Not for me,' I said. 'And certainly not with you. Now get out of my room.'

'You 'eard the lady. Get out while the going's good,' said a threatening voice behind us, and Queenie loomed up like an avenging angel. She had a water jug in her hand. 'Now, do you want this broken over yer 'ead or what?'

'Well, I can tell when I'm not wanted,' Johnnie said and made a hasty exit.

'Queenie,' I said, sitting up again and brushing myself off, 'sometimes you are worth your wages after all.'

'Who was that man? Bloody cheek, coming into your room like that,' she said. 'Nasty slimy type. I'm going to bring my mattress and sleep on your floor in the future. And you tell your Mr Darcy and he'll punch the daylights out of him.'

'I don't think we'd better do that,' I said.

'He was worried about you, you know. He says to me, "Queenie, go and sit with her. See if you can get her to eat something." So I brought you the tray. There's a lovely soup and some game pie and black coffee.'

'I'll try the black coffee anyway,' I said and then fell asleep with Queenie sitting on the end of my bed.

Chapter 16

Gorzley Hall
December 24, Christmas Eve
Awoke feeling rather confused and not too well. Reminder to self: Never touch alcohol again, especially not elderberry wine.

I opened my eyes and wondered why the daylight hurt me so much. Then vague recollections of the night before crept back. Not only of my drunkenness but of the danger I had felt. And I had been too drunk to be vigilant. I opened my bedroom door. The house was suspiciously quiet. I should have stayed awake and alert last night. I should have told Darcy my suspicions instead of . . . My cheeks turned flaming hot as I remembered some of the things I said to him. If someone had died during the night, it would be my fault.

Even the Wexlers had not leaped up at the crack of dawn after the previous night's festivities. I suspected I wasn't the only one taken by surprise at the strength and amount of the alcohol consumed. I washed, dressed and came downstairs to find the Rathbones breakfasting quietly on toast and black coffee. I decided that was all I could manage too and was just trying to swallow a morsel with marmalade on it when the door opened and Monty, Badger and Darcy came in, laughing as if they were in the middle of a good joke.

'So the bishop said, "Not during Lent,"' Monty finished and the other two laughed even louder. They went over to the sideboard and started helping themselves generously to everything that was there while I looked around to see if there was another way out of the room or I could disguise myself as a standard lamp. Before I could attempt either, Darcy came and sat beside me.

'Good morning, my lady,' he said. 'I trust you slept well?'

I flushed bright red as I saw his eyes laughing at me. 'Remind me never to drink elderberry wine again,' I said.

'Good God, you didn't actually drink any of those old biddies' wine, did you?' Monty said in a horrified voice. 'They are notorious for it around here. Lethal. Positively lethal. And the elderberry is worse than the dandelion. Of course, the parsnip is the real killer.'

At the mention of the word 'killer' I found that I was no longer laughing. I remembered the sense of danger I had felt as we walked from my mother's cottage.

'Is everybody all right this morning?' I asked.

Monty was still grinning. 'I suspect the other guests feel rather the way you do,' he said. 'If they all knocked back that wine they'll have glorious headaches.'

Monty and Badger devoured their food as only young college men can and excused themselves to go outside and hurl around a rugby ball. I went to go too, but Darcy grabbed my wrist. 'What did you mean by asking if everyone was all right?' he said softly. 'Did you suspect that might not be the case?'

'It's these unexplained deaths,' I said. 'One each day since I arrived. The man shot in the orchard, the garage owner who fell off a bridge, the old lady found gassed – and yesterday there was also a horrible incident in Newton Abbot. A telephone operator was electrocuted when she tried to plug in her headphones.'

'That doesn't sound right,' Darcy said. 'There would be no way that electric wires would be anywhere near telephone wires.'

'That makes it four deaths in four days,' I said. 'So I couldn't help worrying that someone might have died this morning.'

'As far as I know we're all hale and hearty here,' he said. 'No corpses lying in the hallways.'

'It's not funny, Darcy,' I snapped. 'It's horrible.'

He reached across and stroked my cheek. 'Yes, I suppose it is. Especially when you've actually seen one of those corpses. But there's nothing we can do about it, Georgie, and it doesn't concern us. Maybe your telephone operator was deliberately killed because she eavesdropped on a conversation, but the others – well, as far as I can see they can't be connected or even be murders. A cluster of sad accidents, that's all.'

His hand slid from my cheek down to my chin and he pulled me toward him to give me a kiss.

'Darcy, not in public,' I said.

He grinned. 'You weren't so modest about it last night, I seem to remember. Inviting me into your bedchamber, suggesting that we run off to a desert island together in full hearing of everyone else. In fact, I had no idea that you were such a hot little piece.'

'Oh, dear.' I put my hands to my face. 'Don't remind me. I feel absolutely awful.'

'Don't apologize. I rather liked it. In fact, I'm looking for a time when you can show me more.'

'Stop it.' I slapped his hand and he laughed. 'Maybe it's your true nature coming out. Maybe you take after your mother after all.'

'God, I hope not,' I said.

'By the way, was that your grandfather we saw last night? Looked exactly like him.'

'Yes, it was. My mother's here too. She and Noël Coward are working on a play together and Granddad came down to help look after them.'

'Your mother and Noël Coward – what an unlikely pair.' Darcy chuckled. 'So she's going back to the theater, is she? The big blond German man is *nicht mehr*?'

'He's gone to stay with his family for Christmas,' I said. 'And between ourselves I see the beginning of the end. I think she's only toying with the idea of acting again. She does so love being adored.'

'Don't we all?' Darcy gave me the most wonderful smile that melted me all the way to my toes.

'Oh, Darcy, you're up. Jolly good.' Bunty stopped short when she saw us together. 'I was wondering if you wanted to go out for a shoot. Oodles of pheasants around here just waiting to be bagged.'

'I think we'd better see what your mother has planned for us,' Darcy said. 'She seems to have the whole thing organized.'

'There's no need for family to have to take part in all her silly fun and games,' Bunty said, latching on to his arm. 'You and I could slip away and not be noticed.'

'Another time, Bunty,' he said. He gave me a swift glance, saw me trying to look indifferent, then cleared his throat.

'Bunty, I think you should know that Georgie and I . . . well . . .'

There was a dreadfully long silence in which I shifted uneasily on my seat.

'I knew it,' she said at last. 'I saw the way you look at her. Oh, bugger. Well. I suppose I'd better be charitable and say "Bless you, my children." I probably wouldn't have been able to marry my cousin anyway. Blast and damnation. How am I ever going to meet anyone decent stuck down here?'

And she stomped out. Darcy and I exchanged a long look. 'I had to tell her,' he said. 'She's been pestering me every second since I got here.'

'I hope her mother won't mind,' I said, trying to look blasé while all the time a voice was yelling through my head that Darcy had acknowledged me as his sweetheart. 'Perhaps she had her heart set on a match too.'

'A match?' Darcy smiled. 'I don't think I'd be described as much of a catch at the moment. A title sometime in the distant future and no prospects for the present. Hopeless, if you ask me.' He gave me another one of those smiles.

Other people began to drift into the breakfast room muttering 'Morning' in a way that indicated they too were suffering from hangovers. I got up. 'I should go and see what Lady Hawse-Gorzley wants me to do,' I said. But before I could leave the room she came in.

'Georgiana dear. The weather's not promising this morning. It may snow again. May rain. Dashed nuisance. So I suggest you round up the young people and get to work on the pantomime.'

'Pantomime?'

'Oh, yes. We always put on a pantomime on Boxing Day. The funnier the better. Ask Bunty for the local jokes. I'll have the servants bring the dressing-up box down from the attic. Always such fun. And we'll keep it down for when we play charades. You can have the small sitting room next to the ballroom.'

She looked around the table. 'Everyone all right? Splendid. Splendid. I'll have the butler put the morning papers in the library for you.'

And she was off again. I looked down at Darcy.

'How are you at pantomimes?' I asked.

'Expert,' he said. 'My Widow Twankey brought the house down.'

'What pantomime is she in?'

He looked shocked. '*Aladdin*. You know – Wishy Washy and the magic lamp and all that.'

I shrugged. 'Sorry, I've never seen it.'

'Never seen *Aladdin*? My dear girl, you haven't lived.'

'There aren't too many pantomimes around Castle Rannoch, you know. And I've hardly ever been in London for Christmas. I think I may have seen *Puss in Boots* once, but I can't remember anything about it.'

'And then there is *Dick Whittington*, isn't there? And *Cinderella*, of course. And *Babes in the Wood*.'

'We'll need one with seven or eight roles,' I said. 'Everyone should have a part.'

'Well, that rules out *Dick Whittington*,' Darcy said. 'I can only think of Dick and his cat.'

'I expect he had a sweetheart,' I said. 'It seems to be one of the requirements.'

'It had better be *Cinderella*,' Darcy said. 'At least we know the story to that one.'

I counted on my fingers. 'Let's see – Cinderella, wicked stepmother–'

'I claim that role for myself,' he said.

'Two ugly sisters.'

'Monty and Badger.'

'The prince, the fairy godmother.'

'The king and the person who carries around the glass slipper. That makes eight.'

'Perfect,' I said.

I rounded up the younger members and presented the idea to them. Naturally Cherie thought it would be boring, Junior thought it would be stupid and Ethel didn't look too enthusiastic. But Cherie brightened up a lot when I made her Cinderella. Ethel agreed to be the fairy godmother and I assigned Bunty to be the prince. As you know, the principal boy in a pantomime is always played by a female in tights, and there is always a comic older woman played by a man. It's tradition. And a lot of pies in the face and that kind of thing.

By the end of the morning we had a rough sketch of our lines and everyone had entered into the spirit of the thing, Ethel proving to be rather sharp and witty and even Junior happy to be made the king. But the more they laughed and joked and tried on impossible costumes the more I tried to fight off a lingering uneasiness. Why had I sensed danger so close to my mother's cottage the night before? A ridiculous notion entered my head. What if one of those convicts knew that my grandfather had been a policeman? Might they want to get him out of the way as their fifth victim?

I could stand it no longer. 'I'll leave you to run through it once more,' I said. 'I have to pop down to the village for a minute.'

I put on my coat, grabbed my gifts and ran all the way down the drive, sliding a little in snow that had started to melt. I hammered on my mother's door. When Granddad opened it I let out a huge sigh of relief.

'Oh, you're all right. Thank goodness.'

'And why shouldn't I be all right?' he asked, helping me off with my coat. 'Fit as a fiddle, me.' And he thumped his chest. 'Come on in, ducks. We've got company.'

I went through into the sitting room and found Detective Inspector Newcombe seated by the fire, a cup of tea in his hand.

'The inspector just dropped in for a chat,' Granddad said.

'There hasn't been another death, has there?' I asked.

'Not that we've heard of,' the inspector said, 'but I'm not at all happy. Those first deaths I could explain, but that poor woman at the telephone exchange – that had to be malicious and intentional. We can't tell any more, because the place burned, but I'd say the wires were deliberately hooked up to kill someone. That's why I came to see your grandfather, miss.'

Obviously it had slipped his mind that I wasn't a miss, I was a milady. 'My chief inspector is off skiing in France so it's all up to me. I know I should probably call in Scotland Yard, but I don't want to do that and look a fool, so I thought that a retired member of the Metropolitan Police Service could maybe give me some pointers.'

He looked hopefully at my grandfather. Granddad tried to look like someone who had been a Scotland Yard expert detective, instead of an ordinary copper.

'Do you have anyone around here who might have a grudge against the people who have died? Anyone who has been a bit off his rocker?'

The inspector shook his head. 'Nobody. It's normally quieter than the grave in these parts – oh, dear, that was a tactless expression, wasn't it? But the occasional robbery, a bit of cattle or sheep stealing, someone beating up his old lady on a Saturday night – that's what crime means to us. This has to be an outsider, and the only outsiders I know are those convicts.'

'There are all the people staying with Lady Hawse-Gorzley,' I pointed out. 'They are all outsiders.'

'Yes, but with no connections to the people who have died, surely?' The inspector sounded shocked.

'I don't think so,' I said. 'Since they've just come from America and Yorkshire and India.'

'I wish they'd hurry up and catch those blasted convicts,' the inspector said. 'Until they are caught I have to believe that they are hiding out on my patch and it's up to me to find them.'

'You've asked everybody in the area to report break-ins or stolen food immediately, have you?' I said. 'They have to eat and shelter somewhere.'

'Exactly. With the kind of weather we've just had, someone must be hiding them, but we've pretty much searched door to door. Most of the local people have lived here all their lives. They're not the kind of people to be harboring criminals.'

'I'm not sure it is your convicts we're looking at,' Granddad said slowly. 'In my time on the force I came up against a lot of criminals. Most of them were not too bright and if they were going to kill someone they did it with the first thing that came to hand – coshing someone over the head with a brick, stabbing them, or shooting, if they had a gun. And they usually chose the same way too. They'd leave behind a blueprint we could identify. If these are murders, they are clever methods of killing – someone with a good brain is killing in very different ways – heaven knows for what reason. Either that or more than one person is involved. So we have to ask ourselves why. Why would a man bother to electrocute someone at a switchboard when he could presumably follow her home in the dark and cosh or stab her? Until we can get inside his head, we're not going to be able to stop him.'

'I suppose you're right,' the inspector said. 'But as it happens these convicts were not your usual thugs. One was a bank teller, reckoned to be the brains behind a big train robbery. Another was an escape artist in the theater. You know, Britain's answer to Houdini. We reckon he was the one who got them out of their shackles. He went bad and turned to safecracking. And the third used to do a comic music-hall act with his wife. The old colonel and the innocent young girl.'

'Sounds harmless enough,' Granddad said.

'I don't know about that,' the inspector said. 'When there was no more money to be made from music halls they started robbing their landladies, or conning them out of their life savings. Some of the old biddies met an untimely end, but we could never prove that this bloke was actually guilty of murder.'

'What happened to the wife? Did she go to jail too?' Granddad asked.

'She committed suicide. Drowned herself off Beachy Head in Sussex.'

'So not from around here, then?'

'None of them were. Driving me mad, that's what it's doing.'

He took a long swig of tea, then set down the teacup.

'I don't think you should be focusing on those convicts,'

Granddad said. 'An escaped convict is not going to go to the trouble of setting up an elaborate death to look like an accident, is he? If you're on the run and hiding, the more time you spend out in the open, the greater the likelihood of being caught.'

'Well, at least there hasn't been a death so far today, touch wood,' the inspector said. 'Maybe he's got the four people he wants.'

'And why did he want them?' Granddad asked. 'It seems to me that they couldn't be more different, and they wouldn't be a threat to anybody.'

The inspector sighed. 'I know. Hopeless, isn't it? But my chief is going to come back from France and bawl me out if I haven't solved it.' He got to his feet. 'Thanks for the chat, Albert. Maybe things have quieted down for Christmas. Maybe even a hardened criminal can't bring himself to kill anyone at such a sacred time. Maybe I can even have Christmas dinner with my wife and the nippers for once.'

As he opened the front door a bobby in blue uniform was coming up the path toward us.

'Oh, there you are, sir,' he said. 'I was sent from the station to get you. There's been a robbery in the high street. Mr Klein the jeweler. They broke in overnight and they've taken his most valuable pieces. He's in a terrible state, sir. Ranting and raving and blaming the police. You'd better come quickly.'

Chapter 17

Inspector Newcombe started down the path toward his motor. 'I hope nobody's touched anything and messed up the fingerprints,' he said. 'A lot of damage, was there? Did they smash the window?'

'Oh, no, sir. There were no obvious signs of a break-in and the pieces they took were in the safe at the back. Sarge reckons it was professionals, all right. Picked the lock on the front door. Knew exactly what they were doing and what they were looking for. Only took some rings with bloody great diamonds in them. And Sarge don't reckon we'll find any fingerprints neither.'

'Aha,' Newcombe said. 'See, what did I tell you? One of those convicts was a professional escape artist, wasn't he? Expert at picking locks. I knew they were still hanging around here.'

'Oh, but that's the other thing I've got to tell you, sir,' the constable said, his cheeks pink with excitement. 'A message just came in that they've caught one of the convicts up in Birmingham. Jim Howard, sir. Wasn't he the one who was the escape artist?'

'Damn,' Inspector Newcombe muttered. 'That shoots down my theory, then. I don't think a bank clerk or a music-hall entertainer would know how to crack a safe. I wonder if the other two were with him or if he knows where they are. I don't suppose he'll squeal on his mates, anyway.' He clapped a hand on the constable's shoulder. 'Come on, then, lad. Let's get back into town. Sorry for rushing off like this, Albert. I'll let you know what we find.'

And he strode down the path to his waiting car.

'At least it's not a murder,' I said shakily, thinking of the polite and charming Mr Klein, who had told me about the fine pieces he'd just acquired from Paris. Maybe he had also mentioned these fine pieces to the wrong person. But at least he was still alive and unharmed.

'And this one shouldn't be too hard to figure out,' Granddad said, staring thoughtfully at the departing car. 'There are only a limited number of criminals in an area like this who possess the skills to crack a safe and have the knowledge to take only the best pieces. Your petty thief who needs extra money for Christmas would have smashed the window and grabbed what he could.'

'So you don't think this crime was related to the strange deaths, do you?' I asked.

He shook his head. 'Don't see how. If the others are murders, then they are the work of a twisted sort of mind. And this is the work of an expert burglar. Probably a known criminal.'

We returned to the cozy sitting room. My mother had appeared, wearing a blue satin robe trimmed with feathers. 'Has that horrid little man gone?' she asked. 'We're supposed to be having a quiet and peaceful Christmas and instead we have nasty policemen tramping in and out of the house all the time. You shouldn't have encouraged him, Daddy.'

'The poor bloke is at his wit's end, ducks. He wanted my advice.'

'I take it you haven't told him you were just a humble copper and not the leading light of Scotland Yard?' She curled herself into an armchair. 'Oh, hello, Georgie, darling. Come and give your aged mother a kiss.'

I did so, then I handed her the package. 'A small Christmas token from me. Not to be opened until tomorrow.'

'Georgie, you shouldn't. How sweet of you. And now I feel terrible because I wasn't expecting to see you until the new year, when I was planning to take you on a shopping spree.' She uncurled herself. 'But you have to have something. Come upstairs and see what you'd like. I know I'm teeny tiny compared to you, but I have some pretty scarves and hats and things.'

'It's all right, Mummy, you really don't need to. . . .'

'Nonsense. I insist. You have to have something on the right day. Besides, I always travel with far too many clothes.'

And she dragged me up the narrow staircase into a frightfully untidy bedroom. It was clear she rarely traveled without her maid and Mrs Huggins wasn't up to the task of keeping a lady's wardrobe in order.

'Help yourself, darling. Anything you'd like.'

My gaze swept around the room, alighting on a lovely cashmere cardigan in a soft rose. Modesty almost prevented me from asking for it, but I reasoned that she had the money to buy a replacement whenever she wanted while I wasn't likely to be offered cashmere again in a hurry.

'Could I try this on?' I asked. 'It looks as if it might be big enough for me.'

'That old thing?' she said. 'Take it, darling. I only brought it in case it was freezing here, but as you can see, it's lovely and warm.'

I tried it on and it fitted rather well.

'You need a skirt to go with it,' she said. 'That tweed you're wearing is hopelessly shapeless. Let's see.' She rummaged in a wardrobe and held up a slim gray crepe de chine. 'This is long on me and you do have a nice little waist.'

After a half hour I came away with the cardigan and skirt, a divine peach silk scarf and a clever little black hat with a jaunty peacock feather on one side. As we left the bedroom the door beside it opened and Noël Coward peeked out.

'I've been finding Christmas presents for Georgie,' my mother said. 'Such fun.'

'Oh, God. Is one supposed to give presents?' Noël said. 'It never crossed my mind.'

'It's all right,' I said. 'I'm afraid I didn't bring a present for you, Mr Coward. I didn't see anything you might want.'

'Dear child, you couldn't afford anything I might want,' he said. 'In fact, my needs are few these days. But I tell you what – I'll write a song for you. How would that be?'

'As long as you give her the royalties, Noël,' my mother said astutely.

'Naturally,' he said smoothly. 'At least half of them. Ah, well, back to work. I've nearly finished that scene, Claire. Can we go through it in a few minutes?'

'I have to get back to the hall.' I gave my mother a kiss on the cheek. 'Thank you so much for the presents. They are lovely. I'll look quite smart for Christmas. See you tomorrow for Christmas dinner, then.'

'I'm not sure if we're coming,' she said. 'Noël doesn't think they'll be our kind of people.'

Back downstairs I gave Granddad his little box and Mrs Huggins her box of toffees. They were both quite moved.

'Fancy, me getting a present from royalty,' Mrs Huggins said. 'Just wait till I tell them back home at the Queen's Head.'

'You're a good girl, my love,' Granddad said, putting an arm around me. 'I wish I'd got a present for you, but I had no idea I'd be seeing you. I hope good things come your way soon. You deserve all the happiness in the world.'

'Actually, having you close by for Christmas is the best present I could have,' I said, giving him a kiss.

I felt a rosy glow as I came out of the cottage. I saw Miss Prendergast hurrying across the street, even though there was no traffic in sight. She was holding her shapeless hat firmly to her head, although the wind was hardly blowing, and she didn't notice me until she almost barreled into me.

'Oh, goodness me,' she said. 'So sorry. Didn't see you. I've just come from the Misses Ffrench-Finch. Tried to cheer them up but they are completely devastated, poor dears. They relied on Miss Effie for everything. She used to boss them around dreadfully but they are lost without her. One feels so sorry for them.' And her voice cracked. She swallowed hard, willing herself not to give in to sentiment. 'I really wish that . . .' she began, then shook her head firmly. 'Can't undo the past, no matter how sad, can one?'

And she went on her way, up the front path to her cottage door. I stared after her. What did she wish? I wondered. That Miss Effie hadn't died, or that one of the other sisters had died in her stead? I continued on my way back to the hall.

* * *

The rest of the day went smoothly enough. The younger set were in good spirits after the pantomime rehearsal and amused themselves playing board games. The Sechrests and Rathbones played bridge, chatting as they did so about this area and their memories of past hunts and regattas and families they both knew. The Rathbones once owned a house nearby for their home leaves but had been forced to give it up a few years ago, when so much money was lost in the great crash of '29.

'The memsahib still misses her garden, of course,' Colonel Rathbone said. 'It's too damned hot to work in the garden in Calcutta.'

'The gardeners do try hard, bless them,' Mrs Rathbone said, 'but it's always a losing battle against the heat and then the monsoon comes and flattens everything.'

'Pity it's not summer or Sandra would love to show you around our garden,' Captain Sechrest said. 'Absolutely devoted to her garden, aren't you, old girl?'

'One has to keep oneself busy while you are away for months,' Mrs Sechrest said and I noticed that she shot a look at Johnnie Protheroe, who was playing some kind of card game with Bunty that seemed to involve touching her knee quite often.

'So how often do you get home?' Sandy Sechrest asked the Rathbones.

'Every five years.'

'How much longer do you think you'll stick it out?' she asked.

Colonel Rathbone frowned. 'Can't really say. Of course I'd like to retire to a little place in a village like this. But who knows if we'll have another blasted war or a native uprising. And who knows what one will be able to afford on an army pension.'

He glanced at his wife, then she looked away. 'That's the problem, isn't it?' Mrs Rathbone said. 'You give your life to the army and they reward you with a pension that a sparrow couldn't live on. It's simply not fair. I should have been like some of the other wives and had an affair with a maharaja and been rewarded for my services with jewels. I know a couple of wives who set themselves up very nicely that way.'

'I wouldn't have minded an affair with a maharaja,' Sandra Sechrest said dreamily. 'They have such lovely dark eyes, don't they?'

I let the conversation wash over me as I pretended to study a magazine, but I found I could not shake off the tension. The day wasn't over yet. There was still time for another death.

Lady Hawse-Gorzley appeared, clapping her hands. 'Time for tea, everyone. We're serving it a little early so that we have enough light to go out and find the Yule log. And I wanted to check who would like to go to midnight mass at our little church, and who would rather do matins tomorrow morning. Oh, and Darcy dear – do you need me to find out the times of masses at the Catholic church in Newton Abbot?'

And there it was – the reminder of the fact I had conveniently chosen to block from my mind. Darcy was a Catholic. I would not be allowed to marry him.

Chapter 18

December 24, evening on Christmas Eve
Can't help feeling excited, in spite of everything that has happened.

I tried to push this worry from my mind as we wrapped up warmly and set off to find the Yule log. Monty insisted that we sing carols as we trudged through the snow. The temperature was slightly warmer today so the snow was turning to slush, which would make it hard to drag the log home on a sled. Sir Oswald and Monty were pulling one just in case, but Bunty was leading one of the farm horses attached to a wagon.

This time we set out on the other side of the house, past a lovely formal garden, its statues decorated with crowns of snow and a snowy rim to the lily pond, then into a wilderness area that led up to Lovey Tor. This part of the grounds was full of old oak trees, bent against the cruel Dartmoor wind, as were cedars, yew trees and even a beech or two. When I paused to look back I saw that we had a lovely view of the house and the village beyond, nestled in the hollow between the hills. We could also glimpse another large house through the trees.

'What's that?' I asked Bunty.

'Oh, that was poor old Freddie's place,' she said. 'I don't know who it will go to now. He didn't have any brothers. Perhaps it will be sold and we'll have frightful nouveau riche bankers who will just come down for weekends.'

'At least you'd have a chance to meet people if they brought house parties with them,' I said and she grinned.

'Maybe they wouldn't be so frightful. I do so want to marry someone rich enough to keep me. I could do without the title.'

'I agree,' I said. 'Titles aren't worth much in the real world, are they?'

'In your case you could presumably marry someone with a real title – you know – a prince or a duke.'

'That's what my family would like. They have already tried to saddle me with a frightful Romanian prince. My friend Belinda and I called him Fishface.'

'But you'd prefer a penniless Darcy.' She glanced back over her shoulder to see Darcy far behind, walking with Monty as they dragged the sled.

'Yes, I would, actually. But it probably won't ever happen. I don't think I'd be allowed to marry a Catholic.'

'That's stupid. I'd jolly well ignore them if I wanted to marry someone I loved.'

'I think it's something to do with the law of England. One can hardly go against that.'

'You'll find a way if you want to,' she said encouragingly. We walked on.

'How much further? I'm tired,' Junior whined.

I glanced back again as a thought struck me. This part

of the property was close to Freddie's house, and what's more, it was full of big, solid trees. If he had wanted to rig up some kind of booby trap then the position here would have been ideal. Why go all the way around to the orchard?

'Here we are,' Sir Oswald called. 'This is the one I thought would do. What do you think?'

We gathered around to admire an enormous log – a great fallen oak limb, actually – then worked together to heft it onto the sled, which promptly sank into the mushy snow and wouldn't move. So we had to use the wagon. Even with all of us lifting and grunting, it was jolly heavy and we were glad that the horse had to transport it down the hill and not us. As we made our way home the light was rapidly fading, bathing the world in a dusky pink glow.

'We will take the log into the house and light it after dinner,' Lady Hawse-Gorzley said, 'and if all goes well it should burn all through Christmas Day to bring us luck.'

As soon as we had taken off our coats and hats, Dickson the butler appeared with a punch bowl of steaming mulled wine and a tray of hot sausage rolls. This time I sipped slowly, warming up my fingers on the glass.

'Right, now we all have more work to do before dinner.' Lady Hawse-Gorzley took control again before anyone could slip away. 'It's time to decorate the Christmas tree. Lights in this box, glass ornaments here, tinsel garlands over there. You should be able to reach the upper portion of the tree by leaning through the banister, and I suggest you boys put the lights and ornaments on the upper part.'

We set to work hanging the delicate ornaments – trumpets and birds, gnomes and balls – then adding the finishing touches of pine cones, sugar mice, tinsel. When the lights were finally plugged in, the tree sparkled with a magical glow and the company broke into applause.

This time we dressed formally for dinner, except for Junior, who joined us in an awful blue-and-white-checked jacket. Mrs Upthorpe and Ethel were sporting their Parisian gowns, which somehow failed to make them look elegant. I know that's uncharitable of me, but I was trying to be an unbiased observer. I also wished that it could have been summer, not winter, as I too possessed a Chanel evening gown – designed for me by Coco herself. But alas it was a light chiffon and quite unsuitable for a winter gathering. And so I was stuck with my aged burgundy velvet. At least I had a strand of family rubies that took the attention away from where Queenie had brushed the fabric the wrong way.

I came into the dining room to see that Lady Hawse-Gorzley had outdone herself tonight. There were two large candelabras on the dining table and their light sparkled from silver and crystal. I could tell the guests were impressed, even the Wexlers. There were place cards at the table and I was seated between Colonel Rathbone and Johnnie Protheroe – which would not have been my first choice of assignment. Sure enough, we were only halfway through the first course, a hearty game soup, when I felt a hand on my knee. I pushed it off and pretended not to have noticed.

The second course came: John Dory in a caper sauce. And to my amazement I felt a hand on my knee again, only this time it was the other knee. Either Johnnie had grown very long arms or the colonel was also a groper. I pushed it away. Across the table I saw Darcy giving me a strange look as if he could sense something was not right. I looked to left and right of me then rolled my eyes. I think he understood and smirked.

A sorbet was served before the main course to clear the palate, and no hands appeared. Then the main course was carried to the table: a splendid baron of beef, with individual Yorkshire puddings, crispy roast potatoes and a purée of root vegetables baked with a crispy top. Conversation lagged as everyone ate. Then, as plates were cleared, not one but two hands landed on my knees again. I decided this had to stop once and for all. I slid both my hands under the table and caressed each hand lovingly, a serene smile on my face. Then I picked up each hand and brought them together, carefully removing my own hands. It took them a moment to realize that they were holding hands with each other. I sensed a rapid movement and then each of the men sitting bolt upright on either side of me. Both had red faces!

The pudding was apple tart with Devon clotted cream, followed by anchovy toast savories. We ladies retired to the drawing room for coffee and were soon joined by the men.

'I think some parlor games are in order, don't you?' Lady Hawse-Gorzley said, and she soon had us playing all the silly old ones like the minister's cat. It was the sort of thing that I, as an only child alone with servants in a big castle, had rarely done while I was growing up, and I loved every moment of it.

Around ten, the Wexlers opted to go to bed, but the rest of us decided to stay up, most of us planning to go to midnight service. A couple of whist foursomes were begun. The rest of us sat near the fire talking. After a while I found I wasn't taking part in the conversation, instead letting my thoughts wander from the robbery today to Darcy's Catholicism. I kept telling myself that it was Christmas Eve and all was well, but so many disquieting things had happened in the last few days that I couldn't fully relax and enjoy the moment. I fought back tiredness and was glad when we were dismissed to change for church.

At eleven forty-five we set off up the driveway, marching two by two like students on a school outing. The dowager countess had declined to come with us, declaring that midnight mass was a papist invention and the only proper celebration of Christmas was matins on the day itself. Captain and Mrs Sechrest decided to join her. I suspected they had both eaten and drunk their fill at dinner and were feeling too comfortable to move. The slushy snow had frozen again and made the going treacherous, but we held on to each other and reached the church without mishap. Apparently the Hawse-Gorzleys had their own pews at the front, because Lady Hawse-Gorzley marched us past the rest of the congregation to the places of honor right at the front where nobody else had dared to sit. I noticed that Darcy had come with us and sat with Monty and Badger in the row behind me.

It was one of those perfect village churches dating from Norman times with a vaulted ceiling and simple altar, and it had that special smell I always associated with old churches – a mixture of mold and old books and polish that was in no way unpleasant. It was also, like most old churches, not heated and our breath rose visibly toward the rafters. Miss Prendergast had decorated it splendidly, with holly in every niche and ivy trailing over the back of the altar. I noticed, however, that the Christmas crèche, at the steps of the Lady Chapel, had no adornment of holly, thanks to Mr Barclay.

The moment I located him, sitting at the organ still and formal in his red bow tie, he struck up with a resounding fanfare that filled the whole church. The choirboys shuffled in, the smaller ones rubbing their eyes and wishing they could be in bed. They looked so angelic in their white robes and red ruffs, and when the organ struck up 'Oh, Come, All Ye Faithful' they sounded angelic too. As we reached the verse that begins, 'Yeah, Lord, we greet thee, born this happy morning,' the church bells began to ring midnight and it was Christmas Day.

After a rousing rendering of 'Hark! the Herald Angels Sing' we walked back up the drive, no longer sleepy but revived by the lively singing. I fell into step beside Darcy.

'I see you came to the church of the heretics with us,' I said, trying to make it sound as if I was joking. 'So tell me, does your Catholic religion really mean that much to you?'

'I came with you because I thought it was polite to my hostess,' he said, 'and also because the law says we don't have to attend mass if the church is more than three miles away and if we are a traveler. The nearest Catholic church is at least ten miles away and I didn't want to put anyone to the trouble of driving me in this weather.'

'Oh, I see,' I said.

'And as to whether my religion means anything to me, I can't say I'm always a devout Catholic, but I try. My mother converted to marry my father, you know. And she became very devout. So I'm conscious of that.'

We walked on in silence while I digested this. As we took off the various layers of coats and scarves, Lady Hawse-Gorzley announced that there was brandy and hot mince pies in the drawing room to warm us up. I was about to go through when Darcy grabbed my arm and held me back.

'It's Christmas Day,' he said, 'and I want to give you my Christmas present.' And he took a small box from his pocket. 'If I'd known you were going to be here, it would have been something rather different and a little more special,' he said, 'but I wanted you to have something, to think of me when I'm not with you.'

I took the box and opened it. Inside was a silver Devon pixie on a pretty silver chain. I started to laugh.

'What's so funny?' he asked. 'Don't you like it?'

'Wait and see tomorrow morning,' I said. 'And I do like it. Thank you.'

'And in case you haven't noticed,' he said, 'I planned ahead. You're standing directly under the mistletoe.'

Then he took me in his arms and kissed me – not a perfunctory meeting of the lips, but a real, warm and wonderful kiss.

Chapter 19

Christmas Day at Gorzley Hall
December 25

I floated up to bed in a rosy haze. Darcy loved me. Nothing else in the whole world mattered. Queenie was lying on my bed, snoring away. Presumably she had been waiting for my return to undress me and had not been able to stay awake any longer. I roused her gently. 'Queenie, you can go to bed now,' I whispered. 'Happy Christmas.'

'Same to you, miss,' she muttered and promptly fell back to sleep again.

'Queenie. You have to go back to your own bed.' I prodded and tried to move her. She merely sighed and turned over. She was too heavy to lift. Since I was full of happiness and Christmas cheer I merely rolled her to one side of the bed, undressed and got in myself.

I woke to the sound of bells pealing jubilantly. Christmas Day. I sat up to see that Queenie was still sound asleep, mouth open and snoring unattractively. I nudged her.

'Queenie. Wake up. It's morning and I'd like my tea.'

She yawned and stretched like a cat, then opened her eyes and looked around in surprise.

'Ruddy 'ell, miss. What the dickens am I doing here?'

'You fell asleep waiting for me and I didn't have the heart to wake you.'

'You're a proper toff, you are,' she said.

'Yes, well, proper toffs usually get their morning tea brought to them by this hour, so I suggest you leap up and fetch it.'

'Blimey, yes. Bob's yer uncle then.'

And she waddled out, leaving me to sit up in bed, enjoying the sound of the bells and the white stillness of the landscape outside my window. Then I put my hand to my neck to feel for my pixie. My fingers closed around him, and I shut my eyes, remembering that kiss. It was indeed a good Christmas.

Queenie was back in no time at all.

'Happy Christmas, my lady,' she said. 'Cook sent up a mince pie instead of biscuits this morning.'

It was warm from the oven and I savored it.

'What will your ladyship be wearing?' Queenie asked, clearly trying to be on her best behavior.

'I believe I'll wear my Christmas present from my mother – the rose cardigan and the long silky skirt and the scarf, with my white silk blouse,' I said. 'Oh, and Queenie – that cardigan is made of cashmere. On no account are you to attempt to wash it, scrub it, iron it or do anything else to it. Is that clear?'

She nodded. 'Sorry about the jersey dress, miss,' she muttered. 'I feel like a fool. You know what my old dad used to say, don't you?'

'Various things, if I remember correctly – that you were

dropped on your head at birth or that you must be twins because one couldn't be so daft.'

She grinned. 'You got it. That's exactly what he said.'

I got up and went to the dresser, retrieving a package. 'Happy Christmas, Queenie,' I said. 'Servants should officially receive their Christmas boxes tomorrow, on Boxing Day, but I think I'd like you to have it now.'

'For me, miss?' Her eyes opened wide.

'It's nothing very special,' I said. 'You know I don't have much money.'

She opened it. It was a black cloche hat to replace the shapeless felt flowerpot she usually wore. She was embarrassingly grateful and wiped away tears. 'Oooh, miss, I ain't never had anything so lovely before. Honest, I ain't. You're such a lovely person. I'm so lucky.'

Oh, dear, when she said things like that I realized that I could never sack her, however awful she was.

Washed and dressed in my new finery, feeling delightfully stylish, I went down to breakfast. Apart from the Wexlers I was again the first one down and I helped myself from a splendid array of dishes. The breakfasts at Gorzley Hall had been more than generous every day but this Christmas spread outdid them. Bacon, sausages, kidneys, eggs, tomatoes, fried bread, smoked haddock – everything one could possibly want. I tried not to take too much, knowing the Christmas banquet that was to follow.

While I was eating, the other guests filed in, one by one, and Christmas greetings filled the air. Lady Hawse-Gorzley appeared when we were all seated to wish us a happy Christmas and to inform us that there was something special in the small sitting room as soon as we had finished eating. Like eager children we filed through to see an impressive snow house sitting on a low table. For those of you who have never seen a snow house, it is made of cardboard to look like an old-fashioned house and is liberally decorated with cotton wool and sparkles to look like snow. Oh, and it's full of presents.

Lady Hawse-Gorzley removed the chimney.

'Lucky dip,' she said. 'Red ribbon means for a man, white ribbon for a woman.'

We dipped, one by one. The presents were all rather mundane – boxes of handkerchiefs and writing paper, appointment books and journals. I was lucky enough to pick one of the latter as I have always kept a diary and this one was particularly grand with a purple leather cover and a lock and key. We thanked her and she smiled, but I could tell she was distracted. As people drifted away I went up to her.

'Is there anything I can do?' I asked. 'You seem a little worried.'

She frowned. 'It's that dratted butcher. He hasn't delivered the geese as he promised. Cook has the stuffing all ready and is waiting to put the birds in the oven. You did tell him that I needed those birds by nine o'clock at the latest, didn't you? And now it's almost ten.'

'It could have snowed again overnight, making the roads difficult,' I pointed out.

'The trouble is we've no way of knowing. The telephones are still not working. I suppose we have enough turkeys to go around, with the stuffing and everything, but I did want those geese.'

'I suppose I could go out and shoot you a couple of swans from the pond,' Sir Oswald said, with deadpan seriousness. 'Would they do instead?'

'Don't be silly, Oswald,' Lady Hawse-Gorzley snapped. 'That's not even amusing.'

'Why, are swans not good to eat?' Mr Wexler asked.

'Nobody's ever tasted them,' Bunty said, giving him a withering look that he could be so clueless. 'Swans are reserved for royalty. In the old days killing a swan was punished by hanging. I don't think they'd hang us anymore, but it's still an offense.'

'Fancy that. How quaint,' Mrs Wexler said. 'You have the quaintest laws over here.'

'That's because some of them date back to the Middle Ages and nobody has bothered to repeal them,' Lady Hawse-Gorzley said. 'Those of you who are going to matins should think of getting ready.'

'Have my car brought around, Humphreys. I do not intend to walk through the snow,' the dowager countess said to her companion, who scurried off like a frightened rabbit.

'Hopeless creature. Don't know why I put up with her,' the countess commented before the companion was out of earshot.

'Maybe we could hitch a ride with you, Countess,' Mr Wexler said.

The countess regarded him through her lorgnette. 'I always think that one should walk whenever possible,' she said firmly. 'Had there not been snow on the driveway I should have never considered wasting petrol and using the car.'

'But since you are using it,' Mrs Wexler said, giving her what she hoped was a winning smile.

The countess did not return the smile. 'Those two young people of yours will grow up fat and idle if you mollycoddle them,' she said. 'What your son needs is a good boarding school. Cold showers in the morning and cross-country runs before breakfast.'

'That's positively barbaric,' Mrs Wexler said, putting an arm around Junior's shoulder.

'Ah, but it made us what we are today,' the countess said, smiling at last. 'Rulers of half the world.' She nodded to the Wexlers. 'I will see you in church.'

As she went out I caught Darcy's eye and moved closer to him.

'Isn't she marvelous?' Darcy muttered to me.

'Come with me,' I said and, taking his hand, I led him from the room.

'Is this a repetition of the other night?' he asked, his eyes challenging mine. 'Are you leading me to your bedroom again?'

'Don't keep reminding me of that.' I blushed.

'Oh, I think I'll enjoy reminding you of it for a long while yet.'

We reached an alcove beside the front hall. I turned to face Darcy. 'I wanted to give you your Christmas present,' I said. 'And bear in mind I bought this before I knew you were part of this house party.'

I handed him the little box. When he had taken off the wrapping I saw the grin spreading across his face.

'Great minds think alike,' he said as he opened the box to reveal the pixie.

'I wanted to give you something, and I thought you needed luck more than most people.'

'How true that is,' he said. 'I could really do with a streak of luck right now. My father has become so difficult. One can't even have a civilized conversation with him. He's all set to sell off the last of the family treasures and won't listen to me. I just feel so frustrated, watching everything my family stood for gradually disintegrate and not able to do a damned thing about it.' He stopped and managed an embarrassed smile. 'I shouldn't go piling my troubles on you, especially not on Christmas Day.'

'I feel the same way,' I said. 'I'm no longer welcome at what was my home and frankly I've nowhere else to go.'

'Two orphans in the storm,' he said. 'Maybe we should do what you suggested in your moment of drunken wisdom – run off to a desert island together and to hell with the whole thing.'

'I don't like coconuts very much,' I said. He wrapped me in his arms and laughed.

Lady Hawse-Gorzley summoned us together again before the churchgoers set out and announced that we should make plans for the Boxing Day hunt in the next village of Widecombe. She hoped she'd be able to supply enough horses for all those who wanted to take part.

'Not us, thank you,' Mrs Wexler said firmly. 'Hunting is a barbaric sport, from what I've heard. Tearing poor little foxes to pieces.'

'They've probably never ridden a horse in their lives,' the countess said in a stage whisper.

'I think I'm a little old for that kind of thing,' Mrs Rathbone said, 'but I'm sure my husband won't turn down a chance to hunt, will you, Reggie?'

'I should say not,' Colonel Rathbone said heartily. 'Tallyho and view halloo and all that. It's what England is made of, don't you know.'

'I don't think we're up to hunting, if you don't mind,' Mr Upthorpe said, 'but we'd certainly like to come along and watch you set off. I've never actually seen a hunt. I bet the young men look really handsome in their red coats.'

'Pink,' the countess said sharply.

'I thought the coats were red.' Mrs Upthorpe looked puzzled.

'They are, but we call it pink.'

'Why call them pink when they're not pink?' Mrs Wexler asked.

'I'm sure the explanation is lost in the mists of antiquity,' Lady H-G intervened before this could go any further. 'Oswald will run you over in the estate car. His leg is playing up again. Still recovering from an injury and the doctor has forbidden hunting.'

Sir Oswald nodded gloomily. 'Blasted quack. What does he know?' he muttered.

'I shall enjoy watching you set off,' the countess said. 'Remind me of the good old days when I had the finest seat in Hertfordshire.'

For some reason the Wexler children found this amusing and were given a ferocious look by the countess. 'I shall, of course, be delighted to offer Mrs Rathbone a place in my motorcar,' she said, making it quite clear that she was snubbing the rest of the spectators.

'And I take it you'll be riding your own horses, won't you, Captain Sechrest?' Lady Hawse-Gorzley said quickly, still trying to keep unpleasantness from developing.

'Oh, absolutely,' Captain Sechrest said. 'We'll pop over to our place first thing tomorrow.'

'I'll drop you off at your place in the morning in the Armstrong Siddeley,' Johnnie said. 'I have to pick up my own nag.'

Mrs Sechrest said, 'Thank you, Johnnie, how kind,' at the

same time as her husband muttered, 'Not at all necessary. Have my own vehicle.'

Lady Hawse-Gorzley looked around. 'So let's see, that leaves the colonel, myself, Monty, Darcy, Bunty – how about you, Badger?'

'I'm not the world's most brilliant rider.' Badger's freckled face turned pink. 'But I'll give it a go.'

'Jolly good. That's the spirit.' Lady Hawse-Gorzley nodded with approval. 'And Georgiana – you hunt, don't you?'

'Oh, absolutely. Adore it, if you can find me a mount,' I said.

'I think we can. We've Sultan if Oswald's not coming, and Star is still game if a little plodding, isn't he? And then there are Freddie's horses. I did approach him about borrowing his extra mounts for our guests before the tragedy, and they'll need exercising by now. Monty, dear, you might take Darcy and go over there this morning to see what's what. Tell the groom we'll want them brought round by eight thirty tomorrow morning.'

'I'm afraid I didn't bring my hunting pinks,' Colonel Rathbone said. 'Didn't know about the hunt, y'know. Can't ride without them. Dashed bad form.'

'I'm sure Oswald will lend you his jacket, won't you, dear?' Lady H-G said firmly. Sir Oswald didn't look too sure but smiled wanly.

'And I don't have my hunting jacket either,' I said. I had brought jodhpurs because one always does.

'You can wear my old jacket,' Bunty said. 'We're about the same size and it's not too shabby.'

'Thanks awfully.' I made a mental note that she was being a frightfully good sport about Darcy.

Having sorted out the universe again, Lady Hawse-Gorzley sent the churchgoers off, found jigsaw puzzles and board games for those who were not planning to hunt, and sent the hunters off to sort out mounts. I took the opportunity to go to wish my nearest and dearest a merry Christmas.

The going was treacherous underfoot with melted snow now turned to ice and I wondered if the hunt would be allowed to take place under such conditions. I was concentrating on not slipping and falling on my bottom when a figure loomed out of the hedge in front of me. I started as I found myself looking at a wild-looking woman – hair unkempt, flowing green skirts and, to my utter amazement, bare feet. She blocked my path, staring at me.

'Happy Christmas to you,' I said uncertainly, unnerved by two eyes, green as a cat's, that stared at me unblinking. 'You must be Sal. I've heard about you.'

'You want to watch yourself, miss,' she said with her deep West Country burr. 'Or you might come a cropper.'

Then she darted through the hedge and was gone.

Chapter 20

I went on my way, a little shaken. I hadn't really believed in Wild Sal until now, but she really existed and, what's more, she had just given me some kind of warning. Had she only meant that the ground was treacherous underfoot or was she hinting at something more sinister?

I could hear Mr Barclay thumping out the organ as I passed the church for my mother's cottage. Good smells of roasting fowl and sage stuffing greeted me from the kitchen as my grandfather opened the front door, and I came through to the sitting room to find my mother and Noël Coward around the fire. I was given a grand welcome for once as they were all remarkably in the Christmas spirit. Even Noël Coward was wearing a ridiculous paper hat on his head.

'My dear child,' he said. 'How good of you to come and visit our humble estate, when I'm sure you have a million and one things to amuse you at the big house. Tell me, what's it like there – very feudal? Do the peasants all tug their forelocks?'

'You'll see for yourself if you come to Christmas luncheon today.'

'Ah, I think Claire and I have decided not to accept the kind invitation, if you would give our apologies. It does become so tiring being adored and having to act like one's public persona when the real Noël is a shy and retiring sort of chap.'

I laughed. 'I don't believe it for a second.'

'I am stung, wounded. Claire, your daughter has inherited your own brutal honesty.'

'I must say, that outfit looks good on you, Georgie. The cardigan suits you better than it ever did me.' My mother opened her arms. 'Come and give your mama a Christmas hug. And Noël tells me I was terribly stingy with my gifts yesterday. Passing on a few old clothes, he called it. He said a big fat check would have been more in order. I pointed out that I'd already promised a shopping spree the moment we're both back in London.'

Noël sighed. 'Then I suppose the generous uncle act is up to me.' And to my delight he handed me a couple of five-pound notes.

'Golly. Thank you very much,' was all I could stammer.

'And I've got a little something for you too, my love,' Granddad said. 'It's nothing grand like that, but I wanted you to have a little gift on Christmas Day.'

I opened the wrapping and inside was a snow globe with a charming little village inside and *A present from Devon* inscribed around the base.

I laughed. 'It's perfect,' I said. 'A lovely souvenir of my visit here.'

'So you've got the hordes arriving for the Christmas banquet, have you?' Granddad asked.

'Yes, I believe Lady Hawse-Gorzley invites half the village. Oh, by the way, I just saw Wild Sal. She really exists.'

'Does she?' Noël Coward looked interested. 'I've been dying to meet her.'

'She's very strange indeed. Walks around barefoot and just stares with these piercing green eyes.'

'Well, she is supposed to be the descendant of the witch who was burned here,' Mummy said. 'Isn't this place fun? I keep telling Noël he should scrap what we're doing and set his play in a crazy village like this one.'

'Not much of a comedy at the moment with all these deaths,' I said.

'Let's hope there isn't another one,' Granddad said. 'Did you hear the ambulance go past about an hour ago? It hasn't come back yet.'

'Oh, no. I suppose driving conditions are terrible today. It's so slippery out there.' I glanced at my watch. 'I should be getting back, I suppose. I'm expected to help entertain and church will soon be over.'

'Have a sherry before you go back,' Mummy said.

'I shouldn't, thanks. I rather fear that the wine will flow copiously for the rest of the day, and I'm still recovering from the carol singing the other night. I believe it must have been the old ladies' elderberry wine.'

They all began to chuckle.

'We have a confession to make about that carol singing,' Noël said at last. 'Your mother made the punch and put a generous amount of rum in it. I tasted it and thought it needed something and added a bottle of vodka. The result, I'm afraid, was rather lethal.'

'It was the final blow for me, I'm afraid. I was blotto for the rest of the evening.'

I went around and hugged them, one by one, then stepped out into a stiff cold breeze. The clouds above

Lovey Tor were heavy and looked as if they might produce more snow any minute. My grandfather walked with me down the path.

'I've been thinking about all these strange deaths,' he said. 'That Inspector Newcombe thinks I'm some kind of Scotland Yard miracle worker, but I have to say I'm completely in the dark. Usually when there is a string of murders there is a pattern to them, but there is nothing to tie these together, nor, as far as I can see, any clues to point that they were actual murders.'

'I don't think Inspector Newcombe is too hot at reviewing evidence,' I said. 'I suspect he didn't dust for fingerprints, make imprints of shoe soles, question witnesses. . . .'

'Hark at you.' Granddad chuckled. 'You're sounding like a proper copper. Young ladies of your station aren't supposed to know about these sorts of things.'

'I've picked up a thing or two along the way,' I said. 'Well, as far as we know there were no deaths yesterday, so let's hope that they've stopped.' I turned as I heard a snatch of garbled 'Good King Wenceslas' shouted loudly into the air. 'Oh, look at Willum. Isn't he sweet?'

And there was Willum, wearing a paper hat from a cracker, cavorting around the village green, interacting with a snowman.

'You'd better go inside,' I said to Granddad. 'You'll catch cold.'

'My chest is so much better down here,' Granddad said. 'Feel as fit as a fiddle, me.'

He looked up as we both heard a distant bell. Not from the church this time, but constant and coming nearer. Then the ambulance came into view, making its way down the winding road. As it came into the village, the village bobby appeared from the police station. The ambulance slowed as it approached and the driver wound down his window.

'Nasty crash over at Gallows Corner,' he called out. 'Van skidded off the road and went down that slope into the river.'

'People hurt?' the policeman called back.

'Only one bloke in the van – Skaggs, the butcher from town – and he was killed outright.'

The ambulance went on its way. Granddad and I looked at each other.

'It seems I was wrong about the deaths stopping,' I said.

'A motorcar crash might have nothing to do with the other deaths,' Granddad said. 'Only too likely if someone was in a hurry on roads like this.'

For some reason I had to swallow back tears. 'He was on his way to deliver geese to us this morning. He'd been told we needed them by nine o'clock, so he was probably driving too fast to get here. Poor man. And what about his family too, on Christmas Day. I'd better go and tell them at the hall what happened.'

Granddad nodded and put a big, comforting hand on my shoulder. 'Happy Christmas, ducks. Don't let it get you down. Whatever's going on down here, it ain't got nothing to do with us.'

As I walked back up the drive I was overtaken by the ancient motorcar containing the two remaining Misses Ffrench-Finch and Miss Prendergast.

'Hop in, do,' they twittered as they opened the door for me. 'Much too nasty to walk today.'

I climbed up and squeezed in beside them. 'Thank you,' I said. 'It's certainly treacherous underfoot.'

'We just heard an ambulance going past,' one of them said.

'I'm afraid there was an accident and a van went off the road,' I said. 'Someone was killed.'

'How terrible,' Miss Prendergast said. 'Was he a local man?'

'The butcher from town. He was delivering geese to Lady Hawse-Gorzley. I expect he was running late,' I said.

'Such a tragedy. On Christmas Day too,' one of the Misses Ffrench-Finch said (I hadn't quite worked out which was which). 'So much sadness at the moment. That man from the garage falling off the bridge on his way home and our poor sister. We debated long and hard over whether we should join the festivities, but dear Lizzie said that Effie would not have wanted us to sit at home moping. Such a tower of strength, our dear Effie. How we miss her.'

'I'm so sorry for you,' Miss Prendergast said. 'If there's anything I can do to help, you know I'll always be here.'

'Most kind, my dear. You have been a great comfort to us. It was a blessing the day you moved into this village.'

We pulled up outside the house.

'I just saw the local wild woman.' I looked down the driveway, thinking that I saw a movement among the hedges.

'Wild Sal? Yes, one does see her from time to time,' one of the Misses Ffrench-Finch said. 'In fact, Cook tells me that she came to the back door on the night our dear sister died. Knocked on the door quite late and asked for food. Cook said it was snowing and she felt so badly that she brought her into the kitchen and fed her.'

The chauffeur opened the door. I alighted first and helped the old ladies out of the motor. But the cogs were whirring inside my head. So another person had been in the house that night after the front door was locked. And not only another person but one who was a descendant of the witch, and who had just given me a strange warning.

Chapter 21

Christmas Day in time for the banquet

Any worries were put aside as we joined in the festivities. I delivered apologies from my mother and Mr Coward to Lady Hawse-Gorzley. There were hot sausage rolls and sherry before the meal, then a gong summoned us through to the dining room, which looked absolutely magnificent, the table decorated with holly, Christmas crackers beside every place. To my intense relief I was not seated between any leg fondlers this time, but with Monty on one side of me and Mr Barclay on the other. The vicar said grace and the feast began.

The first order of business was the pulling of crackers. This happened with a lot of popping and exclamations as contents went flying across the table, but everyone ended up with a paper hat, some kind of toy or game or musical instrument and a riddle. We put on the hats, which looked very silly indeed on most of us, then tried the riddles on each other as the first course was brought in: it was smoked salmon decorated with watercress and thin brown bread.

Next followed a spicy parsnip soup, and then the turkeys, three of them, resplendent and brown on platters, were carried in and expertly carved by the butler at a side table. They were accompanied by chestnut stuffing, roast potatoes, Brussels sprouts, carrots, baked parsnips and gravy. Conversation lagged as we ate.

'Well, I declare, this is better than any turkey I've eaten at home,' Mr Wexler said at last.

'I had hoped to have roast goose as well,' Lady Hawse-Gorzley said, 'but the butcher let me down, I'm afraid.'

'Oh, but didn't you hear that he met with an accident?' Miss Prendergast said. 'His van went off the road and plunged down a slope. The poor man was killed.'

Lady Hawse-Gorzley went white. 'No. I didn't hear. How terrible. Now I feel awful for insisting that he come out this morning.'

'Not your fault, my dear,' Sir Oswald said gruffly. 'Roads are icy. Could have happened to anyone.'

We tried to get back into our previous good humor.

'So, Colonel Rathbone, did you ever hunt when you had a house here?' Johnnie Protheroe asked. 'I don't recall seeing you.'

'Haven't been home in the winter in years. When we do take home leave, it's usually in the summer,' the colonel said. 'We try to avoid the hot months in India.'

'Where exactly was your house?' Mrs Sechrest asked.

'Over Crediton way,' Mrs Rathbone said quickly.

'Strange that we never bumped into each other,' Mrs Sechrest said. 'Porky and I have lived in these parts all our lives.'

'Well, Devon's a big county, isn't it?' the colonel said. He turned to Mr Barclay. 'Splendid organ playing, by the way.

I like an organist who thumps it out properly. And good old hymns too.'

Mr Barclay nodded and smiled. He seemed out of his element here, looking around nervously. I deduced he must have come from a humble background and this was confirmed when he muttered to me, 'It's very grand, isn't it? I'm always terrified of making a social faux pas, aren't you?'

'I often do,' I said. 'I'm quite good at shooting my meat across the table when I try to cut it or slipping off my chair. And it's usually when I have to dine with the relatives too.'

'Your relatives must be old-school sticklers then,' he said.

'Her relatives are the king and queen, Mr Barclay,' Monty said, grinning as Mr Barclay's face turned puce.

'I had no idea. Nobody told me,' he gasped, then took a swig of his wine and promptly choked on it, spattering wine on the white tablecloth.

I felt rather sorry for him and tried to ask him about his own family. It turned out he had a twin brother who played the piano professionally. 'He plays at concert parties and summer stock on the piers. My brother wanted us to do an act together called Pete and Pat, flying fingers at the ivories, but I was not prepared to sink to that level, even if he does make good money.'

When we were replete, the remains were cleared away and the Christmas pudding was carried in, flaming, with a sprig of holly on top.

'Hey, Ma, it's on fire,' Junior shouted. 'Should someone throw water over it?'

The countess gave him a withering look. 'Don't you dare,' she said.

The flames died down and Sir Oswald cut the first piece.

'Watch out for all the damned silver bits and pieces that my wife insists on putting in it,' he said.

'Silver bits and pieces?' Mrs Wexler asked.

'Old English custom,' Lady Hawse-Gorzley said. 'There are always silver charms baked in the pudding. You'll find a horseshoe, a thimble, a ring, a button, a boot, a pig, oh, and some silver threepenny pieces as well.'

'And what are they for?' Mr Wexler asked.

'I'll explain when we find them,' Lady Hawse-Gorzley said.

The pudding was served with brandy butter. After a couple of mouthfuls Ethel called out, 'I've got the horse-shoe.'

'Very good. That means good luck in the coming year,' Lady Hawse-Gorzley said.

'And I have a boot.' Mrs Rathbone held it up.

'Very apt. It means travel, of course,' Lady Hawse-Gorzley said.

'Does it really? How lovely,' Mrs Rathbone replied with what looked like a wistful smile.

Mr Upthorpe and Johnnie found threepences, which meant money. Badger found the button, which made everyone laugh.

'The bachelor button, Badger. It means you're not going to get married.'

'Thank God for that,' Badger said.

Suddenly the colonel, seated just across the table from me, turned red, his eyes bulged and he clutched his throat.

'He's choking!' his wife shouted.

Badger and Johnnie leaped to his aid, thumping him on the back. My heart stood still. Was this the death that had been planned for today? I realized that I had been uneasy ever since the wild woman had given me that warning. The colonel was flailing now.

'Somebody do something!' Mrs Rathbone screamed.

The other men at the table were now on their feet, standing helplessly as the flailing grew weaker and the colonel pitched forward onto the table, knocking over his wineglass and sending the contents flowing across the white tablecloth like a river of blood.

Chapter 22

Still at the Christmas banquet

As we stared in horror, there was one thought going through my mind. Until now these deaths had not touched this house. The crash of the van had probably been just an unfortunate accident – someone going too fast around an icy curve. So were we now witnessing the death that had been selected for Christmas Day?

Johnnie grabbed the colonel around his ample waist and attempted to lift him from the table. As he did so something came flying out of the colonel's mouth, landing on the table. The colonel gave a great gasping breath, coughed and sat up again.

'He's all right. Thank God.' Mrs Rathbone fought her way to reach him. 'Oh, Reggie. You're all right.'

'Don't fuss, woman,' the colonel said. 'Of course I'm all right.'

'One of those damned charms,' Sir Oswald said. 'I knew you'd kill someone one day, Cammie.'

'You gave us all a scare there, old fellow.' Johnnie handed the colonel a glass of water.

'Something got stuck in my throat,' the colonel said.

'One of those charms, I expect.'

'Which one was it?'

Johnnie retrieved it from the table with his napkin. And he laughed. 'The pig, old fellow. It means you're a bit of a glutton.'

'Reggie, I keep telling you that you bolt your food,' Mrs Rathbone said.

We all laughed and the tension was broken. The rest of us ate very carefully now and finally my teeth struck against something hard.

'Oh, look, Georgie's got the ring,' Monty called out.

'Next to be married, my dear,' Lady Hawse-Gorzley said. I tried, unsuccessfully, not to blush or to meet Darcy's eye.

The meal concluded, a little more subdued, with port, nuts and tangerines all around. We were just sitting with coffee in a state of stupor when Lady Hawse-Gorzley clapped her hands. 'Everybody into the drawing room quickly,' she said. 'I wasn't watching the clock and we almost missed it. Hurry now.'

'Missed what?' Mr Wexler said.

'The king's broadcast. It's almost three o'clock.'

We marched through to the drawing room. The radio came to life with much crackling and then a voice said, 'His Majesty the King,' and the national anthem was played. We British subjects immediately rose to our feet. The Americans looked at us with amusement but then followed suit. We sat again as the king's deep, ponderous voice came through the air, speaking slowly and carefully, greetings of goodwill from Sandringham to his subjects around the world. The others listened in rapt silence. I was conscious that he didn't sound well. I thought of the times I had been with His Majesty at Sandringham, his favorite house, and he'd been sitting with his stamp collection at the table from which he was now broadcasting, and a feeling of warmth and pride came over me that we were part of the same family.

'And to think that you actually know him,' Mrs Wexler said when the speech ended. 'I suppose you've actually been to those royal castles and palaces?'

'Many times,' I said.

'And what's he like, your king?'

'A little fearsome to start with. Not very patient and likes everything done properly, but he's essentially a kind man and he cares so much about England and the empire. I think he's literally worrying himself to death.'

They tiptoed away from me as if I'd suddenly turned into someone new and dangerous.

Soon the older members of the party fell asleep in armchairs while we younger ones went for a walk.

'I think it's going to rain,' Bunty said. 'That's good for the hunt tomorrow.' She turned back to me. 'I hope you're a good rider, Georgie. We went to look at Freddie's stable this morning and his horses are decidedly frisky – and big.'

'I'm a pretty good rider,' I said modestly – my governess having drilled into me that a lady never claims accomplishments.

We walked across the grounds and up through the bare woods, pausing to look back on the house and the village. As I stared down at the orchard a thought crossed my mind so quickly that I didn't have time to grab on to it. Something about the trees. I turned to stare at the neighbor's estate behind us. Something about why those particular trees might be important.

Darcy fell into step beside me. 'You look rather shaken up,' he said. 'Is something wrong?'

'That incident with the colonel,' I said in a low voice, not wanting the others to hear. 'I thought he might be today's designated death.'

Darcy gave me a quizzical look. 'Designated death?'

'There's been one a day since I arrived, except for yesterday. And the butcher's van already went off the road today, killing him. So I thought that might have been a true accident and this was the death that was planned.'

He took me aside so that we were standing together under the branches of a large fir tree. 'What exactly are you saying, Georgie – that someone has been planning a death a day? For what reason?'

'I've no idea.'

'And do you think these deaths are random people or intentionally selected?'

'There doesn't seem to be any rhyme or reason to them – a butcher, an old lady, a garage owner, a switchboard operator and the man who owned that estate. What could they possibly have in common?'

'Have the police ruled out that they were accidents?'

'I think the inspector is suspicious, but he has no proof, as far as I can tell, that any one of them was not an accident.'

Darcy frowned. 'It may be that this part of the country is just going through an unlucky period. Serial killers don't usually work this way, if that's what you're imagining. They want the police and the public to recognize their handiwork. They usually have a signature modus operandi – think of Jack the Ripper in London. A classic case. Always killed prostitutes in exactly the same gruesome way.'

I shuddered as he went on. 'One of the ways they get a

thrill out of this is believing that they are smart enough to outwit the police. So why kill in a way that makes it look like an accident?'

'I don't know,' I said. 'I can't understand anything about it, Darcy. I'm almost ready to believe in the Lovey Curse. That strange wild woman gave me some kind of warning today. And she's the direct descendant of the witch, isn't she?'

'Georgie, come on.' He shot me an amused look. 'That's village superstition. You are a young woman of the world. You don't believe in witches or curses.'

I tried to smile too. 'It's just that – I'm frightened. I can't help feeling that it's closing in on us and that eventually the killer will strike here.'

'Don't worry.' He put an arm around my shoulder. 'I'll take care of you.'

'That's not the point, Darcy. I feel that somehow I must take care of everyone else. I feel that I have to solve the puzzle before it's too late.'

He turned me to face him. 'Sometimes you worry too much,' he said. 'Leave this to the police and enjoy your Christmas. We're here, we're together and we're having a great time. Think of it – you could, at this moment, be sitting down to Christmas dinner with your sister-in-law.'

I laughed. 'Where they will be sharing one chicken between them and huddling together to keep warm. It's poor Binky I feel sorry for, surrounded by Fig's family.'

Darcy took my hand. It felt wonderful to walk through snowy meadows, feeling the warmth from his hand sending tingles all the way up my arm.

We arrived back to find that tea had been laid out in the drawing room, and that it included the most magnificent

Christmas cake. The icing had been made to look like a snow scene and decorated with little ceramic figures of tobogganing children, ladies with fur muffs, skaters, snowmen. Not surprisingly, nobody felt much like eating, but we all attempted a slice of cake. The Misses Ffrench-Finch asked if they could take their slices of cake home with them as they couldn't eat another mouthful. A generous portion was wrapped for them, and one for Miss Prendergast, and the three ladies took their leave.

Miss Prendergast was overcome with emotion. 'You are too kind, Lady Hawse-Gorzley, too generous. Such a good person. I don't deserve . . .' She paused, putting her hand over her heart. 'When you have no family, nobody else in the world, it means so much to be part of a celebration like this.'

'Then let's hope there are many, many more,' Lady Hawse-Gorzley said, thumping the hand that was extended to her. We duly waved as the old ladies were helped into their car and went home.

Then Lady Hawse-Gorzley produced the indoor fireworks and we passed a jolly hour around the fireplace watching pieces of paper turn into writhing snakes or glowing different colors and finally all holding sparklers. When the last firework was lit, the vicar suggested that we play charades until supper. The dressing-up box was carried down into the study across the hall from the drawing room and we were divided into teams. I found myself on Monty's team with Badger, Mrs Upthorpe, Captain Sechrest, and Cherie Wexler. Monty had to explain to Cherie that we select a word and act out the syllables. If the audience can't guess the word through the syllables, we act out the whole thing.

We rummaged through the props until Badger found an

old cow horn. 'We could do "cornucopia," ' he said. 'First syllable is "corn." Second is "you" and third is "cope." And then for the whole we'll produce fruit from the horn and keep eating it.'

This was agreed upon. I was designated to be an old lady in a gray wig, hobbling around, then taking off my shoe and rubbing my toes. They dressed me up in a hideous tippet, wig and hat. Out I went, walking as if my feet hurt me, then taking off my shoe and massaging my toes with an expression of relief.

'Feet . . . foot . . . hurt . . . sore!' came the calls from the audience.

Monty came out to do the next syllable. He simply pointed dramatically at a member of the audience. He chose Mr Barclay, who turned bright red. I experienced a fleeting feeling of agitation – that something had happened that I should have noticed but didn't. I tried to analyze. Something to do with corns? With Mr Barclay? Definitely something I had just seen. . . .

It was no use. We proceeded to the last syllable. Mrs Upthorpe was the harried mother, wearing an apron, while the other members of the team were her awful children – Captain Sechrest dressed in a school cap and tie, Badger in a smock with a frill around his neck and a giant dummy and Cherie with a big bow in her hair. They came out on their knees, howling and tugging at their mother's skirts while she pretended to cook, lay a table and generally act as if she was harassed. This scene got a good laugh, but nobody guessed it. So we had to bring out our horn and take imaginary fruit from it. Then, of course, it was guessed right away.

The next team went out to dress up and I sat there, mulling over the idea that I had just missed something important, something that might shed some light on the strange events in Tiddleton-under-Lovey. Then Lady Hawse-Gorzley's team came out. Their word was 'dandelion,' which of course we got very quickly – the moment Colonel Rathbone crawled around roaring and trying to eat Bunty, in fact.

We played the game several times more before we went through to supper. This was a spread of cold food, so that the servants could have their own Christmas party. I still didn't feel like eating much, but the array of cold beef, cold ham, veal and ham pie, Cornish pasties and assorted pickles was very tempting. It was washed down with more wine or local cider, and finished with liquors, chocolates, nuts and dates.

At last, full of food and Christmas cheer, we all went to bed. Even the Wexlers could find nothing to complain about and Junior declared it 'a real swell Christmas.' I was inclined to agree with him. It had been a marvelous Christmas Day, and if only a man had not driven his van off the road to his death, it would all have been perfect.

Chapter 23

Boxing Day at Gorzley Hall
December 26
***Off to the hunt. Looking forward to a good ride. I hope I get
a decent horse.***

I was awakened to cold gray light by Queenie with a tray of
tea.

'Morning, miss. They told me to get you up early because
you've got to go on one of them fox hunts,' she said. 'Rather
you than me, sitting on a horse in this weather.' She put
down the tray. 'What was you thinking of wearing?'

'I have only brought one set of jodhpurs with me, Queenie,
so I don't think there is much choice. My warmest jumper
to go with them, and Bunty is lending me a hunting jacket.'

I looked out the window to see the orchard vanishing into
mist and Lovey Tor not even visible. At least it wouldn't have
frozen overnight if the mist had come in. I dressed and went
down to find coffee, tea, pasties, sausage rolls and mince pies
laid out on the sideboard for the early risers. One by one the
other hunters came in and helped themselves to something

to eat and drink. From outside the window came the clatter of hooves, a sound that always sends a shiver of excitement through me. I have always adored hunting, even though I do feel sorry for the fox. I suspect that hunting must be in my blood – and the fox is usually smart enough to get away.

Bunty came in, with a black velvet jacket in her hands. 'I've an extra black crash cap too if you want to match,' she said. 'I hope you'll be all right. Freddie's horses are both a little crazy, you know. He was often seen flying through the village because one of them had bolted with him.'

'Thanks a lot,' I said. 'That sounds most encouraging.'

'He was never a particularly good rider,' Bunty said. 'I expect you'll be fine. You should go out and get first dibs on the one you like.'

'Is one less skittish than the other?'

'No idea,' she said. 'I've never ridden them.'

Thus encouraged, I went out to see a groom holding two leading reins, on the ends of which were a tall bony gray and a chestnut that was stamping and snorting like a war-horse, its breath hanging in the cold air like a dragon's fire. I noted the double bridle and the size of that tossing head and decided on the gray.

'Her be Snowflake, miss,' the groom said as he attempted to give me a leg up into the saddle. 'Her got a right mean streak and a will of her own, if you don't mind my saying so. She can be a right cow at times. Always tries to give me a nip when I'm brushing her. I told the master he should get rid of her, but for some reason he were fond of her.' He shook his head. 'Never did have good judgment, poor bloke.'

After a lot of dancing around on Snowflake's part I finally managed to get into the saddle and Snowflake spent the next five minutes trying to buck me off. I noticed Badger watching, his eyes wide with terror.

'I think I might bow out,' he said to Monty.

'Rubbish, old bean. We've got a mount that's docile as a kitten for you. Bunty and I learned to ride on old Star. He's a bit of a plodder but sure and safe. You'll be just fine.'

They went around to the stables and soon a procession came out. Lady Hawse-Gorzley led the way on a magnificent bay hunter, then Monty and Bunty. Behind them rode the colonel on a large, almost black hunter I presumed must be Sultan, and then Badger on a round animal not much bigger than a pony. Darcy came out and gave me a look as he swung himself effortlessly into the saddle of the warhorse. It snorted and pawed a couple of times but it was quite clear that it recognized Darcy as the master. He tried to ride over to join me but Snowflake backed away.

'Them two don't like each other much,' the groom called. 'Leastways, she don't like no other horses at all. Like I said, a right cow.'

'I'd come and say good morning, but I think I'd better not,' Darcy called as Snowflake skittered again. 'Will you be all right?'

'As long as no horses come near me and nothing else spooks her, I suppose so,' I called back, trying to sound more breezy than I felt.

'Off we go, then,' Lady Hawse-Gorzley called and we set off down the drive and through the village, our hoofbeats echoing dramatically through the misty stillness. Nothing else stirred as we passed the green. The villagers were enjoying sleeping late for once. The road took us over the hill and through deserted moorland until we heard the baying of hounds and the clatter of harnesses ahead of us and came to a lonely pub where the hunt was assembling, a splendid-looking mass of red and black coats and well-groomed horses. There were already a good number of riders and spectators assembled and the publican was going among them passing out stirrup cups of hot grog. My cheeks and fingers were already stinging with cold and I needed no second urging to drink one myself.

'Ah, Lady H-G, you've brought your guests, I see.' A dapper little man with a Ronald Coleman mustache rode up to us. He was mounted on a good-looking gray and both rider and horse were immaculate.

'Good of you to let them join us, Master,' she said.

'Well, let's hope they all know how to ride, what? And the rules of the hunt. I'm a stickler for rules, as you should know.'

'I do, Master. Believe me, I do,' she said and turned back to the rest of us. 'This is our master of hounds, Major Wesley-Parker. Major, this is Colonel Rathbone. Do you military men know each other, by any chance?'

'Can't say that I've had the pleasure,' the major said, extending a hand to the colonel. 'Which regiment, sir?'

'Bengal Lancers. Finest fighting force in India,' the colonel said.

'Bengal Lancers, what? Then you must know old Jumbo!'

'Jumbo?'

'Everybody knows old Jumbo.' He paused. 'Jumbo Bretherton, the brigadier.'

'Oh, Brigadier Bretherton,' the colonel said. 'I never knew him as Jumbo.'

'Didn't you? Thought everybody called him Jumbo.'

'Not his junior officers,' the colonel said.

I had been riding at the back of the group, since

Snowflake reputedly loathed other horses, and I had had a chance to observe the others. I watched the colonel now. Shouldn't someone with the Bengal Lancers have a better seat? I wondered. Wouldn't half his days be spent in the saddle? And why didn't he know the nickname of his brigadier? And why did nobody know him if he'd previously had a house in the area? Something I had heard came back to me – that one of the escaped convicts had had a music-hall act in which he had played, among other things, an elderly colonel. Could he possibly be hiding out under our noses playing the part of the colonel again? In which case, who was the woman with him, posing as his wife, since we'd been told the convict's wife had committed suicide when he was sent to prison? At least it would be worth mentioning my suspicions to Inspector Newcombe. Then I had to turn my attention to the matters at hand as another horse approached Snowflake and she danced away, eyes rolling. Final stragglers arrived, including Johnnie Protheroe on a fine-looking hunter and the Sechrests, also well turned out and riding with flair.

'Here we are, Master, all present and correct,' Johnnie said, touching his crop to his cap.

'No high jinks this time, young Protheroe,' the master said.

'Wouldn't dream of it, Master.' Johnnie grinned as he swung his horse into the group. The horn was sounded. The last stirrup cups were drained. The hounds, who had been sniffing around, tails wagging, suddenly were all business, moving off excitedly.

'Off we go, then,' the master shouted, turning back to us. 'And remember, it's dashed misty out there. I don't want anyone winding up in a bog. And if we go anywhere near

Lovey Tor, stay well to the right of Barston Mere. Nasty bog on the far side. Got it? Jolly good.'

We set off on a broad track across fields. Sheep scattered at the sight of us. Through a copse, and then suddenly the hounds picked up the scent. Their excited baying echoed through the mist. Off they went in full cry and we followed at a lively canter. Snowflake lived up to her reputation, trying to veer off to one side when any horse came near her, and it was all I could do to keep up with the other horses. We came to a low stone wall and she cleared it in a giant bound. As we dipped into a valley we were swallowed up into thicker mist. Snowflake veered off to the left as another horse came up on one side of us. It was the master on his gray – the whiteness of the horse making him almost invisible in the mist. I fought to hold her head and let him go ahead. I could hear the hounds what sounded like far ahead now, off to my left. I urged the horse into a gallop up a steep slope, with dead bracken and rocks around us. Suddenly a row of grotesque black shapes rose out of the mist, looking like giants with arms outstretched to grab us. Snowflake reacted by skidding to a halt and then rearing up. It was all I could do to keep my seat and it took me a while to calm her. And to calm myself too, as my heart was thudding until I realized that I was looking at a row of stunted Scotch pine trees, bent because of the wind, and behind them mist curling up from what looked like black water.

We stood still while I tried to get my bearings. I heard a sound that might have been a cry from a bird or the distant baying of a hound. I had no idea which direction the sound was coming from. But what I did begin to feel was a growing sense of danger, of being watched, hunted. I turned the horse around, peering into the mist, but it was so thick that the grass was swallowed up within a few feet of me. Suddenly a white shape rose up to one side. There was a loud flapping noise and something like a ghost seemed to come at us. That was enough for Snowflake. She took off again, this time to her right, while I fought to control her. Suddenly another flapping shape stepped out of the mist. The horse shied, skidded to a halt, and nearly threw me.

This shape with its waving arms was now identifiable as Wild Sal. 'You don't want to go that way, miss,' she said. "Tis dangerous that way. You'd wind up in the bog and that would be the end of you. Go back the way you came and then take the downward track. That'll set you right.'

'Thank you,' I called, but she had already vanished.

I made my way back, the horse moving cautiously, and I could feel the shudders of apprehension going through her flanks. As we approached the Scotch pines I looked to see what logical explanation I could find for the white flapping shape that had so startled us. I could make out something white moving through the mist. Then I heard a jingling of harness, the soft muted sound of hoofbeats on turf, and heaved a sigh of relief. I wasn't so far from the others after all. A white horse loomed out of the mist and it took me a minute to notice that it was riderless.

In spite of Snowflake's protests I managed to get close enough to grab the reins.

'Hello!' I called into the mist. 'Anyone out there? Do you need help?'

Silence met me, followed by that strange flapping sound echoing back from an unseen crag. I wasn't going to wander into trackless moor so I took Sal's advice and followed the track down the hill, leading the gray. It followed me reluctantly and I thought this might have something to do with my horse's bad temper until I turned around and noticed it was lame in the left foreleg. I went more slowly. As I came down the hill I met other riders coming toward me.

'Lost the scent at Downey Brook,' one of them called, 'and the mist is so dashed thick that we're packing it in. No sense in risking breaking a leg.' The man came closer, riding a big, solid dark horse. He stopped when he noticed the horse I was leading.

'I say. That's the master's horse, isn't it? Where is he?'

'I don't know,' I said. 'I found the horse wandering in the mist.'

'Whereabouts?'

'Up there.' I pointed to the track I had just descended.

'But that's Barston Mere,' he said. 'What were you doing up there?'

'I became separated from the rest of the hunt,' I said. 'I thought I was following the master. Something spooked my horse and by the time I'd controlled it I hadn't any idea where I was.'

'It's not like the master to come off,' the man said. 'Damned fine horseman, and his horse can jump anything you put in front of it.'

'The horse seems to have injured its foreleg,' I said. 'It's limping badly.'

'I can see some blood. Maybe cut itself trying to jump a wall,' the man said. 'Maybe fell at a jump. The master can be a trifle reckless at times. Still thinks he's twenty-one.' And he laughed, a dry *haw haw* sound.

Other riders had now caught up with us.

'The young lady says she found the master's horse up beside the mere,' he said.

'We'd better go and take a look,' someone else suggested,

'but for heaven's sake stay together. We don't want to lose anybody in the bog.'

We made our way slowly up the hill, calling as we went. No sound answered us. As we reached the top of the hill, the mist suddenly stirred and parted and I found myself looking at a sheet of black water, upon which a group of swans was swimming peacefully.

A swan, I thought. Maybe that could have been the white flapping thing that came at us. Probably defending its territory. I had known swans to be aggressive before. I wondered if it had similarly attacked the master and caused him to be thrown from his horse. We picked our way around the lake until we came to an area on the far side where the grass was an unusually bright green. Having grown up on the Scottish moors, I knew a bog when I saw one and I knew what would happen to anyone foolish enough to venture onto that bright green grass. He would instantly find that his feet were trapped in thick, sucking mud. He would feel himself sinking. The more he struggled, the deeper he would sink. I had known bogs to swallow a horse or a steer in a few minutes.

We sat on our horses, not moving, just staring at the green grass as it merged into black water.

'You don't think . . . do you?' someone ventured to say at last.

'Not possible,' someone retorted. 'The master knows this area like the back of his hand. He warned us himself to stay clear of the bog, didn't he? He wouldn't have gone anywhere near it.'

'And yet his horse was found up here,' someone else pointed out.

'Well, there's no sign of him now,' the second speaker

declared. 'My bet is that he tried to jump too big a wall and the horse threw him, then took off on its own.'

'That's what I'd surmise too,' another rider said. 'Let's divide up and search the entire area.'

We were divided into teams of two and set off in different directions. After an hour or so of combing the wild and rocky terrain, calling futilely, we assembled again, with disappointing results. Nobody had seen any trace of the man.

'Of course he could have been knocked cold and is lying among the bracken,' someone said.

The big man who had organized the search shook his head. 'He wouldn't be out cold for a couple of hours, surely.'

'Then he could have recovered, realized he'd lost his horse and made his way down to the road on foot, hitched a lift and gone home.'

'Yes. Perhaps he did that,' several voices agreed. Everyone seemed eager to prove that their worst fears had not come true. Lady Hawse-Gorzley assembled us and we made our way home, hardly saying a word.

As we rode, Darcy urged his mount closer to me. Snowflake was too tired to protest by now and allowed her stablemate to come up beside her.

'It's one rum do after another, isn't it?' he said. 'They said you were the one who found the horse, is that right?'

'I did. Up by that bog.' I shuddered. 'I only hope he didn't come a cropper there. Not an end I'd want for myself.'

'If he got stuck, why didn't he yell?' Darcy said. 'Sound carried rather well today. I could hear the hounds when they were miles away.'

'That's true,' I said. 'And I was up there, quite close to him. I would have heard.'

'You don't gradually sink into a bog and do nothing,' Darcy said. 'Surely there would be some sign of a struggle.'

'Not necessarily. I've known a bog to swallow a Highland steer in a few minutes, although the poor thing did bellow a lot. By the time we reached it, it was too late and nobody could do anything.' I shuddered at the memory of it, watching those terrified eyes as the huge beast finally disappeared beneath the surface with a horrid sucking sound.

'Everyone said he was a good rider, and he certainly knew the area well,' Darcy said. 'What would have made him go near the mere he'd warned us against?'

'Something could have spooked his horse,' I said, and I told him the story of the white flapping thing that came up at me and how it had taken a while to regain control of Snowflake.

'A swan, you think?' Darcy nodded thoughtfully. 'They can be quite aggressive, I know, but when a man is riding his own horse, he should be able to calm it down right away.'

'There was one other thing,' I said. 'I saw Wild Sal up there. She looked like a pale flapping thing too. She stepped out right in front of my horse and stopped me from going in the direction of the bog. She showed me the right way back to the road.'

'Wild Sal, eh? What was she doing wafting around on the high moor?'

'Doesn't she have a cottage somewhere up there?' I asked.

Darcy shook his head, smiling. 'This village is too much, isn't it? Wild women and village idiots and aged spinsters . . . it's almost like a caricature of ye olde English village. Hard to believe it's real.'

That's it exactly, I thought. It's hard to believe it's real. Even harder to believe that every day somebody dies.

'You know what they'd say, don't you?' I turned to him. 'They'd say it was the Lovey Curse taking a person every day until the end of the year.'

'Now that,' Darcy said with a smile, 'is definitely hard to believe.'

'It's not funny, is it really?' I said, swallowing back the lump in my throat. 'I mean, every day somebody dies. It's as if a giant hand is hovering over us, waiting to snatch up the next victim.'

Chapter 24

Still December 26, Boxing Day

We reached Gorzley Hall and I gladly handed Snowflake back to her groom. She aimed a parting kick at me. Those who had not taken part in the hunt greeted us with enthusiasm, wanting to know if we'd killed a fox. Of course they hadn't heard about the master and we had to tell them.

'Do this many accidents usually happen in this part of the world?' Mr Upthorpe demanded. 'I'd always thought the countryside was a quiet, boring sort of place. If I had this number of things going wrong in my factories, they'd shut me down.'

'I assure you that our corner of the countryside is usually most peaceful,' Lady Hawse-Gorzley said. 'Why don't we all go up and change and then meet for sherry before lunch in the library?'

When Queenie had run a bath for me I had her return Bunty's jacket before she could somehow ruin it. Then we went down for a late lunch.

'You'll find we are eating simple meals today,' Lady Hawse-Gorzley said. 'It's Boxing Day, you see. The servants are allowed to spend the day with their families.'

The simple lunch was quite adequate: a hearty soup, then more pasties and cold meats and game pies, followed by a large sherry-laden trifle. I would have liked to visit my grandfather to tell him about this latest occurrence, but Lady Hawse-Gorzley asked me to run a skittles tournament in the ballroom and thus keep everybody happily occupied until teatime.

'Dashed glad you're here,' she said to me, drawing me closer to her. 'Frankly, I rather wish that I hadn't invited them for this long. Seemed like a good idea at the time, with the hunt and the Lovey Chase and the Worsting of the Hag and all that. But ten days of them – not only feeding them but entertaining them, too. It's a bit much, isn't it? And they are such a frightfully dreary bunch. No concept of entertaining themselves.'

I noticed that the colonel limped off for an afternoon snooze while Johnnie and the Sechrests had not reappeared after riding their own mounts back to their respective homes. However, the rest of them had a good cut-throat game of skittles and today made short work of the rest of the Christmas cake at teatime.

We were just finishing the last crumbs of food when Sir Oswald came in, still dressed in his 'mucking out the pigs' outfit.

'Damned police fellow has shown up again,' he said. 'Wants to talk to young Georgiana.'

'Me?' I think it came out like a squeak.

'I've put him in my study.' Sir Oswald gave me a commiserating smile.

I went through and found Inspector Newcombe sitting there. He rose to his feet as I came in.

'Oh, good afternoon, my lady,' he said, 'and please forgive me for calling you "miss" last time. Slip of the tongue, I'm afraid. And I'm sorry to disturb you on Boxing Day, but I wanted to ask you some questions about the man who disappeared during the hunt today. I'm told you found his horse, up by Barston Mere.'

'I did,' I said. 'It was just wandering aimlessly and it had obviously hurt itself, because it was lame in the left foreleg.'

'Did you see what happened before that? Where he might have fallen off?'

'No, not at all. He passed me some time before and my horse was being so antisocial that I rather lost touch with the rest of the hunt and found myself alone with no idea where I was. Then my horse was spooked by a horrible flapping noise and a big white thing came at me. I suspect now it might have been a swan on the lake, but at that point I didn't even know that I was near any water.'

'So you saw no trace of where he might have fallen?'

I shook my head.

'Nobody else anywhere near?'

'Well, yes. I saw the woman they call Wild Sal. She stepped out in front of my horse and told me I was going the wrong way and set me on the right path down. If she hadn't appeared, I might have ended up in the bog.'

'Ah,' he said, nodding.

'You think that's what might have happened to the master, don't you?' I asked.

'My men have been up there with dogs, scouring the moor all afternoon, and have not found a trace of him,' he said. 'Now I've looked at the horse and its foreleg is quite badly

cut. And what's more, there were bits of bracken caught
in its mane, so I have to assume it fell at some stage. And
the other strange thing – the cut is quite a clean one. Not a
skinned knee, which would have happened if it had clipped
the top of a wall.'

He looked at me, waiting for me to say something. 'And
we found some traces of blood between two Scotch pine
trees.'

'I saw that row of trees,' I said. 'I wouldn't have ridden
between them myself. Too many branches sticking out at
odd angles. But if the master did–' I paused. 'A clean cut,
you say. Is it possible that somebody put a trip wire between
those trees? They say he was rather reckless – so somebody
might have guessed that he'd take that route – a short cut
really.'

Inspector Newcombe was staring at me, frowning. 'If
that's the case then we're looking at a deliberate act of
malice, if not of murder.'

I nodded. 'I fear so,' I said.

He gave a deep sigh. 'Until now I kept telling myself that
these deaths were just an unfortunate string of accidents.
But now I had better face facts and admit that there is either
a deranged killer or a clever one, or both, operating on
my turf. And I'm buggered – I mean, I'm dashed – if I can
understand what the motive could be.'

I paused before I said, 'You don't possibly think that Wild
Sal might have had anything to do with it, do you? She
stopped me from going where the master had gone. Did she
know that there was a trip wire waiting for me?'

The inspector brightened up considerably. 'You know,
you may be right. There's one thing I've just remembered. I
went to look at the place where that van drove off the road

yesterday – and I did see some footprints in the snow nearby. Bare feet, they were. And I commented to the lads and one of them said, 'Oh, that's just the crazy woman who lives in Tiddleton. She runs around barefoot all year.' He paused as his brain processed the next step. 'And you say she stepped out right in front of your horse? What if she stepped out right in front of that van? He'd swerve to avoid her and on that icy road he'd plunge straight down into the river, wouldn't he?'

'In which case I should mention one more thing, or rather two more things,' I said. 'The first time I met her, she gave me a sinister warning. She told me to watch my step or I'd come a cropper. I took it to mean slipping in the snow, but it could have been more than that. She could have been warning me to keep my nose out of her business. And one of the Misses Ffrench-Finch told me that she'd found out that Sal came to their kitchen door on the night their sister died. She was asking for food and the cook felt sorry for her and let her in. Maybe she had a chance to slip upstairs and turn on the gas then.'

The inspector got to his feet. 'Right you are. You've put my mind at rest, Lady Georgiana. A good little head on your shoulders, that's what you've got. Well, I'm off right now to find that woman and bring her in. Then finally I may be able to have one peaceful day with my family over Christmas.'

He left with an almost jaunty spring to his step. I didn't feel so jaunty; in fact, I felt sick inside. Had I just condemned Wild Sal on entirely circumstantial evidence?

It was in a pensive frame of mind that I went back to join the house party. If Wild Sal really was the killer, had she warned me to mind my own business or was she warning me that I was on her list? In which case how did I get there? I tried to analyze that list of people who had died, but I could find nothing in common among them, however hard I tried. If you had wanted a random sample of people you'd find in a country village, they would be that sample.

I was in no real mood for fun and games but Lady Hawse-Gorzley had rallied everyone while I was being questioned and had a makeshift stage set up for the pantomime. The performers were already getting into their costumes and were all laughing and joking as if nothing untoward had happened. I was glad I didn't have a part to play and tried to look jolly as Darcy, Monty and Badger made everyone laugh as the stepmother and two ugly sisters. Ethel proved to be a witty fairy godmother and frankly stole the show. Nobody remembered their lines but everybody but me seemed to have a good time and they all declared they were famished by the time we changed for dinner.

The cook had certainly not stinted with the food she had left for us. The main part of the meal was a big turkey curry, with all the accompaniments, preceded by a spicy lentil soup and followed by a whipped cream dessert that slipped down wonderfully. I thought the curry was most tasty. The Wexlers and the Upthorpes eyed it suspiciously, never having eaten curry before. The colonel took one bite, then turned to his wife. 'Call this a curry?' he said. 'Where we live a good curry is hot enough to singe your eyebrows – you ask the memsahib. Our cook, Mukergee – splendid fellow, been with us forever – he's a Bengali and he thinks all English are sissies because we can't take it any hotter.'

'Well, I'm sorry, but this is plenty hot enough for me.' Mr Upthorpe wiped his brow. 'You're welcome to your foreign food, Colonel. Give me a good English roast meat and two veg any day, that's what I say.'

'I enjoyed some fine curry lunches when I stayed with my

friend the viceroy in Delhi,' the countess declaimed when silence had fallen. 'I must say, I miss them and I find this a real treat.'

Lady Hawse-Gorzley beamed. 'Thank you, Countess. It's nice to know that one's planning is appreciated, and I know that Cook will be delighted with your compliment.'

After the men had had their port and cigars and joined the womenfolk for coffee it was suggested that we play sardines and I was sent off to hide. I chose the linen cupboard and squeezed under the bottom shelf. Almost immediately the door opened and somebody squeezed in beside me.

'Finally we get a chance to be alone together,' Darcy whispered, nuzzling a kiss at my neck.

'How did you find me so quickly?' I whispered back.

'Have to confess I cheated. I saw which direction you were heading and I remembered your fondness for linen cupboards. And I'm not wasting any more time talking,' he added before kissing me. It was cramped and awkward and utterly blissful. I'm not sure how long we were alone together before the door opened again and another figure slipped in beside us. 'Found you, you little minx,' said Johnnie's voice. 'You can't get away from me this time. I have you trapped.'

'I should point out that's my waist you are grasping, not Georgie's,' Darcy said. I giggled as Johnnie hastily moved away.

'Well, I never did,' he muttered. 'How did you find her so quickly, O'Mara?'

'Let's just say I have good instincts,' Darcy said, 'and I see now that those instincts were right and I needed to protect her from cads like you.'

'It's a Christmas party game, old chum. Only a bit of fun, what?'

Their talking was overheard and soon more and more people crowded into the cupboard until the door would no longer close and the game was declared over. Darcy winked at me and held me back as we trooped down the stairs. 'Next time we need not try too hard to find anyone,' he whispered, 'and nobody will notice we're missing.'

I have to confess I didn't need much persuading, and when the others scattered around the house Darcy and I ducked into Sir Oswald's study and picked up where the last kiss had ended.

'It's been so long,' Darcy murmured.

'And whose fault is that? I've been stuck at Castle Rannoch. You, on the other hand, were seen entering the Café Royal recently.'

'Do you have your spies on me?' he laughed. 'I did go to the Café Royal. I had to meet a man who had a small assignment for me. As it happened I turned it down. Sailing a little too near the wind for my taste.' He looked at me with sudden longing. 'I wish I could find a normal, everyday sort of job and make a decent living, enough to support a wife and family.'

'You'd be bored in a normal, everyday sort of job.' I tried to make light of it.

'I'm serious, Georgie,' he said. 'You know I'd ask you to marry me if I could support you. I'm trying as hard as I can, but there are no jobs for fellows like me – I don't even have the connections to be sent out to the Colonies.'

'I know, it's hard,' I said. 'I feel the same way. Fig doesn't want me around and refuses to let me stay alone at Rannoch House and I've nowhere else to go, unless I marry the next prince or count that my royal kin produce for me.'

'Maybe you should,' he said. 'I can't expect you to wait for me forever.'

'Darcy, you know I couldn't. If I can't marry someone I love, I'd rather stay a spinster. Perhaps I'll take up a wicked life like my mother.'

He laughed, shaking his head. 'You're not the type, my darling. You've inherited your great-grandmother's moral barometer . . . although after that display the other night, I'm not so sure anymore. Would you have invited the lecherous Johnnie into your bed if he'd escorted you upstairs?'

'Don't tease, and you know I wouldn't. In fact, he came into my room, hoping to take advantage of me while I was drunk.'

'Did he, the bounder? And what did you do?'

'I wasn't capable of doing much, but Queenie threatened to hit him over the head with my water jug.'

'I like Queenie. I'm sure she's not much use as a maid, but she has grit, doesn't she?'

Footsteps ran past the door. Darcy stopped talking, then whispered, 'Why are we wasting precious time talking?' and kissed me again. But this time my mind wasn't fully on the kiss. I knew that I hadn't told him that I wouldn't be allowed to marry him anyway.

Chapter 25

December 27
I'm beginning to agree with Lady H-G. This party has gone on long enough. I'm wishing I could get away from here, before the next awful thing happens. It's like having a sword of doom hanging over us and I feel so powerless.

It was a glorious bright morning with the sun sparkling on the snow-clad Lovey Tor. At breakfast Lady Hawse-Gorzley announced that she and her family had to attend the funeral of Miss Ffrench-Finch but suggested that the chauffeur drive those who were interested around the local beauty spots, to show them the sights in this part of Devon. They could stop for lunch in an old pub in a historic village. The Upthorpes and Wexlers both wanted to do this. The countess declared that she had spent childhood holidays in Devon before anyone else in the room was born and had no need to see it again. Badger thought he might want to come along for the ride (having become, I suspected, rather enamored of Ethel Upthorpe, or at least of Ethel Upthorpe's money), but Lady Hawse-Gorzley stopped him.

'You'll want to start training for the Lovey Chase with the other boys, surely, Badger?'

'The Lovey Chase? What's that?' he asked suspiciously.

'Remember I told you, old fruit,' Monty said. 'All the young men of the area compete in a steeplechase. Have to run around the course and jump over the fences, wearing a dashed ridiculous saddle. And the crowd places bets, just like a real horse race. I actually won a couple of years ago when I was just down from Eton and remarkably fit.'

'Before you went to seed at Oxford,' Bunty commented. 'It's awfully good fun, Badger. Nobody takes it seriously.'

'And it's quite historic. Goes back to 1700, I believe – when there was a powerful Catholic family in the area and Catholics were not allowed by law to own horses. So they invented their own alternative horse race with their own sons.'

'Absolutely fascinating,' Mrs Rathbone said. 'Can't wait to see it. I adore these old English traditions, don't I, Reggie?'

'Is it only for the young bloods or can an old codger like me take part?' the colonel asked.

'Reggie, you are not going to make a fool of yourself stumbling over fences while wearing a saddle,' Mrs Rathbone said.

'Well, I'm to be a contender,' Johnnie Protheroe said. 'Don't care if I have passed forty. How about you, Sechrest?' This was clearly thrown out as a challenge.

'Might just take you up on that,' Captain Sechrest said.

'So I thought you young men might want to go out and view the course, practice the jumps and all that,' Lady Hawse-Gorzley said.

'Absolutely,' Darcy said. He looked at me. 'I hope you plan to bet a large sum on me.'

'Are you fit enough to win?'

'I haven't seen the competition yet.' He chuckled. 'If we're up against some strapping young farm lads, then I don't know.'

'Oh, it's only for the sons of good families,' Bunty said. 'We don't allow the riffraff to join in.'

'Bunty dear, do try to be a little more diplomatic in the way you put things,' Lady Hawse-Gorzley said.

'I don't see why you make such a fuss,' Bunty said, tossing her head. 'It's not as if there are any of the riffraff present, is it? And I think it's jolly unfair that they don't allow girls to compete. I was rather good at cross-country running at school.'

'Come and offer advice then, Bunty,' Darcy put an arm around her, then looked back at me. 'Are you coming too? We'll need a cheering section.'

'I thought I might spend some time with my mother and grandfather, if everyone is occupied elsewhere,' I said.

'Splendid idea, Georgiana,' Lady Hawse-Gorzley said. 'You've hardly had a chance to enjoy your own relatives. Those staying here are planning to play bridge this morning. Mrs Sechrest can't survive more than two days without a bridge game, can you, Sandra?' Mrs Sechrest smiled prettily.

'I'm going with the guys,' Junior Wexler said, breaking away from his mother. 'It's boring seeing old things.'

'And I think I'll come and join the cheering section,' Cherie Wexler said, her eyes on Darcy. 'It might be fun. Are you coming, Ethel?'

'I'd rather sit in a warm motor than stand in the freezing cold,' Ethel Upthorpe said. 'There might even be shops open if we go through a town.'

So I waited until the estate car had set off loaded to the gills with sightseers and the young Adonises had gone to their steeplechase training before I headed down the driveway to my mother's cottage. My mother and Noël Coward were hard at work – at least, Noël was hard at work. My mother was lounging in peacock blue pajamas, a long ebony cigarette holder in her hand, nodding agreement occasionally as he tossed off another line. So Granddad and I decided to go for a walk before lunch.

'The inspector stopped by earlier this morning,' Granddad said. 'It seems that they've arrested that Wild Sal person. Caught her going back to that hovel she lives in up on the moor last night. Said she put up a terrible fight, like a wild animal.'

I nodded. For some reason there was a lump in my throat and I couldn't speak. She had almost certainly saved my life by warning me away from the bog. And I couldn't help wondering what she had been like before and what it must be like to live apart and have absolutely nobody in the world. Perhaps I identified with her a little.

'And of course it makes sense, now that we think of it,' Granddad went on cheerfully. 'She roams all over the moors, doesn't she? And she's clearly quite crackers. Probably didn't even care who she was bumping off. Probably hears voices or something like that. They often do, don't they? Well, at least the inspector can breathe easier now, and it won't even go to trial. She'll be sent off to an asylum, poor thing.'

We walked on, past the village shop, which was open again today and doing a good trade in newspapers and cigarettes, and past the pub, where a group of local people were standing gossiping, presumably about the arrest of Wild Sal. They looked up warily as we walked past.

'I'm glad it turned out to be a mad person,' Granddad said, 'because I couldn't for the life of me find any link between the people who had died and the way they were killed. It didn't tie in with any case I'd ever worked on in my long years with the force.'

'You're walking quite fast,' I said. 'The country air is making you a lot better.'

'You're right, it is,' he agreed.

'You should think of moving down here. Get a little cottage in a village like this.'

'Oh, no, ducks. Wouldn't suit me at all,' he said. 'I'm from the Smoke. Born and bred. I know where I belong.'

I looked at him with concern, realizing how much I loved him and relied on him. In fact, he was the only person in the world I could rely on – certainly not my flighty, self-centered mother, or even Darcy, who was never around for more than two minutes. Why would Granddad want to go back to London where the air was so bad for his chest and could lead to an early grave? I tried to dispel gloomy thoughts. He was here with me now and we were enjoying ourselves. That was all that mattered.

By the time we came back to the cottage there were wonderful smells coming from the kitchen and Mrs Huggins's head poked out. 'I've some sausage rolls in the oven if you need a bite to eat before your meal,' she said. 'The gentleman upstairs is particularly fond of my sausage rolls. He told me I was a dab hand with pastry, and of course he's right. I've always had a way with pastry, ain't I, Albert?'

'You have, my dear,' he said.

She smiled at him fondly.

Mummy and Mr Coward came down to join us for

wine and sausage rolls. Mummy had changed into a skirt and cashmere jumper, but Noël was still in his dressing gown.

'I made another of your favorites, Mr Coward. A steak and kidney pie,' Mrs Huggins said.

'Mrs Huggins, you are an angel in disguise, sent from heaven to bring me happiness,' Noël said.

Mrs Huggins blushed charmingly. I wondered whether she might have landed herself a permanent job as Mr Coward's cook and what Granddad would think of that.

'Noël, are you sure you're not Irish?' Mummy said. 'You are full of blarney.'

Noël reached for the decanter and poured himself a glass of red wine. 'I speak from the heart, Claire.'

'Darling, you don't have a heart. Everyone knows that.' Mummy reached forward to pour herself a large glass of red wine. The steak and kidney pie, served with cauliflower in a parsley sauce, was absolutely delicious, as was the jam roly-poly that followed.

'Good simple English cooking at its best,' my mother said. 'How I long for this sometimes, when I am stuck with that rich German food.'

'I couldn't agree more,' Mr Coward said. 'There are times when one simply can't face another schnitzel, or even another bite of caviar. Of course, it's really the longing to go back to the security of the nursery, isn't it?'

We finished the meal with coffee and nuts and dates around the fire.

'This really is most delightful,' Mummy said. 'I shall be loath to leave and travel back to those big drafty rooms at Max's house and all that entertaining and boring German parties.'

'You know, Claire, I really do believe you're looking for an excuse to leave that brute,' Noël said.

'He's not a brute.'

'He's a German and all Germans are brutes at heart.'

'He adores me, Noël, and you know how much I like to be adored. And he is very rich and generous. But you're right. There is only so much time that one can spend in Germany without longing to escape – especially now that that dreadful little Hitler man seems to have taken control.'

'He won't last, my darling,' Noël said. 'He can't last. He is comic beyond belief. You'll see. Someone with more military bearing will arise and topple him. Maybe even your Max might like to take over – then you could be Frau Führer.'

'If you're in Mr Coward's play then you'll be stuck in England, won't you?' I said. 'It's bound to be a hit and then it'll run forever.'

'Of course it will. Anything I write is a hit,' Noël said. 'And then we'll take it to America, where everyone will adore us.'

'Oh, yes. Do let's.' Mummy's face lit up. 'I really do think it's time I went back to the stage. It's been so long. Do you think my public will have forgotten me?'

Noël took her hand. 'As if they could, my darling. They have been yearning for your return.'

I glanced at my grandfather and he winked.

The grandfather clock in the hallway struck four. I stood up. 'I should go back to the hall, I suppose. They'll all be returning from their various expeditions.'

'Apart from the ones who have been felled along the way by the Lovey Curse,' Mr Coward said callously.

'No, that's all taken care of now,' Granddad said. 'Remember the inspector told us he'd arrested the madwoman.'

Noël sighed. 'How I love this village. A resident mad-woman and old spinsters and a village idiot and a pub called the Hag and Hounds.'

'And don't forget about the Lovey Chase,' I said and gave them all the details.

'We absolutely can't miss that, can we, Claire?' Mr Coward said. 'And I rather think we're coming to your fancy-dress ball tomorrow night, since we can be in disguise and nobody will recognize us.'

'Oh, yes, I'd forgotten about the fancy dress ball,' I said. 'You should see the ballroom. It's absolutely lovely.'

'I don't know what we'll do for costumes,' Mummy said. 'I don't suppose there is a costume shop in Exeter that can send something over by tomorrow. One will just have to improvise, I suppose, if you really insist on attending, Noël.'

'I do, darling. Absolutely adamant about it. Wouldn't miss it for the world.'

I glanced at his elegant face with its sardonic smile. One never knew with people like him if they were being serious or if this was thinly veiled sarcasm.

'Toodle pip, everyone,' I said, blowing a kiss. As I opened the front door I saw a man getting out of a motorcar. 'It's the inspector again,' I called back to the others. 'I wonder, has Wild Sal confessed?'

The inspector came up the path with slow, measured tread. 'Well, it seems I spoke too soon,' he said. 'We've got Wild Sal in custody and now I've just heard there's been another death.'

Chapter 26

My mother's cottage
Still December 27

'Another murder?' my mother asked. 'How positively thrilling. People are dropping like flies.'

The inspector frowned at her. 'Not sure about the murder part, madam. It was some miles away, on the other side of Bovey Tracey, which is why I didn't hear about it until now. A farmer's wife was found lying in the milking shed. Apparently she was kicked in the head by the cow she was milking. Any other time I'd think this was just a nasty accident. Now I just don't know.'

'You'd better come in and let Mrs Huggins make you a cup of tea,' my mother said. 'You're looking quite haggard.'

'I know. This whole thing is driving me mad. My chief gets back in a few days and he'll think I've done nothing.'

'But you've had nothing to go on,' my grandfather said, ushering the inspector to the armchair by the fire. 'I mean, there's not been one of these deaths that one could pinpoint as a murder. No signs of foul play, no motive at all, was there?'

The inspector nodded. 'You're right. No clues, no motive, no sense at all. To start with I thought it might be those escaped convicts, killing because someone had spotted their hideout. But that wouldn't explain a switchboard operator in town, would it? And an escaped convict wouldn't go to the trouble of setting up a trip wire for someone's horse. He'd have been able to stay hidden very nicely in that kind of mist without doing anything. No – that horse's leg has opened my eyes, so to speak. That was a deliberate act of malice. I don't know if it was aimed at a particular person or just at the hunt in general, but it was certainly aimed at felling a rider.'

'Did you find the actual tree where the trap was laid?' I asked.

'My boys might have done so by now, but quite frankly they've been stretched to the limit, what with finding this Wild Sal and bringing her in. My, but she was a little tiger. Put curses on my men too, like someone possessed by the devil – scared the daylights out of some of them, I can tell you.'

'If you look at it logically,' Noël Coward interjected in his bored upper-class drawl, 'you still couldn't come to the conclusion that you were looking at a string of murders. The horse's leg is the only sign of outside intervention – unless you found telltale boot marks around that tree in the orchard or signs of a scuffle where the man fell off the bridge.'

'To tell you the truth, sir, we bungled both of those,' the inspector said. 'That first one with the man in the tree – well, we just took it to be a stupid accident, see. So we walked around a bit and left our footprints all over the place. Same goes for the man who fell off the bridge. Didn't occur to us that they were crime scenes to begin with.'

'Why would it?' Granddad said. 'You don't expect someone to be lurking and pushing people off bridges in this part of the world.'

'You do not, sir,' the inspector agreed. 'But after eight days of one death per day, I have to believe that someone is behind this.'

'Not one death per day,' I interrupted. 'There was no death on December twenty-fourth, remember?'

'You're right, my lady.' He wagged a finger in my direction. 'But there was a crime, wasn't there? The jewelry shop in Newton Abbot was broken into. I don't suppose that had anything to do with the deaths. In fact, I'd have said that someone needed extra money for Christmas except that it was clearly a professional job – safe cracked with no problem and only the best stuff taken – some really expensive gold rings.'

'So have you given up on the idea that the convicts were to blame?' Granddad asked.

'I think I have to, sir. The deaths have been so spread out now that I can't believe escaped convicts could have covered so much ground on foot without being seen. And then there's the question why. If you'd just escaped from Dartmoor Prison your one thought would be to get as far away as possible and then lie low, wouldn't it?'

'You said they'd recaptured one of the convicts, didn't you?' I asked.

'They have, my lady, and they're holding him in a cell up in Birmingham until they can bring him back here.'

'Did he have anything to say about his fellow escapees?' I went on.

'He thought the other two were planning to head straight for London. Leastways, that's what he said. If he knows more, he's not spilling the beans. They don't usually rat on each other.'

'So this woman who was kicked in the head – have you seen her yet?'

'I haven't. They rushed her to the hospital because she was still breathing, but unfortunately she died on the way there, and nobody got a chance to see how she was lying or to examine the shed as a possible crime scene. By now those cows have probably walked all over the spot where she was found.'

'It seems to me this all comes down to why,' Granddad said. 'Why these particular people.'

'I agree with you, sir,' the inspector said. 'And believe me, I've asked myself that question over and over. But they've nothing in common. They'd certainly not have mixed socially, would they? I mean a master of hounds and a switchboard operator and a butcher. I'll wager they didn't even know each other.'

'I presume you've been through your case files to see if you've any antisocial or violent blokes in the area?' Granddad asked.

'I've done that. We've our share of lads who are soft in the head, like that poor chap you've got in the village here, but nobody who's shown any inclination to kill people.'

'It could be someone who has come down from London for the Christmas holidays, I suppose,' Mummy said.

'I don't think that's likely, madam,' the inspector said. 'You see, whoever it was knew an awful lot about these people. He knew where the hunt was likely to go. He knew that Ted Grover took a short cut home over that bridge when he'd been to see his lady love. He even knew that Mr Skaggs would be making an early morning delivery in his van and would be coming around that dangerous bend.'

'If indeed those people were his targets,' Mr Coward said, waving his cigarette holder at the inspector. 'What if he just wanted the thrill of killing and it really didn't matter who fell off the bridge or whose van went off the road?'

'Don't say that, sir,' the inspector groaned, 'because if that is true, then we've no way of ever catching him.'

'You will,' Granddad said. 'I've dealt with a lot of criminals in my life, some of them remarkably clever men, but they always slip up in the end. Get too cocky, see. Like leaving the evidence on that horse's leg. Until that moment you could say that every one of those deaths was an accident. Now you know that at least one wasn't.' He looked up. 'I take it you haven't found the bloke who fell off that horse?'

'We haven't.' The inspector shook his head sadly, 'And not for want of trying. My boys have scoured those hills, and we've had the dogs out, and not a trace of him. We have to assume that he went down in that bog, poor bloke.'

An absurd idea was passing through my mind. What if someone had wanted to disappear, to make it look as if he came off his horse in the mist and wandered into the bog? It sounded so far-fetched that I didn't like to say it, but I thought I'd ask a little more about the master of hounds when I got back to the hall.

Mrs Huggins appeared with a tea tray loaded with generous slices of Christmas cake.

'I should be getting back,' I said reluctantly and made for the door again. 'See you tomorrow at the fancy dress ball.'

'You won't recognize us, we'll be in such brilliant disguises,' Noël Coward said. 'And watch your step as you walk up that long driveway. So far the killer hasn't attacked anyone from the hall, but it might be only a matter of time.'

'Noël, don't say things like that.' My mother slapped his wrist. 'Walk with her if you're worried about her.'

'What, and have to walk back alone in the growing darkness? Not for a million pounds, my dear. It's not for nothing that my last name is "coward."'

'I could accompany you, my lady.' The inspector made signs of putting down his teacup. 'But I don't think there's any need to worry. You're not from around here, are you? The killer or killers only seem interested in people from these parts.'

'That's encouraging, isn't it?' I gave them a bright smile and departed.

I made it back to the hall without incident, although I have to confess, I did turn sharply every time there was a rustle in the bushes. When I reached Gorzley Hall I found that the wanderers had returned. The members of the sightseeing party were full of enthusiasm for what they had seen and were relating their experiences to the boys who had been training and to the bridge players.

'And we saw Buckfast Abbey. And we actually heard the monks chanting,' Mrs Upthorpe said. 'It was like stepping back into the Middle Ages.'

'And all those cute little villages and humpbacked bridges,' Mrs Wexler agreed.

'And we saw the Dartmoor jail,' Mr Wexler reminded her. 'My, but that's a grim-looking place. I'd want to escape if I were sent there.'

'Don't forget the ponies,' Mrs Wexler reminded him. 'We actually saw the famous Dartmoor ponies.'

'You saw ponies?' Junior Wexler showed interest for the first time. 'Like wild ponies, you mean?'

'We sure did. Running up the mountainside in the snow.'

Mrs Wexler paused to ruffle her son's hair. 'But how did your training go, son?'

'Swell. I thought the fences would be big, but they are only this high.' He held his hands about eighteen inches apart. 'Anybody could jump over them.'

'Tea is ready when you've all had a chance to change,' Lady Hawse-Gorzley said, and as they went up the stairs to do so, she sidled over to me. 'Any news from the outside world? One feels so cut off without a telephone still.'

'They've arrested Wild Sal,' I said.

'Wild Sal. Good God. So she *was* the one. I might have known. She is a direct descendant of the hag, after all.'

'Not so fast,' I said. 'Since her arrest, there has been another death.'

'Where?' She looked up sharply.

'On the other side of Bovey Tracey, I think the inspector said. And it might have nothing to do with the other deaths. A farmer's wife kicked in the head by a cow as she was milking.'

'Well, that has happened before, hasn't it?' Lady Hawse-Gorzley dismissed this. 'Such unpredictable creatures, cows. I expect they'll find that this one really was an accident and that Wild Sal is responsible for at least some of the others.'

She gave me a nod of satisfaction, then bustled off again. Everyone fell upon tea with enthusiasm, then we didn't do much before dinner apart from tackling a large jigsaw puzzle of a Dutch skating scene. Ethel and her mother were wearing gorgeous new dresses for dinner – Schiaparelli, if I was not mistaken – and I noticed Badger's eyes light up when Ethel came into the room. Perhaps the investment in this house party would pay off for the Upthorpes and they would get their daughter married into the upper classes. I put the subject of marriage firmly from my mind. It was too worrying to consider.

After the previous night's simple curry dinner, this was a lavish affair, befitting a grand house party. Smoked salmon followed by a rich oxtail soup and then pheasant for the main course.

'What kind of bird is this?' Mr Wexler asked, prodding it with his fork.

'I was so disappointed that I couldn't provide you with goose for Christmas Day that I decided to make up for it with pheasant,' Lady Hawse-Gorzley said. 'Truly the most delicious of the game birds, I always think.'

Nobody argued with that – the meat swimming in a dark brown gravy with mushrooms and tiny onions around it and thin crisps of potato to accompany it. We ate in near silence. The pheasant was followed by an apple crumble and clotted cream, then a local strong cheddar and biscuits. We passed a quiet evening playing records on the gramophone and one or two of us made an attempt at dancing.

'You'll have plenty of opportunity to dance tomorrow at the ball,' Lady Hawse-Gorzley said.

I went to bed and fell asleep straight away. I woke to see the moon shining on me and realized that I needed to face the long walk to the lavatory at the end of the corridor. As I came out of my room I stopped, staring down the hallway ahead of me. A figure in white appeared to be floating slowly down the dark hall. I wondered if this was a Gorzley ghost that nobody had seen fit to mention. Having grown up at Castle Rannoch, I wasn't particularly scared of ghosts. We had plenty of them in the family, including my grandfather's ghost playing the bagpipes on the ramparts – an apparition I hadn't personally experienced. I crept silently behind the figure until I could see it was a woman with long dark hair spilling over the shoulders of a white nightgown.

Then suddenly she stopped outside a door, put her hand on the handle and eased it open before going in. By now my eyes were accustomed to the darkness of the hallway and I saw who it was. It was Sandra Sechrest. I told myself that she had also been on a nocturnal walk to heed the call of nature, and felt like a fool, until I realized that the room she had slipped into so silently was not her own but Johnnie Protheroe's.

Chapter 27

December 28
***I've started counting the days until I can go home, which is
silly because I'm with Granddad and Darcy and frankly I
haven't a home to go to.***

When I awoke the next morning I looked out at a landscape
blotted out by mist and the first thought that came to me
was, I wonder who is going to be killed today?

The fact that this came to me so readily was shocking.
How could I have possibly come to accept that one person
would die every day in this little part of Devon? And anger
flooded through me. Right there, as I stared out through the
window at the ghostly bare branches of the orchard hovering in the mist, I made a decision. This could not be allowed
to continue. Someone had to do something about it, and
since the inspector was clearly incapable, it was up to me
to use the expertise at my disposal and catch the murderer.
I had my grandfather, with all his years of experience at
Scotland Yard, and I had Darcy, who worked, I was sure, as
some sort of spy. And I had assisted in a small way in some

important cases. It was about time we did a little detective work ourselves.

I was already dressed by the time Queenie appeared with a tea tray – more of the tea in the saucer than the cup, I have to say. Her good intentions to be a perfect maid were rapidly slipping back into her normal behavior.

'Blimey, you're already up,' she said. 'I needn't have bothered to come up all them stairs with the tea if I'd known.'

'You came up the stairs because one of your duties is to bring your mistress her morning tea, whether she wants it or not,' I pointed out.

She gave me a look as she put it down, none too gently, on the table. 'Nasty old day,' she said, 'and I don't know about you, but I'm ready to go home. Do you know what they're saying in the servants' hall? They're saying that there's a Lovey Curse and one person will get struck down every day until New Year. I tell you, it ain't half giving me the willies.'

'I don't think you have to worry, Queenie. It's only local people who are cursed,' I said.

'Oh, well, that's all right, then, ain't it?' A beam spread across her round red face. I wished I could be as easily satisfied as she was.

I came into the breakfast room to find Darcy sitting alone at one end of the table while the Rathbones and Upthorpes were busy working their way through enormous piles of kedgeree at the other. I slid into a seat beside him and he looked up, smiling. 'Good morning,' he said.

'Do you think you could possibly borrow Monty's motorcar today?'

'You want to escape for a tryst?' he asked, his eyes teasing me.

I lowered my voice even though the distance between us

and the other diners was considerable. 'No, I want to help solve this ridiculous business before any more people are killed.'

He looked surprised and a trifle amused. 'You are suddenly turning into the Sherlock Holmes of Rannoch, are you?'

'Darcy, be serious, please. The local detective inspector is a nice enough man but he's quite out of his depth. You know a thing or two about questioning people and judging who might be lying, and my grandfather – well, he's dealt with all kinds of gruesome cases during his years on the force. So I thought we might at least take a look for ourselves at the sites where these things happened.'

'Aren't you supposed to be my aunt's right-hand woman? Are you allowed to vanish for a day when you should be running skittles tournaments and things?'

I regarded him frostily. 'You sound as if you don't want to come with me. Fine, if you don't want a chance for us to spend time together . . .' I began to stand up. He grabbed my arm to hold me back.

'Don't be silly. You know very well that I'd love any chance to spend time with you. It's just that I'm not sure we should interfere in local police business. We don't know the people or the territory. I can't see how we can be of any use whatsoever.'

'Darcy, you haven't spoken with Inspector Newcombe. I have. He admits that he is flummoxed. He's been popping in on my grandfather asking for advice every two seconds. Of course he wants help, and if my grandfather had somebody to motor him around he might be able to solve this.'

'Very well,' he said, looking around as if trying to make up his mind. 'I suppose I could ask Monty, but I'm none too sure about the lie of the land around here.'

'There are such things as maps,' I said. 'I'll ask Sir Oswald for one.'

'So what are we going to do about this fancy-dress ball if we're gone all day? Aren't we supposed to be creating costumes?'

'I happen to know there is a whole row of costumes hanging in the attic,' I said. 'I suggest you and I slip up there before the others and grab something.'

'Slip up to the attic and grab something. That sounds interesting.'

'Darcy!' I glared at him.

'My, but you're testy today,' he said.

'Because I'm feeling really angry and frustrated that people are being killed and nobody is doing anything to stop it,' I said. 'We have to help, Darcy. How many people will have to die otherwise before Scotland Yard sends someone down to take charge?'

'I suppose the point is that, from what we can tell, we have no evidence that any of the deaths was a murder.'

'My grandfather says there is no such thing as coincidence. Do you really believe that so many accidents could happen in one small part of Dartmoor, with a death every day?'

'I agree it does sound far-fetched. Unless you believe in the Lovey Curse.'

'Do you?'

'Of course not.' He gave a half-embarrassed laugh. 'But I'm dashed if I can see how these deaths have anything to do with each other. I mean to say, if you were going to kill a chap, would you wait until he was up a tree? And the man who pushed that garage owner off a bridge was most likely the wronged husband, not an outsider. And if someone turned on the gas to kill the old woman, it was probably one of her sisters, tired of being bossed around.'

'But what if it wasn't? What if it was a clever killer with a motive we haven't yet fathomed?'

He put an arm around my shoulder. 'Georgie, think about it – do you really believe we can do anything that the local police can't?'

I chewed on my lip, something I tend to do when I'm not sure of myself. 'I just thought that if three of us put our heads together and looked at the sites in order, then something would occur to us.'

Darcy stared past me, out the window, then he pushed away his plate. 'All right then. I'll go find Monty.'

'We have to choose costumes first,' I said. 'Come on. Let's see if we can sneak up to the attic without being noticed.'

Darcy gave a reluctant sigh, then took my hand. We crept up several flights of stairs, each one less grand than the one before, until we reached a set of steep wooden steps to an attic. The place was illuminated only by the light coming in from some dormer windows, and items covered in dust sheets looked ominous in the darkness. Having grown up in a really spooky castle, I'm not normally afraid of such things, but the way they stirred in the draft we let in was unnerving and I was glad I had Darcy with me.

'Here they are,' I said and threw the dustsheet off a rack of costumes.

'Let me see, what do I want to be?' Darcy examined them one by one. 'Not a gorilla. Too hot. Caveman? I might fancy that. Then I could drag you across the room by your hair.'

'Which, in case you haven't noticed, is not long enough to do that,' I said. 'Besides, there is no cavewoman outfit.'

'You could be a second Wild Sal,' Darcy said. 'Look at

this airy-fairy outfit. I'm sure you could waft around if you wanted to.'

I held it up. 'I don't think I'm the wafting type,' I said.

Darcy was staring at the floor. 'Someone else wanted to get first dibs on costumes, I see. Look at the footprints. Someone has been up here before us.' He pointed at the row of neat footprints in the dust.

'Probably just Lady Hawse-Gorzley or one of the maids sent up to make sure the costumes were brushed and clean.' I put back the Wild Sal outfit.

'Pity there's no Charles the Second,' Darcy said, 'because you could borrow some oranges from downstairs and be Nell Gwyn in this dress.' He held it out to me. 'Rather a daring bodice, don't you think? But then, Nell never did mind displaying her oranges.'

I could see that we were getting nowhere. 'Look,' I said. 'How about this? We could go as gypsies. I'm sure there are red scarves and big golden earrings in the dressing-up box downstairs.'

'I wouldn't mind being a gypsy,' he agreed. 'I've always rather fancied the outdoor life.'

'Good. Then that's settled.' I handed him an outfit with baggy trousers, lacy white shirt and black waistcoat. 'Let's go find Monty.'

Darcy sighed and followed me down the stairs.

Chapter 28

December 28

A half hour later we had picked up my grandfather and were ready to embark upon a day of detecting.

'We should start with the first death,' I said. 'You don't happen to know which tree in the orchard it was, do you?'

'Haven't got a clue, ducks,' my granddad said. 'But we could take a butcher's if you like.'

'A butcher's?' I asked.

'Butcher's hook – rhyming slang for look.'

'I'll never get the hang of rhyming slang,' I said. 'It seems to take twice as long to say something as the actual word it represents.'

'Ah, well, the object is that the toffs don't understand what we're talking about,' he said. 'Rhyming slang and then back slang before it. Private language in a crowded city.'

'Oh, I see.'

'I don't see any point in going to look at the orchard,' Darcy said. 'We know that the police trampled all over it.'

'We could question the man's servants,' I suggested.

Darcy glanced at my grandfather. 'What do you think, sir? Georgie wants to do this, but I don't want to be accused of stepping on the toes of the police.'

'Well, that inspector has asked for my advice, but I'm not so sure we should go questioning people behind his back,' Granddad said. 'And anyway, I heard from the inspector that nobody in the house knew anything. They didn't hear the shot. They didn't know he'd gone out. I gather the servants sleep in another wing altogether and he normally didn't get up before nine.'

'Well, that's a lot of good,' I said. 'I wish we knew who his friends were and whether he'd told any of them that he was planning this prank.'

'What would that prove?' Darcy asked. 'He probably told quite a few people that he was planning the prank. If he wasn't about to carry out some kind of stunt, what on earth was he doing up a tree with a shotgun and wire?'

I sighed. 'This isn't going to be easy, is it?'

'Because if these are murders,' my grandfather said, 'then someone has put a lot of thought and planning into making them look like accidents.'

'What kind of person would do this?' Darcy asked.

'Obviously a brainy type,' Granddad said. 'A loner. Quiet sort, I'd say. And if he really has planned to kill these specific people, then I'd say he's the kind who'd carry a grudge, maybe for years. A crime spree like this must have taken months of planning.'

'What if it's a woman?' I asked. 'Wild Sal fits those characteristics, doesn't she?'

Granddad nodded. 'It could be that the farmer's wife, kicked to death in the dairy, was a genuine accident. We'll just have to see if there are any more deaths. If there aren't, then bob's your uncle. Wild Sal it is.'

'We should be moving along if you want to cover all of the crime scenes,' Darcy said. 'The second one – the man who fell off the bridge.'

'We can hardly ask the publican what time Ted Grover left, if he was dallying with the publican's wife,' I said.

'But we could ask some of the other men,' Granddad said. 'There's a couple of them sitting outside the pub right now.'

We went over and I hung back, letting Darcy and my grandfather do the talking. They joined me soon after. 'They say that nobody saw him leave. He definitely wasn't in the bar at closing time, so he must have left well before that. Could have been round the back with the publican's missus.' My grandfather paused. 'And they were surprised he fell off the bridge because he didn't seem to be drunk.'

There was a clear footpath from the pub across low-lying fields. It was muddy from melted snow and we picked our way carefully until we came to the clapper bridge – just slabs of granite laid over standing stones across the stream.

'Easy enough to fall off here, if you were unsteady on your pins,' Granddad said.

'But they didn't think he was drunk,' I said. 'And if he fell into the stream, it's deep enough that he wouldn't have hit his head on a rock, and the icy water would have sobered him up in a hurry.'

'I suspect the stream is much deeper now than it was a few days ago,' Darcy said. 'All that melted snow.'

'That's true.' I stared down at the swiftly flowing waters, trying to picture a man's body lying there; trying to spot a rock that could have killed him. We made our way back to the road and went to look at the house of the Misses Ffrench-Finch.

'We do know that Wild Sal was admitted to their kitchen on that night,' I said.

Granddad shook his head. 'Do you think she'd know about things like turning on gas taps if she lived wild on the moors? And more to the point, would she have any idea about cross-wiring a switchboard?'

'I suppose that's true,' I said. 'It would take a person with experience of electricity to make sure someone was electrocuted when they plugged in headphones.'

We made our way around the house to the side with Miss Effie's window, and sure enough there was a very large footprint in the flower bed right beneath the window.

'Looks like a large Wellington boot to me,' Granddad said. 'A very large one. Doesn't that half-witted bloke wear big boots?'

'Willum? Yes, but we know he was here the day before Miss Effie died. He helped them carry in packages and get the decorations down from their attic. He could quite possibly have had to fetch something from the shed.'

'Via a flower bed?' Darcy asked.

'Maybe he wanted to peek in a downstairs window,' I suggested. 'He's very childlike.' I looked over to the shed behind the main house. 'Oh, and look. There is a ladder propped against the shed. Perhaps he had to fetch that to put up the Christmas tree.'

Granddad stared at the ladder, then at the wall. 'If that was extended, it would reach close to that bedroom window.'

'It would,' Darcy agreed. 'Now all we have to do is find out who used it, turned on the gas and came down again without being seen.'

'You're being sarcastic again,' I said.

'I just think this is a fool's errand,' he said. 'Maybe Sherlock Holmes could look at the smallest of clues and know everything, but we can't. We can't question everybody in nearby towns, look through police records, hospital records – all the things one would need to do to come up with possible suspects for a murder like this. And even then – if our murderer is a twisted reclusive chap, brooding and plotting from his bedroom, we may have no way of finding him until he makes a mistake.'

'You think he'll make a mistake?' I asked.

'They always do in the end,' Granddad said. 'He can wipe away fingerprints, work hard to make every death look like an accident, but in the end he'll slip up.'

'I'd still like to look at the other crime scenes for myself,' I said. 'And since we have the car, why not?'

'Because it's cold,' Darcy said.

After a mile or so I had to agree with him. Monty's motor was an open-topped Alvis Tourer, so we were exposed to the freezing wind. It wasn't so bad in the front seat, behind the windshield, but I was perched in the poor excuse for a back seat and the wind hit me full in the face. We sat huddled together as we climbed a hill and then down again into Newton Abbot. I noticed that Klein's Jewelers had a notice saying *Closed* on the front door. The robbery had clearly upset Mr Klein enough that he hadn't felt like opening his shop again. We found the telephone exchange with two girls working at a makeshift switchboard at a table, while the other end of the room was a blackened mess of burned-out wires. We made Darcy our spokesman, sensing correctly that girls like that would be more willing to talk to a handsome man. And after his initial questions they glanced at him shyly and said they'd do anything they could to help 'poor Glad.'

'I always said she had it coming,' one of them said, looking at the other for confirmation. 'She loved to listen in on the calls and she was a terrible gossip, wasn't she, Lil?'

The other nodded. 'I told her she was going to get in trouble one day for repeating things like that.'

'Did she ever repeat to you any of the things she'd heard?' Darcy asked.

'She did sometimes – you know, if someone was seeing somebody else's wife. She liked that kind of thing. Crazy about the pictures, she was – romance and drama.'

'So you think that what happened to her wasn't an accident?' I asked carefully.

'I don't see as how it could have been,' Lil said. 'I mean, who would ever connect up electric wires to a telephone switchboard? Only someone who didn't know what they were doing, and nobody like that has ever been in here. We ain't had no kind of work done, or outsiders in here.'

'There was that man about the clock,' the other girl reminded her.

'Oh, right. A man came in the other day – day before poor Glad's tragedy, it were. Said he was sent to repair the clock. He weren't here long, fiddled about a bit and then he went.'

'What did he look like?'

'Nothing much. About forty-something, I'd say. Thin bloke. Big mustache. Glasses. Wearing overalls.'

'He didn't give his name or say who had sent him?'

'We were busy. He seemed to know what he was doing, and he said he'd been sent from the town hall, so we left him to it.'

'Thank you,' Darcy said. 'You've been most helpful.'

'Do you reckon they'll ever catch the person what did this?' Lil asked.

'We hope so,' Darcy said. 'Oh, and tell me – did Gladys have anyone who might have carried a grudge against her? An old boyfriend, maybe? A neighbor she had annoyed?'

They frowned, thinking. 'Like I said' – the other girl glanced at Lil before speaking – 'she did like to gossip so maybe that got her in trouble. But she weren't the sort for boyfriends. Not much of a catch, you might say. She got her romance from the cinema.'

'Should we go to the town hall?' I asked as we came out again to the busy high street. 'They'd know who was sent to repair a clock, wouldn't they?'

'I don't see how that could have any bearing on Gladys,' Darcy said. 'If he'd rigged up the switchboard to kill somebody while he was there, he'd have killed one of the other girls before Gladys came on duty in the early morning.'

'You know what I'm thinking?' Granddad commented. 'They let us in and chatted to us easily enough. Who is to say that people don't often pop in for a chat and that they don't even remember them afterward?'

'Good point,' Darcy said. 'Emphasizing that we're on a wild-goose chase.'

'Fine,' I said angrily. 'You've made it quite clear that I'm an idiot and we're wasting our time.'

I started walking fast toward the motorcar. Darcy hurried to catch up with me. 'Nobody says you're an idiot. I just don't think we have any way of achieving what you hope to achieve. We're amateurs, Georgie. We have no access to police records.'

'He's right, ducks,' Granddad said. 'The only way to solve

this, in my thinking, is to find a local person who has shown himself in the past to be antisocial or warped or hostile. You know, the kind who writes letters to the local newspaper about his neighbor's radio being too loud or the greengrocer raising the cost of potatoes. I think we'll find each of the victims teed him off in a way that wouldn't bother you or me.'

'Then could we go through the past issues of the newspaper and see if anything stands out?'

'That would take days,' Darcy said. 'And I expect the police are already thinking along those lines.'

I sighed. 'All right. Let's go home. I give up. There's no point in looking where the butcher's van drove off the road because anyone could have hidden behind a big rock and jumped out to make him swerve. And I was the one who found the master of hounds's horse and the only person I saw up there was Wild Sal and she's behind bars.'

'Then let's go back, have a good lunch and forget about it,' Darcy said. 'No, don't look at me like that. I'm not being callous, just realistic. And who knows, maybe we'll come to the end of the day with no more deaths.'

'We could drive over to that farm and see where the farmer's wife died,' I said as we reached the motor and Darcy opened the door for me.

'And question the cow?' Darcy said.

My grandfather laughed. For some reason I couldn't find it funny. I climbed into the car with a haughty 'I'm not amused' expression still on my face.

Darcy touched my hand. 'Smile, Georgie. You can't carry this on your shoulders. What could we hope to learn from looking at a cow barn? The only thing that would be interesting to see is whether the doctor agreed that death was caused by a single kick to the head.'

'I wonder whether he has a surgery in this town or was called in from Exeter.' I was already looking around.

'It wouldn't be right to go and see the doctor without permission from the inspector,' Granddad said. 'I'm sorry, love, but I agree with Darcy. There ain't much more we can do on our own. Best go back to your posh house and enjoy yourselves.'

Darcy revved the motor and we drove back to the hall. I sat fuming with frustration, but I knew in my heart they were right. If only I had something to go on, some vital clue, some thread that linked the deaths. As we drove I tried to rack my brains about things I might have seen. There had been a couple of occasions when a thought had passed through my head, too fleetingly to grab on to, that I had just witnessed something important. But I could no longer remember what those moments were. As a detective, I was a hopeless failure.

Chapter 29

Still December 28
Suffering from near frostbite.

When we arrived back at Gorzley Hall we found everyone in a state of excitement about the ball. The clatter of a sewing machine came from a back room and I gathered that one of the local women had been conscripted to make alterations. People were rummaging through the dressing-up trunk, calling out things like, 'Will this do?'

Junior Wexler ran past. 'I'm going to be a Redcoat!' he called. 'I'm going to borrow a real uniform and a real gun.'

'Oh, there you are, Georgiana.' Lady Hawse-Gorzley appeared in the doorway, looking frazzled. 'I wondered where you had disappeared to.'

'I went out with Darcy and my grandfather to see if there was anything we could do to help solve these murders,' I said.

She glanced around in case any guests were within hearing distance. 'I thought you said they'd arrested Wild Sal,' she whispered.

'They have. But a farmer's wife died after Sal was in jail.'

'The whole thing is extraordinary and unbelievable,' she said, shaking her head. 'Especially in our little neck of the woods. Did you discover anything?'

'Nothing at all,' I said. 'I feel quite frustrated, but we've nothing to go on.'

'It's not your problem, my dear. You are supposed to be having fun with everyone else. You have your costume for tonight, I hope. All the best ones have been snapped up. Oh, and I hope you don't mind – I had a word with your maid and asked her to help Mrs Upthorpe and Mrs Rathbone dress tonight. Our Martha can help Mrs Wexler and Bunty.'

I tried not to let my face betray that being dressed by Queenie might be something fraught with danger. Should I perhaps warn Mrs Upthorpe and Mrs Rathbone that my maid had in the past done such things as setting fire to her employer?

'What about Mrs Sechrest?' I asked. My mind went immediately to that white figure creeping down the corridor in the night.

'The Sechrests have gone home and will be dressing there. I wonder what she'll wear this year. She always goes in for frightfully elaborate costumes. Last year she was Nell Gwyn.' I tried not to smile at this.

I went to find Queenie to try to instill in her the fear of God and dismissal from my service, but she seemed pleased with herself that she was going to act as lady's maid to all and sundry. 'They don't have no more proper maids like me here, so her ladyship actually begged me to help them get dressed.'

'She had no idea what you're like, Queenie. Please try not to do anything too stupid, for my sake.'

'I always try, miss. It's just that sometimes things happen.'

At least she hadn't been asked to dress the dowager countess.

I went through the dressing-up box and found my red scarf and gold earrings, then I noticed a long black wig and added that. It's amazing how a difference in hair color changes a personality, isn't it? When I tried on the costume I looked quite sultry, like a Mediterranean temptress. I was rather pleased with my choice, especially as Darcy would be my gypsy partner.

Lady Hawse-Gorzley served a high tea at five, as we would be having a late supper at the ball. This included boiled eggs and Welsh rarebit as well as the usual tea fare and took me back to nursery days when Nanny and I would share such a meal in our own little world. How long ago that seemed now.

Around seven everyone dispersed to prepare for the ball. I told Queenie I could dress myself and sent her off to help the other ladies. As I stood alone in my room I realized that the day was almost over and nobody had died. Maybe our surmise had been true after all – the farmer's wife had been an accident and Wild Sal had been responsible for at least some of the other deaths. I felt a great wave of relief sweep over me. I realized that I had been almost holding my breath, waiting for the next stroke of doom to fall. I was almost ready, only fiddling with tying the scarf around my false locks, when I heard an awful scream. I came flying out of my room, as did those around me. The scream was coming from the far end of the hallway and we raced down it, flinging open a door.

The sight inside was not a pretty one. Mrs Upthorpe was standing in front of a mirror, wearing a Marie Antoinette costume and screaming her lungs out while Queenie stood behind her with a look of terror on her face.

'What's wrong?' I asked.

'The stupid girl has zipped me,' she shouted, her broad North Country vowels coming through in this moment of stress. 'Now she can't get it open again.'

That didn't sound too bad until I saw that what Queenie had done was to catch a fold of Mrs Upthorpe's copious skin in the teeth of the zip fastener and, being Queenie, to keep on tugging. It took several minutes and a great deal of comforting of the distraught Mrs Upthorpe before we managed to release her back from the zip fastener. There was an ugly red welt that was bleeding in places where the teeth had been.

'Queenie, go and ask the butler for first aid supplies,' I said.

'No, don't send that girl. She'll probably come back with caustic soda or weed killer,' Mrs Upthorpe wailed.

'I'll go,' I said and dragged Queenie out with me. 'How could you?' I demanded as soon as we were clear of the room. 'I asked you to be careful.'

'I was,' she said. 'I ain't too used to them zip fasteners and I thought it was just stiff. How was I to know I'd got her caught in it? She don't half have a lot of flesh.'

I sighed. 'I suppose you'd better go help Mrs Rathbone, since Lady Hawse-Gorzley promised you would,' I said.

'I already been with her. She sent me away because I stuck a hatpin in her bum by mistake.'

'Queenie!'

'It didn't make her bleed or nothing. And she shouldn't have turned round so quickly. I don't know why she made such a fuss.'

'What am I going to do with you, Queenie?'

'I never mean no harm, miss,' she said, staring at me with those big cow eyes.

'I know you don't. But you're a walking disaster area all the same.'

I brought Dettol, cotton wool and Cuticura cream to Mrs Upthorpe, who was finally pacified when she saw that the wound would be hidden by the fabric of her dress. Downstairs I could hear the sound of motorcar tires on the gravel as the first guests arrived. I put on the finishing touches to my costume and went down to the ballroom. What an incredible transformation had taken place. The chandeliers in the ceiling were ablaze with electric lights while around the wall tall candelabras sparkled with real candles. Small white-clothed tables, gilt chairs and large potted plants created an air of elegance and on a dais at one end a band was playing a jazz tune. Nobody was dancing yet, but various guests in an interesting array of costumes stood chatting – I saw a black cat, a fat schoolboy and Cleopatra, and someone was even the gorilla. Captain and Mrs Sechrest were among them, he dressed as King Neptune and she as a water sprite with yards of flowing tulle and a sea-green wig, all dotted with pearls and shells. I noticed Johnnie Protheroe eyeing her. He was dressed as a knight of the Round Table, probably Sir Lancelot, and I thought it was a pity the Sechrests hadn't chosen to come as Arthur and Guinevere.

Then the Wexlers came in, he dressed as a cowboy, she as an Indian. Cherie, as a Spanish señorita, looked as if she were about to die of embarrassment. Only Junior seemed to be having a good time, and he went around poking people with his gun. I hoped the Wexlers had checked to make sure it wasn't loaded. The Rathbones and Upthorpes joined us, she still looking pale and suffering. Badger, dressed as a cat burglar, made a beeline for Ethel. The band struck up 'On the Sunny Side of the Street' and couples moved onto the dance floor. I experienced that moment of panic I always feel at balls – that I'll be the only wallflower after everyone else has chosen a partner. It's quite an irrational fear, as I suspect I'm asked to dance as often as anyone else, but I can't stop it.

Ethel bounced past with Badger, whose dancing looked more enthusiastic than skillful. Monty was with the no-longer-pouting Cherie. I saw Bunty, as a Jane Austen heroine, looking around hopefully and her eyes lit up as Darcy crossed the floor. But to my secret delight he headed straight for me. 'My brown-eyed gypsy maiden, I presume,' he said and held out his hand to me. We danced. It was heavenly.

The ballroom filled with people I didn't know, then some I did. I saw the Misses Ffrench-Finch sitting with Miss Prendergast, the vicar and Mr Barclay at a table in the corner. They were not in costume but were enjoying themselves watching the spectacle, nodding in time to the music. I remembered that my mother and Noël Coward had promised to come so I searched until I spotted them. He was a maharaja, with darkened face, impressive curly black mustache and huge turban, and she was a veiled Eastern beauty. I went over to them between dances.

'You recognized us,' my mother said in a peeved voice. 'We thought we were incognito.'

'You are my mother,' I laughed. 'I recognized your eyes beneath the veil. Mr Coward was harder to detect because of the mustache.'

'I know, isn't it splendid? We found it in Woolworths.

And this is much more grand and civilized than I expected,'
Noël Coward said. 'I thought it would be full of clodhopping
peasants.'

I danced with Darcy again and then with Monty and
even once with Johnnie Protheroe, who held me very close
indeed, although he kept glancing across at the lovely Mrs
Sechrest. Then we had a Paul Jones, in which ladies and men
circle each other and each lady must dance with the man
opposite her when the music stops. I found myself dancing
with the man with whom I had conversed about the master's
horse at the hunt.

'Rum do the other day, wasn't it?' he said as he twirled
me around. 'Still no trace of him. Must have ended up in
the bog, poor chap. What a way to go and who would have
thought it of someone like him? Knew the country around
here like the back of his hand.'

I nodded. 'It's horrible.'

'They're saying that someone put up a wire to deliberately trip his horse. If I find the blighter I'll personally put
my hands around his scrawny neck and strangle him.' He
realized that he was shouting, gave an embarrassed cough
and resumed dancing. 'Can't let a thing like that ruin our
evening, can we?' he added.

At around ten a 'Post Horn Galop' led us in to supper – a
magnificent buffet with cold poached salmon, cold chicken,
a York ham and a cold leg of pork with sage stuffing, as well
as various pies, pasties, jellies, blancmanges and petit fours.
I wondered how the gorilla was going to eat, but I couldn't
spot him.

After supper the music became slower and fewer couples
took to the floor. French doors had been opened, as the
room was becoming rather warm, and I suppose there must

have been a sudden gust of wind because I heard a shout and a scream. I looked around just in time to see one of the candelabras toppling over. Sandra Sechrest was standing beside it. She tried to get out of the way but it fell onto her trailing skirt and we watched in horror as those yards of filmy tulle went up in flames.

Chapter 30

Still December 28
A horrible ending to the day.

Sandra Sechrest screamed as the flames engulfed her. There
was a horrid crackling sound and a smell of acrid smoke as
the long shimmering wig burst into flame. Futilely she tried
to run. For a long moment nobody else moved. Then several men sprang into action. Johnnie Protheroe reached her
first. He flung her to the floor, locked her in an embrace and
rolled over with her.

'Get away from my wife, you swine,' Captain Sechrest
bellowed.

'I'm saving her life, you damned idiot,' Johnnie shouted
back as he staggered to his feet and stamped on the last of the
flaming fabric. His face was streaked with soot and his gorgeous knight's outfit was now also scorched and blackened.

The two men stood there glaring at each other while Sir
Oswald, Darcy and a couple of others were down on their
knees around Mrs Sechrest. She was moaning and sobbing
hysterically and she looked horrible – a blackened, frizzled

mess of charred fabric and hair. Someone covered her with a tablecloth.

'Is the telephone working again?' Bunty asked. 'We should call for an ambulance.'

'We can't afford to wait for an ambulance,' Sir Oswald said. 'I'll drive her to the hospital myself.'

'I'll come with you, Dad,' Monty said.

'And I want to be with my wife,' Captain Sechrest said, pushing in front of Monty.

'Lift her carefully. She's in a lot of pain,' Sir Oswald said. 'I'll go and get the motor.'

We watched in silence as the somber procession left the room in eerie silence. Mrs Sechrest no longer moaned.

'Awful. Absolutely shocking. I can't believe it.' Voices murmured around me.

'How can that have happened?' someone asked.

'That open French window. Must have blown over the candelabra.'

Miss Prendergast had made her way over to the spot and was down on her knees. 'That melting wax is ruining your lovely parquet floor, Lady Hawse-Gorzley,' she said as she attempted to pick up the still burning candles. 'We should do something about it quickly.'

'Be careful, Miss Prendergast, or you'll burn yourself,' Lady Hawse-Gorzley said. 'The servants will take care of it.' And indeed a footman and a maid were hurrying toward the smoldering wreck.

A couple of guests helped them to right the candelabra. I watched them struggling with it. What sort of wind could have blown over a heavy object like that and yet not have blown out the candles? And then, of course, the next logical thought: Was it possible that the killer had struck again, just before midnight? I looked around the room, trying to picture where Mrs Sechrest had been standing when it happened. Close to that open French door, obviously – which meant that the killer could have crept in from the outside, giving the candelabra a push at the right moment, and then vanished again. Either that or he was still in the room. I looked from person to person, trying to see if anyone was showing undue interest or even emotion. But all the faces appeared stunned and shocked. What's more, most of them were disguised beyond recognition. A perfect setting if you wanted to kill somebody.

Johnnie Protheroe had been one of those carrying Mrs Sechrest to the motorcar. He came back, white-faced.

'God, I need a drink,' he said. 'Something stronger than punch.'

'I'll get you a brandy,' Lady Hawse-Gorzley said. She summoned the nearby footman. 'A brandy for Mr Protheroe, and hurry.' He sprinted off.

'I can't believe how quickly her outfit went up in flames,' Johnnie said.

'That kind of fabric is horribly flammable,' said Lady Hawse-Gorzley. 'I suppose we were stupid to open the French doors, but people were complaining they were too hot. In fact, I believe she was the one who was complaining.' She paused. 'No, it was her husband who came over and said his wife was too hot, could we open the doors.'

The band leader approached from across the floor. 'Do you want us to resume playing, my lady?' he asked reverently.

She looked at Johnnie. 'I really don't think anyone will feel like dancing after this, do you?'

'No, I'd send them home if I were you.'

I felt I had to say something. 'Wait a minute,' I said.

'Shouldn't someone go for the police before you let people leave?'

'The police?' Johnnie looked alarmed.

I felt self-conscious with everyone's eyes on me, and flushed scarlet. 'I mean, after all these strange deaths, we should consider the possibility that these accidents are not accidents at all.'

'You mean someone deliberately pushed that candelabra onto Sandra Sechrest?' Lady Hawse-Gorzley glared at me in disbelief. 'That's not possible. These are my invited guests. I know them all.'

Johnnie shook his head. 'I don't think it was possible. I was watching her and she was standing alone. Actually, I was plucking up courage to go over and ask her to dance, in spite of that bear of a husband of hers. But there was nobody within three or four feet of her.'

'There was nobody standing near the candelabra?' I asked.

'Well, her husband was hovering nearby, I suppose,' Johnnie said.

I really didn't want to consider the next thought – that Captain Sechrest has just found out about his wife's affair with Johnnie Protheroe and was taking his revenge. I had seen what an emotional and quick-tempered man he could be. Maybe he did it in a sudden rush of jealousy and then instantly regretted it. But at last I was looking at a crime for which there was a clear motive. I glanced around the room, wondering if I should voice this opinion or keep quiet. I saw Darcy coming back in, having helped to carry Mrs Sechrest to the motor.

'I was just saying that I thought the police would want to take a look before we let the guests go home,' I said. 'What do you think?'

It was clear this hadn't occurred to him either. He glanced up with a shocked expression. 'You're not trying to suggest that this is the next attempt at murder, are you?' He shook his head. 'No, that's going too far, Georgie. We can see how it happened. The wind blew over the candelabra. Mrs Sechrest was unlucky enough to be standing in the wrong place. Accidents with fire happen all the time, don't they?'

'Yes, but . . .' I locked eyes with him, trying to convey that I suspected more than I wanted to voice out loud. He picked up the cue.

'Well, I suppose there was an open window, which meant anybody could have sneaked in from the outside. Is your telephone working?'

'It wasn't the last time we tried, but I believe the police station in the village has its line up and running again.'

'We were about to leave anyway, Lady Hawse-Gorzley.' Mr Barclay had come over to join us. 'Might we be of assistance and relay your message to the police station?'

'Most kind, Mr Barclay. And I'm so sorry that a merry evening has had to end in such tragedy.'

'We are sorry too,' Miss Prendergast said, helping one of the Misses Ffrench-Finch across the room. 'But it was a splendid evening and we are so grateful that you allowed us to be part of it. I did so enjoy watching the dancing, and the lovely buffet.'

'Yes, indeed,' the two Misses Ffrench-Finch twittered.

And so they departed. Other guests hovered around, not sure what to do next.

'Should we also be toddling along, Lady H-G?' the huntsman who had danced with me asked. 'I'm sure nobody feels much like dancing after witnessing such a shocking thing.'

'I'd be grateful if you stayed a little longer, Mr Crawley.

The police are being summoned and they may want to get statements from witnesses.'

'Police?' Crawley spat out the word. 'What the deuce have police to do with this? It was an accident, madam. I actually saw the damned thing fall. Nobody near it, I can attest to that.'

'Then perhaps if you'd be good enough to stay, and any others who saw the actual accident, we can allow everyone else to go home.'

'And I to my bed,' the dowager countess said. 'That woman was asking for trouble with all that trailing fabric near live flames.' And she stomped off, clearing a way through the crowd with her stick.

'I think we should go to bed too,' Colonel Rathbone said. 'This has quite upset my wife and she's not a well woman.'

My mother sidled over to me. 'Noël wants to stay in case anything exciting happens, but I feel it's too, too ghoulish. I can't get that image out of my mind – that poor woman going up in flames. I said to Noël, "That could have been me." I'm sure this fabric is just as flammable as hers.' She put her hand up to my cheek and patted it. 'We'll see you tomorrow, I suppose. Noël is frightfully keen to watch the ridiculous Lovey Chase thing. I expect it's all those young men in shorts and singlets that excites him.' She cast a wicked smile in Mr Coward's direction as she went to join him.

One by one the guests departed until the ballroom had that abandoned feel of the day after a party. I took Darcy aside and murmured my suspicion to him. He frowned, considering this. 'Frankly, if he'd wanted to do away with her, a simple cigarette to her skirt would have done the trick, wouldn't it?'

'Maybe,' I said. 'Maybe he wasn't taking any chances.

All those candles at once meant that her costume would catch fire in many places. And there was a chance she'd be knocked out as well, therefore not able to do anything.'

'You're a grizzly little thing, aren't you?' He slipped his arms around me, gazing down at me fondly. 'And I was so looking forward to my last waltz with you – a chance to dance cheek to cheek.'

'There will be other chances, I hope,' I said. 'Right now I wish we could escape from here. Until now it was people we didn't know. Now it's finally come here. I can't stop wondering who will be next.'

One of the footmen was about to close the French doors. 'I don't think you should touch anything until the police arrive,' I called to him. He looked startled, but stepped away. I went over to stand beside the candelabra. 'Was this exactly where it stood before?' I asked.

The footman looked around the room at where the other candelabras had been placed. 'Pretty much, my lady. Maybe a few inches to the left.'

I went to move it and couldn't. It was too heavy for me. And as I held the shaft in my hand I looked down and saw something moving in the strong wind that was now blowing icy cold air into the room. I dropped to my knees. 'Look at this,' I whispered to Darcy. It was a small piece of black thread caught on one of the curly legs of the candelabra.

Chapter 31

Inspector Newcombe arrived about a half hour later. He looked bleary-eyed and grumpy, as if he had been roused from his bed. He took statements from those who had seen the candelabra topple. Nobody recalled seeing anyone standing nearby. I suddenly thought of the person in the gorilla suit I had noticed at the beginning of the evening. I hadn't seen him since supper. I mentioned him and no one had any idea who he was.

'Any other time I would have guessed it was old Freddie, if he hadn't . . . you know,' Mr Crawley, my hunting friend, said. 'Just the sort of thing he'd do. Probably would have swung from the chandeliers too.'

Nobody had seen the gorilla leave. He hadn't appeared at supper. Certainly he hadn't been seen standing any-where near the candelabra, so the inspector dismissed him as unimportant. A constable was dusting around the French door for fingerprints. I waited until the inspector went over to examine the candelabra, then brought his attention to the piece of thread that had been caught on one of its legs.

'You're suggesting that this was attached to the candelabra and at the right moment someone tugged it over?' he asked.

I nodded.

'It's a thin sort of cotton to shift a great thing like that.'

'I suspect it's something like button thread, which is quite strong,' I said, fingering it. 'But the candelabra is clearly top-heavy and the least little jerk might have achieved the desired effect.'

He stared at the open door, the candelabra and the spots of melted wax still on the floor.

'So you want me to believe that someone rigged up a way to topple the candelabra in the hopes that Mrs Sechrest might come and stand in the right spot sometime during the evening? That seems like a long shot to me, especially when it might be rather hard to stand anywhere alone in a crowded ballroom.'

I sighed. 'I agree, unless she wasn't particularly the intended target. If someone just wanted to cause mischief and chose a target at random, that would be different.' Or if her husband wanted to get rid of her, he'd simply push the candelabra over onto her, I thought, but I couldn't bring myself to say those words. Instead I said, 'We have to assume this was today's intended death, don't we?'

'Ah. Do we?' He rubbed his chin, which was in clear need of shaving. 'I had a word with the lord lieutenant of the county and he decided we shouldn't call in Scotland Yard on this matter. It was his feeling that we can't prove we're looking at a single murder here. We've no motive, no clues, no weapons.'

'What about Wild Sal? Presumably you arrested her because she was seen near the spot where the master of hounds vanished and her footprints were seen where the van went off the road.'

'Ah,' he said again. 'I've had to release her. The lord lieutenant felt that we had no real evidence against her. Purely circumstantial, he said.'

'What about the wound to the horse's leg? We know that was deliberate.'

'Not necessarily. Could have been trying to jump a wire sheep fence and hit the top strand.' He tried to give me a kindly look. 'Look, we could speculate that some of the deaths were intentional – that telephone switchboard incident is definitely fishy, if you ask me. So maybe the telephone switchboard girl had overheard something she shouldn't and needed to be silenced. Blackmailing someone, perhaps. I could go along with that. Maybe the old lady had been bullying her sisters or someone else in the house and they turned on the gas tap. That would make sense too. But there was no possible connection between them, was there? The lord lieutenant said he felt that we were just looking at a run of unlucky accidents, and that such things happen from time to time.'

'So you won't investigate this as a potential crime?'

He rubbed his chin again. 'When I thought that the convicts might be responsible, I did try to find forensic evidence of a crime at the scenes. Didn't come up with anything, though. But there would be no reason for a convict to risk going into the middle of a busy town, where he might be spotted, to cross-wire a switchboard, and no reason for him to be anywhere near the farm where the woman was kicked by a cow.'

'So maybe that one could really have been an accident,' I conceded.

'We've no witnesses to any of the incidents, unless you count tonight. I've tried to take fingerprints but the room with the telephone switchboard was badly burned. There were no strange prints in the old lady's bedroom. And the rest of the deaths happened outdoors. So until I find someone lying with a bloody great knife stuck in his back I'm afraid I'm going to have to drop the idea of a mass murderer at work. I never quite believed it, anyway. Didn't make sense, did it?'

'I suppose not,' I said, fighting back my anger. 'So how long are you going to let these deaths continue? Until January? February? Summer? The local population will be seriously depleted by then, won't it?'

He winced as if I had struck him and immediately I felt bad. He was just doing his job, following orders from much higher up, and I wasn't actually angry with him. I simply was frustrated that none of us had managed to do anything to stop people from dying.

'I think we should all go to bed,' he said. 'We're all tired and there's nothing more we can do here tonight.' He summoned the constable who had been dusting for fingerprints, and the two of them left. Darcy came to my side as I made my way up the stairs.

'Cheer up, old thing,' he said and put his arm around my shoulder. 'I know it's upsetting to see something like that, but there's nothing more we can do.'

'We just have to wait for someone to die tomorrow, is that what you are saying?'

'I'm saying that there is a perfectly good police force in the village and we need to leave it to them. Oh, and we watch our backs too, just in case.'

'It's lucky we're not from around here, isn't it?' I said.

He looked down at me. 'Well, I suppose you can say I have local ties. My mother was born in Devon. Lady Hawse-Gorzley's my aunt.'

'Yes, but you are not known to the killer, are you? If it is one person, he must have a reason for choosing these particular people. It must be some kind of vendetta.'

'Do you believe he was here tonight? In the ballroom?'

I stared ahead as we reached the top of the staircase and the long corridors stretched away from us into darkness. 'There was that man in the gorilla suit. Nobody knew who he was and we didn't see him toward the end of the evening.'

Darcy frowned. 'If he's as clever as he appears to be, then I think you should not interfere. I don't want some "accident" happening to you.'

I rested my head on his shoulder as we walked down the hall. We reached my bedroom. 'Good night.' I turned to give him a kiss on the cheek.

'Is that it?' he asked. His hands grasped my shoulders and he pulled me toward him, his lips coming to meet mine in a demanding kiss. I felt myself responding to him, my body melting against his as his arms slid around me, crushing me to him. When we broke apart breathlessly, I remembered where we were.

'I don't suppose we should be doing this in the corridor,' I whispered. 'Someone might come.'

He looked down at me. 'Then let's continue somewhere more private.' He opened the door to my room. 'Oh, good, your maid has conveniently gone to bed.' His eyes were dark with desire as he gazed down at me and went to usher me inside my room. I hesitated, suddenly unsure. What was wrong with me? I asked myself. This was Darcy, the man of my dreams. Wasn't this exactly what I wanted? And hadn't I begged him to stay a few nights ago? Then without warning I burst into tears – as much of a shock to me as it was to him.

'That's what she did and look what happened to her,' I blurted out.

He closed the door hastily behind us, then his arms came around me. 'Wait a minute. Who did what?'

'Mrs Sechrest. I saw her creeping down the hall to someone else's bedroom, and now she's probably dead.'

'You think the killer is striking down sinners?' he asked.

'I don't know.' I was still blubbering.

He was trying not to smile as he stroked my black gypsy hair back from my face. 'You are adorable sometimes,' he said. 'I'm sure that tonight's horrible tragedy upset you. It upset all of us. But you're not in the same boat as Mrs Sechrest, are you? She is married to someone else. And you and I care about each other, don't we?'

'I know,' I said and sank down onto my bed, my face in my hands. 'It's just that . . . it's all been too horrible. So many horrible things happening. I don't feel safe.'

He stood looking down at me tenderly and then he said, 'It's all right. I probably need a good night's sleep if I'm to compete in that ridiculous race in the morning.' He bent to kiss me gently on the forehead. 'Sleep well. And Georgie – I don't think I've actually said this before, but I'm saying it now. I love you.'

I looked up at him. 'I love you too,' I said. He was about to walk away when I grabbed his hand. 'Don't go,' I whispered and pulled him down to the bed beside me.

He sat looking at me for a moment, then he removed my gypsy wig and ran his fingers lightly through my own hair. 'Don't worry,' he said. 'I'll take care of you, my little gypsy lass.' Then he started to undo the buttons on my lacy white blouse. Improbably, I found myself wondering if Queenie had fallen asleep or, heaven forbid, she was attempting to undress one of the other ladies. I didn't hear any screams, so I had to conclude it was the former. Darcy slid the blouse from my shoulders then drew a finger gently down my front, tracing lightly the curve of my breast. I felt a strong surge of desire that wiped all thoughts of Queenie or anyone else from my mind. I wanted him. I wanted him badly.

His hands had just moved around to the catch of my brassiere when the door opened suddenly, sending a stream of light into the room and making us both look up, blinking.

'I came to undress you, my lady,' Queenie said stiffly, 'but I see that the gentleman is already helping you.'

Darcy got to his feet. 'Lady Georgiana was distressed by tonight's tragedy,' he said. 'She needed comforting.'

'Comforting, is that what you call it, sir?' She looked at me. 'Should I go away again, then?'

Darcy looked down at me and smiled. 'No, it's all right, Queenie. You can take care of your mistress. She's had a long day.'

He blew me a kiss and he was gone.

'Sorry about that, miss,' she said. 'I didn't mean to interrupt nothing.'

'Mr O'Mara only escorted me to my room because I was upset,' I said primly.

'Go on,' she said, giving me a nudge. 'You were going to have a bit of the old "how's-yer-father," weren't you?'

'Queenie,' I said severely. 'That is not how a lady's maid talks to her employer. You may go. I'll finish undressing myself.'

'I didn't mean no harm, miss,' she said.

'I'm tired,' I said. 'Just go.'

She closed the door and I sat in the darkness, not moving. All the unsettling events of the day flashed through my mind, followed by one overwhelming fact: Darcy loved me. A smile came over my face until I let the worry surface from the depths of my consciousness. He loved me. I loved him. But we couldn't ever marry.

Chapter 32

Gorzley Hall
December 29
Day of the Lovey Chase but beastly weather. I hope nothing will go wrong. I wish Darcy wasn't taking part in it.

I was awakened by Queenie with a tea tray.

'Morning, my lady,' she said. 'Bloody awful day. Fog so thick it reminds me of back home in London. I don't half wish we was there now.'

I looked out the window, where only the first trees in the orchard were visible and Lovey Tor didn't exist.

'Oh, crikey,' I said. 'I wonder if they'll be able to run the Lovey Chase in this weather.'

Queenie put down the tray on the bedside table. 'I'm sorry I barged in on you last night,' she said. 'I should have scarpered off and left you to it. He's a bit of all right, ain't he? The cat's whiskers, I'd say.' And she gave me a wink.

'Queenie, I doubt that any other lady's maid in the world would speak to her mistress the way you do.'

'Like what, miss?' she asked. 'I was only having a nice little chat with you. Friendly, like.'

I was about to say that we were not friends, she was my servant. But I couldn't do it. I got out of bed and sighed. I had to accept that she would never learn, that she would never be employable elsewhere and that I was stuck with her.

'It's going to be freezing watching that race,' I said. 'You'd better put out my warmest jumper and my tartan trousers. This is one of the occasions when I wish I owned a fur coat.'

'You could always borrow mine, miss,' she said.

I tried to keep a straight face. Queenie's ancient fur coat was mangy and spiky and made her look like an aged hedgehog. 'Awfully good of you, Queenie, but I think not,' I said.

I was in the midst of getting dressed when a bell rang in the hallway outside my door. 'One hour to the start of the chase,' Lady Hawse-Gorzley's powerful voice called. 'Everyone needs a hearty breakfast today so get a move on.'

I finished dressing and went downstairs; I met Darcy going into the breakfast room.

'Did you sleep well?' he asked, a challenging smile in his eyes.

'I did, thank you.' I noticed he was dressed in thick corduroy trousers and a big fisherman's jersey. 'You're not going to run the race in those clothes, are you?'

'I have my racing gear on underneath,' he said. 'And I will not reveal it until I really have to. Frankly, I'd like to back out, but it would be rather letting the side down.'

We helped ourselves to a generous breakfast and joined others at the table. The mood was remarkably cheerful considering what had happened the previous night. Johnnie Protheroe came to sit beside me. 'You've heard the news, have you? Captain Sechrest called in on his way from the hospital this morning. Sandy has some nasty burns but they are not life-threatening. She's going to be all right.'

'That is good news,' I said, and I saw the relief in his face. He really cares about her, I thought. He cares about her and she's married to someone else. What a complicated world this is. And then I realized something else. If this was yesterday's planned murder, then the killer had finally made his mistake. His victim was going to live and she might have some idea why she was a target.

Breakfast finished, we wrapped ourselves up in scarves and hats and walked down the drive. Mist swirled about us and the bare bones of trees loomed like giant skeletons. However, there was already a festive atmosphere in the village, with bunting strung between buildings and signs to a car park behind the shop. On the far side of the village green some booths had been set up. We went through a gap in the hedge and were charged fourpence admission by a young Boy Scout. Folding seats had been set beside what looked, through the mist, like a real racetrack, only the fences were, as Junior had described, two feet high at the most. Quite a few people had arrived from elsewhere and the stalls selling hot cider, roasted chestnuts and baked potatoes were doing a good trade. So were the bookies. I could see on a blackboard that Monty appeared to be the current favorite. Darcy was at ten to one. I joined the line for one of the bookies and placed my bet on him.

'Isn't this kind of gambling illegal?' Mrs Wexler asked.

'It's for charity,' the vicar said hastily. 'The restoration of the church, you know. And you'll see that the police are well represented in the crowd.'

I left the seats for the older people and stood behind one of the booths, which offered some shelter from the bitter cold. Mist swirled in, swallowing up the tents and then revealing them again. All around me people were laughing, but I couldn't join in their festive mood. All I could think of was that this mist was a perfect opportunity for a killer, and that Darcy would be among those running out there.

'Yoo-hoo, Georgie!' I turned at the sound of my name and spotted two gorgeous mink coats coming toward me. Mr Coward and my mother, both looking equally glamorous, came to join me. 'Hello, my darling.' My mother kissed me about three inches from my cheek. 'So what happened after we left last night? Any news on the poor woman?'

'Nothing much happened. The police decided to call it an accident and the good news is that she's going to be okay.'

'Strange sort of accident,' Mummy said. 'Someone must have bumped into that candle thingie, either accidentally or on purpose. It couldn't have been blown over. Surely it was too solid.'

'I agree,' I said. I looked around. 'Is Granddad here?'

'Mrs Huggins wouldn't let him out of the house. She said it would be too bad for his chest. She's taken to bossing him around lately, I notice.'

'She has her eye on him,' I said.

'Well, why not? Poor old dear. He needs some companionship in his old age,' she said.

'You'd welcome Mrs Huggins as a stepmother?'

A spasm crossed that perfect face. 'Well, if you put it that way, it might be a tad embarrassing. But she does cook well and I find it a comfort to know she's looking after him.'

'He could do with more money.' I decided to be frank.

'Darling, do you think I haven't tried? He claims it's all

German money and he won't touch it. Always was stubborn, you know.'

The sound of a drum interrupted this conversation and the Boys' Brigade band marched in, playing 'The British Grenadiers.' An announcer with a megaphone got up onto a makeshift dais.

'Ladies and gentlemen, welcome to the two hundred and thirty-third running of the Lovey Chase,' he boomed. 'Presenting this year's contestants: From Widecombe, Tony Haslett. From Little Devering, Roland Purbury. From right here in Tiddleton, Monty Hawse-Gorzley. Visiting us from Shropshire, give a hand for a very good sport, Mr Archibald Wetherby. . . .'

The flaps of a big tent were drawn back and out came the most extraordinary apparitions. They were wearing white woolen long johns and long-sleeved woolen undershirts. On their heads were ancient plumed helmets like those worn by the dragoon guards and around their waists were small saddles, with stirrups hanging down to their knees. I don't think I've ever seen anything more ridiculous. There were shouts, jeers, taunts as the young men came out, one by one.

'From Bovey Tracey, Mr Jonathan Protheroe. And from Ireland, the Honorable Darcy O'Mara.' Darcy caught my eye for a brief second and gave me an embarrassed grin.

'Runners to the starting gate, please,' the announcer shouted. Everyone cheered now. 'Five times around the track,' he continued. 'No cheating and cutting corners or running around the jumps in the fog. Anyone not playing fairly will be disqualified.'

The runners lined up along a ribbon laid on the ground. Their breath rose into the frigid air and they looked like a row of warhorses, ready for battle. One of the boys from the band stepped forward with his bugle and sounded the call. The starter waved his flag and they were off. It was soon clear that the saddles and flying stirrups were a bally nuisance. These danced and flew around, hitting other racers and getting in the way as they tried to jump. There was a collision at the first jump as Badger and a hefty lad tried to jump it at the same time. More cheers and jeers. And then they were swallowed up into the mist.

I found I was holding my breath, peering into the mist at the ghostly shapes of the runners. I heaved a sigh of relief as they reappeared a minute later with Monty and Darcy at the front of the pack, together with a slim youth. Badger and Johnnie Protheroe came lumbering up toward the rear of the pack.

Behind me two men were chatting. 'You have your money on young Monty, then? I'm not so sure myself. Don't know if he has the stamina.'

'Who else is there?' the other male voice said. 'If poor old Freddie Partridge had been alive, I'd have backed him. Always a good sport, old Freddie. Who'd have thought he'd shoot himself, what?'

I was holding my breath again, not because I was thinking of the racers this time, but because something incredible had just dawned on me. Something so obvious and simple that I wanted to shout out loud. Freddie Partridge. I believe I had heard his last name before, but it had never really registered. I peered to my right, through the mist, trying to make out the shapes of the first trees in the orchard. And in my head I heard Sir Oswald saying clearly, 'It was a pear tree.'

'Oh, golly,' I said out loud. Freddie had been the first of the deaths and he was the Partridge in a pear tree.

Chapter 33

December 29
The Lovey Chase.

I wasn't even conscious of the race continuing. I vaguely heard cheers as the racers thundered past us, stirrups jangling. But suddenly it all made sense. It all fitted perfectly: Ted Grover had been to visit his lady love, the publican's wife. They were the two turtledoves. And the Misses Ffrench-Finch of course were the three French hens. And Gladys Tripp – she was a calling bird, wasn't she? My heart was hammering so loudly I was sure it must be echoing around that field. And the five gold rings? Mr Klein, the jeweler – the only one the murderer had not tried to kill, for some reason. Mr Skaggs the butcher had been bringing us the geese – which were not a-laying, but a-lying, which might be significant. And the master of hounds had disappeared into the mere where the swans were a-swimming. . . .

And golly, it was true. My instincts were right. The previous night's affair was no accident. Mrs Sechrest was one of the nine ladies dancing, which meant . . . my eyes were suddenly riveted to the track again . . . that these were the ten lords a-leaping.

The first runners emerged from the mist, their breath now ragged and gasping as they came toward us. Monty, Darcy and the thin lad were running neck and neck. One by one the others straggled behind them, fighting for breath. One of them stopped to throw up, then staggered on.

'Last lap,' someone shouted and the crowd cheered them on.

I wanted to leap out and shout for them to stop, but by the time I had plucked up my courage, they had vanished into the mist again. The crowd fell silent. You could feel the anticipation. Then out of the mist came two figures – Monty and Darcy, still running neck and neck. As they reached the finish line Darcy seemed to slack off or Monty put on a surge and he crossed the tape first.

I made my way through the crowd to Darcy. 'Well done, old thing,' I said.

He leaned on me, gasping for breath. 'I wouldn't want to do that again. These stupid saddles are heavy and the stir-rups kept flying up and hitting me.'

'But you came second. That was wonderful.'

He looked up with a grin. 'Well, I thought it was wiser that Monty should win. It is his home territory, after all. Only right that the locals should be able to cheer their landowners.'

I stared at him and had to smile. 'Darcy, you're a snob at heart after all, aren't you?'

'Well, I am going to be Lord Kilhenny someday. I have to get used to the idea.'

I kissed his freezing cheek. 'I'm very proud of you anyway.'

There were renewed cheers as the other runners staggered

in, one by one. I found that I was breathing easier. The race was over and nothing had happened. Then somebody said, 'Where's old Johnnie?'

'Johnnie Protheroe?' another of the runners said. 'He was with me last time I looked. Didn't he come in yet?'

The feeling of doom returned. Several people started back along the course.

'Knowing Johnnie, he probably decided he'd had enough and he's nipped across to the pub,' someone chuckled.

We passed one jump, then a second and a third. Then someone said, 'My God – what's that?'

One of the ridiculous helmets was lying to one side of the track. And there was Johnnie lying half concealed under the hedge that bordered the field. Hands dragged him out. Someone said, 'He's fainted. Get some brandy.'

Then someone else said, 'He hasn't fainted. He's dead.'

'Someone run and get Dr Wainwright. He's over by the tent.'

A couple of younger lads ran off. I stood staring down at Johnnie's dead face. He looked so normal, so peaceful, that I expected him to open his eyes at any moment and say, 'Fooled you all, didn't I?'

But he didn't. The doctor arrived, puffing and panting, his black bag in his hand. He dropped to his knees beside Johnnie and started to examine him. After a while he looked up at the considerable crowd that had now gathered around them. 'Heart,' he said. 'Clearly a heart attack. The fellow was on heart medication, you know. I warned him that he should be taking it easier but he still acted as if he were twenty-one. Someone better call for the ambulance.'

He rose to his feet again. I went over to him. 'Doctor, in

light of all these strange deaths around here, don't you think the police should be called in?'

He gave me a cold stare. 'I've been practicing medicine for thirty years. Do you think I don't recognize a heart attack when I see one?'

'But just in case?'

'An autopsy will be done, of course,' he said. 'But I'd like to wager with one of these bookies here that I am right. The chap had a dicky heart. He overextended himself. Simple as that, young lady.'

The St John Ambulance boys were in attendance in case of accidents and they now arrived with a stretcher. As I watched the body being carried away, the increasingly familiar feeling of dread overwhelmed me. I now knew what the deaths meant and why they were happening to fit in with the Twelve Days of Christmas, but I was not one bit the wiser about why these people were chosen or who had planned this awful farce. Darcy had removed the saddle and helmet and was now dressed in his jersey and corduroys.

'Poor old Johnnie,' he said. 'A bit of a cad, but I rather liked him.'

'In spite of everything, so did I,' I said. 'And I've been trying to make the doctor see that his death was not a heart attack. At least they're going to conduct an autopsy.'

'You think this was today's planned murder, then?' he asked. 'You are not going to budge from your belief that these are planned killings, are you?'

'Because I now have proof that they are,' I said. 'Come over here.' I took his arm and led him away from the crowd. Then I told him exactly what I had figured out. He stared at me in growing wonder. 'A partridge in a pear tree. Of course. Why didn't we see that?'

'Because everyone referred to him as "old Freddie." I believe I did hear his last name once, but that was before I saw his death as any more than a freak accident, so it didn't sink in.'

'Well, you've cracked it now, haven't you? Brilliant,' he said.

I looked past him to the happy revelers, the journalists taking pictures of the winner and copious amounts of either beer or cider being drunk. 'But we are no nearer to solving it, are we? We know that some twisted mind is enjoying a little joke at the expense of people's lives, but we have no way of knowing who or why. They are still such a strange assortment of victims and the killer has been clever enough not to leave evidence.'

'He has left evidence,' Darcy said. 'Two people are still alive. Mr Klein was apparently not harmed, and Mrs Sechrest is going to recover. We have to contact the police right away and have them talk to the survivors. Maybe they will know why someone might have wanted them dead.'

'He didn't want Mr Klein dead,' I said. 'He only took valuable jewelry from him.'

'Either he thought that would be an appropriate punishment for Klein or he had planned a murder that for some reason didn't happen.'

'Let's go see Mr Klein right away, shall we?' I took his hand.

'We have to tell all this to the police first,' Darcy said.

'Since when were you so law-abiding?' I demanded. 'You are the one who taught me how to crash wedding parties and who does all kinds of suspect things around the world.'

'Those are different. This is dealing with people's lives, Georgie. And also it's my aunt's family. I have to do the right thing when I'm staying with her.'

'Very noble,' I said. 'Well, all right. Let's borrow Monty's motor again and go find the hopelessly thick inspector. We can get away now, while they are all celebrating.'

I glanced across at Monty, now drinking something from a large cup while the crowd cheered. We moved silently toward the gap in the hedge, slipped through, then hurried across the village green, up the driveway and around to the garages. A few minutes later we were driving toward Newton Abbot at a snail's pace, with Darcy peering forward through the mist. Luckily nobody else was foolhardy enough to attempt driving in this weather.

'So let's think,' Darcy said, raising his voice over the considerable noise of the engine. 'What does all this tell us about the murderer? Why did he wait until Christmas?'

'So that he could kill twelve people in twelve days?'

'But why? It's clearly his little joke, isn't it?'

'He's punishing each of them for a reason. Maybe Freddie played one of his pranks on him. Ted Grover was committing adultery. Miss Ffrench-Finch – well, I'm sure old ladies can be annoying. Gladys Tripp listened in on private conversations and gossiped afterward. We don't know anything about Mr Klein or the butcher or the master of hounds or the farmer's wife, but Sandra Sechrest and Johnnie Protheroe were carrying on together.'

'So someone who sees himself as the hand of God, striking down those who have sinned?' Darcy asked. 'Obviously someone with a clever brain to carry out these things and make them look like accidents.'

'But not all that well educated,' I said. 'Remember he mixed up "lay" and "lie." His six geese were not a-laying, they were a-lying.'

'Poetic license, my sweet. He couldn't make everything fit the poem exactly, could he?'

The cold wind stung my face as the Alvis flew along the lane. I shivered, partly with cold and partly with apprehension. 'We have no proof that these were all intended victims.'

'Oh, I think we have to assume that they all were, because we know that some of them were. Freddie Partridge, for example. His death was not only planned, but planned elaborately to happen so that the twelve days would finish on New Year's Eve.'

'Not the correct twelve days of Christmas, by the way,' I interrupted. 'They are supposed to start on Christmas Day and finish on Twelfth Night.'

'Then the killer must have had a reason for starting when he did. Maybe when he knew everybody would be assembled for the house party.' He paused. 'I wonder how they managed to get Freddie Partridge into the pear tree. And look at the trouble the killer went to to finish off poor Gladys Tripp. That took skill. The man is good with his hands as well as his brain. And brazen enough to risk going into a telephone exchange in the middle of a busy town. A formidable opponent.'

'And who, one has to presume, was at the ball last night, waiting for the right moment when Mr Sechrest stood beside the candelabra.'

'My aunt will have the guest list. We can hand that to the police.'

'I don't suppose it would have been too hard to sneak in unnoticed. There was that gorilla. Nobody knew who was in that costume.'

'We have to assume it was the same gorilla suit we saw hanging up in the attic. Maybe someone in the family knows who borrowed it. Maybe someone did leave a clue inside – a strand of hair or the smell of a particular talcum powder, for example.'

'That's a long shot,' I said. 'I think our best bet is motive. Why did he want to kill these people?'

'Not just for fun – unless he chose Freddie Partridge for his name and the method of killing was more important than the victim. But that would indicate a true madman and I don't know how one begins to trap such a person.'

We had been climbing a long, winding slope and came suddenly to a steep bend at the crest. 'Didn't see that coming,' Darcy said as he swung the motorcar around it, faster than he intended.

'I believe this is where Mr Skaggs went over the edge, coming from the other direction.' I looked down that steep, rocky slope until it vanished into mist and I shivered. Someone was out there who could kill at will, leaving no trace, and was waiting to strike again the next day. According to the song he had two more victims planned . . . and the last two had been members of our house party.

I was very relieved as the first houses of the town appeared through the mist and we drove into the main street. Ghostly shapes darted in and out of shops, swathed in scarves against the bitter cold. We stopped outside the police station and went in.

'I'm afraid Inspector Newcombe isn't here,' said the constable on duty. 'No, I couldn't tell you where he's gone, but I believe it was some kind of meeting he had to go to. And I couldn't say when he'd be back.'

I asked for writing paper and wrote a note for him, telling him that we'd come up with something very important concerning a case and needed to speak with him as soon as possible. As I sealed the envelope I experienced a sudden flash of satisfaction that I had been proved right after all. Now Inspector Newcombe would have to admit that the deaths were not accidents and they were linked and one person was doing the killing. Not bad for an amateur. Now if only I could come up with a motive. . . .

I handed the envelope to the constable with strict instructions that it be given to Inspector Newcombe immediately and we came out into the eerie stillness of the street.

'Do you fancy a cup of coffee and a bun before we go back?' Darcy asked. 'There's a little tea shop across the street.'

'I think we should go to visit Mr Klein first, don't you?' I said. 'He might hold the key to this whole thing.'

'I'm not sure if we shouldn't leave that—' Darcy began but I cut him off.

'Look, if Inspector Newcombe isn't available to do it, then I don't think any more time should be wasted. Someone's life could be at stake.' I was already striding down the street toward the jeweler's shop. Darcy caught up with me. 'We're not interfering, we're helping,' I said. 'And if Mr Klein doesn't want to talk to us, at least we can send him to talk to the police.'

'Since when did you become so forceful?' Darcy said. 'I remember you as a meek little thing when we first met.'

'I don't think I've ever been meek,' I said. 'Remember, I do come from a great-grandmother who was rather forceful herself. Maybe I was just reticent when we first met – I didn't quite trust you.'

Darcy laughed. 'Good judgment. My one aim was to get you into bed, and I can't believe I haven't succeeded yet. I must be developing a conscience.'

'I do want to, Darcy,' I said. 'It's just that the moment never seems to be right.'

He grinned at me. 'We'll make a moment even if I have to whisk you off to Brighton to do so.'

'Mr and Mrs Smith?' I joked.

'How about Mr and Mrs O'Mara?'

Ah. There was the rub. I tried to say, 'I can't marry you,' but I couldn't. Instead I joked, 'I suspect I'll have a good long wait, then, until you're ready to settle down.'

'Who knows,' Darcy said, giving me a questioning look. 'Stranger things have happened.'

We reached the jeweler's, but it was closed. 'I don't believe it's opened since the robbery,' I said, peering through the window into the dark interior.

'There's a front door to one side,' Darcy said. 'Maybe he lives over the shop. Try knocking.'

We knocked. We even rang the doorbell, but nobody came.

'Not at home,' Darcy said.

I stared up at the window with the curtains drawn across it. 'Who would go out on a day like this?' I asked.

Darcy and I looked at each other. 'You don't suppose . . . ?' we said in unison.

Chapter 34

In the town of Newton Abbot, Devonshire
December 29

Darcy gave one last volley of knocks on the front door. As we were walking away, a window opened above the next-door haberdashery shop. An elderly woman's face looked out.

'You're wanting Mr Klein, are you? He's not there, my dearies,' she said. 'Leastways, I haven't seen him since I got back from my daughter's yesterday. I knocked to give him a piece of my daughter's Christmas cake, but nobody answered so I think he must have gone away.'

'Any idea where he might have gone?' I asked.

She shook her head. 'He has two daughters, I remember, but I couldn't tell you where they live. He's a very private man. Keeps himself to himself and it's hard to get a word out of him.'

Darcy and I exchanged a look as we walked away. 'We'd better go back to the police,' I said. 'He could be lying there dead on the floor and nobody would know.'

The constable at the police station listened politely but clearly wasn't taking us seriously. 'Lots of folks go away over Christmas,' he said. 'I don't think you should worry yourself unduly, miss.'

'But we have reason to believe that the robbery of his store was linked to all these strange deaths. You know – Gladys Tripp, Mr Skaggs.'

'And how might that be, miss?'

'It's too complicated to explain now,' I said. 'I'm sure Inspector Newcombe would act immediately if I told him what I now know.'

'We can't just go breaking in someone's door on the off chance that something might not be right,' he said.

'Not even if a person may well be lying dead inside, murdered?'

He shifted uncomfortably. 'I'm all alone here at the moment. Can't leave the station unattended, can I? Besides, I can't do nothing without my sergeant's permission.'

'And where is he?'

'It's his day off, miss. Can't bother him on his day off.'

I had a growing desire to slap him but I fought to stay calm. 'So if a major crime happened now, if someone ran down the street shooting people, you'd just watch because you're all alone in the police station?'

I felt Darcy dig me in the side. The constable considered my question, not recognizing it as sarcasm. 'Well, miss, if a man ran down our street shooting at people, I reckon I'd be bound to try and stop him, wouldn't I? But if the gentleman you're talking about is already dead, then an hour or so more won't matter much to him, will it?'

In the face of such reason I had to back down.

'So you have no way of contacting Inspector Newcombe

at all? You couldn't find out where his meeting is being held?'

The constable considered this. 'I suppose I could put through a telephone call to the main police station in Exeter and they might know how to find him, but he wouldn't half be mad at me if I brought him back here for nothing.'

'I can promise you it's not for nothing,' I said. 'We now have proof that all those deaths were murders, you see.'

'You don't say!' He stared at me, wide-eyed.

'And another man has died this morning and more people will go on dying unless the murderer is stopped.'

'Well, I never. Who'd have thought it around here?' he said. 'I don't recall there ever being a murder in these parts. Just like London, isn't it?'

'So will you try to contact the inspector for us, please?' I asked.

'I'll do my best, miss,' he said.

'We shouldn't wait around any longer,' Darcy said. 'They'll worry where we've got to. And I've borrowed Monty's motorcar without permission. The inspector will come out to us as soon as he gets your note.'

'I should add something about Mr Klein,' I said, and on the back of the envelope I wrote, *Mr Klein doesn't answer his door. Suspect he may be dead inside his flat. Constable refused to break down door to find out.*

Then reluctantly we had to drive back to Tiddleton-under-Lovey. The field where the chase had taken place now had an abandoned feel to it, with bits of bunting flapping in the wind and the ghostly shapes of booths looming over the fence. Johnnie's roguish face swam into my mind and I remembered the others teasing him about entering the race because of his age. He had felt himself immortal then. I squeezed my eyes shut in an attempt to blot out the pain.

We put the motor back in the old stables beside the house and went in to find everyone in a mellow mood after the exertions of the race and the large amount of alcohol consumed. Cherie and Ethel had now attached themselves to Monty and Badger and were sitting beside them on a sofa. The adults were drinking coffee and looking bored. Lady Hawse-Gorzley waylaid me in the passageway.

'Oh, there you are. I suspect you slipped away with my nephew, you naughty girl.' She wagged a finger, but she was smiling.

'We tried to find Inspector Newcombe,' I said. 'We discovered something he ought to know.'

She brushed back her hair from her face in a distracted gesture. 'These deaths – I'm really beginning to believe in the Lovey Curse. I can't explain them any other way. And Wild Sal was out there at the Chase today, dancing around as bold as you please. It would not surprise me one bit if she were a witch.' She paused, then managed an embarrassed smile. 'Oh, I know one is supposed to be modern and pooh-pooh anything supernatural, but in this part of the world we take the supernatural seriously.'

'I don't think she's responsible for these deaths,' I said.

'Then how can they be explained?' she snapped. 'Seeing poor Johnnie today . . . I've known him all my life. We used to play together when we were children. Am I really to believe that he suffered a heart attack?'

'I think we'll find out that he was murdered,' I said. 'I think we'll find that these were all well-planned murders.'

She glared at me fiercely. 'Then who will be next?' she

said. 'Shouldn't I send my guests away now rather than expose them to this kind of danger?'

'I think your guests are safe. It seems to be only local people – people about whom the killer knows an awful lot.'

She shuddered. 'Horrible. Horrible. I worry about Oswald. He often goes off alone, tramping all over the estate. He takes the dogs with him, but they can't protect him, can they?'

I put a tentative hand on her arm. 'We may be near to solving this,' I said. 'I suggest we keep everyone close to the house for the rest of their time here.'

'What about the Worsting of the Hag?' she said. 'They'll want to take part in that, won't they? It's the big event.'

'What exactly happens?'

'On New Year's Eve every year, everyone goes from house to house around the village, banging on pots and pans and drums, making noise to drive out evil spirits. It's supposed to be the re-enactment of the time when they chased the witch around the village before they caught her on Lovey Tor. Always great fun.'

'But dangerous,' I said. 'How can you protect people out in the dark?'

She shrugged. 'We'll have to enlist the help of the police, won't we? We can't stop the festival. It's been going for two hundred-plus years.'

She peered into the sitting room. 'Oh, God. What are we going to do with them? Look at them – just sitting there, waiting to be entertained. I do wish I hadn't undertaken this stupid farce.' She looked at me for understanding. 'You've probably heard by now that they're all paying guests.'

I nodded.

'We needed the money, you see. Things have not been

going well and this seemed like such a good opportunity.'
She sighed. 'But I wish to God we had never done it. I even
began to wonder whether these deaths were some kind of
punishment for not accepting our lot.'

'I'm sure they're not,' I said. 'Look, why don't I go and
set up another skittles tournament for them? And maybe we
could ask Mr Barclay to give them an organ concert in the
church. He plays very well.'

'What a splendid idea. Thank you, Georgiana. You've
been a big help to me.'

I didn't think I'd been that much of a help at all and I suddenly felt awkward about accepting money from her. After
all, I was having a far better Christmas than I would have
had at Castle Rannoch. Actually, I'd have paid her to be
away from Fig!

After lunch I took Mrs Upthorpe, Ethel and Mrs Wexler for
a walk with me to see Mr Barclay. I didn't feel like going
anywhere alone anymore and they all seemed at loose ends.
All the way down the drive they chatted about fashions and
dressmakers and ladies' magazines until I felt quite left out.
Sometimes it's hard to be penniless.

Mr Barclay's eyes darted nervously when he saw us standing on his doorstep.

'Well, this is an unexpected pleasure. A peeress of the
realm in my humble cottage,' he said, but he didn't look very
pleased. He invited us into a neat, old-fashioned front parlor
that looked as if it hadn't been touched since his grandmother's day, and offered us tea. It seemed rude to refuse
and we sat uncomfortably while he kept apologizing for
not having anything suitable to offer us to accompany the
tea. If only he'd known we were coming, he said, he'd have

baked something. When he heard the reason for our visit he perked up no end.

'Oh, how kind of you,' he said. 'What an honor. I shall be thrilled, positively thrilled. Now you've given me a challenging task – what piece of music to play. What a delicious dilemma, isn't it?'

We set the time of the concert for three o'clock the next day ('Not after dark, if you please; the church lighting is so poor and my hands won't work when they get too cold') and were glad to take our leave.

'Poor little man, I feel rather sorry for him, don't you?' Mrs Upthorpe said when we could finally take our leave. 'Such a lonely life. Probably has nobody in the village to talk to.'

We arrived back to a second, and more satisfying, tea. The day seemed to drag on and on, with no news from the inspector. We played charades again before dinner, but this time it felt as if nobody's heart was really in it and nobody had the urge to dress up, after the previous night's horror. We had just gone up to change for dinner when there was a tap on my bedroom door. I opened it to find one of the maids.

'If you please, my lady, that police inspector has come to see you,' she said. 'I've put him in the master's study.'

I hurriedly finished dressing and went down the stairs. Inspector Newcombe had been pacing the room and spun around as I entered.

'I came because my constable impressed upon me that you had something terribly important to tell me. A matter of life and death, I believe was how he put it.'

I nodded. 'But first what of Mr Klein? Did anyone go and see what had happened to him?'

'We did,' he said, eyeing me coldly. 'And it turned out he's been staying with his daughter in Torquay. We felt like a lot of right charlies, I can tell you.'

'So he's all right, then?'

'Perfectly.'

I let out a sigh of relief.

'Do you mind telling me what made you think he wasn't all right?'

'Because he should have died on the twenty-fourth,' I said. 'He was the gold rings.'

And I explained what I had figured out. He listened, at first with a smirk on his face, but then a frown formed on his forehead and his expression grew grimmer and grimmer as I went along.

'It's positively bizarre,' he said at last, 'but I have to admit it certainly fits. And if you're right, then the man who died today did not have a heart attack.'

'Maybe he did,' I said. 'If the killer knew he had a weak heart and was on medicine, he could easily have tampered with the dose. He has been staying here so you'll probably find his medicines up in his bedroom. I suggest you take them with you for testing.'

The inspector looked at me suspiciously. 'Where do you get these ideas, a well-bred young lady like you?'

'I've had some experience with murders,' I said.

'Do you go around actually seeking them out for fun?' He shook his head. 'I've heard of you bright young things stealing policemen's helmets, but this takes the cake.'

'Certainly not. I hate them, but I've been involved in a few. I'd much rather not.'

He perched on the edge of Sir Oswald's desk. 'All right, then, my lady. If you've figured out how these deaths are linked, perhaps you'd be good enough to tell me who might be playing this little game with us.'

'I wish I could. Somebody local who knows everybody's habits. Somebody with considerable skills and a twisted mind. Somebody with a grudge against a lot of people.'

He sucked in air through his teeth. 'And how are we to find out who that might be?'

'He has made two mistakes,' I said. 'Mrs Sechrest and Mr Klein. He has let them live. They may have some idea of who might want them dead.'

'Right,' he said. 'I don't think Mrs Sechrest will be up to talking much yet, but I could go to see Mr Klein tomorrow.' He looked at me almost coyly. 'Do you think the retired gentleman from Scotland Yard might want to accompany me?'

'He might very well want to,' I said. 'And I'd like to come along as well, if I may.'

'Well, given that you're the only one who has made any headway with this puzzle, I can hardly say no, can I?' He stood up again.

'And my friend Darcy O'Mara. I know he'd want to come along too.'

'This isn't a blooming bright young things' charabanc outing,' he snapped, then seemed to remember to whom he was speaking and checked himself. 'I'm sorry. Didn't mean to fly off the handle like that. But if you want my advice, my lady, the fewer people who know about this, the better. If the murderer is lurking around here, word will get back to him somehow or other and it may put more people in danger. I agreed to taking you, because you've figured it out, but no more. And I'd be grateful if you didn't mention our excursion to anybody.'

I took a deep breath. 'All right, I suppose.'

'I'd best be getting along, then. Another long day and the

missus isn't pleased. Says we've had no Christmas at all this year. But that's the nature of the job, isn't it? I told her she knew what she was getting when she married me. For better or worse, eh?'

I escorted him up to Johnnie Protheroe's bedroom, where he took several medicine bottles. Then I accompanied him to the front door.

'Remember now.' He wagged a finger at me. 'Nobody else is to know at this stage. All right?'

I closed the door and went to join the others for sherry. I could hardly contain my excitement. Finally we were getting somewhere, and I was being allowed to join in. I was no longer the annoying amateur. It was quite satisfying. It was only as I entered the salon and saw Darcy's back, as he talked with Monty and Badger, that I felt the full implication of leaving him out of the next day's little jaunt. I reasoned that he hadn't really shown much interest and was all for leaving the investigation to the police. But I still didn't like the thought of going off without telling him. How was I going to explain this away?

He seemed to sense my presence and came over to me. 'What did the inspector say? Was he impressed with your detective abilities?' he asked, drawing me aside so that we couldn't be overheard above the buzz of conversation.

'He was.' I managed a bright smile. 'And he's found that Mr Klein is staying with his daughter. He's going to see him tomorrow.'

'Splendid,' Darcy said. 'Now I hope you're satisfied. I said it was a good idea to leave this to the police.'

I attempted a bright smile, but I felt too sick and worried at dinner to eat much of the delicious leg of lamb and golden syrup pudding.

Chapter 35

December 30
Lovely day so far. Going to see Mr Klein and excited at the
chance of this horrid riddle finally being solved. I just hope
he can set us on the right track before someone is killed
today.

In contrast to the previous day's damp and gloomy fog, the
weather was sparkling and clear. Remnants of snow still
clung to the top of Lovey Tor and the sky looked as if it
were made of blue glass, with the bare bones of trees etched
upon it. I dressed, grabbed a hurried breakfast and then set
off down the drive, having told Lady Hawse-Gorzley that I
wished to visit my grandfather.

I was nearing the front gates when someone stepped out
in front of me, barring my way. It was Wild Sal and she was
staring at me with those strange bright green eyes.

'You're still here, are you?' she said. 'You'll leave right
now if you know what's good for you.'

'Why is that?' I stared back defiantly.

'You're not wanted in these parts. Outsiders like you only

cause trouble. You're the one who set the police on me, aren't you? You got me locked up in that little cell.'

'I only told the police that I'd seen you up near where the master of hounds disappeared, that's all,' I said. 'I was asked if I'd seen anybody and I could hardly lie. Besides, you saved me from falling into the bog. I told them that too.'

She looked at me strangely. 'He went into the bog, and good riddance too,' she said. 'Hunting poor defenseless foxes.'

'Did you string the wire that tripped up his horse?'

'Me? Why would I want to harm a horse? I love all creatures, except humans, that is.'

'But you saw him fall off his horse?'

'No, but I saw someone putting him in the bog.'

'Who was it?'

'Couldn't tell you that. Big bloke, all wrapped up, wearing some kind of hood. And I reckon the other one was already dead, 'cos he just lay there and let the bog suck him up.'

'Why didn't you get help?'

'Too late by then. Once the bog gets you, you goes down fast, and like I said, I reckon he was already dead.'

'Why didn't you tell this to the police?'

'I did, but they weren't interested. I couldn't describe the bloke, see, couldn't tell if he was young or old or anything. Just that he were a big, strapping chap.'

'And you saw that van go off the road, too?'

'No, I heard the noise and I got there too late. It was already smashed to bits down in the stream.'

'So you didn't see the same man there?'

'Didn't see nobody,' she said.

I phrased my next question carefully in my head. 'Sal, do you know anyone in these parts, anyone at all, who would do terrible things like this?' I gave her an appealing look. 'He has to be stopped before he kills more people.'

'I don't have much dealings with people. Keep myself to myself, that's what I do,' she said. 'They don't trust me and I don't trust them. But there's plenty of folk don't deserve to live.'

'But you might be in danger too. You might be next.'

'Not me,' she said. 'No one around here would ever dare touch me. They're afraid of the Lovey Curse.'

'I'm going with the inspector today,' I said. 'With any luck we'll know who is doing this by tonight.'

I saw her look at me strangely and I found myself wondering if she was the killer after all. Hadn't she just said that there were plenty of people who didn't deserve to live? But how had she managed to cover so much ground? How could she possibly have known about the butcher driving on the road from Newton Abbot, or got to a farm on the other side of Bovey Tracey? And how would she be strong enough to drag a body into the bog?

As I went to take my leave, another thought struck me. 'Sal, on the night that the old lady at the big house died, you went to the kitchen for food, didn't you? You didn't see anyone else, did you?'

'When I was leaving, I did see Willum,' she said. 'He was going round the side of the house to their back garden.'

I paused, digesting this. 'Did you speak to him? Did he say what he was doing?'

She shook her head. 'No. I didn't speak to him. I just went my way and left him to it. Willum often does jobs for people.'

'I must go. I'm supposed to be meeting people,' I said.

'Remember what Sal just told you,' she said. 'You watch yourself, miss. And if you had any sense, you'd go home now, before it's too late. Sal sees danger in your future.'

I was still strangely shaken by the time I arrived at the cottage and found the inspector and my grandfather standing together beside the big black police motor. Granddad and I got into the back seat while the inspector rode in the front, next to his driver.

'It should be a nice ride to Torquay today,' the inspector said. 'Better than driving in that awful fog yesterday.'

'I hope your meeting went well,' I said.

'Have you been keeping tabs on me?'

'Of course not.' I flushed. 'Your constable said you'd had to go for a meeting.'

'Of a sort,' he said. 'The prisoner they recaptured in Birmingham has just been returned to Dartmoor Prison. I went to talk to him.'

'And did you learn anything?'

'Not a dicky bird. He still maintains that they split up as soon as they reached the road, and he thought the other two were both heading for London. As for how he made it to Birmingham and where he got his civilian clothes, he's just not talking.'

'You won't get convicts to squeal on each other, unless there is something in it for them,' Granddad said.

'I just met Wild Sal,' I said. And I told them about her seeing the body dragged into the bog and the fact that she'd seen Willum in the Ffrench-Finches' back garden.

'Willum? The simple-headed one?' The inspector stroked his chin. I noticed he'd shaved that morning. 'I can't see him having the wit to pull off crimes like these. He's like a big kiddie. No, I think we'll find we're dealing with a real smart aleck, the sort of man who thinks he's the cat's whiskers and that society hasn't appreciated his talents. You know, the quiet bank clerk who feels that he's been overlooked.

Probably doesn't have friends. Probably spent months or years planning this.'

'Rather like the man you described to us, then,' I said. 'You said one of the escaped convicts was a bank clerk, had brains and was ruthless.'

'Yes, I did.' Inspector Newcombe considered this. 'But he'd have no reason to stick around these parts. And what's more, I'm sure he doesn't have any local connections either. No, my betting is that he's safely back in London.' He turned to look out the window as we swung around a hairpin bend on the hill. 'But there are plenty more like him. The Great War turned some of them cuckoo, didn't it? Came home from the trenches and were never the same.'

We reached the crest of the hill and had a lovely view ahead of green fields and copses, farms nestling in hollows and in the far distance a sparkling line of sea. The road dropped from the moors until we were driving through the tamed landscape of the coast. Torquay looked positively Mediterranean in the sparkling sunshine. There were palm trees along the front and couples strolling, taking me back to my time in Nice. But the couples here were bundled in great coats and scarves, betraying that the weather here was not exactly balmy. We left the expensive hotels and souvenir shops until we reached a more humble backstreet with semi-detached houses and children playing on the pavement outside.

My heart was racing as we walked up the front path and the inspector rapped on the door.

'Mrs Goldblum? Detective Inspector Newcombe, Devonshire Constabulary. I telephoned you last night,' he said. 'Your father is still here, I hope?'

'Yes, he's here, but I don't want him upset.' The thin and

rather gaunt-looking middle-aged woman frowned at us. 'That robbery has quite unnerved him. He fled from persecution in Russia as a young man, you know. He remembers the Cossacks burning his village and killing his parents. He said he has felt safe in England until now.'

'I quite understand,' Inspector Newcombe said. 'Let us hope that we will soon apprehend the person who did this and he can feel safe again.' He saw her looking at us. 'This gentleman is a former detective from Scotland Yard, who I hope can help solve this quickly.'

'And I'm his granddaughter,' I said quickly, before anyone could give my full name and title.

'I don't know why it might take all these people to solve a simple robbery.' She was now glaring at us suspiciously.

'It might turn out to be not so simple,' the inspector said. 'It may be tied to other crimes in this area. So if we could please speak with your father?'

She stood aside to let us into a narrow front hall. 'He's in the back parlor. It's easier to heat. I'll make us some tea.'

We went through to a small room crammed full of furniture. Mr Klein was sitting in an armchair beside a roaring fire. He got to his feet, looking at us nervously.

The inspector held out his hand. 'Mr Klein. Detective Inspector Newcombe. We met the other day in connection with your robbery. And these are two acquaintances who have been helping me.'

'Good of you to come, Inspector,' Mr Klein said. 'Please, take a seat, all of you. I recognize the young lady from my shop the other day. Any news on the robbery yet?'

'Not yet, I'm afraid, but we may be closer to solving it.'

We sat, I perched on an upright chair away from the fire, leaving the two men to sit close to Mr Klein.

'I'd be so happy if you could find out who broke into my shop,' he said. 'I haven't slept a wink since, you know. If someone had smashed a window and grabbed a few items, it would have been one thing. But letting himself into the store with no sign of a break-in and then opening my safe – well, that's something else entirely, isn't it? I won't feel safe again until he's found and arrested.'

'That's exactly what we hope to do, Mr Klein. And we have reason to suspect this wasn't just a simple robbery. It may be linked to a chain of crimes, some of them murders. So in many ways you're lucky to be alive. And I suggest you stay with your daughter until we tell you it's safe to go home.'

'Goodness me.' Mr Klein put a hand to his heart. 'You have your suspicions then, do you, Inspector?'

'We're hoping you can help us, Mr Klein. We suspect there must be some kind of vendetta motive behind this, so I'm asking you to think. Has there been anyone with whom you've crossed swords, anyone who has written you a nasty letter? Anyone who might want to punish you in any way?'

'Because I'm Jewish, you mean?'

'Not at all. None of the other victims was a Jew.'

'Well, that's a relief, anyway. I always told myself that was one thing I could count on in England. And as to your question – no, I can't think of any enemies. I keep myself to myself. Don't make trouble. Don't get involved in town politics. Never had a nasty letter that I can remember.'

I moved toward the edge of the sofa. 'Mr Klein, do any of the following names mean anything to you?' And I began to recite them. He shook his head after each of the first few.

'Gladys Tripp. Now, that name rings a bell. Where have I heard it recently?'

'She was the telephone switchboard operator who was killed last week.'

'In a fire at the exchange, wasn't it? That's right. I remembered her name from before.'

'Before what?' Inspector Newcombe asked.

Mr Klein frowned. 'Maybe I've run into her around town? Go on. What were the other names?'

'The next person was the master of the local hunt. Major Wesley-Parker.'

Mr Klein looked up suddenly. 'Dapper little man with a mustache like that dreadful Hitler fellow? Thinks a lot of himself?'

'That's right,' I said.

'Oh, I remember him all right,' he said. 'I served on a jury with him several years ago. He was an officious person. Took charge from square one. Bossed us all around. Wanted everything his way.'

'A jury?' Inspector Newcombe exchanged an excited look with us.

'That's right. Come to think of it, that telephone lady must have been on it too. At least, there was some woman who chattered nonstop, inane stuff. I believe her last name was Tripp.'

'Think carefully, Mr Klein,' Inspector Newcombe said slowly. 'Who else can you remember on that jury?'

'Let me see. A refined older lady who locked horns with your hunting chap. There were a couple of people who never said a word – a large countrywoman, I remember, who looked distinctly out of place and uncomfortable. Did her knitting all the time. Click of knitting needles was most annoying. Then there were a couple of younger men who wouldn't take anything seriously. That Major Whatsit did get annoyed with them. "You're a disgrace to the county set," he said.' And Mr Klein chuckled.

'Freddie Partridge. Johnnie Protheroe?' I asked.

'I really can't remember names, if I even knew them. You don't ever want to get too friendly with fellow jurors. It's such an unreal situation that you just want to do the job and get out of there. At least, that was the way I felt. And most of them ignored me. I'm the sort that people overlook.'

The inspector cleared his throat. 'Mr Klein, what was the nature of the case? And the name of the defendant?'

'Now, that I do remember,' he said. 'It was quite interesting, actually. He'd been a well-known music-hall artiste. Had fallen on hard times since the demise of the music-hall and had taken to swindling old ladies out of their life savings. The prosecution wanted us to believe that he'd killed more than one of them. His last landlady had died from a fall down the stairs, but there was no real proof that he'd actually pushed her.'

'And his name, Mr Klein? Do you remember his name?'

'His name was Robbins.'

Chapter 36

The inspector got to his feet, slamming his fist into his open hand. 'I knew it. I knew my instinct was right all along.'

'You know him, then?' Mr Klein asked.

'Oh, yes, I know him. He's one of the convicts who recently escaped from Dartmoor. We've been looking for him.'

'My life, already,' Mr Klein said. 'You're telling me that the man who broke into my shop and took those rings was that same Robbins?'

'Almost certainly so.'

'Then I'm lucky I wasn't murdered in my bed.'

'You are very lucky, I agree. In fact, you're the only one he hasn't attempted to murder, most of them in ingenious ways.'

'Oh, he was a slick one, all right, from what we heard of the way he got around these old ladies. Knew how to charm people. Smarmy, that's what I called him, but some of the ladies believed him. I don't quite approve of having ladies sit on juries, if you don't mind my saying so. Not enough experience of the outside world and too easily swayed by a charming smile.'

'What did he look like, Mr Klein?' I asked.

'We know what he looked like. We have his mug shots,' the inspector said.

'I wanted Mr Klein's impression of him,' I said.

'Well-built chap, good solid jaw. Quite a big man and, as I said, charming smile. Charming manner altogether. If you'd believed him, butter wouldn't melt in his mouth.'

'I take it you haven't seen him recently?' the inspector asked. 'He didn't come into your shop, for example?'

'Oh, no. I'd have remembered him, I'm sure,' Mr Klein said. 'A person like that you don't forget so easily.'

We took our leave then.

'Well, that's a turn-up for the books, isn't it?' the inspector said. 'If we're to believe him, that Robbins fellow is still hiding out in these parts and bumping off the members of the jury, one by one.'

'He still has two to go,' I said. 'We need to find out who the other members were before it's too late.'

'That trial would have been at the Crown court in Exeter,' the inspector said. 'The local magistrate's court wouldn't have touched a case like that.'

He turned to his driver and we swung onto the main Exeter road.

'What I want to know,' my grandfather said as we negotiated the narrow streets near the center of town, 'is how he obtained all this local knowledge if he was locked away in Dartmoor Prison. Someone from around here must have found out about the details of the people he killed.'

'The same one who is hiding him, presumably,' I said.

'Doing a bloody good job of it too,' the inspector said. 'We went door to door in all those local villages when the convicts escaped, but nobody claimed to have seen hide nor hair of them.'

The car came to a halt outside the court buildings and we followed the inspector inside. We were passed from one department to the next until we found where archives of court cases were stored. And then we waited, sitting on a hard wooden bench in a drafty foyer. At last a young man came back with a sheet of paper. 'This is the one you wanted,' he said. 'Robert Francis Robbins. Convicted November 22, 1928.'

We read it eagerly. 'Who is Agnes Brewer?' Granddad asked.

'The farmer's wife. Already dead.'

'That just leaves Stewart McGill and – oh.' I stopped, mouth open.

'Peter Barclay,' Granddad said. 'Isn't he the quiet little chap who plays the organ?'

'That's him.' I looked at the inspector. 'Do you have any way of telephoning the police station in Tiddleton and having some kind of guard put on Mr Barclay?'

'I'll do it from the station here,' the inspector said. 'And we need to find out where this Mr McGill lives. We have an address for him and it's in Exeter.'

We drove with a growing feeling of dread to Mr McGill's address. It was in a rather shabby backstreet of terraced houses right on the pavement with no front gardens. We knocked on the front door and a young woman opened it. She looked unkempt, with a baby on her hip.

'Mr McGill?' the inspector asked.

She stared at him defiantly. 'No. You've got the wrong number. The name's Perkins.'

'How long have you lived here, Mrs Perkins?'

'Just over a year. What's it to you?'

'I'm a police officer,' Inspector Newcombe said coldly and

noted the reaction in her eyes. 'You don't happen to know where to find the people who lived here before you, do you?'

'No idea.' The baby started to wail. 'Look, this isn't a good time. He wants his bottle and the bigger ones want their dinner.'

'We're looking for a Mr McGill who used to live here,' the inspector said. 'It's vitally important we contact him. A matter of life and death.'

She shrugged, still not interested. 'You can ask the old bat at number 14,' she said. 'She's always snooping out through her window, minding other people's business. She might know.'

We went across the street. I saw a lace curtain twitch before the inspector knocked on the door. Soon after, the door was opened an inch or two and a sharp-nosed face looked out.

The inspector repeated his question and the door was opened wider to reveal an old woman in a flowery pinny and carpet slippers.

'You're not going to find him, are you?' the old woman said triumphantly. 'He's gone. Hopped it.'

'Gone where?'

'Out to his daughter in Australia. His wife died and he packed up and went. Three or four years ago now.'

'Now, that presents an interesting problem for Mr Robbins, doesn't it?' the inspector said as we returned to the motor. 'I wonder if he's planning to go out to Australia to seek out the last jury member.'

'Hardly on the twelfth day,' I said. 'He wouldn't even have time to leave England by then.'

'Then what's he going to do on the twelfth day?' my grandfather said. 'I rather think he's the type who'd want a big finale.'

None of us had an answer to that one.

We left the city of Exeter behind and rolling countryside stretched ahead of us, with the snowcapped tors as a backdrop. 'So the big question is, who has been hiding him?'

'It might be worth checking with Wild Sal again,' I said. 'She sort of threatened me this morning. Nobody goes near the place she lives up on the moors, do they?'

'My lads were there to apprehend her,' the inspector said. 'Hardly more than a sheep byre – stone walls, dirt floor and not enough room to swing a cat. Nowhere to hide him there.'

'But if they'd seen you coming, there are plenty of places to hide up on the moor until you'd gone, aren't there?' I suggested.

'What exactly do you know about this Robbins?' Granddad asked. 'Used to have a music-hall turn, didn't he?'

'He did. In fact, he was quite popular at one time. I gather it was a sort of magic act with his wife, sleight-of-hand stuff, but the difference was that it was a type of comedy act too and they played various characters. His most famous one was apparently an old colonel, trying to impress a coquettish young girl, played by his wife.'

'You know, I think I saw him once,' Granddad said excitedly. 'At the Hammersmith Empire. The old colonel and the young girl. That rings a bell. They were quite good. Clever and funny too. What were they called?' He sucked through his teeth, thinking.

'I believe it was Robbie and someone.'

'"Robbie and Trixie, Tricks and Chuckles," that was it,' Granddad said. 'I did see them. The old colonel and the young girl. He was trying to impress her, producing flowers out of her hat, money out of her ear. So did you say that his wife killed herself?'

'Right after he was convicted,' the inspector said. 'Left a

note. Said she couldn't handle the shame of it or go on living without him. So she drowned herself near Beachy Head. Walked out into the sea, and you know what the currents are like around that headland. The body was never found.'

I stared out the window, trying to control my racing thoughts. The old colonel. Was he actually staying at Gorzley Hall at this moment? Colonel Rathbone had claimed to be a colonel with the Bengal Lancers, but he didn't look comfortable in the saddle. And he hadn't known his commanding officer's nickname. But Mrs Rathbone? She didn't look as if she'd ever been an entertainer. But was it possible the old colonel's wife hadn't died after all? I wondered whether to voice my suspicion to the inspector, then decided that I should talk it over with Darcy first. He knew people in London who could check on such things. I'd tell him instead.

As we drove down the hill and into the village we saw the constable talking to someone outside the police station. The inspector wound down his window. 'Did you get my message, Jackson?' he asked.

'I did, sir.' The constable came over to us. 'I went round to Mr Barclay's house, but he wasn't there. I've been keeping an eye open for him, but I haven't seen him all day.'

'I want him found, Jackson. The man may be in danger. Now go and ask around the village if anyone has seen him, understand? I'll just drive this young lady to her front door and then we'll come back to help you.'

'It's all right. I can walk from here,' I said.

'No, my lady. Given what we know now, I don't want you walking anywhere alone. In fact, when I get back to the village I'm going to question everyone again. Someone must have spotted Robbins. Someone must know something and I mean to find out who is hiding him.'

It was his insistence on driving me to the hall that made me realize the danger we all might be in. If Mr Robbins had been plotting and planning his vengeance during his years in prison, he wouldn't take kindly to anyone who was trying to get in his way. And he had proved clearly that he was literally able to kill with no trace and under all our noses.

As I entered the hall I was met by Darcy, striding out from the drawing room with a look of thunder on his face.

'Where the devil have you been?' he demanded.

I stepped back, recoiling from this unexpected wrath. 'I went out with my grandfather and Inspector Newcombe. We went to find Mr Klein and you'd be amazed what else we discovered—'

'And you didn't think of telling me?' His eyes were still blazing.

'I wanted you to come too, but the inspector refused. And he made me promise not to mention it to anyone else. I felt terrible. I did tell Lady Hawse-Gorzley.'

'Yes, that you'd gone to see your mother,' he snapped. 'Can you imagine how worried I was when I went down to the cottage and you and your grandfather were not there and your mother had no idea where you had gone?'

'I'm sorry,' I said. 'I really am. I did try to include you.'

His expression softened a little. 'I'm not angry because I couldn't come,' he said. 'I always felt that police business should be left to the police, as you know very well. It's just that I was worried about you. I thought you might have been kidnapped or bumped off because you were interfering. You can't imagine what went through my mind.'

I touched his shoulder tentatively. 'Darcy, I said I'm sorry. I wanted to tell you but I'd been asked not to.'

'You could have at least let me know you were safely with the police.'

I was beginning to feel defensive. 'You have plenty of secrets from me, don't you? I don't even know what you do when you go off on your little jaunts. Don't you think I worry about you?'

He smiled. 'You do have a point there. But I know how to take care of myself.'

'So do I,' I said.

He slipped his arms around my waist. 'Well, you're home and you're safe. So let's forget about it. Are you allowed to tell me what happened?'

'You'll never believe this.' I led him down a long hallway until we were far from other people and told him everything.

'The man must be completely mad,' he said at last. 'Killing off jurors one by one, in such an elaborate fashion. What for? What can it accomplish?'

'He's a showman, Darcy. He wants to go out with a bang. Maybe he has no desire to live now that his wife is dead, and no desire to go back to that horrible prison.'

'Signing his own death warrant, you mean?'

I nodded. 'And there's something I want you to do,' I said, and I voiced my suspicions about the colonel.

He stood there, frowning. 'Yes, I think I know someone who can find that out for me in a hurry,' he said. 'Do you really think it's possible that he's been here among us, all this time? It doesn't seem possible. How has he managed to go in and out to kill people at odd times?'

'It's a big enough house. I'm sure it's possible to slip out without being seen.'

'Extraordinary. I'll send a telegram right away. And in the

meantime stay well clear of him, understand? I don't want him to get any hint that you know.'

I nodded. As we came back to the front foyer Lady Hawse-Gorzley was coming down the stairs. 'All ready for the concert, then?' she asked brightly. 'Is your dear mother coming too?'

'I'm not sure,' I said. I'd completely forgotten about the concert and remembered now that Mr Barclay would be playing for us.

'Dress warmly,' she called after me. 'It's always freezing cold in that church. I don't know how the poor man manages to play the organ with frozen fingers.'

I put on a scarf and hat and joined those assembling on the driveway. Colonel Rathbone announced that he and his wife would not be joining us, as she wasn't feeling too well. The dowager countess said that she'd heard organ concerts at St Stephen's in Vienna and St Nicholas Cathedral in Leipzig and really didn't need another one. Monty and Cherie also expressed little interest, but Monty was told by his mother that he was expected to attend. Cherie walked beside him, sulking and loudly proclaiming that churches were boring.

We turned onto the path beside the village green and were nearing the gate leading to the church when we heard the most bloodcurdling scream coming from inside. We ran up the path. The church door was open and screams continued to come from inside. As we went in we were met by Miss Prendergast running toward us, her face a mask of terror.

'It's him,' she gasped. 'And he's . . . and I thought . . . and I touched him, and . . .'

She held out her hands and they were covered in blood.

Chapter 37

She had stopped screaming but a strange noise continued – a sort of moaning sigh that echoed around the church. We looked past to where her gaze was focused. Mr Barclay was lying across the keys of the organ and blood was trickling down one side of his face. The noise appeared to be coming from the organ itself and I realized that it was the dying breath of air coming from the organ pipes.

'My God,' Lady Hawse-Gorzley exclaimed. 'It looks as if part of the roof has fallen on him.' On the floor beside him was a large chunk of masonry that seemed to have come from the top of the vaulted ceiling.

Someone was dispatched to the police station. Lady Hawse-Gorzley rapidly escorted her guests away from the scene. 'Monty, take them back to the house and give them a brandy,' she said. 'I'll have to stay until the police get here.'

I couldn't take my eyes from the dead man. We had known he was in danger. We had put a police guard on him and nevertheless the killer had struck at will again. It was almost as if he were a supernatural being who could move among us invisible and undetected. I was shaken from my troubling thoughts by Miss Prendergast's gasping sobs.

Lady Hawse-Gorzley patted her on the back. 'Nasty shock, I know. You'll be all right,' she said briskly. 'What you need is a stiff drink.' She saw me. 'Georgie dear, why don't you take Miss Prendergast to your mother's cottage? She shouldn't be left alone and the police will want to talk to her when they get here.'

'All right,' I said. I took the woman's arm. 'Come along, Miss Prendergast.'

She allowed herself to be led out of the church, along the path to my mother's cottage. I explained briefly what had happened and brought her inside. My mother had been sitting by the fire with a cup of tea. I thought she wouldn't want a strange older woman in her cottage but she instantly switched into full Florence Nightingale mode.

'You poor dear thing. What an awful shock,' she said. 'Come and sit down. Daddy, get her a glass of brandy.'

'Oh, no spirits, thank you,' she said as the glass was placed in her hands. 'I rarely touch alcohol.'

'Go on, down the hatch,' Granddad said. 'It'll do you good.'

'If you insist.' She gave him a wary glance before sipping it.

'I'll make you a nice cup of tea, love,' Mrs Huggins said. 'Your face is as white as a sheet.'

'So would yours be if you'd just found someone lying dead in the church,' Mummy said. She still had that caring smile on her face and I realized that she was playing the part because she wanted all the ghoulish details. She was finding these murders thrilling. For her it was a big game.

Miss Prendergast shuddered. 'I still can't believe it was real,' she said. 'I saw him lying there and I thought he'd fallen asleep and I went to wake him and my hands were all sticky.' She held them up, showing the dried blood on them. 'So awful. I warned the vicar about the state of that church. The masonry is crumbling in several places. It was only a matter of time before it fell on someone. But poor Mr Barclay.' She looked from one face to the next, imploring us to understand what she was feeling. 'I must say we didn't get along very well. He did like his own way, you know, but I would not have wished that on anyone. And he did play the organ very well, didn't he?'

'Yes, he did,' I said.

'I feel so guilty. All those unchristian thoughts about him. Especially about the holly around the crib. And now he's gone.'

'Here's your tea, my ducks,' Mrs Huggins said. 'And a slice of my good plum cake. That's what you need right now.'

'You are too kind,' Miss Prendergast said. 'I don't know what's going on here. I moved to this place thinking it was a little haven of peace after looking after my dear mama for so long. And now so many tragedies at once. It almost seems as if the place is cursed, doesn't it?'

'I'm sure it will all stop soon,' I said. 'The police have found out who is behind these deaths and they are hot on his trail.'

'Behind the deaths? You mean they were not accidents?'

'Absolutely not. Horrible murders, every one.'

Miss Prendergast clutched her hand to her breast. 'Murders? In Tiddleton? It's not possible. I can't live here any longer. I shall never feel safe again.'

'Don't you fret, ducks. The police will get him,' Granddad said. 'It's only a matter of time. And then everything will be right as rain again.'

'But I will have so many dreadful memories, won't I? Miss Effie, Mrs Sechrest, Mr Protheroe, and now Mr Barclay. I shall never sleep again.'

I noticed that Noël Coward had come in to join us. He also enjoyed good drama.

'So where did you come from, my dear?'

'Bournemouth. Mummy had a nice house there. We lived very happily together until she died.'

'Bournemouth? I know it well. Where exactly did you live? Did you go to the theater much? I once performed there.'

Miss Prendergast tried to get to her feet. 'Look, I know you're all being awfully kind, but I'm too upset to chitchat right now.'

'Of course. We understand,' Mummy said.

'I think I should go home. The police will want to talk to me, I expect.'

'I'll walk you home,' I said.

There was a great amount of activity going on outside the church. An ambulance. Two police motorcars. Several policemen, one with a dog. Miss Prendergast shuddered. 'It's like a nightmare, isn't it?'

I nodded. 'You go inside and lock your door, just in case.'

As we reached her gate, a man in uniform was just coming out. I thought it was another policeman until I saw it was only the postman.

'Oh, there you are, Miss Prendergast,' he said. 'I was trying to deliver another parcel for you. Didn't just want to leave it on the step. Another late Christmas present, I expect.'

'Yes, I expect it is. Thank you.' She took the package from him.

I watched with interest. I thought she said she had no one in the world. Then I saw that the package came from a firm in London. Maybe she'd been ordering little gifts for herself.

'Thank you again,' she said to me, then she almost ran up her front path and I heard the bolt being shot on her front door.

All of Lady Hawse-Gorzley's guests were assembled at tea, but I noticed that nobody felt much like eating.

'I'll never get these awful images out of my mind, as long as I live,' Mrs Upthorpe said. 'First poor Mrs Sechrest and now that organist. I think we should go home now, Arthur, and not wait for the New Year.'

'Oh, but we have to stay for the last event, Mummy,' Ethel said, her eye on Badger. 'Only one more day.'

'How do I know that we'll be safe? I can't believe that they were accidents.'

'They weren't,' I said and felt all those eyes upon me. 'We now know that it was one of those escaped convicts behind all these deaths. They were all clever murders. But don't worry. The police will soon have him.' I sounded more optimistic than I felt. If he had evaded us all so far, what chance did the police have now that there were no more people left to kill? If he had fulfilled his mission and killed off his jurors, surely he'd be out of this area right away.

'I'm so sorry this had to spoil your lovely holiday here,' Lady Hawse-Gorzley said. 'After we went to so much trouble to make everything perfect for you.'

There were murmurs of understanding from those around her. Mrs Wexler even patted her knee, which brought an astonished look from Lady H-G. I took a scone and went to sit beside Darcy. 'Am I forgiven for worrying you?'

'Now do you see why I was worried?' he said. 'That man couldn't have been killed long before we arrived in the church. The blood was still running. That meant that the murderer was probably still somewhere close by, watching us. He may even have been in the church somewhere.'

'I don't know why nobody has seen him,' I said.

'If he adopted various characters as part of his stage act, then he is probably a master of disguise. We may have walked right past him and not recognized him.' His gaze went across the room to the colonel, now sitting eating calmly beside his wife. She did not look so serene. She looked decidedly pale, in fact. Had she realized what he was doing, perhaps?

'When do you think you'll get an answer to your telegram?' I asked.

'Shouldn't take too long to check War Office records,' Darcy said.

Tea concluded. Nobody felt much like doing anything, but I noticed that they all chose to sit together in the drawing room, rather than go off alone. I couldn't blame them. I shared their fear.

Darkness fell and reluctantly we went up to dress for dinner. Queenie was waiting in my room, wide-eyed with a mixture of fear and excitement. 'They say someone got killed again, miss,' she said. 'Had his head bashed in with a great lump of rock. Blimey, what a place, eh? Give me the old East End any day. Do you reckon we're safe here, in this house?'

'I hope so, Queenie. I think the murderer is only targeting specific people and he doesn't know us, so I have to assume we're safe. Just don't go wandering around outside.'

'You bet yer boots I won't, miss,' she said. 'I ain't that stupid.'

At that moment there was a thunderous knock at the front

door. I urged Queenie to hurry with the fastenings on my dress, then I went out to peer over the gallery to the hallway below.

'Telegram for a Mr O'Mara,' I heard the boy's voice announce.

I went to find Darcy and we stood in the front hall together while he opened the telegram. It said, COLONEL RATHBONE RETIRED BENGAL LANCERS TEN YEARS AGO.

'We should call the police,' I said.

Darcy shook his head. 'We'll confront him before dinner. At least hear what the man has to say for himself.'

'Isn't that a little dangerous? He might be a cold-blooded murderer.'

'I hardly think he'd be able to do anything surrounded by so many people. And Monty, Badger, myself, we're all pretty strong.'

'What if he has a gun?'

'In his dinner jacket pocket? Besides, he hasn't shot anybody yet.'

'Well, all right,' I said, 'only be careful.'

'Pot calling the kettle black.' He smiled at me.

One by one the dinner guests assembled for sherry. They stood together in little groups, talking in low voices. Hardly the loud, laughing group of a few days ago. It was clear that everyone wanted to go home.

'The memsahib was all for leaving tonight,' I heard the colonel say. 'But I told her I'd never run away from a charging tiger in Bengal. Why should we run away now?'

'Quite right,' the countess said. 'My sentiments exactly. I will not allow one horrible little convict to spoil my holiday. Who knows if I will ever have another Christmas like this one?'

Darcy and I moved into the group. 'So when did you last face a charging tiger, Colonel?' Darcy asked.

'When? Let me see. Not that long ago.'

'Was it at the London Zoo?' Darcy asked.

'What the devil are you talking about?' The colonel's face flushed red.

'Because you are an imposter, sir,' Darcy said. 'I just received a telegram from the War Office. Colonel Rathbone left the Bengal Lancers ten years ago.'

I expected him to bluster, but he deflated like a balloon. 'Quite right,' he said. 'No sense in pretending any longer. I did it for the memsahib, you see.' He turned to look at his wife, who was sitting with Mrs Upthorpe on the sofa. Her face was a mask of granite. 'She hasn't been at all well. In fact, those doctor wallahs don't give her long to live.'

'I don't understand,' I said. 'You really were in the Bengal Lancers?'

'I had to retire ten years ago,' he said. 'Caught some damned tropical disease. We had to come back to England and live on a pitiful army pension. Quite a shock for both of us, I can tell you. Lost my savings in the crash of '29 so we're reduced to living in a shabby little rented house in Fulham. No luxuries. Just about enough to eat. But when the doctor gave us the bad news, I decided that my wife deserved one last splendid Christmas – the kind she always talked about, the kind she had as a child. So I sold a lot of my Indian mementos and we splurged on this. I don't regret it either. She's had a splendid time.'

He looked across at her again and they exchanged a lovely smile.

Chapter 38

December 31, New Year's Eve
The Worsting of the Hag tonight. Will anyone be killed? If
so, who? I can't believe he'll do nothing on the twelfth day. I
wish I were going home. . . . No, I don't.

My stomach was in a tight knot the moment I awoke to the
sight of Queenie's large bulk looming over me. In fact, I had
woken with a jolt, conscious of warm breath on my face. In
my half dream it was the Labrador of my childhood, Tilly,
who used to sit by my bed, waiting for me to wake up. I
opened my eyes to see a large face close to mine. I gasped
and tried to sit up. Then I saw it was only Queenie.

'What on earth were you doing that for?' I asked. 'You
scared the daylights out of me.'

'Sorry, miss. You were lying there so still, I wanted to
make sure you were still alive.'

'Thanks a lot,' I said. 'The sight of you a few inches away
from me might well have given me heart failure.'

After that first scare I couldn't shake off the tension.
Something was going to happen today, I was sure of it. But

I couldn't think what, and to whom. As I sat writing my morning entry in my diary, I wished I could go home right then. Then of course I knew that was rubbish. I didn't want to go back to Fig and her family, and it was no longer my home. I didn't have a home any longer. After this I really had nowhere to go. Frightening thought. And also I'd soon be leaving Darcy. I knew that before I left I must pluck up the courage to tell him I couldn't marry him. And that was the one thing I didn't want to do.

The whole household still seemed to be suffering from the shock of finding Mr Barclay yesterday. People sat separately at breakfast, not talking. I knew I was supposed to be the social organizer, but frankly I couldn't think of anything to cheer them up. Mrs Upthorpe looked positively sick. Only the countess ate a hearty breakfast and seemed in good spirits.

'Such gloomy faces,' she said. 'It's New Year's Eve. Time for celebration.'

'But it doesn't seem right, with that poor man not in his grave yet,' Mrs Upthorpe said.

'It wasn't as if we knew the man, after all,' the countess said. 'These things happen. I lost my husband. A big shock. Not at all pleasant, but I got on with it. I don't hold with all this moping. Death is a fact of life. It's going to come to all of us sooner or later.'

'We're just hoping it's not sooner,' Mr Wexler said. 'I don't want my family in any danger.'

'Of course they're not in danger,' the countess said. 'Who'd want to kill you?'

I managed a poached egg on toast and was just finishing when Darcy came in. 'I have to send another telegram,' he said. 'Fancy a walk to the village after breakfast?'

'All right.' I got up. 'Are you not breakfasting?'

'I ate hours ago. I've been out for a ride with Monty. Lovely morning. Frost on the grass.' He stared out the window as we walked from the room. 'God, I miss my horses, don't you?'

'I've been at home, so I've been able to ride,' I said.

'Lucky you.'

'Not much lucky about being at Castle Rannoch, I can assure you.' I grinned.

'And you'll go back there after this?'

'I've nowhere else to go,' I said. 'I don't know what I'm going to do. They don't want me there. I'm not allowed to use the London house. I may find myself as lady-in-waiting to one of the royal great-aunts.'

'I know people,' Darcy said. 'I should be able to find something better than that for you.'

I managed a hopeful smile. 'Really?'

'It's a bugger, isn't it?' he said. 'This having no money.'

'Not a word I'm usually allowed to use,' I said. 'But it is an absolute bugger.'

'We'll work it out somehow. Even if I have to get a job in a bank or behind a sock counter in a gentlemen's outfitter's.'

This made me laugh. 'You'd probably plot to rob the bank.'

'Nonsense. I've sworn to the straight and narrow these days.' Then he stopped and looked ahead. 'Isn't that your mother?'

A figure in a long mink coat was coming up the drive toward us. And a short, stocky figure beside her. 'And my grandfather,' I said. 'It's a little early for a social call.'

Mummy spotted me at the same time and waved. 'Yoo-hoo, darling! We were just coming to see you.'

They waited until we joined them. 'Is something wrong?' I asked.

'It's Miss Prendergast,' Mummy said. 'We're worried that something has happened to her.'

'Oh, no.' Darcy and I exchanged a glance.

'Well, I felt sorry for the old biddy,' Granddad said. 'She had that awful shock yesterday. So I got your mum to come with me to see how she was doing this morning and nobody answers the door. We wondered – well, if anything might be wrong. Have you heard from the inspector this morning?'

'I haven't seen anybody,' I said. 'You didn't happen to see her when you were out riding, did you?' I asked Darcy.

He shook his head. 'We went up on the moors. Nowhere near the village.'

'Oh, no,' I said. 'Poor Miss Prendergast. She is a bit of a busybody, isn't she? I hope she didn't see something that put her in danger.' And immediately it crossed my mind that she had been the first person into the church. If the killer had been in the process of making his getaway, had she caught a glimpse of him? Had he thought she'd seen him? In which case she had sealed her fate.

'We'd better go and take a look,' Darcy said. We walked back down the drive together at a quick pace.

'Strange woman, isn't she?' Mummy said, taking quick and dainty little steps on her high platform shoes to keep up with us. 'I wouldn't have thought she was the type prone to hysterics. Always acted like one of those capable and no-nonsense females.'

'Well, she had just found a body,' Darcy pointed out.

'And you say she was a lifelong spinster?' Mummy went on. 'I'd swear that woman was no virgin.'

We looked at her with interest. 'Why do you say that?'

'The way she sat, darling. I noticed her particularly at that ball. She sat with her legs crossed, leaning back in her seat. Spinsters always sit bolt upright with their knees together.'

We had to laugh, but she went on. 'They do. You know it's that upbringing thing – their mothers drummed into them that the best form of birth control is to put a sixpence between your knees and keep it there.'

We were still laughing as she continued. 'And there was something else I noticed yesterday. I don't think she's as old as we think. Did you see her hands? She didn't have old hands. Look at your Granddad's' – and she lifted one of his hands for my inspection – 'wrinkles and age spots. Not at all nice. But hers were smooth and elegant.'

'Perhaps she just took care of them.'

'You can't prevent age spots, no matter how much care you take.'

I tried to digest what this meant and then something struck me, like an explosion in my head. 'Cornucopia,' I said, making them stop and look at me. 'One of the words when we played charades. For the first syllable we had someone hobble like an old woman with corns. That was just after the two Misses Ffrench-Finch had crossed the room with Miss Prendergast. And later I had recalled that the first two walked exactly as we had depicted in the game, but Miss Prendergast strode out.'

'So if she's really younger than she wants us to think,' Darcy said carefully, 'what do you think that means?'

'That she's not who she claims to be,' Mummy said. 'What's the betting she's hiding out here?'

That stopped us all in our tracks at the bottom of the driveway.

'A package came for her yesterday,' I said. 'From a firm in London. Angels. Any idea who they are?'

'I know that name. I've used them a thousand times. They're well-known theatrical costumers,' Mummy said.

'Is it possible that she's been hiding Robbins all this time, right under our noses?' Darcy said.

'Then who is she? We were told that his wife killed herself right after he was arrested. She couldn't stand the shame,' I said.

'Killed herself by walking out into the ocean and the body was never found,' Darcy reminded me. 'That's an old trick for anyone who wants to disappear. So Mrs Robbins is dead and Miss Prendergast, elderly spinster, comes to live in a Devon village, near where Robbins is in prison and where she can plan everything they are going to do when he breaks out.'

'Oh, crikey,' I said. 'She was the first person on the scene when Miss Ffrench-Finch was found dead in her bed. It was Miss Prendergast who turned off the gas and opened the window.'

'So that there would be a legitimate reason for her prints to be on everything,' Granddad said.

'And yesterday in church,' Darcy went on, waving his arms excitedly now, 'no wonder she had blood on her hands. She had just killed Barclay herself.'

Granddad wagged a finger at us. 'You need to let Inspector Newcombe know about this right away. This is not something you should tackle yourself. They are nasty customers and may well be armed. I'll go into the police station and you three behave as if nothing has happened.'

'Darcy and I will go and get a newspaper at the shop,' I said. 'I can ask there if anybody has seen her this morning. Willum's usually out and about.'

Darcy took my hand and we sauntered across the village

green, two lovers out for an early morning stroll. In the shop we bought our paper and inquired about Willum.

'Willum? He's come down with a nasty cold, my dearie,' Willum's mother said. 'I'm keeping him in bed today with a mustard plaster on his chest. Always had a weak chest, you know, so I can't be too careful. Mind you, he's so disappointed he'll miss the celebrations tonight. He does so enjoy all that noise.'

'Please give him our best,' I said.

'I will, and I told him he can watch the fireworks on the green from his window, so he's happy about that. Easy enough to make him happy, that's one good thing.' And she smiled as she handed Darcy his change.

'Has Miss Prendergast been in for her paper this morning, by the way?' I asked casually. 'She wasn't home when my mother called on her a little while ago and we wondered if she was all right after that shock yesterday.'

'Wasn't that just terrible?' Willum's mother folded her arms across her ample bosom. 'A shock for all of us here. Mr Barclay's been part of this village for twenty years now. There's some that weren't too fond of him, but he was always polite enough to me. Who would have thought that part of the church would fall down like that and kill him?'

'It didn't,' Darcy said. 'Somebody killed him deliberately, and tried to make it look like an accident.'

'Well, I never,' she said. 'What is the world coming to? Not even safe in our own village now, are we? I'm glad my Willum is inside where I can keep an eye on him.'

'Don't worry, it will all be over soon,' I said. 'Now that the police know who they are looking for, they'll soon catch them.'

'I hope so. I do hope so,' she said, shaking her head.

* * *

We then hurried back to the hall to alert the Hawse-Gorzleys while we waited for news from the inspector. Lady Hawse-Gorzley stood staring out the window.

'You mean one of those convicts has been committing all these murders with the help of his wife, who was disguised as Miss Prendergast?' she said. 'God, I need a sherry. How about you?'

'It's a little early,' I said, 'but given the circumstances . . .' I accepted the glass she held out to me. The liquid felt warm and comforting as it slipped down. 'So until these people are caught, I think we should make sure that all your guests stay safely in the house,' I said.

She turned to me then. 'You don't think anyone here is in danger, do you?'

'I don't think so,' I said. 'If he has been killing only the jurors from his trial, they are all dead now, except for one man, who went to Australia.'

'That's a relief,' she said. 'But I suppose he could get desperate if cornered and who knows what he'd do. The man must be stark raving mad.'

'No, I think he's cool and calculating,' I said. 'He's been plotting this all the time he was in prison, I suspect. Or he and his wife have been planning it between them. I don't know how involved she was and whether she was a willing party to all this. I remember that she tried to express regret to me several times, saying how sorry she was that someone had to die. Of course that could have been an act and she could be the cold, brutal one for all we know.'

Lady Hawse-Gorzley sighed. 'Such a farce,' she said. 'And for what? The jurors were only doing their duty. I know I've had many unpleasant tasks as a magistrate.' She turned to the window again. 'My husband is out on the estate some-where. Someone should find him and bring him inside.'

'Darcy already went to do so,' I said.

'Such a kind boy,' she said. 'Well, not really a boy any longer, is he? It's hard for me to think of him as grown-up. I remember him fondly as a child – such a little rogue.'

'Still is,' I said.

'I notice you two are fond of each other. Any plans to marry, do you think?'

I took a deep breath. 'I'm afraid I can't marry him.'

'Why ever not?'

I took a deep breath. 'I'm part of the line of succession. I can't marry a Catholic by law, and I don't think he'd be prepared to give up his religion.'

She looked amused. 'My dear girl. It's not as if you're going to be queen one day, is it? Just renounce your claim to the throne, say you're not interested, and they can step over you.'

'I can do that?'

'Why not? Even kings have abdicated before now. One might do so again.'

Suddenly, in spite of everything we'd been through, the world was a brighter, more wonderful place.

'I never wanted to be queen anyway,' I said.

We looked up as one of the maids came in. She curtsied. 'My lady, the policeman is here to see you again.'

Before Lady Hawse-Gorzley could say, 'Please show him in,' Inspector Newcombe strode into the room.

'Sorry to barge in on you like this, Lady Hawse-Gorzley,' he said. 'But I just wanted to come up and tell you that they've flown the coop. We had to break in the cottage door and they've gone. Taken any incriminating evidence too, although there are signs that Robbins was living upstairs.'

'Nobody saw them leave the village?' I asked.

'They must have had a vehicle hidden nearby and crept away sometime during the night. I can't get over that Prendergast woman. Had us all fooled, didn't she? If she was that good an actress, why didn't she make money legitimately on the stage?'

'She wasn't that good,' I said. 'My mother saw through her.'

'Well, we're talking of a superior actress there, aren't we?' he said with a smile. 'But I'm hoping they won't get far. We're sending out alerts for them all over the country and at all the ports. We'll catch 'em eventually, you'll see. And then they'll both hang. And good riddance too.'

'So he's not going to finish the twelve days,' I said. 'I'm surprised.'

Lady Hawse-Gorzley had been standing there silently. Now she said, 'Did you say the man's name was Robbins? Not Robert Robbins, by any chance?'

'That's right. One of the three convicts who escaped.'

'What an unpleasant man he was,' she said.

'You knew him?' the inspector asked.

'Oh, yes. I presided as magistrate when he was first arrested,' she said. 'He came up before me on extortion charges, but I could see there was more to it than mere extortion. I was convinced he'd killed at least one landlady, so I handed him over to the Crown court.'

My heart was thumping loudly. 'Oh, no.' It came out as a whisper. 'Then you're intended to be the twelfth victim. You're the one he's been waiting for.'

Chapter 39

Still New Year's Eve
Nobody dead yet.

It was the inspector who spoke first. 'Right. That settles it. You're staying in the house and we're putting a police guard on you until Robbins is caught.'

Lady Hawse-Gorzley shook her head. 'Oh, no, Inspector. Don't you see – this is our only chance to catch him. I'm afraid I must carry on as planned tonight. I must offer myself as bait.'

'You can't do that,' I said.

'Why not? If tonight passes without my presence, he'll just slip away and probably be on the next boat out of England. I want him caught, Inspector. I want to make sure that this time he doesn't escape the noose on a technicality. I want him hanged. And her too. She was part and party to all this.'

'You've got guts, my lady, I'll say that much for you.' The inspector nodded grimly.

'I'm one of the old school,' she said. 'We were brought up to do our duty.'

'It might just work,' he said. 'We'll provide you with a police guard, of course. You'll be protected all the time.'

'They should be disguised as our guests,' I said. 'If Robbins and his wife can use disguises, then so can we. They mustn't get any hint that we are waiting for them.'

The inspector nodded approvingly at my suggestion. 'So what exactly happens at this little beanfeast tonight?' he asked.

'We all assemble on the village green, then we go from house to house banging on pots and pans and making a lot of noise. It's to drive out evil spirits for the coming year. Wonderfully primitive.' And she smiled. 'And then we reassemble outside the pub for hot toddy and baked potatoes and sausages and there are fireworks on the village green.'

The inspector was frowning. 'That sounds like the most challenging kind of situation possible to try to protect somebody. If Robbins doesn't want to get close and reveal himself, there's plenty of chance for a shot in the dark. I'm beginning to think it's too risky to contemplate.'

'Nonsense,' she said, tossing her head like an impatient mare. 'We have no choice, Detective Inspector. If you let him slip through your fingers tonight, he'll be gone.'

The inspector stroked his chin. 'I'm not sure I can round up enough men. We'll need a good number, and backups sitting in vehicles nearby in case he makes a break for it.'

'But they mustn't be obvious,' Lady Hawse-Gorzley said. 'They must be laughing and having a good time with the rest of us, not appearing to look around.'

'Not an easy task,' he said.

'Darcy and I will keep watch,' I said. 'We'll pretend to be having our own private tryst and not necessarily keep up with the rest of you.'

The inspector looked at me sharply. 'I don't want you exposing yourself to any danger either. By this time he might well be feeling desperate, especially if he senses that we're on to him. And he might be armed.'

'Darcy will look after me,' I said. 'He's been in worse situations than this.'

'Has he?' Lady Hawse-Gorzley looked interested. 'We always wondered what he did with himself. What does he do, exactly?'

'He won't tell me,' I replied with a smile.

The sound of voices could be heard in the hallway outside. Lady Hawse-Gorzley looked around. 'My husband,' she said in a hiss to us. 'He is not to know anything about this. I absolutely forbid it.'

At that second Sir Oswald strode into the room. 'So that damned twittery woman was really an actress all along, was she? Well, I never. Had us all fooled. And harboring an escaped convict too. Hope they catch the pair of them. Coming here and eating my food!' He stomped across the room, scattering mud from his boots. 'I know what I'd like to do with them – feed 'em to my pigs. That's what I'd do.'

'Now, don't upset yourself, Oswald,' Lady Hawse-Gorzley said. 'And we have the inspector here.'

'What?' He stared at Inspector Newcombe as if he'd just seen him for the first time. 'How do you do,' he said brusquely. 'Damned funny business.'

I took my cue and led Darcy away down the hall to tell him what had been proposed. He wasn't at all happy about it. 'I don't know if I want you exposed out there. If either of them suspects you had something to do with their being discovered, he might take a pot shot at you too. Or she might. Who knows whether she's the mastermind behind this.'

'But if Lady Hawse-Gorzley is willing to risk her own life, I can hardly not do my part, can I?' I said. 'After all, Geordie Lachan Rannoch followed Bonnie Prince Charlie into battle. I can't let the side down.'

'What happened to Geordie Lachan Rannoch?' he asked with an expression of amused tenderness.

'He was hacked to pieces, unfortunately, but that's not the point.'

'The point is that the Rannochs should have learned a little sense since then.'

'You'll be there to keep an eye on me.'

'I'm tempted to make you wear a saucepan lid inside your coat, in case someone shoots at you.'

'Well, everyone is going to be carrying pots and pans, so I don't see why not.' And we both laughed, a trifle nervously.

But the day seemed to stretch on endlessly. The other guests felt it too, although they were not apprised of what might happen that evening. We dined well. Lady Hawse-Gorzley served leg of pork, with the most wonderful crackling, sage and onion stuffing, baked onions, roast potatoes, cauliflower cheese, and apple pie to follow. We lingered over coffee and liqueurs and afterward let off the last few indoor fireworks. Then around eleven we put on coats, hats, scarves and gloves and we all trooped down the driveway, each of us armed with a saucepan or lid and a wooden spoon to beat on it. Others were already assembling on the village green. The first thing I noticed was how hard it was to recognize anybody under all that outerwear. They might all be policemen or one of them might be Robbins. He was a big chap. That's all I knew. And I took heart in the fact that those assembled seemed to know each other.

More and more people came to join us and I spotted

Inspector Newcombe, wearing a red balaclava and matching red scarf. Then the publican came out of the Hag and Hounds.

'People of Tiddleton-under-Lovey, the time has come,' he announced. 'I charge you all to rid this place of ghosts and ghouls, of witches and warlocks, of all manner of enchanted folk who would do us harm.' He gave a mighty beat on a big gong. In reply came a barrage of sound from the crowd. Saucepan lids were crashed together. Spoons beat on pots and a great cry rose from the crowd. It was an eerie sound that made the hairs on the back of my neck stand up. A sound that belonged to another age and time. If I'd been an evil spirit, I'd have vanished then and there. I hoped Robbins would take the hint if he was anywhere around. I searched the crowd but saw nothing unusual.

Then the crowd launched into a chant of sorts. I couldn't make out the words and decided that it must be in an old, long-forgotten tongue – Old Cornish, maybe. We were close to the Cornish border. In its way it was as unsettling as the cry had been. We set off, chanting, dancing, banging our noisemakers, first through one house and then another. Darcy and I deliberately hung back and watched Lady Hawse-Gorzley and Inspector Newcombe go ahead of us. We moved across to the cottages on the other side of the green. My mother and grandfather were standing at the door, smiling as everyone trooped inside and then out again. I noticed that Miss Prendergast's cottage was avoided. Perhaps everybody sensed that true evil still lurked in there.

Through the vicarage and then on to the cottages on the other side of the village. Nothing strange happened and I began to believe Robbins had really fled. Then up the driveway to Gorzley Hall. In through the front door, around the foyer and out again, while the servants stood on the stairs, laughing and clapping along. We waited by the front door as the first revelers came out again and began their long trek back down the drive.

I noticed Willum's startling red hat as he lumbered down the side of the column, nodding and dancing in his clumsy way, like a giant in a child's fairy tale. Then suddenly it hit me. I ran and grabbed the inspector.

'That's not Willum, it's Robbins,' I shouted. 'Willum's in bed with a cold.'

The inspector didn't waste a second. 'That's him, men. Get him.'

At those words the fake Willum drew out a gun and fired directly at Lady Hawse-Gorzley. She stumbled and fell as he took off into the darkness. The noise of the crowd turned to howls as they pursued him.

'Go and get help from the hall,' I shouted amid the chaos. I dropped to my knees beside Lady Hawse-Gorzley. 'And summon a doctor.'

Darcy took off back to the hall.

Lady Hawse-Gorzley grabbed my hand. 'I'm all right. Help me up.' She attempted to stand but couldn't quite manage it. 'The impudence. Thank God I'm wearing my old sheepskin coat. The hide's thick enough to stop any bullet.'

I opened the top buttons on the coat and saw that the white fleece around the shoulder was black with blood. 'You're bleeding badly. Just lie still until help comes from the hall.'

'Funny,' she said, 'I don't feel a thing.' And then she fainted.

Chapter 40

Around Lovey Tor
New Year's Eve

I looked up nervously as feet ran across the gravel toward us. But they had come to help Lady Hawse-Gorzley. Then she was being picked up and carried back up the drive. I followed behind, feeling sick and scared. In spite of everything, we hadn't managed to protect her. Surely she wasn't going to die, was she? I'd grown rather fond of her during these twelve days at her house. I just hoped they'd caught Robbins by now and that he would hang.

Suddenly I felt alone and exposed in the darkness and quickened my pace to catch up. I gasped and spun around as someone grabbed my arm. Wild Sal was standing beside me. 'Come on, miss, quick,' she said. 'That woman – the bad one. She's getting away. She's heading for the moor.'

She took my sleeve and started to lead me across the lawn and through the trees. I looked around for Darcy or someone else I recognized. 'Tell them that the Prendergast woman is heading for the moor,' I shouted to the last stragglers who were milling around on the driveway. 'Find Inspector Newcombe.'

'Come on. We'll lose her,' Sal hissed impatiently, staring ahead as if she could see somebody I couldn't in the darkness. She grabbed my arm. Our footsteps crunched through frosty dry bracken as we came out onto the wild upland. What a lot of noise we make, I thought and instinctively glanced down at our feet.

'You're wearing shoes,' I said. And even as I said the words out loud I realized the truth. She wasn't Sal at all. She was dressed in flowing robes like Sal. Her hair hung around her face and over her shoulders like Sal. But the face beneath was quite different. Before I could say anything I felt something hard shoved into my side.

'You have to stop being so trusting,' the woman said in her own voice, far coarser and more common than Wild Sal's. 'You're all so bloody stupid around here. Now get moving.'

The thing in my side didn't feel sharp. Not a knife, then. A gun.

'What do you want with me?' I tried to make my voice sound calm and in control. 'You could have gotten away by now and nobody would have noticed.'

She gave a little cackle in her throat. 'You're my ticket to freedom, duckie. We always planned to take a hostage and you were too good to turn down. Keep moving.'

And she prodded me forward. We stumbled upward in complete darkness, falling over rocks until we came to some kind of path, then we moved along more rapidly. Suddenly the woman froze.

'Hold on,' she said, listening, and sure enough we heard feet crunching up through the bracken toward us. 'Don't move. Don't make a sound,' she whispered. 'I've killed enough people recently that one more won't be no trouble at all.'

I heard her cock the gun. It's Darcy, I thought. He's come to save me and he's going to be shot. I made up my mind. I was going to shout out a warning and run as soon as he got close enough. Then a voice whispered, 'Trix, is that you?'

'Over here,' she called back and Mr Robbins himself came toward us. 'Lost them easy enough,' he said. He had now shed his Willum disguise and was dressed head to toe in black, including a black balaclava so that he blended into the darkness of the night with only his face hovering, disembodied, which somehow made the whole thing more alarming. I was shivering now, and not just with cold. He came closer and noticed me.

'Who's this?'

'We got ourselves a good hostage, Rob. She's the one I told you about – relative of the king.'

He came up to me, took my chin in his hand and grinned at me.

'Well done, Trix. She should be good for a safe passage to South America.' He gave my head a nasty tweak as he released me. 'Come on, then, let's get moving. The motor's this way, down behind that pub.'

I looked around me and saw no lights. The valley now lay hidden in mist. It was creeping upward toward us, moving like a live thing.

'Mist is coming in,' he said. 'All the better for us. They'll never find us now. Safe to use this, I think.'

He turned on a small torch, shining it on the ground around us. We started to move to our right. Far below us we heard a deep baying.

'They've got dogs, Rob,' Trixie said nervously.

'Don't matter. They'll never catch up with us in this.'

We plunged forward into mist. I felt its icy dampness on my face and all sound seemed to be deadened, apart from the heavy tread of Robbins's boots. I was trying to stop the rising panic I felt. If I ran off into the mist, would they shoot me before I could get away? If we were ambushed when we reached their motorcar, they'd shoot me without a moment's hesitation.

'Where's that bloody lake?' he muttered. 'We don't want to go anywhere near that. I almost copped it when I had to drop that toffy-nosed hunting bloke into the bog.'

'We should be well to the right of it if we stay on this path,' she said. 'It will drop down behind the pub soon.'

Far below us a dog howled again, an eerie sound that seemed to echo all around us. I remembered that the hound of the Baskervilles hunted on this very moor. Right now I'd have welcomed the sight of him.

We plunged on in silence. Then Robbins said, 'We should be right above that pub by now. The path should be starting to go down.'

But it didn't.

Then Trixie spoke. 'I don't think this is a proper path. It's just an animal track.'

'Then where is the damned path?' he snapped back.

'How should I know?'

'You're the one who has had five years to scout out the place. Hurry up, I'm freezing.'

'You're freezing? I'm freezing in this stupid get-up.'

Then through the darkness I thought I heard a flapping sound. The others heard it too.

'One of them bloody swans,' Trixie said. 'If the lake's

over there then we must have swung too far to our left. No wonder we didn't find the right path. Come on. This way.'

She took the torch from him and struck out to her right. Robbins gave me a rough shove and forced me ahead of him.

We forged ahead in silence, stumbling now that we no longer had the least semblance of a path to follow. Mist swirled, cleared, then closed in again. It was a world of unreality and I lost all track of time. It felt as if I had been stumbling forward for eternity.

Suddenly the mist parted again and he cried out, 'You stupid cow. You're leading us astray. Look, that must be the tor over there. We're going down the wrong side.' And with that he strode out ahead of us. Trixie jammed the gun into my side again. 'Get going. Keep up with him.'

We half ran, half stumbled as he vanished into the mist. Suddenly we heard him swear.

'Watch your step,' he called back. 'I'm into a bloody bog.' We heard him swear again under his breath. Then he shouted, with panic in his voice, 'Trix, I can't move my feet. Give me a hand.'

'Where are you?' she called. 'I can't see you.'

'Over here.' The voice echoed and bounced from unseen peaks.

She swung the torch around, but the light couldn't penetrate the mist.

'For God's sake, woman, get a move on. I'm bloody well sinking.' His voice sounded desperate now.

'I can't see you.' Her voice was full of fear. 'Keep talking.'

'I'm sinking, damn it. Come and get me out of this infernal thing.'

She started running, first left, then right, like a frightened animal. 'Robbie, where are you?'

'Here. I'm here.'

She must have remembered me because she turned to grab my arm and drag me with her. Suddenly we stumbled upon a frightening scene. Only a few yards away from us Robbie Robbins was now up to his waist in the bog. He was thrashing and struggling but he had nothing around him but liquid mud. Trixie screamed, dropped the torch and ran forward. 'Oh, my God. Oh, no. Robbie.' She plunged toward him and grabbed his hands, trying with all her strength to pull him clear. The torch fell propped against a clump of grass, throwing an eerie light on the scene.

'It's no use,' he said. 'You're not strong enough to pull me out. I'm done for. Save yourself now, Trix. Go on, run for it. Take her with you.'

'I'm not leaving you, you bloody fool. Try harder. Move. Kick.'

'I can't move a bleeding thing,' he said. 'My legs are held fast. Run for it, Trix. If they catch you, you'll swing.'

I could see she was hesitating. The spectacle was horrendous to watch – the bog silently sucking him down. She let go of his hand and then she shrieked. 'It's got me, too. I can't move my feet.'

Although it looked as if she was standing on grass, she was in bog above her ankles.

She turned back to me. 'Help me,' she called.

I stood there in a moment of absolute indecision. I was free. I could run away now and leave them. It was what they deserved, after all. They hadn't thought twice when they turned the gas tap on a poor old woman or smashed Mr Barclay's head in with a piece of masonry. The Lovey Curse was taking its revenge. I started to walk away, but I couldn't. However despicably they had behaved, I could not leave anyone to die. I told myself I could run for help, but I knew it would be too late. I took a deep breath and stepped gingerly onto the tufted grass that edged the bog.

He was now almost up to his neck, his eyes bulging in terror. She was in past her knees. I felt my own feet beginning to sink as I chose the tufts of grass to stand on. 'Here, give me your hand.'

I reached out to her and felt her bony hand grasp mine. It was like being held by a skeleton. 'Try to get one leg free,' I urged.

She grunted and groaned. 'I can't move them an inch,' she said. 'Pull harder.'

I took both her hands and pulled. It seemed that her struggles were only making her sink more quickly.

'I'm going, Trix. Damn it. What a bloody stupid way to end it,' Robbins called. She let go of me to turn back to him. 'No, Robbie. No!' she screamed, trying to grasp at his face, his hair. We watched in silent fascination as the mud rose over his mouth. We heard him cough and splutter. Then it was past his eyes and then there was a horrible sucking sound and the bog claimed him completely.

'Oh, God,' she whimpered. 'I don't want to die like that. You have to get me out quickly.'

I grasped her hands again, but she was now up to her thighs. Suddenly she realized that it was impossible. She was caught.

'Well, if I'm going, then you are too,' she said and she gave a mighty jerk, catching me off guard and sending me sprawling forward into stinking mire. I tried to scramble to my feet but she still had my hands in a grip of iron and I felt the pull of the bog gripping my legs. I wriggled and strained, trying to break her grip on me. I heard her laughing.

'I guess you won't be marrying a prince anytime soon,' she said.

Darcy, I thought. Why did I send him off to the house for help? Why hadn't he sensed I'd be in danger? Why wasn't he here when I needed him? And now I'd never know what it was like to make love to a man, to be married, to have a child. . . . I felt hot tears stinging on my frozen cheeks. If only I can hang on somehow until she's sucked under, I thought. That will surely break her grip. But I pictured a dead hand locked onto mine forever as I was sucked down with her. Not a pretty image. I wriggled and squirmed closer to her so that our arms were no longer outstretched. I felt instantly that the mud was more deadly here and knew I only had a few seconds to act. Without warning I pulled myself up toward her with all my might and sank my teeth into her hand. She yelled and instinctively let go. I floundered, scrabbled, slithered out of reach.

'You little devil,' she snarled. 'But it don't matter. You're going down too, and serves you right.'

I tried to maneuver myself around, so that I was facing away from her, but my legs from the knees downward were held fast. It was utterly frustrating to have nothing firm to hold on to. I made for a clump of grass and grabbed at it, only to have it break off in my hand. At that moment the torch gave out, leaving us in total darkness. Then a voice near me whispered, 'Don't struggle. Lie flat. Spread yourself out on the surface.' I looked around, trying to see where the voice had come from, but I could see nobody through the blackness; indeed, it seemed as if the voice had come from inside my head. I obeyed it, recoiling from the cold touch of the mud on my chin. Now that my weight was not on my feet, I felt I could move my legs again. Then the voice came again. 'Swim. Slowly. Gently. Big strokes. Breaststroke, like a frog.'

It was not easy to do anything gently, but I managed to maneuver myself around, away from Trixie. I could hear her wailing and cursing. 'Oh, God. I don't want to die. Somebody save me. Somebody!'

Then what looked like a rope of shimmering silver came flying out across the bog to me. It landed within reach and the voice said softly, 'Hold on.' I reached for it, held and felt myself moved forward. Within a yard or two I was scraping against tufts of grass, firmer ground. I got to my knees and dragged myself forward with the last of my strength.

Unseen hands helped me up and I stood there, gasping, feeling the heavy caking of mud drying on me in the cold wind.

'You're all right now,' the voice said and I could make out Wild Sal – the real Wild Sal – standing beside me.

'You saved my life. How can I ever thank you?' I said.

'You tried to save her,' Sal said. 'When she deserved to die. Well, now she's getting what she deserves. Now she knows what it feels like.'

We both peered out into the darkness where Trixie Robbins was thrashing and screaming. 'Help me! Get me out!'

'Is there no way we could help her?' I asked.

'Only if we had planks, which we don't,' she said.

'Is your rope not long enough to reach her?'

'I don't have no rope,' she said.

'But you threw it to me.'

'Just the piece of cord I tie around my middle,' she said. 'It ain't but a yard or more.'

An image of the shining silver rope flashed across my mind. Surely it had been longer than that, and almost moved with a life of its own?

'We can't reach her,' she said. 'She'd go to the gallows anyway. This is Nature taking her revenge.'

Trixie's last moments seemed to go on forever: the cursing, the spluttering, the pleading and the last horrible choking sounds. They will probably be in my head forever. She had only just vanished into the bog when we heard the baying of hounds and the tramp of feet and the first policemen appeared.

'You're too late,' I said, feeling stupid tears running down my cheeks. 'They've both gone into the bog. I would have gone too, but Wild Sal saved me.'

I turned to her, but she was no longer there.

Chapter 41

Midnight on New Year's Eve and the first moments of a new year

It seemed to take an eternity to walk back down to the village. I stumbled along in a nightmare of what I had just lived through. A young policeman held my arm and helped me along, saying encouraging things, but I couldn't shake those images from my mind. I thought about Wild Sal and how she had vanished when the police arrived. Had she really been there at all? Was she really a witch after all? I remembered the voice that had seemed almost to be inside my head. How could she have whispered to me over such a distance? But one thing was sure – somebody or something had saved my life. I was still here. The bog had not taken me.

An explosion rocked the night, then another. I recoiled in horror, wondering if this was a last act of vengeance set up by the Robbinses – blowing up the village that had sheltered them. But then a rocket burst into brilliant color over my head. It was only the fireworks at the end of the evening.

Rhys Bowen

More flashes and crashes could be heard as we came down the last of the slope.

'I've got the young lady with me,' my policeman shouted. 'She's all right.'

People started running toward us, one running more quickly than the rest. Darcy swept me into his arms and held me so tightly that I thought he'd crush every bone in my body. 'Thank God,' he muttered, his lips on my face and hair. 'I was worried out of my mind.'

'How is your aunt?' I asked. 'Is she going to be all right?'

'Only a flesh wound, luckily. The nerve of the fellow, shooting her in front of us all.' Then he released me a little, looking down at me. 'And what were you thinking, going off with that woman on your own?'

'I thought she was Wild Sal,' I said. 'She told me Miss Prendergast was getting away and we had to stop her. It was stupid of me, and it was a trap anyway. She was really Robbins's wife and they wanted me as a hostage.'

'Where are they now?' he demanded.

'Dead. Both of them drowned in the bog. It was horrible, Darcy. I was nearly sucked down with them. I would have died if Wild Sal hadn't appeared and rescued me.'

'I've a good mind to take you over to a convent in Ireland and lock you up there until we can be married,' he said, half laughing. 'That is, if you want to marry me someday.' He paused. 'I didn't get the feeling you were too keen on the idea last time we spoke about it.'

'Because I thought I couldn't marry you and I didn't know how to tell you,' I said.

'You can't marry me? Why? And don't tell me you're engaged to Prince Siegfried again.'

I had to laugh. 'I'm part of the line of succession,' I said.

'English law prevents a claimant to the throne from marrying a Catholic.'

'Then I'll give up my religion if that's what it takes,' he said.

'You don't have to, Darcy, and I wouldn't want you to. But it's all right. Your aunt said I could just renounce my place in the line. I hadn't realized I could do that.'

'You'd give up the throne of England for me?' he asked, his eyes challenging mine in the darkness.

'Darcy, I'm only thirty-fifth in line,' I said. 'Unless there is a particularly big epidemic I don't think there's any danger of my becoming queen. And besides, the answer to that question is yes. I would give up the throne of England to marry you. Only you haven't asked me properly yet.'

'You're right.' He went down on one knee, oblivious to the people milling around us. 'Lady Georgiana of Glen Garry and Rannoch, will you do me the honor of becoming my wife?'

And I, who prided myself on never crying, cried for the second time in one evening.

'I can't think of anything I want more,' I said.

Around us the crowd broke into applause, and, as if on cue, the church bells began to ring.

Darcy took me into his arms. 'Happy New Year,' he said and he kissed me.

Chapter 42

New Year's Day, January 1, 1934
Everyone is going home today. I wonder where I will go?

Queenie didn't come in with her tray until after ten o'clock the next morning.

'That Mr Darcy told me to let you sleep,' she said. 'My, but he's a bossy one, ain't he? And they are saying you're going to marry him. You really going to let him boss you around all your life?'

'Yes, I am, I suppose,' I said.

Downstairs there was an end-of-term feel, with guests exchanging addresses, promising to write and to come for a visit. The Upthorpes had been invited to America. Cherie and Monty were going to write to each other daily. Badger was going to stay with the Upthorpes. Even the dowager countess had melted a little and invited Colonel and Mrs Rathbone to come to tea when they were all back in London.

'I don't get much company these days,' she said. 'I'd welcome a chat to share memories with old India hands.'

So all was well, except for poor Johnnie Protheroe and

Mrs Sechrest. I felt terribly sad about Johnnie. He was the sort of man one couldn't help liking, in spite of his wicked ways. And I wondered if the fire would leave Mrs Sechrest permanently disfigured. She had certainly lost a man she really cared about and life would never be the same for her.

Bunty came up to me after breakfast. 'Just been for a brilliant ride with your intended,' she said. 'You're a lucky stick, you know. I'd always hoped . . . but I suppose cousins really shouldn't marry, although they do it in royal circles all the time, don't they?'

'That accounts for all the insanity.' I smiled. 'Luckily my mother brought in an infusion of good common blood so my children should be all right.'

She smiled. 'I'm glad you're going to be my cousin. I asked Mummy if you could stay on here, after everyone else has gone. It's dashed lonely and boring here. And Mummy said you'd be more than welcome, anytime.'

'That's very kind of her. Actually, I don't know what I'm going to do when I leave here. I'd like to stay, but I don't want to be dependent on other people all the time. I want to make my own way in the world. Darcy and I won't have the money to marry for ages and I want to do my part. Now I've been a social hostess once, maybe I'll find a similar job somewhere. Without the bodies, that is.'

She nodded. 'It was rather awful, wasn't it? Poor Mummy, with her plans for the perfect English country Christmas. Who would ever have thought everything could go so horribly wrong?'

'Actually, everyone seems to have had a good time, in spite of everything,' I said. 'I know I did. And the best thing is that those awful Robbins people didn't succeed with their twelfth victim.'

'You're right. And Mummy's talking about getting up to say good-bye to everyone this morning. Daddy is trying to persuade her to stay in bed, but you know what she's like when she puts her mind to something.'

'I suspect stubborn determination runs in the family,' I said, noticing Darcy coming across the foyer with a piece of paper in his hand and a frown on his face.

'I've just had a telegram,' he said, waving it at me. 'I'm afraid I'm wanted back in London straight away. I may be going back to South America.'

'Is it going to be dangerous?' I asked, looking at him with concern.

He smiled. 'I know how to take care of myself better than you do.'

'All the same,' I said, 'I wish you didn't have to go.'

'So do I, but I don't have much choice.'

We stood looking at each other, our gaze not faltering, and so many unspoken things passing between us.

Bunty coughed. 'Well, I'd better go and leave you love-birds to the mushy stuff,' she said.

'How long will you be gone?' I asked, trying to sound bright and cheerful.

'I don't know. Not too long, I hope.'

'I wish . . .' I began.

He stroked my cheek. 'I know. I wish too. But we have something to look forward to now, don't we? By hook or by crook I'm going to make enough money to set you up as Mrs Darcy O'Mara in the style to which you're accustomed.'

'Oh, please, no. Not another Castle Rannoch.' We both laughed and he slipped his arms around me. 'I don't want to make this official until I've spoken with my father,' he said, 'so let's keep it to ourselves, shall we?'

I nodded, trying hard to master a brave smile. He leaned toward me and his lips brushed mine. Then he stroked my cheek. 'I'd better go and pack. Monty's driving me to Exeter to catch the express.'

I watched him walk away, longing to call after him, to run after him, to beg him to take me with him. But I forced myself to behave as a lady should.

One by one the guests departed. Lady Hawse-Gorzley made an effort to come down and see them off. The doctor had told her to stay in bed, but she insisted on doing the right thing, as she put it. Stubbornness definitely did run in the family. When the car headed down the driveway for the last time she turned to me and took my arm to walk back up the steps and into the house. 'I shouldn't say this, but thank God they've gone,' she whispered. 'It was a bit of an ordeal, wasn't it?'

'But fun too,' I said. 'I had a lovely Christmas in spite of everything. I think you did splendidly and gave them a perfect old English Christmas just like they wanted.'

She patted my hand. 'Thank you, dear. Most kind of you. I did try hard. And between ourselves, I don't think we actually made much of a profit, but we did eat and drink very well, didn't we?' She closed the door behind us. 'You know, when these deaths started happening, I kept asking myself whether I was being punished in some way for trying to make money out of a sacred holiday. And when I was shot, I really did ask myself if it was the Lovey Curse.'

I chuckled. 'Don't be silly. If anybody was the victim of the Lovey Curse it was the awful man who shot you. At least he and his wife got their just deserts, didn't they?'

She nodded. 'It's hard to imagine someone could be so warped as to cleverly plot the deaths of twelve innocent people.'

'But speaking of the Lovey Curse,' I said, 'I'd like to do something for Wild Sal – send her some clothes or food or something. She saved my life, you know.'

'She wouldn't accept it, my dear. We have tried in the past and she rejects all help. She'll probably go on living wild like that until she's ninety.'

'I don't suppose I'll see her again, but do thank her for me when you see her,' I said. 'And now, if you don't mind, I'd like to see what my mother is doing. It would be just like her to up stakes and vanish without saying good-bye.'

'Of course, my dear. Off you go, then. Just a simple supper tonight. Thank God.'

I was just walking down the drive when I met Inspector Newcombe's car coming toward me. The car stopped and he got out.

'Just the person I was coming to see,' he said. 'You're not off yet, are you?'

'I was just going to visit my mother and grandfather,' I said. 'I'm not sure when they are leaving.'

'I've come to get an official statement about last night from you,' he said, 'but I can interview Lady Hawse-Gorzley first. How are you feeling today after your ordeal?'

'Never felt better, thank you.'

'Whoever thinks that the aristocracy are useless and frail should take a look at you,' he said and chuckled. Then he looked at me, stroking his chin. 'You had a lucky escape last night. Not many can say they've walked away from that bog. And it takes care of the pair of them nicely, doesn't it? Saves us the trouble of hanging them.'

I nodded, not trusting my voice to speak. The images were still too raw in my mind.

'All the same,' he went on cheerfully, 'I'd have liked the

chance to question them. To know exactly how he managed to pull off all those murders without being caught. It took talent and skill, I'll give them that.'

'They used disguises, I'm sure,' I said. 'I expect they moved around disguised as Willum and Wild Sal, knowing that nobody would have paid them any attention.'

'Too crafty for their own good,' he said. 'Oh, well. Now we'll never know, will we? I'll stop off at your mother's cottage after I've talked with Lady H-G, then, shall I? I'd like to say good-bye to your grandfather. A proper old-fashioned gent, isn't he? I wish there were more like him on the force these days.'

I went on to the cottage and found that my mother was packing up to leave too.

'I've had a telegram from Max,' she said. 'He is coming to London to meet me. He had a gloomy Christmas and missed me dreadfully. And frankly I've had enough of country living. I mean, it's fun to play at cottages and simple English food for a while, isn't it? But then one longs for a good nightclub and caviar and the things that make life worth living.'

'Will you be going back to Germany right away?' I asked.

'Actually, I'm going to persuade Max to rent a house in London for a while.'

'So that you can finish working on the play with Mr Coward?'

She glanced up the stairs and I recognized that expression. 'I don't think this play is going to work out somehow,' she said, sotto voce. 'Noël really does want to hog all the best lines, darling, and I've only just found out that he sees my character as a mature woman. I ask you – me, a mature woman? Well, really!'

And she made a dramatic exit. My grandfather and I exchanged grins.

'So you'll be heading back to Scotland, will you?'

'I hope not,' I said. 'I'm going to try to find another job. I wish I could come and stay with you, but . . .'

'Of course you can't, my love,' he said. 'We live in different worlds, you and me. But you're always welcome to come and visit.'

'At least you've got Mrs Huggins.'

He made a funny face and stepped nearer. 'Between you and me and the gatepost, she's beginning to get on my nerves. Fusses over me like an old hen. I don't mind it when she's next door, but not under the same roof.'

'Well, I suppose it's good-bye, then.' I wrapped my arms around his neck. 'It's been a sad day. All these good-byes.'

Granddad stroked my hair as if I were a small child. 'I expect you'll keep turning up like a bad penny,' he said fondly.

Mummy appeared at the top of the stairs again. 'Georgie, I've just had a brilliant idea. Noël suggested I write my autobiography. Won't that raise some eyebrows!'

'Are you sure you should?' I started to laugh. 'Won't there be an awful lot of husbands who have to do some explaining to their wives?'

'Darling, I'll be discreet. I'll only include the really juicy ones. But listen to my brilliant idea. Why don't you come to London with me and you can be my secretary. Can you use a typewriting machine?'

'I'm afraid I can't.'

'No matter. I'll buy you one and you can learn and I'll scribble down my thoughts and you'll tidy them up for me. How about it?'

'Sounds like fun,' I said.

I was fully aware as I said the words that working with my mother was not going to be easy. But living in a house in London, with proper heat and decent food, was definitely preferable to the only other alternative – time spent in a bleak Scottish castle with Fig. What's more, I'd learn to use a typewriting machine and develop a real skill, more useful than where to seat a bishop at a dinner table. And I'd be in London, on the spot, the moment Darcy reappeared in the country. All in all, the future hadn't looked brighter in a long while.

The next morning Sir Oswald, Lady Hawse-Gorzley and Bunty came out to see me off. The latter two hugged me fondly and begged me to come back soon. What an incredible stroke of luck that I'd seen that advertisement and dared to answer it, I thought as I waved through the rear window. The car took me and Queenie to the station and we caught the train going back to London. The Devon countryside flashed past the train window, with the snow-clad tors of Dartmoor in the background, until they merged into the Somerset lowlands and green fields, and Tiddleton-under-Lovey was just a memory.